"With *Wounded Prey*, Sean Lynch delivers a hell for leather, wild ride of a debut with the 'been there done that' authenticity that lifts it above other thrillers. I just added Farrell and Kearns to my short-list of favourite characters, and Vernon Slocum to my worst nightmares!"
  Matt Hilton, bestselling author of the Joe Hunter series

"If you love a good thriller, you'll blaze through this one, and personally, I can't wait for the next Farrell and Kearns novel! What a great debut!"
  My Bookish Ways

"This is a great debut and I certainly look forward to more."
  The Eloquent Page

"Sean Lynch understands his heroes and what drives them, and while they have considerable skills on their side, Slocum is a true monster, his reign of terror is shocking, and he really does seem larger than life. Be prepared to go to the dark side in this harrowing, fast-paced thriller."
  Kristin Centorcelli at Criminal Element

"With its smooth prose, plausibly flawed characters and brilliant central villain, *Wounded Prey* is a welcome addition to the crime landscape. It's a read-in-one-sitting kind of book, and promises great things for Lynch down the line."
  Russel D McLean in Crime Scene Scotland

"*Wounded Prey* is a non-stop thrill ride of a book. Unrelenting, brutal, scary ~~and~~ ~~~~ ~~~~crawling in its depictio̶~~~~ RY ~~~~nny, warming a~~~~

  *Tony Hea~~~~

ALSO BY SEAN LYNCH

Wounded Prey

SEAN LYNCH

THE FOURTH MOTIVE

EXHIBIT A
An Angry Robot imprint
and a member of the Osprey Group

Lace Market House
54-56 High Pavement
Nottingham
NG1 1HW
UK

www.exhibitabooks.com

An Exhibit A paperback original 2014
1

A catalogue record for this book is available
from the British Library.

ISBN 978 1 909223 09 7
Ebook ISBN 978 1 909223 11 0

Set in Meridien and Franklin Gothic by Argh! Oxford

Printed and bound by CPI Group (UK) Ltd, Croydon, CR0 4YY

This work is dedicated to dogwatch patrol-jockeys everywhere; those brave souls who prowl the night armed with a pistol and a prayer.

CHAPTER 1

Paige Callen didn't see the man until he was upon her.

Her attention had been focused on a flock of seagulls that were grazing on remnants of bait left by beach fishermen the night before.

Not that she would have noticed the man, anyway. The most pleasant aspect of her dawn jog along Shoreline Drive each morning was her ability to tune out the rest of the world, if only for a while, and lose herself in the music piping into her head via the earphones of her bright yellow Sony Walkman cassette player. It was Monday morning, so she'd chosen something a little more upbeat to jumpstart her mood for the impending workweek. *Appetite for Destruction*, the debut album from a two year-old band called Guns n' Roses, was recommended to her by a co-worker. Most of the Guns n' Roses songs on the cassette Paige found a little raucous for her tastes, but "Sweet Child o' Mine" was beginning to win her over.

At 6am, the beach was almost always desolate. Paige would rarely encounter another runner. If she did, they invariably would plod by, like her, oblivious to the rest of the world.

As usual, Paige was clad in nylon shorts topped by an oversized UC Berkeley sweatshirt. Her long, freckled, and muscular legs continued into the tops of her running shoes. She eschewed socks. It was mid-September and she wouldn't need to wear sweatpants for another month.

Paige ran east along the water's edge. Even without Axl Rose wailing in her ears, the soft, damp shore beneath her feet effectively muffled the sound of approaching footsteps.

Paige felt rather than saw a brief flash of movement over her left shoulder. Before she had time to react, she was shoved forward with tremendous force. With the air rushing explosively from her chest, she went sprawling to the wet turf and landed on her stomach. Once more, before she could recover, her attacker pounced. He straddled her back, pinning her down. What little breath not torn from her lungs by the initial violent shove was now completely gone.

Choking and struggling, Paige tried to look over her shoulder at the person holding her helplessly to the ground. Her assailant responded by pushing her face savagely into the dirt. As a tide of panic rose within her, Paige realized she was going to be suffocated face first in the soil. She gasped and thrashed but was trapped. She tasted the silt of the Alameda beach.

A gloved hand released its hold on the back of Paige's neck and ripped the stereo headphones from her ears. The same hand grabbed her long blond ponytail and pulled her head back sharply out of the sand. She gasped for air. Both her arms were held against her sides by the weight of the person atop her. Paige's eyes watered but not enough to wash away the soggy grit embedded over her eyelids.

Paige knew she was about to be raped. But in her overwhelming fear for her life, rape seemed strangely insignificant. She tried to convince herself that maybe another jogger had witnessed the assault and phoned the police, but quickly realized this was wishful thinking. She'd been jogging on the beach almost every day at this time for the seclusion it provided. And that's exactly what she had today: seclusion.

"Hi, Paige. Betcha never thought you'd see me again, huh?"

A man's voice. Deep and raspy; the voice of a heavy smoker. Paige could detect no hint of an accent, and her tortured brain struggled to find something familiar or identifiable in its tone. The assailant's use of her name and implication of previous contact set her into an even deeper panic.

He knows my name. This isn't random.

Paige felt another sharp pull on her ponytail.

"That's right, you fucking whore; you know me," he said, as if reading her mind. "But I didn't come here for a reunion. I came to make you a victim. Never been a victim before, have you?"

Suddenly, the weight on her back lifted. She instinctively tried to get up. In the same motion, Paige brushed a forearm across her grime-covered eyes to clear her vision.

Before Paige could open her eyes, however, she was struck a sharp blow over her left ear by a hard, heavy object. Though not knocked unconscious, the force of the strike flipped her over and put her flat on her back, dazed. She reflexively touched the place on her head that had suffered the impact, and when her eyes finally focused, she saw blood staining her fingers.

Paige looked up to see her attacker standing over her. He was wearing a gray hooded sweatshirt and pants to match. The hood blended nicely into the ski mask covering his face. He was Caucasian, by the glimpses of skin she could see around his lips and eyes, and of medium height with a thin build. In one gloved hand was a large black revolver, held loosely at his side. She realized the weapon was the object he'd struck her with.

The man stared down at Paige, chuckling. His laugh was a harsh staccato. Then he stopped grinning, leaned over, and leveled the revolver directly at her forehead. The distance from the end of the barrel to Paige's skull was no more than a few inches.

The hole at the muzzle gaped at her. Paige tried to look at the man and away from the black tunnel of the revolver barrel but couldn't pry her eyes from the gun. She could feel herself trembling, convulsive shudders she was certain were visible to the ski-masked figure looming over her.

"So long, slut," the man said in his raspy voice.

Paige could see the revolver's cylinder rotating as the man slowly began pulling the trigger. She knew she was about to die.

Paige squeezed her eyes shut as a sob escaped her lips. The revolver fired.

CHAPTER 2

At the sound of the doorbell, retired judge Gene Callen rose from his breakfast table and limped toward the front door. He reached for his cane leaning against the doorway. He'd been using the cane more with each passing year, though he had started limping on his return from the Pacific theater in 1945. As a junior officer aboard the carrier *USS Sargent Bay*, Callen had endured the unpleasant experience of being wounded during the Iwo Jima campaign. The shrapnel damage to his right knee hadn't been more than a nuisance as a younger man, but as he approached his seventieth birthday, the war wound reared its arthritic head with a vengeance.

The Judge hobbled through his large house toward the front door as the chimes sounded again.

"I'm coming," he said, forgetting whoever was ringing the doorbell was beyond his voice.

His house, or mansion as some would describe it, was on Dayton Avenue, in the heart of Alameda's Gold Coast. A widower, and retired from the Superior Court in the City and County of Alameda, Judge Callen shared his home with a part-time housekeeper. Though it was only a little past 7am, Judge Callen had risen and dressed, and was enjoying his coffee and morning paper as had been his custom for over forty years.

Despite his age, the Judge was a remarkably vibrant man. And despite the cane, he stood ramrod-straight and sported a full head of white hair. Up until a couple of years ago, when his declining leg began severely limiting his mobility, it had been his habit to take daily walks at this time of day. The degrading condition of his gait the past couple of years had left him happy to get to his breakfast table each morning without intolerable pain.

The Judge opened the door to find a uniformed Alameda police officer standing on his porch.

"Good morning, Your Honor," the officer said. "I'm sorry to disturb you at this hour, but there's been some trouble with your daughter. I need you to accompany me to the hospital."

"What is it? What's happened to Paige?" His heart skipped a beat.

"She's been attacked," the cop answered. "I don't think she's badly hurt. I've been ordered to escort you to the hospital. That's all I know. The sergeant can give you more information when we arrive."

"Then let's go," the Judge said, grateful Paige was alive but filled with dread at the word "attacked". He stepped forcefully through the door and pulled it shut. Ignoring the anguish in his leg, he pushed past the startled police officer and strode down the walk toward the patrol car parked in front of his home.

The Alameda Hospital was on Clinton Avenue, only a few scant blocks from Callen's residence. Within a couple of minutes, he was clambering out of the patrol car, which had come to rest at the emergency room entrance. Waiting to greet him was a tall, middle-aged man in a suit, with a thick mustache and blow-dried hair. Callen recognized him as an Alameda police detective.

"Judge Callen," the man said, offering his hand. "I'm

Detective Sergeant Randy Wendt. I'm with APD's Homicide/ Robbery Unit. I believe we've met before."

"I remember you," the Judge said curtly, shaking his hand. "Where's Paige? How bad is it?"

"Follow me and you can see for yourself."

Wendt led Callen into the ER and to one of the treatment rooms. There, surrounded by two people in hospital garb, sat Paige. She was still wearing her running attire and was coated head to toe in sandy grime. She had a blanket wrapped around her shoulders and sported a large shiner over her left eye. A patch of bloodied white gauze was being held over her left ear by one of the attendants. Paige's face was an ashen color, and oddly enough, her forehead was covered with a bright, phosphorescent orange stain over a nasty bruise. At her father's entrance, Paige looked up.

"Dad–"

"Paige; thank God. Are you OK? What happened?"

The woman holding the patch over Paige's head motioned angrily for the Judge to leave. It was then Callen noticed she wasn't a nurse but a physician. She was busy sewing stitches over his daughter's ear.

Wendt took his cue from the attending doctor and firmly ushered the Judge out of the examining room.

"C'mon, Your Honor," he said. "You can speak with your daughter after she's been treated. Let's get a cup of coffee. There's a break room down the hall; we can talk there." He escorted the red-faced Callen to a room with a table, a refrigerator, and an industrial-sized coffee machine.

Judge Callen sat down heavily and put his face in his hands. Wendt poured a cup of coffee and placed it on the table before him.

"What happened?"

Wendt sat across from the Judge. "We're not sure yet. It only went down within the past hour. We're still piecing it together. Paige was pretty out of it when she was brought in, so details are sketchy."

"Was she...?"

"No," Wendt reassured him. "As far as we can tell, Paige was not sexually assaulted. But she was definitely attacked and terrorized."

"What do you mean by 'terrorized'?" The Judge looked up; his emotional moment had passed. He was all business now and sought the facts of the case.

Wendt wasn't surprised. Like most cops in the San Francisco Bay Area, he knew the Judge's reputation well. A figure of legal prominence since the mid-Fifties, Callen's exploits as a Municipal and Superior Court Judge were as legendary as the fiery man himself.

"Iron Gene" Callen was a controversial and colorful character in the history of the notoriously tolerant criminal justice system of the San Francisco Bay. A staunchly law-and-order magistrate and fierce champion of the death penalty, Callen had made his name during the turbulent Sixties. He was well known throughout San Francisco Bay Area jurisprudence for his tendency toward maximum sentences when dropping the gavel. Criminals who had the misfortune of finding themselves before Judge Callen could count on the full weight of whatever the law allowed him to penalize them with. This made him popular with cops, prosecutors, and victims, but reviled by defense attorneys, criminal-rights advocates, and quite often the press.

The Judge's clout wasn't entirely in the legal arena, either. Callen's early inroads into Alameda real estate had earned him both great wealth and a formidable reputation as a shrewd businessman. Only his lifelong disdain for politics prevented him from rising to what many believed was his true calling: a seat on the California legislature.

He'd been personally asked to run for political office first by Governor Reagan, and again by President Reagan.

Judge Callen's flame had diminished somewhat with the death of his wife several years ago, and his retirement from the Bench, not surprisingly, came shortly thereafter. Their only child, Paige, was his pride and joy. Paige had followed in her father's legal footsteps and obtained her law degree from Berkeley's Boalt Hall. Through Judge Callen's clout but without Paige's knowledge, she was hired as a deputy district attorney for the County of Alameda straight out of law school. Though not yet twenty-nine years old, Paige had been assigned to the City of Alameda municipal courthouse for a little over three years of the five she'd been a deputy DA.

"This is what we know," Wendt began. Callen folded his hands over his cane.

"Apparently, your daughter was on the beach for her morning jog," Wendt said. "Same route she takes every day."

"A habit instilled during our morning walks when she was a child," Callen said. "Go on."

"Paige was running when struck from behind by an unknown assailant. She was listening to music. She didn't hear him approach due to her headphones. The guy was wearing a hood and ski mask. She could tell he was Caucasian and thinks he's at least twenty-five or thirty years old. He knew her name and implied Paige should know him."

"Accomplices?"

"Paige didn't see one. Doesn't mean there weren't any. He pushed her face in the sand, and she believed she was going to be suffocated."

The Judge's face became taut, but inside him a fury began to build. He remained outwardly composed. "Continue."

"The suspect struck her with the barrel of a revolver. He made a point of showing her the gun. Then he aimed it at her head and said, 'Goodbye', or something similarly final. He wanted Paige to believe she was going to be killed."

Hard lines formed around Callen's mouth. In a hoarse but calm voice, he asked, "Why isn't she dead, Sergeant?"

"It was a paintball gun, Your Honor."

"A paint gun?"

Wendt shook his head. "This type of paint gun isn't used to paint a house or car. It's an air gun manufactured to look and handle like a real gun, but instead uses compressed air to fire a ball of dye intended to mark its target. Survivalist types and gun nuts use them in simulated war games. Our departmental SWAT team sometimes uses them in training. They're not uncommon, and can be acquired at many sporting goods stores."

"That's the orange gunk I saw on Paige's face?"

"Right."

"I don't get it," Callen said. "Why would someone assault Paige, choke her, hit her, and then shoot her with a harmless ball of paint?"

Wendt paused, choosing his words carefully. "Your Honor," he started, "remember when I used the word 'terrorized' a moment ago? These paintball guns look exactly like a real gun. For all Paige knew, she was about to be executed. That's what I meant by 'terrorized'. It was deliberate. He was trying to make her think she was going to die."

Most of the color left the Judge's face. He reached down with none-too-steady hands and took a sip of coffee.

"I want this man found," he said.

"We do, too. It looks pretty bad for the cops in this town if our own deputy DA is assaulted and the crook gets away with it. But we don't have much to go on. There are no witnesses and no physical evidence. We don't even have a motive."

"What about the criminals she's prosecuted?" Callen asked. "Isn't that the logical and obvious place to start?

"In theory, Your Honor, I would agree. But reality is a different story. Paige has been a deputy DA, here and in Oakland, for over five years. She's prosecuted hundreds of cases. You want me to go through every case she's ever handled in Alameda Superior Court? Even if I had the manpower to do that, which I don't, how do we know when we find him? Besides, we don't even know if the attack is linked to her job. It could be anyone from an ex-boyfriend to a random creep who spotted her and took a fancy. Unless we can narrow the scope of the suspect pool, the possibilities are endless."

"So you're going to do nothing? Is that it?" This time it took greater effort for the Judge to maintain his impassive demeanor.

"Hell no, Your Honor. I'm going to do everything I can to nail this bastard. But you've got to be prepared for the worst."

"What do you mean, 'the worst'? I don't like the sound of that."

Wendt let out a slow breath and sat back in his chair. "What I meant is that our best chance to get this guy is probably going to be in the act. If he tries again and if we're ready for him."

"And if you're not?" Callen demanded.

"He may never try again," Wendt offered. "This might have been a one-time deal. Or maybe we'll get a break and it'll turn out to be an ex-boyfriend or someone else from her past. All I'm saying is there aren't any certainties. We'll do the usual investigative stuff and interview Paige's neighbors and co-workers. We'll check the local sporting goods stores for recent paintball gun purchases. But I don't want you to get your hopes up. We don't have much at this point."

"I know how police investigations are conducted, Sergeant," Callen said sternly, his eyes flashing, "and I'm more than aware of their limitations."

"I didn't mean to imply you didn't," Wendt said.

Callen cooled his stare. Like Wendt, he sat back in his chair.

"I'm not trying to argue with you, Sergeant," he said, deliberately softening his features and tone to conceal the plans he was already hatching to take matters into his own hands. "I'm just an old man trying to protect his only child. I'm confident your department will do everything within the law to bring justice to bear."

In truth, the Judge wasn't confident. A lifetime of watching criminals escape justice on a daily basis had left him with no illusions about what the police could do to protect his daughter.

Wendt was immediately on guard. He knew Judge Callen's reputation too well to swallow the sudden switch from challenge to condescension, and he could see the plotting lights in the older man's eyes when he spoke. The detective sergeant sympathized; if someone threatened one of his kids, he'd do anything he could, the law be damned, to keep them safe. But he had a job to do, and keeping the victim's father from interfering in a felony investigation was part of it.

"I know what you're thinking, Your Honor," he said. "You need to leave this to us. You understand that, don't you?"

"I understand perfectly." The Judge stood up. "Don't let me keep you from your work, Sergeant. Thank you for explaining the status of the case to me."

Wendt stood also. "I'm sorry for what happened to your daughter. Know that we'll be giving this case top priority. If there is anything I can do for you–"

"Actually, there is," the Judge cut him off. "I'd like to be kept apprised of the investigation as it progresses. Say, a daily phone call?"

Wendt knew he didn't have the power to refuse the Judge's request. He was more than aware his police chief and Callen were thick as thieves, and even if he were to decline to reveal the details of the investigation, the well-connected old judge could easily obtain the information from any number of other sources within the department. At least if the daily report to Callen was coming from him, Wendt could edit the information as needed.

"Of course. Call me anytime." He handed the Judge one of his business cards.

Judge Callen started for the door. With some effort, he pivoted on his cane and turned back to the Alameda detective.

"I have one more question, if you don't mind?"

"Not at all," Wendt replied warily.

"Do you believe, professionally or personally, that the attack on my daughter today is a 'one-time deal' as you said?"

Wendt studied his fingernails for a moment before answering.

"No, Your Honor. He'll be back."

"I thought the same. Good day, Sergeant."

CHAPTER 3

Ray Cowell cursed loudly and slammed his fist into the dashboard of his Hyundai sedan as the flashing blue lights of an Alameda police motorcycle reflected in his rearview mirror. He braked sharply and checked his speedometer, which read an unpleasant forty-four miles per hour. Ray pulled to the curb and eased his car to a halt.

The motorcycle, a big Harley-Davidson, pulled in behind his car and its rider dismounted. Ray glanced nervously at the gym bag sitting innocently on the passenger seat next to him. The motorcycle officer, a broad-shouldered Caucasian with a light complexion, was almost at his door.

"Good morning, Sir. May I see your driver's license and registration, please?"

Reaching for his wallet, Ray replied, "Certainly, Officer. Did I do something wrong?"

Accepting the license, the cop ignored Ray's question until he had ensured the image adorning the document matched the face of the car's driver.

"I stopped you for speeding, Sir. Do you know how fast you were going?"

"I was only doing twenty-five, Officer. That's the speed limit here on Lincoln Avenue. I know because I take this route every day to work."

"Sir, I clocked you on radar at over forty miles per hour.

I'm going to have to issue you a citation. Please wait here."

Ray felt his blood begin to boil. As the motorcycle cop turned to walk back to his bike to write the ticket, Ray got out of his car.

"Hey, Officer, wait a minute–"

The cop whirled to face Ray with a speed that startled him.

"Sir, I told you to remain in your vehicle. It's for your own safety and mine."

The cop strode from Ray to his Harley, opened the saddlebag, and brought out a black leather citation book. He began to write.

"Officer," Ray called out, his voice rising. "I wasn't speeding. This is total bullshit. Why don't you fill your quota with somebody who deserves a ticket? You only pulled me over because I'm a white guy and have the money to pay the fine. Why don't you hassle one of the niggers or Mexicans? Why are you picking on me?"

The cop ignored the racist jab and continued scrawling his citation. Ray wouldn't let it go.

"That's right. You heard me. I know how gutless you cops are. Too afraid to pull over a nigger or a car full of Mexicans, so you hammer the law-abiding taxpayer. You only pulled me over because I'm white," he repeated.

"That's odd," the cop replied sarcastically. "My radar gun must be malfunctioning. I had it set on 'Asian'." He made an elaborate gesture of picking up his radar gun and examining it. "My mistake; the radar gun is working fine." He looked directly at Ray. "It was set on 'Asshole'."

Ray fumed. He took several steps towards the officer. The cop set the radar gun and his citation book down on the motorcycle seat.

"I already told you to remain in your car."

"It's a free country. I'll stand wherever I want." Ray's

entire body was pulsing with fury. He folded his arms and glared at the cop.

The Alameda cop strode forcefully up to Ray. Ray suddenly noticed that while the cop was about his height of five-foot-ten-inches, he was at least thirty pounds heavier than Ray's one hundred and fifty-five pounds. Most of it looked like muscle.

"You're right; it's a free country," the cop said, "and you can stand wherever you want. But if you take one more step closer to me, you're going to be enjoying your freedom in the hospital. And then jail. Do I make myself clear?"

Ray was trembling with rage but held his tongue. The last thing he needed was to get arrested. It had been such a good day until now, and he didn't want to ruin it with his temper. His temper was always getting the best of him; that's what his ex-girlfriend Maritay used to say.

"I'm sorry, Officer," Ray said, his tone calmer. "I'm upset. I think you're making a mistake on my speed. I just went to court last month on another bogus ticket one of your buddies gave me."

The cop finished his citation and extended the book and a pen to Ray.

"Press hard; you're making three copies. If I've made a mistake, we can hash it out in court. This isn't the time or the place."

"You're right," Ray said, signing the ticket with a flourish. "I'll see you in court. I want your name and badge number."

The cop peeled off the yellow copy of the citation and handed it to Ray. "My name and badge number are already on the ticket. Have a nice day." He walked backwards to his motorcycle, keeping Ray in sight.

"You have a nice day too, Officer," Ray said. Under his breath, he muttered, "I hope you crash your motorcycle and get crippled for life."

The cop grinned and fired up his Harley. Apparently, he had heard Ray's muttering. He kicked his bike into gear and sped off.

Ray stood in the street and clenched his fists as the motorcycle roared away. He crushed the ticket into a ball in his hand and got back into his car, slamming the door.

After several minutes, Ray was calm enough to drive. Making sure to remain at the speed limit, he continued west on Lincoln Avenue and then north on Constitution Way, which took him into the Posey Tube.

Once through the Tube and into Oakland, Ray guided his Hyundai west through the metro traffic until he reached the Port of Oakland complex. He parked in the Maersk Shipping parking lot on Ferry Street. As he got out of his car, he grabbed the gym bag from the passenger seat.

Opening the trunk, he tossed the half-open gym bag in amongst the spare tire and assorted tools. A small amount of sand was leaking from the partially-zipped bag. Ray took a moment to zip the bag fully closed, cursing as the ski mask inside briefly fouled the zipper.

Closing the trunk, Ray nodded to the gate guard and headed into the office. Passing other busy shipping clerks, he entered his cubicle and sat down behind his cluttered desk. Seconds later, the head of a co-worker poked around the edge of the partition. Ray disliked all of his co-workers, and this one was no exception.

It was just Ray's luck that his closest cubicle neighbor was constantly inflicting his musical choices on the office via a cheap clock radio on his desk. This morning, as if the workday weren't already going badly enough, Ray was being subjected to the annoying warbles of Terence Trent D'Arby. Ray despised today's top 40, MTV video crap. His preference was for the Sixties folk music of his youth on the oldies station.

"Morning, Ray. Boss already noticed you're late. Thought I'd warn you. Good luck with an excuse."

Ray lit a cigarette from a pack in his desk drawer, and extended his middle finger as his co-worker turned his head. When he was sure the unwelcome intruder had gone for good, he removed a piece of typing paper from inside his desk, carefully using his handkerchief to prevent leaving any fingerprints. He inserted the paper into his typewriter. Still using the handkerchief, he produced a plain white business-sized envelope and placed it next to the typewriter. He began typing.

It had been a good day. Despite that prick of a cop and a speeding ticket, it had been a splendid day. And it was shaping up to be a damned good week. Ray would make certain of that. This week would be one to remember.

One for the books.

CHAPTER 4

Paige came downstairs clad in a pair of jeans and a sweater dug out from the closet in her old room. Her hair was still damp, and she'd tied it up with a wide band taken from a collection of hair accessories she had left over from her high school days. The hairband did an adequate job of concealing the bald patch over her left ear created by the ER doctor when she shaved away her locks to sew the gash there. The hairband, coupled with her lack of makeup, gave Paige the appearance of looking much younger than her twenty-eight years.

The Judge was seated in the kitchen and looked up when he saw Paige. A mostly empty glass of scotch was on the table in front of him next to a just-opened bottle of Dewar's. He stood when she entered.

"Sometimes," he said, "you are the spitting image of your mother."

"It's the hairband, Dad," Paige said. Her nose wrinkled when she saw the bottle.

"Maybe it adds to the effect," he said, sitting down again, "but it's still true. You look more like I remember your mother every day. Can I pour you a drink? Might do you good."

Paige sat down. "You know I don't drink very often; especially on workdays."

Judge Callen stiffened. "You're not going to work today; I forbid it."

"I have a caseload, Dad," she said, consciously tempering her reply. Paige hated it when her father patronized her with his courtroom tone. "I've already missed a preliminary hearing this morning, and the afternoon's booked solid."

"Surely after what happened this morning you can take the afternoon off? My God, you were–"

"It's not a big deal," she interrupted her father. "I'm OK. I've handled far worse crimes than this one."

"Horseshit," he countered. "You were the victim today, not an impassive third party processing the victim through court. There's a difference."

Paige struggled to maintain her cool. Her body ached, her head hurt, and she was still rattled from the attack. She didn't need another argument with her father on top of it all.

"That lunatic is still out there," the Judge went on. "Maybe he'll be at the courthouse, waiting for you there? Maybe he's been following you for some time? He called you by name; that's what the detective said. I'm worried."

Paige could indeed see concern behind her father's eyes. She knew him as an aloof, impassive personality who prided himself on his gruff, professional demeanor. It was said of Judge Callen that he once sentenced a man to the gas chamber and ordered the bailiff to bring donuts and coffee in the same breath.

Yet Paige noticed since her mother's death two years ago and his subsequent retirement, the Judge seemed increasingly frail. More fatherly and less the imposing figure of discipline and propriety who had ruled her life as firmly as his courtroom.

"Dad, this guy is just some kind of a nut. I'll probably never hear from him again. Anyway, I'll be damned if I'm going to let a lowlife thug scare me. I'm not afraid of this jerk."

Even as she spoke, she knew she was lying. She had been terrified beyond anything she'd ever experienced before and would be looking over her shoulder for a long time to come.

"Besides," Paige said with a certainty she didn't feel, "I'm confident APD will identify and arrest him soon."

The Judge's brow furrowed in doubt. "Who are you kidding? The cops don't have squat, and you of all people should know it. For this creep to get caught would take one of three things. One, he'll turn himself in. Not likely. Two, somebody else will turn him in. Possible, but still highly unlikely. Three, he'll get caught in the act. Assuming someone is there to catch him at the time of the attack, which is of course at his leisure and discretion. And further assuming he is caught in the act before doing you harm."

"So what do you want me to do? Dig a hole and hide in it? Move to Tibet?"

"One thing you could do," the Judge said, averting his eyes, "is move back here to the house. You'd be safer here where I could keep an eye on you."

"I'm not moving back home, Dad. How many times do we have to go over this?"

Ever since the death of her mother, the Judge had been trying to entice Paige into moving back into the mansion. She was currently residing in a condominium on Bay Farm Island, adjacent to the Harbor Bay health club. Judge Callen never tired of dropping hints that the house was too big for him to maintain, even with Mrs Reyes, his housekeeper, coming every other day. And though Paige visited her father for lunch at least once a week, he never relented in his not-so-subtle demands for more of her time.

"You know I enjoy spending time with you here at the house. But I have my own life. I need my space."

Paige couldn't believe her own ears. She sounded like a college freshman ditching her first boyfriend, instead of a nearly thirty year-old deputy district attorney working for one of the largest counties in California.

The Judge stared forlornly at his feet. Paige stood, wrapped her arms around him, and gave him a hug. "Dad, I love you. And I know you believe you're looking out for my best interests. But I'm a big girl now; I can handle this."

Judge Callen grinned, a warm glow spreading across his craggy features. He adored his daughter Paige and, despite his best efforts, could not restrain himself from using every opportunity to convince her to move back home with him. He knew it was a flagrant indicator of old age but did it nonetheless.

Paige disentangled herself from her father. "I've got to get to the office. I'll barely have time to run home and change before lunch is over."

"I wish you'd reconsider taking the day off."

"Bye, Dad," she said, ignoring his question and giving him a peck on the cheek. She started for the door. "I'll need to borrow your car; mine's still at the beach. I'll bring it back tonight."

"Keep it as long as you like," he said.

"Thanks."

"Paige," the Judge said, "I want you to know I love you. I'd do anything to ensure your safety. Anything."

Paige turned back to her father, puzzled at the odd look on his face. She couldn't remember ever seeing that expression before, and it momentarily alarmed her.

"Of course I know you love me. Are you OK?"

"I'm fine."

The Judge waited until he heard his Mercedes pull out of the garage, and the garage door close, before retrieving his cane. He lumbered to his study and sat down behind his large mahogany desk. There he opened the top drawer and withdrew a worn and elegantly embossed address book. Putting on a pair of reading glasses extracted from his pocket, he thumbed through the book until he found the number he was seeking. He reached for the phone on the desk and dialed a series of numbers.

"Bayfront Realty," a woman's voice answered. "May I help you?"

"I'd like to speak to Sandy Altman, please."

"I'm sorry, but Mr Altman is in a conference. May I take a message?"

"Yes. Could you relay to Mr Altman that Judge Callen called? I need to speak with him; it's rather urgent."

"Please hold," the woman's voice said. "I'll see if Mr Altman can be interrupted."

A moment later another voice came on the line. "Gene? That you?"

"Yes, Sandy, it's me. If I called at a bad time–"

"Hell no, Gene. I've instructed my secretary to tell everybody I'm always in a conference; that way, I can screen the deadbeats. What can I do for you?"

"Sandy, I have a favor to ask. It's personal and important."

"You name it; heaven knows I owe you."

"You owe me nothing," the Judge replied. "But I have a serious problem. Somebody is stalking Paige. She was attacked this morning."

"Oh my God; is she all right?"

"She's all right for now, but this stalker is a real psychopath. He beat her up and shot her in the head with some kind of a toy gun. She believed at the time it was a real gun and she was going to be executed."

"Paige must have been petrified," Altman said. "Was it a random thing?"

"Apparently not. The bastard called her by name and said something menacing about meeting again."

"The cops have any idea who this dude is?" Altman asked.

"Not a clue." The Judge paused, carefully choosing his next words. "Sandy, I can't sit on my hands waiting for the police. We both know how that usually works out. Not when Paige's life is at stake."

"I understand. You think this creep is going to make another try?"

"I don't know," Callen said. "I'm not going to take the chance."

"I wouldn't, either," Altman said. "What can I do?"

"I need your help. I want you to reach out to somebody for me. One of your friends."

"Just give me the name, Gene," Altman said, "and I'll have him on your doorstep."

"I want to meet Bob Farrell," Judge Callen said.

CHAPTER 5

"Bless me Father, for I have sinned," Bob Farrell said.

"May the Holy Spirit visit you and fill your heart with contrition," the priest's paternal voice responded through the confessional partition. "How long has it been since your last confession?"

"Twenty years or more," Farrell reluctantly admitted. "Johnson was in office. It was before I shipped out to Vietnam."

"The Catholic church welcomes you back," the priest said. "You may begin your confession."

"I've done something pretty bad," Farrell began after a moment. "I'm not sure I'm ready to confess it yet."

"The sacrament of confession is a powerful thing. You'll feel better after you unburden yourself of your sins."

"If you say so," Farrell said. "Well, here goes; I broke into somebody's house today."

"That's a very grievous sin," the priest acknowledged.

"You don't know the half of it," Farrell quipped. "It was your house."

"My house... What kind of a sick joke is this?" the priest demanded.

"No joke, Padre," Farrell said. "You are Father Mulroney, aren't you?"

"I am," came the hesitant reply.

"And you live in the rectory behind this church? Your roommate is a fluffy white cat?"

"How did you know that?"

"It was your place I burglarized, all right. Don't worry about the cat; I locked it in the bathroom so it wouldn't get out."

"Who are you?"

"I thought my confession was supposed to be confidential?"

"I'm not going to stand for this," the priest announced. He tried to exit the confessional booth but found he couldn't budge the door.

"I wedged a chair under the doorknob before I entered," Farrell told him, as he listened to Father Mulroney rattle the confessional door in a futile attempt to get out. "I'm afraid you're not going anywhere."

"You filthy thief," Mulroney said. "Let me out."

"Don't you want to hear the rest of my confession?"

"I do not. But I'm sure the police will."

"The San Francisco police are already on their way."

"What are you talking about?"

"I called the cops from your home telephone, as a matter of fact. I phoned in an anonymous tip that somebody just kicked in the front door to the rectory here at the church. I even told the police dispatcher I heard screams coming from inside the residence. When the SFPD rolls up, they'll find your door smashed in. They'll have to go inside to check on your welfare. Probably be here any minute."

"What do you want?" Father Mulroney challenged. "Why are you doing this?"

"You forgot to ask the most important question, Father," Farrell said, putting an unfiltered Camel between his lips and lighting it with a worn Zippo. When he finished lighting his smoke, Farrell kept the flame burning, illuminating the darkness of the confessional. "Don't you want to know what I took?"

"Who are you?" Mulroney asked again, his voice wavering.

"Let me show you what I took from inside your home," Farrell said, ignoring the priest's question. He extracted a Polaroid photograph from his pocket and held it up to the screened partition separating the priest's and confessor's compartments. The flickering glow of the cigarette lighter brought the photograph into clarity. The image showed a naked Caucasian man in his late fifties with gray hair and sideburns. The man sported a distinct eagle tattoo on his shoulder, a goatee, and an erect penis. Lying next to the man was a nude Hispanic boy who couldn't have been older than ten or eleven years old. The boy appeared drugged.

"Excellent likeness of you, wouldn't you say?"

"Where did you find that?" Father Mulroney asked in a hoarse voice.

"You know exactly where I found it, Father Mulroney. It was with a bunch of similar Polaroid photographs inside an old shoebox. You know the place: in your bedroom closet, under the false panel beneath the carpet. It was in there with your camera, and your stash of homosexual porn magazines, and your dildo, and your bong, and that little tin throat-lozenge box full of weed. I found your methamphetamine and amyl nitrate, too."

"You planted that stuff to disparage me."

"Oh come now, Father," Farrell chuckled, exhaling smoke. "Who's going to believe somebody planted twenty or thirty naked pictures of you with little boys?"

"Those pictures aren't mine," Mulroney declared.

"Whatever you say, Father. Isn't telling a lie a sin?"

"It'll never hold up in court," Mulroney insisted, desperation creeping into his tone. "Anything you found in my house is inadmissible as evidence in a court of law because you obtained it illegally."

"Spoken like somebody who's been accused before," Farrell said. "That's where the cops come in. Whatever contraband the police find when they enter a residence for a lawful purpose – say, investigating a reported burglary – is, in fact, admissible in court. Especially if that evidence constitutes a potential felony. And rest assured I left all your goodies out in plain sight. If the San Francisco police department sent Officer Ray Charles with Stevie Wonder as his backup, they'd find it."

"I can get money," Father Mulroney pleaded.

"Is that how you beat the rap at your parish in Albuquerque? What about Wichita? And Duluth? The bishop must have had your back, or you had something over his head, because you kept avoiding prosecution and got reassigned to new parishes in new states. I checked. But you're not very smart, Padre; you keep mementos."

"Parents don't want trials," Mulroney said in a defiant voice. "They don't like to go to court. Nobody wants their child to be shamed in public. No one will testify. And I have a right to face my accusers."

"That kind of intimidation might have worked in the past, Father, but not anymore." Farrell took a deep drag on his smoke and exhaled through his nostrils, snapping his Zippo shut. The darkness returned. "Anyway," he went on, "who said anything about a court of law?"

Outside the church, a series of car doors slammed. Men's voices barked and there was the sound of several pairs of running feet.

"That would be the police, I'm guessing. Any minute now, Your Holiness, they'll enter your burglarized house with the noble intent of rescuing you. Boy, are they in for a surprise."

"You son of a bitch," Mulroney's voice hissed.

"Good heavens, Father," Farrell exclaimed. "Such language. And in God's house."

"I won't let you do this," the priest said from behind the partition.

"I already did it," Farrell said. "By the way, you haven't finished hearing my confession."

"Fuck you."

"Is that my penance?" Farrell retorted. "Because if what I've seen in your photo collection is any indication of how you absolve people of their sins, I'll stay a sinner."

"Fuck you," the priest snarled again.

Farrell opened the confessor's compartment and stepped out. He took a moment to ensure the folding metal chair he'd taken from the choir was still firmly jamming the priest's compartment closed. He rapped on the door with his knuckles.

"Hey, Father Mulroney," Farrell called out. "Don't blow a gasket in there. Once I get down the street, I'll put in another anonymous call to the San Francisco police department. I'll let them know where you are. By then I assume the cops are going to want to talk to you anyway."

"You can go straight to hell."

"Probably. Aren't you curious why I chose that particular photograph, out of all those pictures of naked boys in your little souvenir box, to show you?"

"I don't care," answered the muffled voice of the priest trapped inside his own confessional.

"You should," Farrell said. "The kid in that picture was an altar boy from your parish in Albuquerque. But you already knew that, didn't you? I say 'was' because he's dead. He committed suicide the day after his thirteenth birthday. Hung himself in his parent's basement. I'll bet you already knew that, too."

"Who are you?" Mulroney asked for the third time, his voice quivering. "A cop?"

"Not anymore," Farrell said, "although you're going to wish I was. I'm the man who was hired by the dead boy's father. It's a tragic story, really. After his son killed himself, his health and marriage collapsed. I guess you could say he went a little crazy with grief."

Farrell could hear the breathing of the priest locked within the confessional become heavier.

"This man," he continued, "operates a very successful sanitation business with his brother, who happens to be an ex-con in good standing with the Mexican Mafia. The brothers have understandably become rather obsessed with finding the person they believe responsible for the boy's death. That's where I come in."

"What are you going to do with that photograph?" Father Mulroney's voice changed to a trembling whisper.

"I'm going to give it to the guy who paid for it, of course," Farrell told him matter-of-factly. "And paid well. I may be a sinner, Father, but I fulfill my contractual obligations."

"They'll kill me," Mulroney said meekly. He began to cry.

"Not my concern," Farrell said.

"Do you want my blood on your hands?" the priest wept. "Do you?"

"I've had bloody hands before," Farrell said truthfully to the confessional door. "I've learned it washes off."

"Not off your soul," Mulroney cried. "Please don't give him the picture." His sobs increased in intensity. "You'll be damned to hell."

"Actually," Farrell smirked around his cigarette, "after the boy's father sees this Polaroid, I bet you'll end up in hell long before me. If I were you and I wanted to keep breathing, I'd confess to the cops, plead guilty, and pray for solitary confinement."

"For the love of God," Father Mulroney's muffled voice hysterically entreated.

"I don't think God has anything to do with it."

"Please; I beg you."

"Thanks for hearing me confess, Father Mulroney," Farrell yelled over his shoulder as he walked away. "I'll say a couple of Hail Marys on the way out." He extinguished his cigarette in the stoup.

"And you were right about the power of confession," Farrell's voice echoed through the church. "I feel better already."

CHAPTER 6

Paige Callen mounted the steps to the Alameda Municipal Courthouse and tried to blend in with the herd returning from lunch. She made it through the lobby unscathed but was accosted immediately upon entering her office.

"Paige, how's it going, babe?"

Paige let out an exasperated sigh. It was the voice of her officemate, Deputy District Attorney Tim Potter.

"I'm fine, Chaz," she said. "And I'm not in the mood for any of your crap."

"Who's giving you crap? And I hate it when you call me Chaz."

"I know."

C. Timothy Potter, as the nameplate on his desk read, shared the office and a county secretary named Carmen with Paige. He had been assigned to the Alameda courthouse from the Berkeley station only a month before. In his late thirties, he was a paunchy man a couple inches shorter than his co-worker. Potter sported a diamond pinky ring to accent his expensively cut suits, the expense being the extra material and effort his tailor exerted to conceal his girth. Tim Potter always reeked too heavily of cologne, and his forehead was scarred from where his latest hair transplant was struggling to find purchase.

Since he had more tenure with the district attorney's

office than Paige, Potter never ceased to affect a superior tone, which was a constant source of irritation to her. Potter was the last person Paige wished to see today, but since she shared a county office with him, she knew it was unavoidable. His clumsy, chronic attempts to woo her were an annoyance on a good day; today, she expected them to be unbearable.

"That's some shiner," Potter remarked as he blocked the path into her office. He stepped up and peered into her face, bringing his own face, and sour breath, uncomfortably into Paige's personal space.

"I'm not in the mood," Paige said, elbowing him aside and entering her office. Potter remained in the doorway, leaning his shoulder against the doorjamb and crossing one ankle over the other.

"Paige," Potter began as she tossed her briefcase on her desk. "I realize almost getting raped is a traumatic event. That kind of thing can really mess with a chick's head."

"Who told you I was almost raped?" Paige said, trying to ignore the sexist remark.

"I heard two cops talking in the hallway say you were attacked," he answered.

"Overheard, you mean."

"I wanted to reassure you that all men aren't bad, you know? Some of us aren't insensitive to the needs of the modern woman. Why don't you let me take you to dinner tonight and show you what I mean?"

"I wasn't almost raped," Paige insisted, wishing she hadn't said it as soon as she had. She wasn't sure it was true and had no desire to be sucked into a conversation with Potter. "As far as dinner, I would rather be kidnapped by pirates and sold into slavery than go anywhere with you."

"Wow," Potter exclaimed, unfazed, as always, by Paige's rebuke. "What kind of weirdo would attack a hot-looking broad like you and not rape her? I mean, what a freak, right?"

"Christ, Chaz; it's nineteen eighty-nine; not eighteen eighty-nine. Could you please at least pretend to not be such a chauvinist asshole?"

"So, if he didn't try to rape you, what did he do?" Potter asked, ignoring Paige's insult. "He must have done something, or else you wouldn't have that bald patch over your ear."

"Listen to the expert on bald patches. Chaz, every time you open that fat mouth of yours, you sound more like the brain-dead pervert you are. Get out of my office and away from me this instant before I call Charlie White."

"I'm not afraid of White," Potter grunted. "Bring him on."

"Suit yourself," a thundering voice boomed. Potter winced and turned around to find the voice's owner, Charlie White, standing behind him. Charlie was the court bailiff and a Bay Area law enforcement legend going back to the days when the law was enforced exclusively with the baton and gun. Charlie had killed more suspects in shoot-outs than anyone in Alameda County history, and was as well-known as any judge on the Alameda County bench. In his late sixties, Charlie packed over three hundred pounds on a six-foot-five-inch frame and had a well-earned reputation as nobody to tangle with in a fight. More than one youthful offender inclined to create trouble in the courtroom learned the hard way that fat old Charlie's bark was far preferable to his bite. Charlie was fiercely protective of Paige, whom he'd known since she was a toddler visiting her father's courtroom. White scowled over Potter.

"You keep your distance," Potter stammered, "or there's going to be trouble."

"You're goddamned right there's going to be trouble, shit-for-brains," the bailiff growled, "and you're going to be on the receiving end."

One of Brown's sausage-sized fingers snaked out and poked Potter's chest like an iron rod.

"You know something, shit-bird," Charlie said to the flinching Timothy Potter, "I used to bounce Paige here on my knee. I know her old man real well, best damned judge to ever pound a gavel. If he knew you'd been harassing his little girl, he'd probably volunteer his legal services in my defense after I popped you like a ripe zit."

Paige suppressed a grin as Potter squirmed beneath the looming deputy. His beady eyes bulged in their sockets as White poked him again for emphasis.

"You better leave him alone, Charlie," Paige said. "If you hurt him, I'll be buried in paperwork for a week."

"You're right, honey," White said casually, lowering his finger and stepping back. "Besides, I don't like to injure anybody so soon after lunch; it causes indigestion."

As Potter tried to reclaim his composure, White turned to Paige. "Heard about what happened this morning. Came by to let you know if you need anything, anything at all, you just holler. Old Charlie will come a-runnin'."

Paige gave Charlie a hug. "I'm fine," she said. "But thank you. It's good to know you're around."

Charlie blushed. "I'd better get going." As he walked out, he turned and pointed at the green-faced C. Timothy Potter.

"I find out about you giving Paige a hard time again, I'll be back to make a balloon animal out of you, Counselor."

Potter nodded as Charlie walked out. He waddled over to his own office and sat down behind his desk, loosening his tie. He glared at Paige, who shook her head.

"I have half a mind to report Charlie to the district attorney," he whined, rubbing his chest. "For assault."

"Go ahead, Chaz; my sexual harassment complaint will be right behind it."

Potter was about to retort when Carmen, their perm-haired secretary, walked in.

"Sorry I'm late getting back from lunch," she announced in her nasal voice. "Had to pick up my dry cleaning." Paige smiled. Potter merely nodded.

No sooner had Carmen sat down at her desk than the phone rang. "District attorney's office," she answered. After a moment she called out, "Paige, it's for you; line two."

Paige plopped into her chair and picked up the phone, punching the illuminated button for the waiting call.

"DA's office," Paige said. "Deputy District Attorney Callen speaking."

"How's the fucking whore this afternoon? I see you made it to work after our little rendezvous on the beach."

Paige's heart rate instantly skyrocketed as she recognized the raspy voice of her dawn attacker.

"Who is this?"

"Like I'd really give you my name. Just called to say 'Hi' and see how you're doing."

"What do you want?" Paige tried to control the tremor in her voice. She hoped it wasn't audible to the man on the other end of the phone.

The caller ignored Paige's question and continued. "Bet you thought you were going to get fucked this morning, out there in the surf, with your face in the sand and your butt in the air. I wanted you to know I had a hard-on, but I didn't fuck you on purpose, even though I could have. Wasn't that considerate of me? But you aren't the kind who fucks on the first date, are you, Paige?"

Paige wanted to slam the receiver down but was frozen. Each word he spoke plunged her deeper into revulsion and anger. She gripped the receiver so tightly her hand trembled.

"What's the matter, Paige; not in the mood to chat?"

"What do you want?" she repeated.

"I'll let you know on our second date, slut," the voice crackled. "Maybe I'll fuck you then. Ciao for now."

The line clicked dead in her ear. She sat, ashen-faced, staring at the telephone as if it were a coiled serpent.

It was several seconds before Paige snapped out of her state of fury and fear. "Carmen, get me Sergeant Wendt at APD right away," she barked, unable to moderate the strain in her voice. "And hold all my other calls."

Timothy Potter, hearing Paige's elevated tone, reappeared in the doorway of her office. "Who was that on the phone? You look like you've seen a ghost."

"Go to hell, Chaz," Paige said, putting her face in her hands.

"Moody fucking broads," Potter said under his breath as he slunk away.

CHAPTER 7

"Raymond, what in the hell are you doing in my bathroom?"

Ray Cowell winced at the sound of his mother's voice and looked up from where he was crouched on her bathroom floor. He was rummaging through the cupboard beneath the sink.

"I asked you a question. What are you doing in my bathroom? Is your toilet backed up again? You need the plunger? I told you before, you wipe with more than one sheet of tissue and sure as the sun shines, you'll have a backed-up toilet. Raymond? Are you listening to me?"

Ray found the object of this search; an industrial-sized can of hair spray. Shaking it, he was pleased to find it more than three-quarters full. He stood up and looked down at his mother.

"Relax, Ma; no need to throw a hissy fit." He held up the can of hair spray. "I need to borrow this for a while."

"What are you gonna do with my hair spray? You ain't sniffin' that stuff, are you? I know that's what kids today are doing; I seen it on Geraldo. You sniffin' chemicals, Raymond?"

"Jesus, Ma, of course I'm not sniffing your damned hair spray. I'm working on a model airplane," he lied. "You spray this stuff over the paint so it won't run."

"Sounds pretty strange to me. Boy your age, still playing with model airplanes. Whyn't you get a girlfriend, Raymond?

You oughta have a girlfriend. Ain't natural, fella your age without a girlfriend."

"Ma, I'm going to be thirty-three years old next month. I'm not a boy anymore. I'm a man. And you know I don't like it when you call me 'Raymond'. I like 'Ray'."

"Raymond is your God-given name and I'll use it whenever I like. If you're such a grown-up man," she nagged, following Ray out of the bathroom, "how come I still cook all your meals? And do your laundry? And how come all you do is sit in that room of yours and read those foul magazines. How come you ain't got a girlfriend, Raymond? Answer me that, Mister Grown-Up Man?"

"Leave me alone, will ya?"

"Sure Raymond, I'll leave you alone. Next time the UPS man comes with one of your packages, I'll be sure and tell him you want to be left alone."

Ray stopped in his tracks. "Ma, did something come today?"

"I don't feel like telling you. But you might want to look on the back porch."

"Goddamnit, Ma," Ray cursed, "how many times do I have to tell you? Don't let the delivery people leave packages on the back stairs. You know what this neighborhood's like."

"Don't use the Lord's name in vain," she admonished.

"Go to hell, you drunk old bag. Leave me alone."

Ray stormed through the kitchen and down the back stairs. He'd heard every one of his mother's lectures countless times before and was not in the mood for another round of her biting tongue. If he'd missed a package because of her foolishness…

He had not. Plopped on the back porch was a large, flat, and relatively heavy cardboard box. The label read ARMO-TECH and bore a Sacramento address. Ray scooped up the box and scurried to his basement apartment. He kept the door locked at all times, and he fumbled with the key as he juggled the cardboard box and the can of hair spray.

Ray lived in the basement apartment of his family home; the same place he'd lived since his birth. The house was a small, one-story bungalow on Pacific Avenue in Alameda, and sat among many others just like it. Since Ray's youth, the once-quaint neighborhood of exclusively single-family residences had degenerated into a series of run-down, ramshackle homes that were now mostly segregated into low-income apartments, overpopulating the narrow street.

Ray remembered how the neighborhood looked as a kid: freshly mowed lawns and gleaming white picket fences. He remembered playing catch with his dad in McKinley Park, only a block away, and coasting the flat streets on his homemade skateboard. He remembered his neighbors, all family men like his dad, working at the Alameda Naval Air Station or in one of the factories across the estuary in Oakland. In those days, everyone in the neighborhood knew each other and would wave as he and his dog Skipper made their afternoon deliveries on his daily paper route.

Ray's dad was especially well liked in the neighborhood, and his memories of his father were always cluttered with images of him chatting with a neighbor about politics, or the weather, or helping someone with a do-it-yourself project. Ray recalled the times he loaned out his push mower, or helped his buddy across the street rebuild the engine of their old Chevy. Those days were the best ever for Ray Cowell.

Ray's mom was thin then and had long, pretty red hair. In those days, it seemed she was always smiling and content to be doing her duty as a wife and mother. She kept busy with decorating projects, or cooking experiments, or playing bridge with the other wives on the block.

It had been an idyllic life on Pacific Avenue, back in the late Fifties and early Sixties of Ray's childhood. But now, as the Eighties drew to a close, the neighborhood had become transformed. Ray's house, like most on the block, was going to pot and desperately in need of roofing work and a coat of paint. The neighborhood itself was no better. Battered cars lined both sides of the street, and chain-link barricades and burglar bars had replaced the white picket fences. The neighbors, too, had changed. Welfare recipients of African-American or Hispanic origin had replaced the largely working-class Caucasian residents of his childhood.

Ray's mother had changed as well. Her once-striking red hair was now gray and matted, and her svelte figure had ballooned over the years to a grotesque parody of her former silhouette. It seemed all she did anymore was drink vodka and yell at him.

Ray hated it when his mother berated him. He was a loyal son and deserved better. His father, had he still been alive, would have been proud. Ray's salary as a shipping clerk at the Port of Oakland had kept the family home from foreclosure all these years. If his mother did his laundry or cooked him a meal once in a while, she should be glad to do it and grateful she had such a hardworking son, a son who kept a roof over her head, food in her belly, and the liquor cabinet stocked.

Ray pushed open his door and went inside. Hanging from the ceiling was an armada of model airplanes suspended by nearly invisible filament. There were Stukas, Messerschmitts, B-17's, Zeros, Spitfires, every conceivable type of civilian or military aircraft from the dawn of aviation to the NASA space shuttle Challenger, which exploded only three years back. There was even a balsa wood replica of the Wright Brothers' famous craft included in the collection.

Ray switched on the light and closed the door. In one corner of the room was a large drafting table, complete with a telescoping lamp. On the table lay the to-be-assembled components of a scale model of the Spirit of Saint Louis. There were X-acto knives and paint brushes of various sizes scattered on the table also, as well as an assortment of epoxies. More than a hundred tiny jars of modeling paint stood at attention in neat rows on a shelf over the desk.

In the opposite corner of the sparsely-furnished room was a sofa bed. Next to it was a nightstand with another lamp, a clock radio, and an ashtray.

Magazines, too many to count, were scattered everywhere throughout the small basement apartment. There were copies of Scale Modeler, Airpower, and Aviation Weekly. There were issues of Popular Mechanics, Guns & Ammo, and Soldier of Fortune. And in a milk crate buried under a stack of soiled laundry in his closet were stacks of Hustler, Screw, and his father's faded Playboy collection.

The water-stained walls were adorned with posters of aircraft in flight and framed black-and-white photographs. Each of these pictures depicted a tall, balding man standing alongside an anemic-looking boy. In one photo, the boy held up a sand shark for the man's inspection. In another, both the boy and man wore scouting uniforms and Native American headgear. In yet another, the boy stood drenched in water and sported a grin. A soggy dog appeared to be struggling in his soapy arms as the man aimed a garden hose at the pair.

Ray tossed the box and hairspray on the floor amidst the scattered periodicals and sat down cross-legged to open the box with a penknife. The first thing that greeted him when the carton opened was an invoice. The document acknowledged his money order and listed his purchase as a "size medium, Class IIA Kevlar vest". The owner's manual with the vest described it as "an improved, lighter, stronger Kevlar armor", which would "defeat .45 ACP, .357, 00

Buckshot, 9mm projectiles, and all lesser threats to National Institute of Justice IIA Standards".

Ray slipped the vest on and fastened the Velcro tabs to adjust the garment. He pounded on the stiff armor with his fist a couple of times and checked himself in a full-length mirror affixed to the inside of his closet door.

Satisfied, Ray slipped off the vest and set it down alongside a number of other items he had laid carefully out on his sofa and covered with a blanket. He checked the other items, taking a mental inventory.

There was a handgun, a Glock model 17, he had purchased the year before at Trader's in San Leandro. Wearing a pair of cotton gardening gloves, Ray had fieldstripped the weapon as described in the manual and thoroughly cleaned and oiled it. Then he loaded the semiautomatic's two magazines to their capacity of seventeen nine-millimeter cartridges each, still wearing gloves to eliminate the possibility of leaving fingerprints on the brass cases.

In a similar manner he'd fieldstripped his father's old M1 carbine, smuggled home from his service in Korea, and lovingly cleaned and oiled the military arm. Like the pistol, Ray meticulously loaded the weapon's multiple fifteen- and thirty-round magazines with fresh .30 carbine ammunition purchased from a gun shop in Fremont months ago. Ray had taken the time to purchase a paratrooper model folding stock for the weapon at an Army/Navy surplus store in San Jose, and had replaced the standard full-length wooden stock on the M1 rifle with the shorter pistol grip. He'd also modified the rifle's canvas sling by shortening it and securing it to the butt of the pistol grip by means of a swivel. This allowed Ray to hang the semiautomatic military carbine over his shoulder like a purse. Concealed under a coat, the weapon could be hidden from view but ready for instant use.

Ray had a pocket-sized police scanner with an earpiece. He'd customized it himself by installing the crystals for the Alameda police radio frequencies.

Among the other items on the sofa bed were a blue nylon windbreaker, several pairs of cotton gardening gloves, baseball caps of assorted colors, two pairs of Ray-Ban sunglasses, and a box of replacement guitar strings. Ray Cowell did not play guitar.

There was also a fanny pack containing several small tools, which included a flashlight and a Philips screwdriver. A paintball pistol, designed and manufactured to resemble a Colt Python .357 magnum revolver with a six-inch barrel, lay on the sofa as well. Next to it were an opened package of phosphorescent orange paint balls and compressed CO_2 cartridges to power the gun.

Ray packed all of the items, including the new vest and hairspray, into a green US Army duffel bag with the name PASCOE, ARNOLD R. stenciled in faded block lettering on the side. He put the bag into his closet and lay back on his now vacant sofa bed to light a cigarette.

Exhaling smoke, Ray contemplated the past. He thought about his mother and what she'd become. He thought about Paige Callen and her father, a smirk spreading slowly across his thin features. Mostly, though, he thought about his own father and what might have been if not for Sissy, and that terrible summer.

The summer of 1964.

CHAPTER 8

Bob Farrell followed Judge Callen into the house's interior.

"Thank you for coming," Callen said over his shoulder as he led Farrell into his study. "I apologize for the lateness of the hour."

"No apology necessary," Farrell said. "Sandy said you wanted to see me about a job. He told me it was urgent."

"It most certainly is." Callen motioned to one of several large armchairs. "But not so urgent as to preclude being a good host. May I offer you a drink?" The Judge thrust his chin at a well-stocked wet bar in one corner of the expansive room. "You look like a thirsty man."

"I've been known to take a drink," Farrell acknowledged.

"That's a good sign," Callen said. "I find it difficult to trust men who don't imbibe."

"A sentiment we share," Farrell said. "Why don't you take a load off and permit me the honor of pouring you one." He could see the Judge leaning heavily on his cane.

"You are a considerate man, Mister Farrell. It's been a long and exhausting day." He slumped into a well-worn, high-backed leather seat. "Scotch over rocks, if you please. And don't spare your elbow."

"I won't." Farrell strode to the bar.

"Sandy speaks very highly of the work you did for him, Mister Farrell."

"What did he say?"

"That you were both effective and discreet," Callen said. "Qualities I admire."

"Sandy's a good man. And the name's Bob." He busied himself pouring two drinks, a Dewar's for Callen and a Kentucky bourbon for himself.

"He was most grateful for what you were able to accomplish for him," Callen added.

"I was glad to help. So, what can I do for you, Your Honor?" Farrell asked once he had delivered the Judge's drink and sat down.

"This morning at dawn, a man assaulted my daughter. She was jogging on the beach here in Alameda. The assailant called her by name and made it clear he would be back."

"Was she—"

"No," Callen cut him off. "She was not sexually assaulted. But he took pains to let her know he could have. He struck her in the head with a pistol, which I've subsequently learned was something called a 'paintball' gun. Then he shot her with it."

"I can only assume your daughter didn't know it was a paintball gun?"

"You presume correctly. She believed she was going to be executed."

Farrell nodded to himself. "Does your daughter have any idea who this guy is?"

"No. She didn't recognize the voice."

"The police have anything?"

"Nothing." Callen shook his head. "Not a clue."

"That's not uncommon this early in the investigation. Of course, it could mean this guy is good, the cops investigating him aren't, or both."

"I agree," Callen said.

"Is your daughter employed?"

"Paige is an Alameda County deputy district attorney. She's assigned to the DA's office here in town."

Farrell's brow furrowed. "Paige? Paige Callen? Your daughter wouldn't be a tall blonde, late twenties, would she? Lots of freckles; takes herself real seriously?"

It was Callen's turn to wrinkle his eyebrows. "She is. How did you know that?"

"We've met before," Farrell chuckled into his drink.

"You two haven't–"

"Hell no; nothing like that. I'm practically old enough to be her father." As soon as he said this, Farrell winced. "No offense, Your Honor."

"None taken," the Judge said sternly. "If I may be so bold, how do you know Paige?"

"I really don't; she knows me."

"Please explain."

"About a year ago, I found myself in some hot water with the Feds. Some of the trouble had to do with things I did here in Alameda. The US Attorney's office was looking to lock me up and throw away the key. I brokered a deal, and all the charges went away. I gather the Alameda cops, and your daughter, who was the deputy DA reviewing those charges, were none too happy I was getting off."

"I'm aware of your past troubles with the federal authorities," Judge Callen said. "I didn't realize Paige was involved from the Alameda County DA's end of things; she never told me."

"How do you know about me?"

Callen smiled. "I may be retired, but I keep my fingers in the game. The senior superior court judge in Alameda County at the time you 'brokered a deal', as you called it, with the federal, state, and county prosecutors, is a protégé of mine. I would call what you 'brokered' more like blackmail and less like a deal. Not many legal settlements of that magnitude are negotiated in this county without my knowledge." He paused for effect. "Then or now."

"Small world," Farrell said. "I wondered why Sandy said you specifically asked for me."

"I did indeed."

"Not being a believer in coincidence," Farrell went on, "I have to ask: does my history, which you admittedly know so well, have anything to do with why you want to hire me?"

"It does."

Farrell took this in, gazing into his bourbon.

"Not a lot of people approve of what I did. Some of them, like your daughter, wanted me jailed for it."

"You did what you had to do, Bob."

"I'm not referring to tracking down Vernon Slocum," Farrell corrected him. "I meant as a superior court judge, how do you feel about me getting off?"

"You took down a monster. You succeeded where the proper authorities failed. You saved lives. And you managed to protect your daughter, your partner, and yourself in the process. An impressive feat. In your shoes, I'd have done the same if I could."

"Your daughter doesn't share your sentiments. I only met her once, at the federal courthouse in San Francisco, when the deal was sealed. She was fit to be tied. She ranted at the federal attorney for several minutes about what a 'gross miscarriage of justice' it was. She believes I should be occupying a cell in a federal penitentiary. Hell, I thought she was going to clobber me right there in the courtroom."

"That's my Paige, all right," Callen conceded. "She's very passionate about following rules."

"You can say that again." Farrell eyed the Judge coolly. "Does your daughter know you want to employ me?"

"Not yet."

"When she finds, out there'll be fireworks."

"I don't care. I want Paige protected. I want to commission you to find out who this degenerate stalking her is." The Judge paused again. "I want him dealt with."

"Those are two different things."

"I don't believe they are. Both achieve the same goal: keeping my daughter safe."

"Two different things," Farrell repeated. "Protecting your daughter and hunting for her stalker are separate tasks. Both are labor-intensive." He tilted his head. "Why not let the police handle it?"

Callen shook his head dismissively. "The police have to play by the rules. Not only do they have to play by those rules while trying to catch this perpetrator, they are simultaneously handcuffed by the requirement to build a legal case against him for prosecution in criminal court. Somewhere behind these considerations is keeping Paige safe."

"For a superior court judge," Farrell noted, "you exhibit a remarkable lack of faith in the criminal justice system."

"Correction: I'm a retired superior court judge. Any allegiance I may have had to the criminal justice system is subordinate to my duty as a father. After reviewing your history and the documentation of your hunt for serial killer Vernon Slocum, which the federal authorities chronicled in minute detail—"

"The Feds are good at that," Farrell cut in.

"—I'm frankly rather surprised at your squeamishness."

"I'm not squeamish about breaking rules," Farrell countered. "Or the law, when it's necessary. I'm just not accustomed to meeting superior court judges who hold similar views."

"As I say, I'm a father first."

"I understand. I have a daughter myself."

"Then you know why I want to hire you."

"Not entirely," Farrell said. "I'm a one-man band. Why not employ one of the larger, established private investigation firms? They have the resources and manpower to handle both a wide-ranging investigation and around-the-clock protection. Surely money isn't a barrier; why hire me?"

Judge Callen drained his scotch and extended the glass to Farrell. Farrell did likewise and stood up, gathering the Judge's empty glass along with his. He made his way back to the bar and busied himself refreshing their drinks.

"You can make mine a double," the Judge said.

"Way ahead of you. You were saying?"

"I already told you I read the full dossier on you, Bob. I know about your nearly thirty years as a San Francisco police inspector. I know about your Vietnam service. And as I already told you, I know all about your blood hunt for Vernon Slocum. I know what you did, why, and how you did it."

"That still doesn't answer my question," Farrell said, handing the older man his scotch. "Why me?"

"I'll do you the courtesy of speaking bluntly," the Judge said. "You're obviously a man who speaks his mind."

"Life is too short to do otherwise."

"Simply put, you, Mister Farrell, are an exceptionally resolute man. You always get the job done."

"I'm flattered by your confidence in me," Farrell said, after taking a sizeable gulp of his own drink, "but that may not be enough. I can't guarantee results. Nobody can. Anyone who claims otherwise, in this line of work, is either incompetent, lying, or a fool."

"Another reason I want you handling this case," the Judge said. "You're a realist. You're not going to blow smoke up my ass and try to placate me with a lot of excuses and bureaucratic double-talk like the police do."

"That's not the only reason you want to hire me, is it?"

"No," the Judge admitted. "It's not."

"It's because I'm a father?"

"Correct. We share a common bond. What would you do to protect your child?"

"What wouldn't I do?" Farrell said, staring again into his drink.

"Precisely why you're the man for this job."

"Judge Callen" – Farrell looked up – "I haven't said I would take this case yet."

"Of course you'll take the case," Callen announced, as if it was already settled. "If it's money you're worried about–"

"It's not money," Farrell said. "When I went after Vernon Slocum, it was personal. Begging your pardon, but this isn't. I cracked a lot of eggs to make that omelet and damn near paid with my life. I almost got my partner killed, and the both of us barely escaped a long prison jolt."

"I am aware of the sacrifices you made," the Judge said. "Remember, I read your dossier."

"I'm not talking about sacrifice, Your Honor," Farrell said. "I'm being practical. You may have forgotten that I forced the Feds and several local DAs like your daughter Paige, into swallowing all the criminal charges we'd accumulated while on the hunt; but they sure as hell didn't forget. Any one of them would jump at the chance to put me on the grill again, with your daughter leading the pack. I'm sorry for your troubles, but I don't need that kind of grief. I don't want to go to prison."

"I am not without influence," Callen said.

"And I'm not unfamiliar with your reputation, Your Honor. 'Iron Gene' they call you. You're owed a lot of favors and have your hands in a lot of pockets. But I'm not sure even your influence is going to do me any good if I find myself in hot water with the Department of Justice or the Alameda County District Attorney's office again."

"Your reservations are understandable. I am prepared to pay whatever fee is necessary to allay your qualms and take this case."

"Maybe I have lavish notions," Farrell pointed out. "What if you can't afford me?"

Judge Callen sipped scotch, his jaw tightening. When he spoke again his voice was quiet and hard. "I am an old man. I have more money than I could spend in several lifetimes. But I only have one daughter." He challenged Farrell with his eyes. "You tell me what it will take to obtain your services and I'll pay. No quibbling and no questions asked. And I'll pay in cash, under the table, so you don't have to worry about the IRS."

"That gets my attention. But there's another thing," Farrell said, meeting the Judge's eyes. "From what little you've told me, your daughter's stalker smells local. If you didn't know it already, I'm persona non grata with the Alameda police."

"I seem to remember reading something in your file about taking two Alameda officers hostage here in town."

"Believe me, at the time I had no choice. If I'd let the Alameda cops arrest me that night, a little girl named Kirsten Ballantine would be dead and hanging from a tree. My point is," Farrell continued, "if I'm going to catch this creep, I'll need to be privy to the official Alameda police investigation. You can bet I'm the last person the Alameda cops are going to want to cooperate with."

"I've already got that covered," Callen told him. "I'll get daily briefings from the sergeant assigned to Paige's case. I can pass that information on to you."

Farrell rubbed his chin and ran a hand through his thinning hair.

"Please take the case, Bob," the Judge pressed, sensing his hesitation. "Paige is my little girl." His voice faded to almost a whisper. "She's all I've got."

Farrell stood up. "All right, Your Honor. I'm your man. But it's going to cost you." He stood up and extended his hand. The Judge waved dismissively at the mention of cost and shook Farrell's extended hand.

"One last thing: I'm going to have to hire some help. Like I said, I can't babysit your daughter and track her stalker at the same time. I want to bring on a partner."

"Run the case however you see fit."

"I'm only telling you because I might need more than money to hire this guy. I'll need your political influence if I'm going to convince him to come aboard. Still game?"

"Not a problem," the Judge assured. "Who exactly do you plan to hire?"

"I have someone in mind," Farrell said.

CHAPTER 9

When Kearns opened his apartment door, the first thing he noticed was the smell of cigarette smoke. The second thing he noticed was Bob Farrell's bony frame seated on a folding chair next to the stack of boxes that served as his makeshift kitchen table.

"Hello, Kevin," Farrell drawled around his cigarette without getting up. "Long time no see."

"I'd ask how you got in here, but I know about your ability to pick locks." Kearns shook his head. "You mind putting that out? I breathe this air."

Farrell ground out his smoke in an empty tuna can, which Kearns recognized as the same one he'd discarded into the trash bin under his sink the night previous. He noticed Farrell's battered flask on the table next to the improvised ashtray. The flask's cap was already open. Farrell's tan raincoat was draped over the back of his chair. "Come in, why don't you?" Kearns said sarcastically. "Make yourself at home."

"Why, thank you," Farrell said. "Don't mind if I do." He gestured with his arm. "Love what you've done with the place. What do you call this décor? 'Early American Grapes of Wrath'?"

"It ain't much," Kearns conceded, looking around the sparse apartment. "But it's home. At least for now."

"You look well," Farrell said, appraising Kearns. "California living must be doing you some good."

Kearns was in his mid-twenties and stood a shade under six feet tall. He had a muscular physique set under sandy-colored military-length hair. He was clad in athletic shoes, warm-up pants, and a pastel-hued, high-collared shirt with the flowery name and logo of a popular health club chain embroidered on the front.

"What's with the monkey suit?" Farrell asked. "You a doorman at a hair salon?"

Kearns looked at himself and chuckled. "Not quite, but close. I work the evening shift at a fitness center. That's what you Californians call a gym."

"Please tell me you aren't teaching aerobics?" Farrell gasped.

Kearns laughed. "Almost as bad. I teach overweight housewives and mid-life cubicle dwellers how to train with weights."

"I'll bet all your female customers swoon over that corn-fed Iowa charm of yours."

"Most of them are old enough to be my grandma," Kearns said. Farrell stood and the men shook hands. "Good to see you, Bob."

"I brought you some beer," Farrell pointed to the tiny refrigerator in what was supposed to be the apartment's kitchen. "Help yourself."

Kearns' studio apartment was located directly over the bar in one of Alameda's most popular taverns. This made the rent cheap but the peace and quiet scarce. Fortunately, it was almost midnight on a Monday evening and the bar had only a few patrons left. On weekends, the raucous sounds of revelers lasted until well after 2am.

Kearns found a six-pack of Anchor Steam inside the fridge and opened one with his Swiss army knife. He sat down on the edge of the bed, which was the only other piece of furniture in the apartment. Farrell resumed his seat.

"So how're you doing, Kevin?" Farrell punctuated his question with a swig from his flask.

"Getting by. No complaints."

"Still going to school?"

Kearns nodded. "I'm a senior now, if it matters. Most of my credits from Iowa State transferred to Cal State Hayward. With any luck, I'll have my bachelor's by Christmas."

"When do you find time to study?"

"That's a good question. I'm up every morning before dawn and at school by seven. I barely have time to commute from Hayward to the gym in Alameda after class in the afternoon, and don't get off work until past eleven. I work double shifts both days on weekends."

"How're the finances holding up?"

"I'm making ends meet," Kearns said, taking a pull from the bottle. "Got no college debt, which is all that matters right now. And as you can see" – Kearns swept the tiny apartment's water-stained walls with his beer bottle – "I'm living a life of opulence."

"I looked in your garbage can when I was searching for an ashtray," Farrell smirked. "Macaroni and cheese and canned tuna ain't exactly an opulent diet."

"It fills the belly," Kearns said.

"That it does. How are the police applications going?"

"Don't ask," Kearns said, rubbing his brow.

"You still running into a wall at the background check?

"Yeah. Eight so far this year. I've still got a couple of applications out. I figure I'll go to an even ten before I throw in the towel."

"I'm sorry, Kevin."

Kearns had been consistently applying to Bay Area police departments for most of the past year. Part of the deal that Farrell arranged with the federal prosecutors was to expunge Kearns' record of arrest and the criminal charges he and Farrell had accrued during their search for Vernon Slocum. But as Kearns soon found out, sealing a record and keeping people from talking about it were two different things.

Each time Kearns applied to a police department, he aced the written test, slam-dunked the physical agility test, and easily managed the oral interview. His experience as a deputy sheriff back in Iowa, as well as his military training, ensured he was always at the top of the hiring list.

As soon as Kearns' application reached the background investigation phase, however, his candidacy as a police recruit would be mysteriously terminated. Eight times in as many months, Kearns received a form letter from the police background investigator stating he was no longer being considered as a viable candidate. No reason was given, and by California civil service rules, none was required.

But he knew the truth. The reason he continued to have his police applications torpedoed was because his name was on a list. A federal list. That wasn't supposed to happen. Kearns could never prove it, but the word had been put out: he'd been blackballed. Farrell knew it, too.

"Kevin," Farrell began softly. "You don't have to live like this. You've got nothing to prove. Move in with me until you find something solid, or at least until you finish your college degree."

"That's a generous offer," Kearns said, "but I can't. You live in San Francisco. If I move in with you, everybody is going to think we're dating." He finished his beer in one long gulp. "Not that I have anything against gay people, mind you," he said. "It's just that you're not my type."

"Too sophisticated for a bumpkin like you?"

"Too shady." Kearns got up to get another beer.

"That's your pride talking," Farrell said, not unkindly.

"Maybe," Kearns conceded, popping the bottle cap with the attachment on his pocketknife.

"So, what's your plan? Keep filing futile police applications until your hair goes gray?"

"I'll give it until I graduate college. If I can't get hired on with a police agency by then, I'll go back in the army, this time as a commissioned officer. At least in the service, I'll have a steady paycheck coming in and a roof over my head."

"That isn't what you really want, though, is it?"

"No," Kearns conceded, "it's not. Did one hitch in the army already; green isn't my color. But it beats the unemployment line." He held his bottle out to Farrell. "To what do I owe an unannounced visit from Private Eye Bob Farrell? And with him bearing gifts?"

"Inherently suspicious," Farrell said, clinking his flask against Kearns' beer. "You're a born detective, Kevin; you just won't admit it."

"Not much to detect," Kearns said. "You're as subtle as a freight train."

"I need your help. On a job."

"Not interested," Kearns said.

"Won't you at least hear me out?"

"There's no point. I quit the private investigation business. I don't want to peek in people's windows anymore or follow deadbeats around. We tried it already, remember? For over six months, I let you drag me all over Northern California playing Dick Tracy, and all it did was make me feel shittier about losing my career as a cop. No thanks, Bob. Been there and done that."

"This job is different," Farrell told him. "It's a criminal matter. Not some low-rent worker's compensation fraud gig, or taking dirty pictures of a philandering husband. It's lucrative, too."

Farrell withdrew a fat envelope from his suit pocket and tossed it on Kearns' cardboard tabletop. Kearns picked it up and thumbed through the denominations.

"There's over ten thousand dollars in here," he whistled.

"Damn right," Farrell said. "That's half my retainer. It's yours if you're with me. There'll be plenty more."

"You're moving up in the world," Kearns said, his eyebrows lifting. He tossed the money back on the table. "Sorry, Bob, but I still have to refuse."

"Why? What do you have against private investigation work? Or is it me?"

"Of course it's not you. I need more, that's all. You forget you have a police pension coming in. PI work is too unstable; too hand-to-mouth. I need to build a future and put away something to fall back on. Private investigation, especially as a freelancer, doesn't pay the bills consistently enough." He gave Farrell a disdainful look. "Or justify the risk."

Farrell appraised Kearns, his eyes narrowing. "This is about Jennifer, isn't it?"

At Farrell's mentioning his daughter's name, Kearns' stomach tightened. Since meeting her during the course of their hunt for Vernon Slocum, a day didn't pass without him thinking of her.

"Huh?" Kearns said, looking away and confirming it was. "What are you talking about?"

"You know exactly what I'm talking about, you redneck. You never were much of a liar." He smacked himself on the forehead with his palm. "Of course; why didn't I see it before? That's why you're busting your ass to get a college degree and a steady job. You don't believe a girl like Jennifer would go for a guy like you if he was a self-employed private eye. Some detective I am; I should have smelled this months ago."

Kearns said nothing in reply, but his eyes told Farrell he was right. After a long pause, he said, "What do you want me to say? That you're wrong?"

"Hey, kid," Farrell put his hand on Kearns' shoulder. "I didn't realize what was going on with you. I'm sorry."

Kearns' shoulders slumped. "When we were trailing Slocum and I met your daughter, I thought she was something real special. Who wouldn't? She's one in a million. But it's more than Jennifer. It's the thought that somebody like her wouldn't give a second look to a guy like me. Not where I am, and what I am, right now."

"I'm an idiot, Kevin. I forgot what walking hard-ons guys your age are."

"Jesus, Bob; that's not what I meant."

"Of course it is," Farrell corrected him. "I know how you young bucks think. Hormones dominate your world. When you get to my age and you start having feelings for a woman, it's easier to keep your little head from controlling your big head. Don't you remember what your drill sergeant taught you?"

"My drill sergeant taught me a lot of things," Kearns said. "Mostly four-letter words."

"He should have taught you 'If you get the urge to marry, quell it. It's much cheaper to simply find a woman you hate and buy her a house.'"

"I seem to remember something along those lines in our barracks discussions," Kearns said.

"After two divorces," Farrell said, "I've come to believe in the wisdom of those sage words. Most of the really important stuff a young man needs to know he can learn from a drill sergeant."

"I agree. And who said anything about marriage?"

"Look, Kevin," Farrell said. "It's not that I don't think you're good enough for Jennifer; problem is, you don't think you are. Besides" – he grinned – "if she turns out anything like her mother, you'll be glad you dodged her."

"If you're trying to console me, you're failing," Kearns said.

"Never mind," Farrell cut him off. "Would you at least consider my proposal?"

"I already declined it."

"Not yet, you haven't. Trust me; you'll dig this job."

"All right, I'll bite. Tell me about it." Kearns sat back down on the bed. "But just because I'm listening to your pitch doesn't mean I'm going back in with you."

"Fair enough. Do you remember last year when we had to go to federal court in San Francisco?"

"How could I forget," Kearns said. "I was afraid they were going to throw us in jail. You kept saying, 'Relax, Kevin', which, coming from you, made me even more scared."

"Very funny. Anyway, do you recall a pretty blond deputy DA from Alameda County who was present in the courtroom? Looked like she belonged on the cover of a magazine?"

"How could I forget her? Full of herself. Thought she was a real hard case. Great legs but a ball-buster. Had a major problem with you, if I recall."

"That's the one."

"What about her?" Kearns asked.

"Her name is Paige Callen. Somebody is stalking her. Attacked her on the beach in Alameda today. Cops got nothing. Looks like a preplanned thing; very personal."

"So how do you figure into this?"

"Her father is Iron Gene Callen," Farrell said. "That name mean anything to you?"

"Should it?"

"Hell yes. He's retired now, and a widower, but in his day, he was the most powerful judge in Alameda County history. I'm talking old-school, political-machine powerful. Reagan tapped him for a cabinet post and he refused."

"Governor Reagan or President Reagan?"

"Both. He's also richer than a pharaoh, owns half the real estate in Alameda and San Leandro."

"He's your client?"

"Roger that," Farrell said. "He wants me to track down the creep who's stalking his daughter. And he wants her protected while I'm doing it. That's where you come in."

Kearns squinted at Farrell. "No offense, but why does this Judge Callen guy want to hire you? If he's the big shot you claim, why not commission one of the large PI firms?"

"Valid question. I asked Judge Callen the same thing. He knows our track record. He wants the job done by a private investigator with a history of this type of manhunt. Someone who knows the territory. Someone discreet. Somebody who finishes what they start."

"Somebody not afraid to get his hands dirty?"

"That could be part of it," Farrell admitted.

Kearns bit his lip. "He hired you because you bagged Vernon Slocum, didn't he?"

"Yes," Farrell said flatly. "He did. And he's willing to pay."

"Holy shit," Kearns said. "I always knew you were crazy, but this is insane; even for you."

"It's just another job, Kevin. Same as any other except it pays more, a lot more. I need your help."

"It's not 'just another job'. You're being hired by the parent of a deputy DA who hates our guts, has the means to do something about it, and would like nothing more than to see you and me showering together in San Quentin every morning for the rest of our lives."

"Kevin," Farrell persisted. "If you come in with me on this case, it's not only money that's going to be coming your way. Iron Gene Callen has serious juice. He's the financial director for the Alameda County sheriff's and district attorney's reelection campaigns. One word from him and you get a no-questions-asked appointment as a sworn deputy to the Alameda County Sheriff's Department. Iron Gene makes a phone call and you're in. You could be in the next academy."

Kearns sat up straighter. Farrell knew he had his undivided attention.

"You already spoke to him about me?"

"Of course," Farrell said. "I told him I needed to bring on a partner. I didn't specifically name you, but I think the old bastard suspects who I was referring to. He's read our entire file."

Kearns leaned closer to Farrell. "What would I have to do?"

"Nothing we haven't done before. Mostly bodyguard duty. Shadow Paige Callen. Be prepared to intervene in the event of another attack. Help me track down the asshole stalking her." Farrell's voice lowered. "Convince him to leave Judge Callen's daughter alone."

"Now I get it," Kearns said. "That's the real reason this Judge Callen guy didn't hire a reputable private investigations firm. He wants this stalker's ticket punched."

"Like I said, Kevin, you're a born detective."

"Shit, Bob, even if I wanted to partner up with you again, I don't even own a gun anymore. Or a permit to carry it concealed. My revolver is still locked away in the evidence room at the Omaha police department."

"Got that covered." Farrell winked. He extracted a folded paper from his inside pocket. "I told you Iron Gene has juice, didn't I? Fill this out and I'll give it to the Judge tomorrow morning. You'll have your CCW permit approved by tomorrow night."

Kearns accepted the form from Farrell. On examination, he found it to be a county application for a permit to carry a concealed weapon.

"A bit of a presumption, wasn't it?"

"Not at all. I need you on this one, Kevin. We're a team, you and me. We both know I can count on you in a pinch and then some. We belong together; like Holmes and Watson."

"More like Martin and Lewis. And I'm still unarmed."

"Not for long," Farrell said smugly. He reached back into the pocket of his raincoat and withdrew a heavy parcel wrapped in an oiled cloth. He thrust it at Kearns.

"Open it. Christmas came early."

Kearns peeled away the cloth to find a large-frame Smith & Wesson revolver with a four-inch barrel. The model number on the barrel read "58" and the caliber was .41 magnum. The weapon had a bit of the bluing worn off at the crown of the muzzle and cylinder, undoubtedly from holster wear, but had been well maintained and smelled of oil. Kearns opened the cylinder to verify the handgun's unloaded status.

"My old uniform duty gun before I made inspector. She shoots straight and hits hard." Farrell handed Kearns a box of fifty hollow-point .41 magnum cartridges and a brown leather belt holster.

Kearns hefted the big wheelgun. "If I get attacked by a charging rhinoceros, this ought to do the trick."

"What do you say? Can I count on your help?"

"Give me a minute to think it over, will you? Last time I signed on with you, I got shot at, beat up, arrested, and carved up like a Thanksgiving turkey."

"That was a fluke. Nothing like that is going to happen on this job. Trust me."

Kearns' jaw dropped. "Trust you?"

"All right," Farrell said, showing his palms. "Poor choice of words."

"This judge who hired you, can he really get me appointed to the sheriff's department, despite the Feds blackballing me?"

"He can. He has the sheriff's and DA's ear."

"OK; against my better judgment, you've convinced me." He took a deep breath. "I'm in." Both men stood up and Kearns extended his hand. Farrell shook it triumphantly.

"I've got a feeling I'm going to regret this," Kearns said. "When do I start?"

"How about now?"

CHAPTER 10

Paige ignored the furtive glances of the other gym patrons and concentrated on regulating her breathing and keeping a steady pace on the StairMaster machine. She realized the large-frame sunglasses she was wearing were out of place inside the health club, particularly before sunrise, but considered them less conspicuous than the purple, crescent-shaped bruise surrounding her left eye.

She was listening to Madonna's new album, Like a Prayer, through the earphones on her yellow Sony Walkman cassette player. The same earphones which had been ripped from her head by a masked man the day before.

Paige had risen even earlier than usual, unable to sleep. Her night had been consumed by sweat-soaked dreams of the attack on the beach, and she'd finally given up on slumber entirely. She opted instead to be at the Harbor Bay health club near her condominium when its doors opened at 5.30am for a pre-dawn workout.

Paige's body ached, her shoulders and back especially, from being body-slammed to the beach the previous day. She might have skipped her daily workout entirely if not for her fierce determination to ignore the assault and get on with her life.

As Paige pumped her legs up and down on the stair machine, she replayed the attack and its aftermath over and over again in her mind. She'd been racking her memory for a recollection of the raspy voice of her assailant, to no avail. Nothing about the man's cigarette-scarred speech was remotely familiar, and she was certain if she had heard that distinct tone of voice before, she'd remember it. Especially after hearing the same voice again on the phone in her office yesterday afternoon.

She'd dutifully reported the threatening phone call to Sergeant Wendt but rejected his immediate demand to come down to her office in person to interview her and take another statement. Paige had had enough of cops by yesterday afternoon, and responded to Wendt's insistence by hanging up on him. She realized it was rude but didn't care. She had a busy afternoon in court waiting for her and wasn't afraid of offending the Alameda cops.

Paige was well aware the Alameda cops nicknamed her "Ice Queen", and not merely for her routine dismissal of certain officers' constant sexual advances. She knew most of the cops felt she undercharged their cases, pled them away too readily, or failed to charge them at all without due consideration for the work they put into them. To Paige, unlike her father, what the cops thought of her mattered not in the least. She did her job professionally, correctly, and by the book, and if some facet of a case was improperly completed, it was usually at the law enforcement end of the transaction. Paige was not about to waste her office's limited time and budget on go-nowhere, bullshit cases which would embarrass the DA and divert her from more pressing criminal matters that actually had a chance of successful prosecution.

Many times over the past couple of years, an outraged beat cop or detective would storm into her office and demand an explanation for what they perceived as her dereliction of duty in failing to prosecute one of their cases.

Each time Paige, would reply in the same manner. "I don't make the rules," she would remind the cop, "I just enforce them." Then she would point out to the simmering officer what problems his case had that resulted in the failure to advance its prosecution. Often, the issue stemmed from investigative oversight, the overzealous cop's bending of the rules, or just plain shoddy police work. Other times, political or financial considerations brought the prosecution to a halt; a harsh reality of working for an elected official who kept his job at the whim of the voting public.

Paige figured she wasn't in her line of work to make friends or secure close-knit relationships with members of the police community. She was there to prosecute criminal cases, when possible, and if the case was weak or poorly prepared, then her duty was to abort it before the case tainted the police agency's reputation, besmirched the DA's office, or unnecessarily added to the already immensely overburdened criminal court system.

Sometimes, Paige wondered if her pathological adherence to following the rules was a reaction to her father's pathological, and legendary, habit of bending them. She wasn't sure.

What she was sure of, was that it was nineteen eighty-nine; not nineteen fifty-nine. The criminal justice system she was part of had no place for backroom deals, kickbacks, and the shady political maneuvers of her father's era. Paige Callen was determined that none of the still-whispered rumors of corruption that had plagued her father throughout his career were going to haunt her. Paige was going to do it by the book. When it came to her law career, nobody was ever going to be able to say she was her father's daughter.

Paige ran a forearm across her brow in an attempt to wipe away fatigue along with her sweat. She'd spent last evening at home in her condo watching television in the hopes she could unwind and divert her thoughts from the day's stark events. Not even Major Dad, 21 Jump Street, or Murphy Brown could distract her from thinking about what had occurred on the Alameda shoreline. And not even aspirin and a long, hot bath diminished the accumulation of aches and bruises left by her attacker. Before finally turning in for a fitful night's sleep, she checked to make sure her alarm was in working order and left the lights on in the hallway, something she had not done since childhood.

Whatever hope Paige held out that her attacker wouldn't return faded the instant she'd heard his voice over the phone. And Sergeant Wendt's repeated reminders to be careful echoed in her mind, convincing her that she should heed the police detective's advice.

Still, a part of her refused to acknowledge further danger from the attacker and persisted in trying to rationalize away the mounting fear that nagged at her consciousness. This was the educated, rational, in-control component of her personality, and its voice was a potent one. As Paige climbed up and down on the StairMaster, in the brightly lit and increasingly crowded health club, that voice, and the logical reasoning behind it, appeared to have the power to overcome the fear she'd experienced since the assault.

But when Paige was alone, like last night, waking to every tiny sound, real or imagined, that rational, in-control voice became a tiny squeak.

This morning, however, refreshed by exercise and the light of day, Paige found her confidence returning. She would be careful, as Sergeant Wendt had admonished. She wouldn't give her stalker a chance. She would remain in public. She would work out at the health club and avoid the beachfront jogs; at least for now. She would notify the police of anything unusual or out of the ordinary. She wasn't going to let herself become a frightened schoolgirl peering behind the closet door for the boogieman. She was an experienced criminal prosecutor, well versed in the world of crime and with no intention of becoming like so many of the victims she dealt with every day in court.

Or so she hoped.

CHAPTER 11

Ray Cowell waited a full five minutes after Paige left her condominium before getting out of his car. He watched her from across the parking lot as she walked down the sidewalk along the tennis courts which separated her condo complex and the Harbor Bay health club.

Once her leotard-clad figure was out-of-sight, Ray lit a cigarette and forced himself to wait longer as the second hand of his Timex swept slowly around. The delay was in case Paige returned, perhaps forgetting something on her way to the gym. "Haste makes waste," his mother used to say before she became a drunk and he stopped listening to her. Ray didn't know if Paige would go to the health club or skip her daily exercise in light of what happened to her yesterday. As result, he arrived early enough to account for either contingency.

Ray left the ignition running and the car's door unlocked. Theft was unlikely in this upscale neighborhood, and he might need to leave in a hurry. Besides, the car was already stolen. After retrieving his gear from the back seat of the car, he was careful not to slam the door. He put out his cigarette in his car's ashtray, pocketed the butt, and strode toward the front door of Paige's condominium.

He was wearing tan coveralls and a San Francisco Giants baseball cap. He also wore sunglasses and a false mustache he'd purchased from a theatrical supply store in Berkeley. The fake mustache made his nostrils itch, and he restrained himself from scratching his nose to abate the irritation; he didn't want the glued-on facial hair to come off. Ray was carrying a small stepladder and had his black nylon gym bag in the grip of one gloved hand. In his pocket was the portable police scanner, and the earpiece adorned his left ear. He was softly whistling Frank Sinatra's version of "Anything Goes".

When he reached Paige's porch, he nonchalantly set down his bag and unfolded the stepladder. He moved slowly, with confidence, and avoided the urge to glance around to see if anyone was watching him; a furtive act that a legitimate workman would not feel compelled to do. Instead, he played the role of the bored repairman busily attending to the day's first service call.

Ray stepped up onto the ladder and withdrew a screwdriver from his bag. The mini-ladder put him within easy reach of the metal alarm box over the front door. The label on the alarm box read "ACME Security Systems" and was above a local phone number. The same logo and phone number were stenciled on the back of Ray's coveralls. He unscrewed the alarm box cover, opened it, and took out the canister of hairspray obtained from his mother's bathroom. Still whistling Sinatra, he sprayed the contents of the industrial-sized can of hairspray into the inner workings of the alarm until it was emptied. He replaced the alarm box cover.

He stepped down from the ladder and walked through the gate leading into the condominium's minuscule backyard. Once there, he stripped lengths of gray duct tape and stuck them horizontally across the width of one window. In less than a minute, the window was covered in tape. Once this task was completed, Ray kicked the center of the pane and then all four corners in succession. The tape muffled the sound of the breaking glass to a dull crunch, and the entire pane fell as one unit into the condominium. No alarm sounded.

Ray climbed through the window into Paige's home. Once inside, he made a quick dash through each room to ensure there were no other occupants or noisy pets, like a bird or cat.

Paige's condo was neat and well decorated with expensive furnishings. Ray wasted no time appreciating her interior design tastes. He made a beeline for the den, for a large antique rolltop desk in one corner. Ray searched the drawers from the bottom up. In the third drawer he found what he was looking for.

This drawer contained writing utensils and stationary. There was a stack of business cards with Paige's name and the Alameda County DA's office logo embossed on them. There was also an address book. Ray pocketed the book, grinning.

Back in the living room, he set down his bag and began to rifle through it. He came out with a can of phosphorescent orange spray paint; the same color of paintball he'd used on Paige the day before. Taking a few seconds to shake the can, he sprayed two words in large, bold, neon orange script on the wall over the fireplace.

Ray returned to his gym bag and switched the spray paint can for a large can of lighter fluid. He liberally splattered the flammable liquid throughout the house. He went from room to room and doused the walls, carpet, and furniture. He emptied the remaining contents of the lighter fluid can on Paige's bed.

With a flick of his Bic, the bed was in flames. Ray lit the sofa in the living room as he passed, scooping up his gym bag and heading for the front door. He unlocked the front door, exited, and closed the door behind him. He grabbed his folding stepladder and went for his car.

Ray made himself walk slowly and resisted the impulse to look back. He reached the car, stowed his tools, and climbed into the driver's seat. The police scanner in his ear was silent.

Ray was several blocks away before the first wisps of black smoke became visible in his rearview mirror.

CHAPTER 12

Paige stood shivering on the porch of what had once been her condominium. Firefighters elbowed past her, going back and forth between her home's interior and their vehicles parked outside. It wasn't only the chilly Bay Area morning causing her discomfort.

Standing next to Paige were Sergeant Randy Wendt and one of APD's property crimes detectives, a Hispanic cop named Bernie Costa. He was the Alameda Police Department's designated arson investigator.

The sweat Paige had worked up on the StairMaster had cooled in the early-morning fog the moment she'd left the Harbor Bay Club. She was walking the short distance home after her workout when she smelled the smoke. She looked up to see the glow of emergency lights up ahead in the fog. Fearing the worst, she broke into a run. By the time she reached the end of the path to her condominium complex, she realized to her dismay that it was indeed her home that was the origin of both the smoke and flashing lights.

Despite the fire trucks, engine, police cars and crowd milling about, it was clear the fire was over. The firefighters scurried busily about but were obviously in mop-up mode.

Wendt was talking to a fire captain when Paige approached him.

"Paige," a startled Wendt exclaimed when he saw her. "Man, am I glad to see you." He spoke into his walkie-talkie, and between the unintelligible police jargon and code numbers Paige heard her own name. She gathered he was notifying other officers that she had been located. Wendt made an apology to the fire captain and turned to her.

"Where have you been?"

"I was at the Harbor Bay Club, working out," Paige said.

Wendt ran his hand through his hair, relief flooding over him. "We didn't know. We thought you may have been kidnapped."

"Kidnapped? My house burns down and you're worried about kidnapping? What the hell is going on here? I was only gone for an hour."

"Paige, I know you're upset about your house, but you've got to realize how lucky you are you weren't home."

Paige walked past the detective sergeant and into her condo. Wendt sighed, counted silently to ten, and followed the irate deputy DA inside. They walked gingerly over the hoses.

"You the owner?" a firefighter asked when Paige entered. She nodded. "Fire started in the bedroom. Looks like an accelerant was used; gas or lighter fluid. If one of your neighbors hadn't smelled the smoke, you wouldn't have a condo anymore. I know it looks bad, but it's not as bad as it looks. Your carpet and rugs are gone, and some furniture, and you're going to have quite a clean-up job ahead of you, but otherwise it's all cosmetic. Your roof, walls, electrical, and plumbing are all OK."

"Accelerant? Lighter fluid? Gasoline? This was arson, wasn't it?"

"I'll take over from here," Wendt cut in before the firefighter could answer. The firefighter nodded and returned to his duties. Wendt turned to Paige.

"This wasn't an accident, Paige. Somebody broke in and deliberately set this fire. The reason I was so relieved to see you is not because I cherish your company. When we got the call and figured out it was your house, we didn't know you weren't here when the place was torched. Once the firefighters confirmed your body wasn't inside the residence, we thought you'd been abducted and the fire set to erase any forensic evidence of what may have occurred to you inside."

The weight of Wendt's words sank in and Paige felt her chill deepening. "You don't think this fire was set by the same guy who attacked me yesterday, do you?" She knew how ridiculous the question was the instant she asked it.

"I don't believe in coincidence," Wendt answered. "Been a cop too long."

"Randy," Paige went on, trying to convince herself the obvious wasn't true. "Fires don't have to be arson. Homes burn down accidentally all the time. Maybe–"

"Turn around, Paige," Wendt interrupted her, his lips pursing.

Almost afraid to, Paige turned around. At first, she didn't see anything but the charred wall over the fireplace. Then she saw what the homicide sergeant was referring to.

On the wall over the fireplace in huge, block letters, were printed two words in orange paint. One word read "Whore", the other "SLUT".

Paige cringed and trembled even harder as chills traversed her spine. She now fully understood Wendt's relief at seeing her, and the tide of fear she thought she'd successfully repressed an hour ago on the StairMaster again flooded over her.

"What if I'd been home?"

"Don't think about that," Wendt said, putting a hand on her shoulder.

"Got something you should see, Randy," Detective Costa's voice called from outside.

Wendt headed for the door, motioning for Paige to follow. She was only too happy to leave the smoky carnage of her condo for some fresh air outside. They found the arson investigator in the backyard near a shattered window.

"This is the point of entry," Costa announced when Wendt and Paige walked up. "I thought at first the firefighters had smashed out the window to vent the smoke, which is standard procedure, but take a look at this."

Costa pointed towards the floor on the inside of the window. "See that? This guy was smart. See how he taped the pane to muffle the sound of breaking in and to make sure it would separate from the window in one piece? That's a pro's trick."

"You're wrong," Paige spoke up. "This window is wired to my alarm. I'm sure I set it before I left. He couldn't have broken the window without setting off the burglar alarm."

Costa shook his head. "I said he was smart. Come over here."

Wendt and Paige followed Costa from the backyard to the porch, where he'd placed a ladder against the exterior wall. The cover of the alarm box had been removed and was lying on the ground at their feet.

"I asked myself the same question, Paige," Costa said. "Why didn't the alarm go off?" He gestured to the alarm cover at his feet. "I took it down to make it easier for the fingerprint technician to lift latent prints, if there are some. But I doubt we'll find any; this guy's too careful to leave prints."

"How did he defeat the alarm?" Wendt asked.

"See for yourself," Costa said.

Wendt climbed the ladder and peered into the alarm box. The interior was covered in a clear, glue-like substance that had hardened and completely immobilized the inner workings of the alarm. "What is it?" he finally asked.

"Aerosol glue, or hairspray, or something similarly gooey. Easy and silent to apply, takes only seconds to harden, and fouls up the clacker real good. Won't work on electronic buzzer-type alarms, only mechanical bell-ringer systems, which are the most common type of burglar alarm around here."

"That means this guy knew what kind of alarm she had," Wendt remarked, stepping down from the ladder.

"That's my guess," Costa acknowledged.

"You're saying this guy cased my house, aren't you?" She didn't recognize the rising tone of her own voice.

"We don't know anything for sure at this stage of the investigation," Wendt soothed her. "It's just one possibility."

"Don't placate me, Randy. This isn't a possibility; it's a certainty."

"Nothing's certain at this point," Wendt said. He noticed several firefighters' heads turning toward the elevated sound of Paige's voice.

"Nothing's certain?" she mocked, her face flushing. "You're kidding, right? It's not certain this creep knew exactly where to find me during my morning jog, and exactly what spot on the route was the most secluded? It's not certain he knew where I work, because he called me there? It's not certain he knows where I live, and even what kind of alarm I have? It's not certain he knows my name, and my schedule, and probably what I had for fucking dinner last night?"

Wendt stood silent, afraid to say anything that would further fuel Paige's tirade.

"The only thing that isn't certain," Paige said, "is if I'm going to survive another twenty-four hours of your department's uncertainty."

"I know things look a little bleak right now," Wendt tried to calm her. As soon as he spoke, he wished he hadn't.

"Bleak? Some thug beats the shit out of me, shoots me with a toy gun, threatens me at work, breaks into my house, and burns me out of my home, all in the span of twenty-four hours, and you call it a little bleak?"

Suddenly, Paige broke into a grin. "I sound like the proverbial hysterical female victim, don't I?"

"I wasn't going to say it," Costa said. Wendt gave him a sharp look.

"You have a right to vent," Wendt said.

"Maybe. But I have no right to take it out on you," she said. "I'm sorry."

"Forget it," he said. She gave the sergeant a weak smile.

"I'm going to my father's house," she announced. "Do you guys need me for anything else?"

"Not right now," Wendt said. "But I'll need to reach you later. Why don't you let me drive you over to the Judge's?"

"I appreciate your concern," she answered, her voice tired. "But you needn't worry. It's only a couple of miles away; I'll be all right." She gestured at her torched condo with a wave of her hand. "What more could happen now? Besides, I'm exhausted. I won't be going in to work today. The wheels of justice will just have to revolve without me."

"That's a good idea. I'd prefer you didn't go to work. I'll stop by your father's house later and let you know how the investigation is going."

Paige's eyes narrowed. "You mean you'll stop by my father's house to check on me and to let my father know how the investigation is going."

It was Wendt's turn to grin. "You don't miss a trick, do you?"

"So long; I'll be at Dad's."

Paige walked across the complex parking lot to her Saab convertible. She was anxious to get inside and fire up the heater. Her chills had become full-body shivers. As she inserted her key into the door lock, she noticed an envelope on the windshield under the wiper blade.

She retrieved the envelope and climbed into her car. Switching on the ignition and turning the heater to full blast, she tore open the envelope. There were no markings on the outside. She presumed it was a note from Sergeant Wendt, placed there before he knew her whereabouts. She was wrong.

As she read the words typed on the plain white paper from within the envelope, her expression changed from puzzlement to wide-eyed horror.

Slut,

How does it feel? Do you like it? Does it feel good? I'll bet it doesn't. I know it doesn't. It never feels good to lose things.

I'm going to take more things from you. I took something from you yesterday. I took something today. I'm going to take more. Until there's nothing left to take.

If you think you can stop me you're wrong. If the cops think they can stop me they're wrong. Your law degree can't help you now.

Don't bother looking over your shoulder. And don't worry about dying yet. I've got plenty of things to take first. You're a slut, Paige, and I'm going to punish you.

Sleep well. Don't let the bedbugs bite.

Until next time, whore

It was a full ten minutes before Paige could compose herself enough to leave her car and turn the letter over to Sergeant Wendt.

CHAPTER 13

Ray Cowell sat chain-smoking in his car. He was parked in the empty lot of the Bay Fairway Hall banquet facility near the golf course. He'd chosen that location because it was the last address on Bay Farm Island before the bridge. No vehicular traffic could exit the island to Alameda without coming under his scrutiny. It was after 8am, and more than two hours had elapsed since he had left Paige Callen's condominium. The morning commute was in full swing.

The car Ray was using was a 1978 Mercury Monarch, in an oxidized blue color. He'd taken it from the vast long-term parking lot at the Oakland airport the evening before. He knew it could be at least several days before the car's owner returned from wherever he was traveling to report the vehicle stolen.

Ray had learned how to hot-wire car ignitions from a mail-order book he'd sent away for after reading an ad in one of his military publications. Over the years, he had learned a great many useful skills from mail-order literature. Ray had learned, among other things, how to kill with a knife the Green Beret way, how to bug a telephone, which poisons were most effective, how to manufacture explosives from common household items, how to convert a semiautomatic weapon to fully automatic, how to obtain false identification papers, and countless other unique martial talents.

"Ray has always been a reader," his mother would tell the neighbors. But that wasn't true. Ray had not always been a reader. As a small boy, books were boring things forced upon him at school. He'd much preferred to be outdoors riding his skateboard, playing catch with his dad, or chasing Skipper down Pacific Avenue over reading a dusty old book. That was before the summer of 1964.

After the trial, he and his mother stayed shut up in the house. Ray would go to school each day and endure taunts and beatings. His mother would go to work and to the grocery store. Beyond those required excursions, neither Ray nor his mother, who reassumed her maiden name of Cowell, ever ventured out of doors. His only friend was Skipper, his beloved pound puppy.

One autumn afternoon, Ray returned home from another hellish day at school to find his mother burying a newspaper-wrapped bundle in the backyard. When he asked about it, she merely stood up and kicked the bundle with her shoe.

To Ray's horror, the parcel contained what was left of Skipper. Skipper's eyes were open and bulged out of their sockets, and his tongue filled his gaping mouth. Pinned to Skipper's collar was a note. All it read were three letters: R.I.P.

"He was poisoned," Ray's mother said harshly. "Found him on the porch. Now don't you start crying. You know I hate crying. What's done is done. Anyway, it's your own damned fault. You shouldn't have let him get out."

Ray ran into the house and buried his face in his pillow as his mother buried the only friend he had in the world. He cried for the whole rest of the day. Sometime during the night, his mother came into his room and sternly ordered him to stop whining like a little baby and be a man. She smelled of vodka, which was becoming more common in the evenings, and was unsteady on her feet.

After Skipper was gone, Ray's only friends became his books and magazines. He spent every waking moment scouring the pages of almost any type of literature he could get his hands on, anything to distract him from the painful reality of his daily existence. His favorite books were about aviation, but he loved military books in general and sports stories. When not devouring the printed page, Ray spent hour after hour meticulously constructing model aircraft; working tirelessly to get even the tiniest detail correct. He spent all his paper route money on magazine subscriptions, books, and model airplanes.

As Ray grew older, he became even more reclusive. His books became his friends, family, and lovers. They taught him amazing things and took him to exotic places. His books did not judge. And like his mother's vodka, they numbed him to the stark reality of his daily life.

His voracious reading had its rewards. Ray excelled in school despite the constant bullying. When he turned sixteen, he got a job at a local electronics store by impressing the manager with his extensive knowledge of hi-fi stereo systems, know-how gained from the pages of countless electronics journals. He brought in extra money repairing appliances and used the additional income to pay for correspondence courses in everything from gun repair to diesel mechanics.

One other consolation Ray allowed himself came, like his other magazine subscriptions, on a weekly basis. But unlike his other magazines, these arrived wrapped in plain brown paper and bore no return address. These magazine he kept stored in a box on the floor of his closet, away from his mother's prying eyes.

In the solitude of his room, with the help of these special magazines, Ray would turn the pages and enter a world of flesh. A world whose inhabitants were always "turned on" and "wanted it". Ray knew it was dirty and he should be punished for reading the "filthy" magazines, as his mother used to call them when she found them in his father's garage, but was locked in a fascination born from his remembrances of Sissy.

In fact, though Ray's special magazines always featured a menagerie of women of different races and appearances, it was the dark-haired, light-skinned women, like Sissy had been, who gave him the most pleasure. Those and the blond-haired ones, with the innocent eyes, like the little girl at the courthouse.

By the time Ray turned seventeen, he had completed his high school equivalency diploma. He asked his mother for her consent to join the army since he wasn't yet eighteen years of age. At first, she refused to sign the enlistment papers, until she learned what his income would be. Once she realized how much money Ray would be sending home, she signed in a flash.

A week later, a pale and skinny Raymond Cowell boarded a bus in Oakland, bound for basic training in Fort Leonard Wood, Missouri. It was the first time Ray had left the San Francisco Bay Area.

Ray was a quiet recruit and endured the rigors of military indoctrination without complaint. He enjoyed basic combat training and was an attentive student. Ever the loner, he eschewed the unity-building camaraderie of the barracks, preferring instead to spend his few free moments rereading his field instruction manuals.

He had enlisted under contract to become an aviation electronics maintenance specialist, a military occupational specialty that would enable him to utilize his already considerable electronics skills, as well as work on the aircraft he had adored all his life. For the first time since childhood, Ray was close to being happy.

But things were not to remain happy for Private First Class Raymond Cowell. Shortly after his eighteenth birthday, and a week prior to graduation at the top of his avionics radar systems class, his military career and all that it promised came to a screeching halt.

By then, Ray had been in the army for almost a full year. He was stationed at Fort Rucker, Alabama, while attending advanced aviation electronics training. He'd made rank quickly and had attracted the attention of several of his senior instructors for his unassuming personality, laser-like focus, and burgeoning electronics skills. As a result, he'd been recommended for assignment to a rotary-wing maintenance unit, highly coveted duty typically not offered to a soldier of his limited tenure. If Ray worked hard, he could be assigned to a helicopter maintenance aircrew. After that, maybe even advancement to warrant officer status and a shot at becoming a crew chief on a helicopter of his own. His boyhood dreams of flight would be realized.

With newfound confidence chipping away at his normally restrained temperament, Ray allowed his fellow graduating classmates to talk him into a night of celebration. The party was to be at one of Enterprise, Alabama's local nightclubs. It would be a night Ray would never forget.

Ray and his classmates went to a club whose patrons consisted mostly of soldiers from nearby Fort Rucker. The place was loud, raucous, and packed with GIs in various stages of intoxication. The club was also brimming with girls.

Ray had never before consumed an alcoholic beverage. His introduction to the world of liquor was shots of tequila washed down with mugs of beer. And Ray had seldom ever spoken to a member of the opposite sex, much less been on a date. It was therefore both strange and exhilarating to find himself for the first time chugging drink after drink and dancing with girl after girl.

As the evening of revelry progressed, his fellow soldiers took turns staggering outside to the parking lot with a girl, to the leers and cheers of his drunken pals. One of the soldiers had driven the group to the club, and his parked car was serving double duty as a makeshift hotel room. After a few minutes, each soldier and his companion, usually wearing sly grins and adjusting their disheveled clothing, would stagger back into the club, this time to the thunderous applause and lewd comments of the crowd. Suddenly it was Ray's turn.

By now, Ray had lost track of the number of drinks he'd consumed and was having difficulty focusing his vision. He realized he was about to have sex; something he'd hitherto only read about in magazines.

Leaning against him was a slovenly, dark-haired girl who said her name was Candy. She insisted she was eighteen years old; a claim few believed but nobody disputed. Ray learned that Candy was a regular at the club, and he'd lost track of the number of times she'd dragged him onto the dance floor. As his buddies raised their glasses and cheered, Candy led him out to the parking lot.

A moment later, Ray found himself sitting in the back seat of his classmate's car, his head swimming and his stomach lurching. His hands felt many times their normal size, and he kept waving them in front of his face in a dazed stupor. Candy, who seemed to hold her liquor far better than Ray, was busy undressing.

Candy removed her bra and lifted her skirt above her waist. She began to undress Ray and struggled with the brass buckle of his class A uniform belt.

Ray was disgusted. He knew this was supposed to be fun, and the curiosity he'd built up over the years was about to be answered, but he found himself repelled by what was transpiring. As he watched Candy tugging his pants down, a wave of repulsion swept over him.

Candy wasn't one of the sleek and silky women from his magazines; she was a short, fat, ugly, drunk girl with a mottled complexion and without even the pretense of femininity. She wasn't even clean.

What Candy lacked in hygiene she made up for in enthusiasm, and she busied herself doing battle with his trousers. As soon as she had his olive drab boxer shorts down, she pounced. Ray fought the urge to puke as Candy's superior weight pinned him to the back seat. She reached down between their collective legs to guide him inside her, but let out a gasp when she found him limp.

"What's wrong with you?" she shrieked in an alcohol-slurred voice. She stared at his shriveled gland. "You some kind of a weirdo? Can't get it up?"

Ray looked down in dismay at his unresponsive penis. The car was spinning.

"Fucking loser," she blurted. "Wait till I tell 'em about this. Can't even get his dick up. Real party animal, that's what you are." She started to climb off Ray. "You aren't a homo, are you?"

Ray bolted upright and smashed his fist directly into Candy's mouth. Blood sprayed from her lips. Both his hands found Candy's throat and he lunged forward, pushing her against the front seat.

"Fucking whore!" he screamed as he choked her with all his might. Candy struggled and tried to yell out, but Ray punched her again and again, returning his fists to her throat between strikes.

"Slut! Whore! You fucking whore!" he howled repeatedly. Blood from Candy's nose and mouth stained his hands. As he alternated between hammering her with his fists and strangling her, Ray noticed that his formerly inert penis was now ramrod straight. He couldn't remember ever being so aroused. He closed his eyes and saw images of Sissy, back in his father's garage, as a boy.

Suddenly, the world turned upside down. The car's doors were wrenched open from the outside, and Ray was roughly grabbed by several pairs of hands. He found himself on the dusty ground of the nightclub parking lot with his pants around his ankles. He sensed a crowd around him and could hear Candy howling hysterically. He tried to stand up but his level of intoxication, combined with the trousers bundled around his feet, hampered him. He struggled to his knees and was just getting his balance, when something hard struck him on the back of the head and the lights went out.

Ray woke up the next morning with the worst headache he'd ever experienced. He was lying on the floor in a cell and covered in his own vomit. The night before was a hazy blur.

It was the end of Ray's military career. Due to Candy's level of inebriation, her age, and inability to coherently testify, formal civilian prosecution was not pursued. But the Armed Forces Uniform Code of Military Justice was not as lenient.

Ray was dismissed from the army with a dishonorable discharge. His military career, along with his dream of aviation, was obliterated. A crushed Ray returned home to California.

Back in Alameda, home was no home. Things had only gotten worse in his yearlong absence. His mother, now unemployed and drunk most of the time, followed him around the house, berating him. With no money, Ray had nowhere to go and no choice but to remain and endure it. The seeds of bitterness planted in the child began to flourish in the man.

Once again, his chances for success and happiness were dashed. Destroyed by a whore. A slut. If only he hadn't gone to the nightclub. If only he hadn't been drinking. If only the slut hadn't made fun of him and called him those names. If only things had turned out different.

If only Sissy hadn't been a slut. And a whore.

If only.

Ray snapped out of his reverie as the object of his vigilance came into view. He tossed his cigarette out the window and put the Mercury into gear as the Saab passed by him on Island Drive. Ray pulled his car out of the empty parking lot and cruised into a position directly behind the convertible. He could see the lone occupant of the Saab clearly as both vehicles crossed over the Bay Farm Island Bridge.

CHAPTER 14

Paige had almost no warning before the impact.

What little warning she did receive arrived in the form of a screeching blue blur that exploded into view from her peripheral vision. In the next instant, she felt a grinding shock and her car skidded out of her control. The Saab completed a full one-hundred-eighty-degree turn before slamming into a signal light at an intersection. Fortunately, Paige was wearing her seatbelt. After the crash, she remained behind the wheel, stunned and shaking cobwebs from her head.

A moment before, she'd been driving to her father's house from the ruins of her own. She was still clad in her damp exercise clothing, and the collision was an unexpected and unwelcome addition to an already bad day.

Paige unbuckled the seatbelt and began to clamber from her wrecked car. The collapsible fabric top of her convertible sedan had offered no protection against the toppled light pole, which sheared during the impact and now occupied the passenger seat of her crunched vehicle. Had the pole landed a foot or two to the right, Paige would have been crushed.

As Paige reached for her car's door handle, the door suddenly opened from the outside. Looking up, she saw a man in coveralls and a ski mask looming her. Before her astonished and terrified mind could react, he reached a gloved hand towards her. There was something in it.

Paige started to scream. The man pressed the object, which looked not unlike a handheld transistor radio, against her chest. A split second later, she was on the ground, her brain scrambled and her body convulsing.

The object was a stun gun, specifically, a Nova model XR-5000, available to virtually anyone by mail order. Used by police officers and civilians alike and powered by a nine-volt nickel-cadmium battery, the Nova stun gun sent forty thousand volts of incapacitating electrical energy into its victims. The Nova typically rendered all but the most drug-crazed and determined attackers instantly and temporarily immobile. It worked even better on already-dazed young women.

Paige looked up from the ground. She could see what was transpiring but was frozen, her limbs unresponsive. She saw a blue sedan wedged against her once-pristine Saab convertible, and a pair of work boots directly in front of her face. She realized she was flat on her back and helpless. Stark panic completely overtook her thoughts. She could neither scream nor move.

The ski-masked face leaned down to within an inch of hers. Paige could smell the cigarette odor on the wearer's breath and recognized the smile behind the mask. She'd seen those nicotine-stained teeth before.

She felt her limbs begin to recover, and tried to move and shout at the same time. The stun gun touched her chest again. When the flashing lights finally cleared, Paige was again on her back and immobile.

"Hi, Paige. Good to see you. Nice tits."

Paige felt a gloved hand roughly kneading her breasts. She wanted to scream; the hand felt like an insect crawling over her.

"We're going to have a lot of fun, whore, before I kill you. You're going to be punished. Come on, slut; we're going for a ride."

Paige wanted to close her eyes and block out the horrifying images before her. But her eyes, the only part of her which seemed unaffected by the stun gun, could not look away. With mounting dread, she felt herself being dragged across the pavement toward the open door of his waiting car.

Paige realized she was being abducted. The fear welling within her sparked a superhuman effort to move the lead weights her arms and legs had become. She started to struggle, and again the dual electrodes of the stun gun descended, jolting her into submission. This time, she was barely able to remain conscious.

Her mind shrieked in agony. She prayed for help, for someone to intervene, but knew as silent sobs racked her body that just like yesterday on the beach there would be no deliverance.

Suddenly, there came the sound of brakes screeching and a car door opening. She felt the hands dragging her across the pavement release her. She landed on her face, unable to break the fall with her numb hands.

Paige desperately tried to roll over on her back again. She could hear the sounds of a fierce struggle and knew that someone had indeed intervened and come to her aid. On her third try, she was able to roll onto her back and view the events transpiring above her.

Paige could see the man in the coveralls rolling on the ground with another, larger man. It was clear from their sprawling posture that the newcomer had hit her attacker in a flying tackle.

She saw both men scramble to their feet. The newcomer, a muscular Caucasian fellow with blond hair who appeared to be in his mid-twenties, seemed vaguely familiar to her. She tried to yell out a warning about the stun gun, but no sound escaped from her lips.

Paige watched impotently as the ski-masked man's hand reached out with the stun gun. The other man blocked the blow with his forearm but caught the leads. Paige heard the static buzz sound again, and the man went to one knee from the shock. Her heart sank.

But the big sandy-haired man did not fall. The electrical pulse had obviously shaken him, but he didn't go down. He shook his head, and as ski mask moved in to zap him again, he punched his adversary directly in the groin.

Ski-mask howled and Paige felt a brief pang of joy. He fell to his knees, both hands over his crotch. The stun gun clattered to the pavement.

It wasn't over. Both men slowly rose to their feet. The blond man's face was pale from the charge of the stun gun. She hoped his opponent was hurt as well.

The man in the ski mask tore open the front of his coveralls and reached a gloved hand inside. In response, the blond man went similarly into his own coat. He came out with a large black revolver and fired as ski-mask emerged with a squat black semiautomatic pistol of his own.

The sound of the revolver was very loud, and the bullet struck ski-mask full in the chest. He staggered back, reeling. To Paige's astonishment, however, he not only didn't fall but recovered enough to raise his own gun and point it at the blond man who had just shot him.

Blondie fired once more, from the hip, as he leaped over the hood of Paige's Saab. Ski-mask opened fire and sent a torrent of bullets in his direction. The sound of the shots from ski-mask's gun weren't as loud as the revolver's, but there were a lot more of them. She lost count of the gunshots as round after round tore into the chassis of her wrecked car. She didn't know how many times ski-mask fired, but it seemed like a hundred. The bullets shattered what was left of her car's windshield and side windows, raining a shower of glass particles onto the pavement.

The next thing she saw was ski-mask running for his car, which still had its engine running. She watched as he ducked into the open driver's door, where only a moment before he'd been trying to drag her inert body. Her attacker was making his escape.

What relief Paige may have felt at her assailant's exit was quickly drowned in a tide of fear as she realized her legs lay in the path of one of the Mercury's wheels. With a Herculean effort, she willed her paralyzed body to roll and scooted clear of the tires just as the blue sedan gained traction and sped away.

As the car fled, the blond man emerged from behind her smashed and bullet-riddled Saab and assumed a two-handed shooting stance. He fired four times at the fleeing blue vehicle with no apparent effect.

Paige felt waves of pain and dizziness flood over her, and her vision blurred. She felt hands again on her shoulders. The fuzzy contours of the blond man's face filled the void in front of her.

"Relax," a faraway vice soothed. "You're safe now."

After hearing his voice, Paige was even more certain she'd previously encountered the man somewhere and was frustrated she couldn't recall where or when. Before she could ponder further on his identity, darkness enveloped her.

CHAPTER 15

Paige walked to her father's door, ignoring Sergeant Wendt, who followed silently behind her. She hadn't spoken a word to him in over an hour. She paid no attention to the blood-red Oldsmobile parked on the curb across the street from the house.

Wendt had driven Paige to her father's from the Alameda hospital emergency room in his unmarked police sedan. It was her second visit to the facility in as many days; she was taken there by ambulance from the scene of the crash and attempted kidnapping. Although she was still a bit woozy from the repeated stings of the stun gun, and now had an abrasion on her nose and forehead to add to the black eye and stitches, she was otherwise unhurt.

Sergeant Wendt had arrived at the emergency room shortly after Paige. As she was being treated, he barraged her with questions until he realized her angry silence was all he was going to get for answers.

Mrs Reyes' eyes widened when she opened the door.

"Paige–"

"It's all right, Mrs Reyes," Paige said, giving the woman a hug. "It looks worse than it is." She was all too aware of her battered and scruffy appearance.

"Come inside," the housekeeper insisted, taking Paige by the arm. "Your father is waiting for you."

Instead of allowing Mrs Reyes to lead her into the house, Paige stopped at the base of the staircase. "Dad will have to wait. I feel like hell. I need a hot shower and to put on some clean clothes." She looked over her shoulder and gave Wendt a contemptuous look. "You can take Sergeant Wendt to see Dad, though; I'm sure he can't wait to give his report."

Wendt shook his head but said nothing. Paige went upstairs. Mrs Reyes led the police sergeant into the study.

Judge Callen was sitting across from Bob Farrell. Farrell was smoking and both men had drinks, even though it was not yet noon. Wendt's eyebrows rose. Farrell stood up.

"Hello, Sergeant Wendt," Judge Callen said. "Allow me to introduce–"

Wendt cut him off. "I know who he is."

Callen looked quizzically from Wendt to Farrell. "We've met," Farrell acknowledged. "How are you, Randy?"

"What the hell is he doing here?" Wendt demanded, ignoring Farrell's greeting.

"I'm sorry, Sergeant Wendt," Judge Callen said in a mock tone. "I didn't realize my guests required your approval."

"You know what I mean," Wendt snapped.

"No, Sergeant Wendt, I don't. Why don't you enlighten me?"

Wendt put his hands on his hips. Farrell smiled like a Cheshire cat and exhaled smoke through his nostrils. The Alameda detective sergeant took a deep breath and counted to ten before answering. He'd been doing that a lot lately.

"Your Honor, I can only assume if this con man is in your parlor, you're thinking of hiring him. I'd heard he was passing himself off as a legitimate private investigator. All I can tell you is hiring Robert Farrell would be a mistake." He looked directly at Farrell. "A big mistake."

"It's nice to see you, too," Farrell said.

"Then I've already made it," Callen said. "Mister Farrell is currently in my employ."

"You don't know what you're doing," Wendt told the Judge.

"Arguably," Callen responded, "neither do you."

"What the hell is that supposed to mean?"

"It means, Sergeant, that while I appreciate the hard work you and the other members of your department are expending to protect my daughter and apprehend her stalker, I felt a little more expertise was called for. I hired Mister Farrell to consult in the matter."

"Expertise?" Wendt pointed an accusing thumb at Farrell. "Him?"

"Yes," Callen said. "Mister Farrell is uniquely qualified to assist in this investigation. You have to admit, this crime appears to be a bit outside your department's capabilities."

"I don't have to admit any such thing," Wendt said. "And if you let him get anywhere near this investigation, you'd better be prepared for the worst."

"Could it get much worse?" Farrell spoke up. "From what I hear, during the past twenty-four hours, the Judge's daughter has been stalked, assaulted, potentially raped and murdered, threatened, harassed by phone at her place of employment, burned out of her home, rammed in her car, assaulted again, and nearly kidnapped. And you think I'm going to fuck up your investigation? At this rate, she'll be dead and buried by sundown."

Wendt's face reddened.

"Mister Farrell's worth has already proven invaluable," Judge Callen said.

"How's that possible?" Wendt asked incredulously.

"Why do you think the Judge's daughter isn't a hostage or dead right now?" Farrell inquired.

"No thanks to you; a citizen intervened," Wendt answered, his suspicion aroused by the insinuation in Farrell's question.

"A passing motorist came to her aid. Paige got lucky."

"I don't believe in luck," Farrell said. "Who was this citizen?"

"We don't know yet. He's refusing to answer questions until he gets an attorney. We're still working on it. I've been with Paige at the hospital."

"By the way, thank you for phoning me from the emergency room and letting me know what happened and that Paige was all right," Judge Callen said. "I'm grateful."

"My pleasure," Wendt said. "As far as the identity of the motorist who rescued Paige, we'll know who he is soon enough. When I called the station from the ER, he was just getting booked. Apparently, he's refused to give his name and was carrying no identification. His car wasn't registered to him, either; it was a rental. We'll get his fingerprints back from the FBI within a few hours. Why do you want to know?"

"I already know who he is," Farrell grinned. "Have you run the serial number on his gun yet?"

Wendt tilted his head. "How did you know he had a gun?"

Farrell's grin widened.

"May I use your phone?" Wendt asked.

"Be my guest," Callen offered, pointing to the phone on his desk with his cane. Wendt picked up the phone and dialed. After a moment's hushed conversation, he hung up. He turned to face Farrell and the Judge. The redness in his face was replaced by bemusement.

"His gun is registered to you," the sergeant said.

"That is correct," Farrell said.

"You put a tail on Paige, didn't you?"

"Correct again."

Sergeant Wendt's shoulders slumped. "How long?"

"Since last night."

"You should have told me, Your Honor," Wendt said.

"I could have," Callen said. "I felt it best to be discreet. Turns out I was right."

Wendt's disapproving gaze bounced between Judge Callen and Farrell, then faded to resignation. "I tried to do the same thing myself. Yesterday afternoon, after Paige got that crank call at work, I requested approval from my command staff to authorize overtime for a couple of our SWAT guys to start shadowing her," he said. "I was hoping to get an answer later today after the command staff meeting." He rubbed the back of this neck. "The SWAT commander was already drawing up an operations plan."

"Unfortunately," Farrell said, "while your department was making plans, Ms. Callen's stalker was executing his." He took a final drag on his smoke and put it out in an ornate marble ashtray.

"As I already noted," Callen said, "I appreciate the effort you and your department are expending on Paige's behalf. But quite frankly, as Mister Farrell has clearly demonstrated by his contribution to the case, your efforts are not enough. Had I not retained him, Paige would at this very moment be a captive" – his voice hardened – "or worse."

"My lieutenant is going to be really pissed," Wendt muttered.

"He shouldn't be," Callen said. "One would think your department would welcome any additional help."

"Normally they might, but not from you," Wendt said, addressing Farrell. "You're not very popular among Alameda cops." He gave Farrell a sideways look. "There are a few cops I work with, and one ex-cop in particular, you would be well-advised to avoid."

"Are you threatening me?" Farrell's smile faded.

"Not at all. Giving some friendly advice."

"That's what you call friendly?"

"What do you expect?" Wendt said. "You took a couple of our cops hostage; you even relieved them of their guns. Did you think they were going to forgive and forget? And then, thanks to some hush-hush deal you worked out with the Feds, you didn't get held to answer for it. One of those cops was never the same. He quit the force not long after your little escapade. Fell into the bottle, lost his family; the whole nine yards. He still has friends on the force. Friends you probably wouldn't want to meet in a dark alley, Mister Farrell."

"I'm sorry for that," Farrell said, "but I'm not sorry for what I did. If I hadn't made that play, a seven year-old Alameda girl would be dead."

"That's bullshit," Wendt countered. "I was the poor bastard who was stuck investigating your mess: the shooting gallery at the Ballantine home, the car chase and crash, and the kidnapping of two uniformed Alameda cops at gunpoint. You didn't have to play it like the lone ranger. If you had called us in the beginning–"

"Kirsten Ballantine would be dead," Farrell finished for him. "You would have bollixed it up just like you did protecting the Judge's daughter today. Cops would have swarmed all over the neighborhood, and Slocum would have smelled them a mile away. It's not your fault, Randy; that's just the way it is. Cops have to follow rules. Bad guys don't. I know; I was a cop for thirty years, remember?"

"That's a load of crap," Wendt said.

"That's a fact." Farrell extracted another unfiltered Camel from an inside pocket and lit it with his worn Zippo.

"Gentlemen," the Judge interceded. "The past is gone. I suggest we put our differences aside and focus on keeping my daughter safe. We still need to identify and apprehend the man determined to hurt her."

"I'm for that," Farrell agreed. "What do you say, Randy? We don't have to be at each other's throats. And we both want the same thing."

"My captain's going to go apeshit when he finds out you're anywhere near this case."

"Let me handle that," Judge Callen said. "I already have a message in to your chief. I expect a return call at any moment."

"Do I have a choice?" Wendt asked.

"Not really," Callen told him. "I've employed Mister Farrell, and I will continue to do so until Paige's stalker is stopped. I'm perfectly within my rights to obtain an outside consultant. I don't plan on interfering with your official investigation."

"You have the right, and the juice, to do whatever you want. But that doesn't mean my fellow cops are going to like it."

"I don't care if I ruffle a few blue feathers, sergeant. I'd rather be loathed by the cops and have Paige safe, than be toasted at the policeman's ball and bury my daughter."

Wendt had no answer to that. "What about him?" he finally said, directing his thumb at Farrell again.

"What about him? As I see it, you're both working to achieve the same goal."

"I'm not so sure we are," Wendt said. "My methods are legal."

"Maybe so," Farrell reminded him, exhaling smoke. "But my methods get results." Wendt again said nothing in reply.

"What can you tell me about what happened this morning, Sergeant?" Callen asked Wendt, deftly changing the subject.

"I'm not comfortable discussing details of an ongoing investigation in front of him."

"I thought your chief had issued you a directive to keep me informed?" Callen said.

"That's right, to keep you informed. Not him."

"Anything you can say to me, Sergeant Wendt, you may say in front of Mister Farrell. He's acting as my agent. If you refuse, I'll only relay your report to him later myself. I've already briefed Mister Farrell on the preliminary information you provided from the hospital about what happened to Paige this morning. Let's try to be adults, shall we?"

"I should have listened to my mother," Wendt said. "She wanted me to become a realtor."

"Please sit down," the Judge said in his paternal voice.

Wendt relented and took a chair. Farrell resumed his seat. "May I offer you something?" the Judge asked the Alameda cop. "A soft drink? I'd offer something stronger, but you're on duty. As you can see, Mister Farrell and I aren't impeded by such limitations."

"One of the perks of being a private consultant," Farrell teased, raising his glass.

"No thanks," Wendt said wearily, rolling his eyes at Farrell. "One of us should probably remain sober."

"Do we know any more about this man after this morning's attack?" Callen asked.

"Yes," Wendt answered. "We know he's put some effort into this. He knew where Paige lived. Knew her routine. He knew what kind of alarm system she uses and how to defeat it. He knew how to break in quietly."

"That's helpful," Farrell commented.

"How so?" Callen asked.

"It tells us something about him. Gives us some insight into his motive."

"Go on," the Judge prompted.

"This guy is smart. He's motivated. Relentless. He's executing a very elaborate plan. He's put a high degree of thought into this operation. He's no goofball who strikes only during the full moon, or some other irrational motive; he's methodical."

"I'm not sure I agree," Wendt said. "He was pretty reckless today. He damned near got caught during the attempted kidnapping. He tried to pull it off in the middle of a busy street at the height of the morning commute. I wouldn't call trying to kidnap a woman in broad daylight in front of dozens of witnesses very smart. That's what I'd call impulsive and reckless."

"It was neither reckless nor impulsive," Farrell said. "It was actually quite clever. His tactic of hitting Paige immediately after she'd left the ruins of her burned-out condo was a bold but sound strategy. He struck when she was psychologically vulnerable."

"What do you mean by psychologically vulnerable?" the Judge asked.

"People generally have an innate sense of timing," Farrell said. "It's how we make order of the world. If a guy gets into an automobile accident, psychologically, he might feel he's immune to another car crash for a while. Like he's met his quota of bad luck. Same thing if he catches a cold; he's just as likely to catch another a week after getting over the first one, but mentally he feels like he's somehow built up an immunity."

"As if he's already had his ration of bad fortune," Callen said.

"Right."

"How does this apply to my daughter's stalker?"

"When I was in Vietnam," Farrell continued, "we learned that the most effective time to counterattack was just after we'd been hit, especially if the attack had been an effective one. Psychologically, the attackers feel it's unlikely a just-defeated adversary will mount a counterstrike. It's called 'initiative'. They don't expect it. That's what happened to your daughter today." Farrell punctuated his conversation with a deep drag on his smoke. "When she drove away from the wreck of her condominium, even though she was distracted and upset, I'll bet the last thing she was thinking about was that she'd be attacked again a few minutes later in broad daylight, on a busy street, on the way to her father's house only a few miles away."

"Paige's guard was lowered deliberately? Is that what you're saying?" Callen posed.

"I believe so," Farrell said. "It's a pattern. Yesterday's dawn attack, the afternoon phone call, and then being smoked out of her home—"

"There was a message inside her condo, and a note on her car," Wendt added. "I see where you're going with this."

Farrell nodded. "I think your daughter's stalker did these things deliberately to put her in a vulnerable state of mind. To lull her. The cops, too."

"The cops?" Wendt exclaimed. "We weren't lulled." He made no attempt to hide his disbelief.

"You sure about that? Alameda's a small town. Where were all the cops this morning when her condominium was burning on Bay Farm Island?"

"All the east end units were at the scene of the fire," Wendt conceded. "The west end units were on the other side of the island. It was at shift change. Morning crew was probably just getting their coffee."

"Where did the kidnap attempt go down?"

"Midtown." Wendt's shoulders dropped.

"Exactly," Farrell said. "You think that was a coincidence?"

"That would mean—"

"That would mean," Farrell interrupted, "this guy knows your department's deployment routine, where the respective beat patrol units are at any given time, and what their response times are from various points on the island. How do you think he knows that?"

"Either's he's got inside knowledge of our department…" Wendt said.

"Or?" Farrell said.

"A scanner," Wendt said. "He's got a police scanner."

"Bullseye." Farrell squinted at him around his cigarette.

"What are you two talking about?" the Judge asked.

"If you listen to the radio traffic on a police scanner," Sergeant Wendt said, "within a short time, even a layman unfamiliar with police procedure can get a pretty good sense of how cops operate and where they're deployed. Police scanners are not expensive and can be bought at electronics stores like Radio Shack. You can even build them yourself from parts if you know what you're doing."

"And you think Paige's stalker has the use of such a device?"

Wendt looked at Farrell and nodded in reluctant agreement. "I think it's very likely," he answered.

"It fits his modus operandi," Farrell said. "This guy is meticulous. He obviously does his homework. He knew your daughter's jogging routine, her work schedule, where she lives, what health club she works out at; and we know he likes electronic gizmos. Why wouldn't he use a scanner?"

"You lost me," the Judge said, further confused. "How do you know he's an electronics buff?"

"The stun gun," Wendt said, snapping his fingers. "Of course."

"That's the device you told me about earlier on the phone? The thing he used to incapacitate Paige this morning?"

"Yes, Your Honor. He left it at the scene when he fled. Unfortunately, the serial number on it was removed."

"I'll wager you'll find no fingerprints on it, either," Farrell said. "Not even on the battery inside."

"I wouldn't take that bet," Wendt concurred. "And like the paintball gun he used on Paige yesterday morning, tracing something like a stun gun, which can be purchased by mail order, is virtually impossible."

"What do you think the odds are you'll find prints on any of the shell casings ejected from the suspect's gun?"

"You briefed Mister Farrell well," Wendt remarked to the Judge. "I didn't realize you knew about the shoot-out." He gave Judge Callen a disapproving glare. "To answer your question, about zero. But at least if we find the gun, we can match the casings up by the markings on the ejector, extractor, and firing pin."

"If you find the gun," Farrell pointed out. "How about the car?"

"It's already been recovered in San Leandro. It was an unreported stolen auto taken from the Oakland airport long-term parking lot."

"Clean?"

"As a whistle, so far," Wendt said, "except for a couple of fresh bullet holes. This guy apparently leaves nothing to chance."

"Essentially," the Judge declared, "despite all that's occurred, we've made no real progress in identifying Paige's stalker?"

"I wouldn't say that," Farrell said. "I think we've learned some things that might narrow down his motive. If we can figure out his motive, it might lead us to him."

"I agree," Wendt said.

"I don't believe it," a woman's voice interjected. Sergeant Wendt, Farrell, and Judge Callen looked up as Paige entered the study. She was wearing a sweater and jeans, and her hair was wet. She was trembling in fury. Her heated eyes were locked on her father and her fists were clenched.

All three men stood up.

"How long have you been eavesdropping?" the Judge asked.

"Long enough," her voice wavered in outrage.

"I told you there'd be fireworks," Farrell said, putting out his smoke.

CHAPTER 16

Ray Cowell's face was contorted in a mask of anguish as he knelt over the toilet. He'd been intermittently vomiting and urinating blood for the better part of an hour, and as a result was dizzy and weak.

He'd driven the stolen Mercury into San Leandro and ditched it at the marina, not far from where he'd parked his Hyundai. He then drove straight home, cursing in agony the entire journey. Once at his mother's house, Ray staggered down the steps to his basement room and collapsed in the bathroom.

The ache in his groin was immense and rivaled only by the stinging in his chest. While the body armor he'd been wearing undoubtedly saved his life, the bullet's impact badly bruised his torso beneath where it struck the vest, possibly even cracking a rib.

Ray stripped his sweat-soaked clothes off and examined his genitals. To his horror, he found his testicles swollen to the size of golf balls. The slightest touch sent shivers of excruciating pain rippling through his body. The pit of his stomach was a burning knot of fire and he felt a constant urge to relieve himself. But when he did, he found the urine pink with blood, and the pain rose to a fever pitch. It hurt so badly he almost fell to the tile floor.

Ray vomited, splattering the floor and walls surrounding the toilet as well as himself. The only sounds emanating from his mouth, besides the noise of his violent retching, were the words "slut" and "whore", over and over.

Gradually, the puking and tremors subsided. By then, Ray was so weak from exertion, he could barely stand. Using the toilet for leverage, he attempted to leave the bathroom. He was in this state, kneeling over the toilet and waiting for the waves of nausea to subside, when the knocking started.

"Raymond? You in there? Raymond?"

The biting staccato of his mother's voice corresponded with a persistent pounding on the door leading upstairs to the main house, a door Ray kept locked at all times due to his snooping mother. Neither the voice nor the knocking would go away.

"Leave me alone," he called out, the effort making his head ache even more. "Go away."

"Your boss is on the phone. You open this door, you hear me? Your boss wants to know why you aren't at work."

"Tell him I can't come in today," Ray stammered weakly. "Tell him I'm sick."

"I will not," his mother's shrill voice insisted. "If you think I'm going to make excuses, you've got another think coming. You're going to tell him yourself. Raymond, open this door right now."

His mother had been trying to gain entry into his basement apartment for years, ever since he'd moved back home. He'd installed sturdy locks on both the upstairs and outside doors to keep her prying nose out, but she never tired of trying to get in. Sometimes after dinner, as he retired to his room, she followed, as if that night, unlike every other, he would allow her admission to his lair. It had become an obsession with her.

Ray pushed himself shakily to his feet and made his way to the upstairs door. The soreness in his bruised chest made breathing difficult, and he was forced to shuffle in a knock-kneed gait to lessen the stinging in his groin created by walking. By the time he reached the door, he had to lean against it for several long seconds to recover his breath and prevent himself from passing out. The pounding on the door continued.

"Raymond?"

"Mother," he began, trying to calm his voice, "I'm very sick. Please tell my boss I'm taking today off on sick leave. I haven't used a sick day in over eleven years; I'm entitled. Please do it."

"No, I won't, Raymond. You're going to have to do it yourself."

The sound of locks unlatching was followed by the door swinging violently open. The victorious smirk on Margaret Cowell's face instantly vanished when she saw her son.

Raymond, pale and stooped, stood shakily before her. His skin was a dreadful hue and he was completely naked. His stringy hair was sweat-plastered over his balding head, and he had vomit-spittle running down his chin onto his chest. But it was his eyes that were the most alarming. They were red-rimmed and glaring, brimming with hatred. For a moment, she didn't recognize her own son.

"Listen to me, bitch," hissed the thing that resembled her son. "You're going to get on the phone and tell my boss that I'm going to be sick for the next couple of days. If you don't and I lose my job, the first thing I'm going to do is kick your stupid, fat, lazy, drunk ass out on the street."

Ray's mother started to respond but kept silent. She had once before witnessed such behavior from her son, and was afraid how he would react if she retorted. She retreated from the basement door and from the foul odor emanating out of her son's room.

"OK, Raymond, if that's what you want—"

"Just do it!" he shouted, slamming the door.

When his mother had gone and he'd relocked the door, Ray hobbled to his bed and collapsed. The aroma of sweat and barf hung heavily in the room, and he rolled his head from side to side to clear the fog from his pain-addled mind. Above him, suspended by fishing line, model aircraft dived and plummeted. His thoughts turned to the events of earlier, and his face twisted into a grimace of rage.

How could he have been so stupid? Why didn't he wait? He wasn't supposed to take her until tomorrow night. That was the plan. He expected her to be driven or escorted to her father's house from the fire by one of the police officers at the scene. But when he saw her drive past in the shiny convertible Saab, all alone, her ponytail flowing in the crisp bay air, it was too good to pass up.

She didn't even see him come up on her from behind, just like on the beach the day before. What a grass-eater!

Ray's dad used to tell him that there were only two kinds of animals on the earth: meat-eaters and grass-eaters. He said grass-eaters were dumb herd animals, like sheep and cattle. Grass-eaters wandered around in groups, always looking down at the ground, oblivious to everything but their next mouthful of grass. Ray's dad said that's why nature made so many of them, because they were easy to prey on.

Meat-eaters, Ray's dad told him, usually hunted alone. Meat-eaters were always on the prowl, warily searching for grass-eaters to feed on. Or for other predators who might wish to consume them. Meat-eaters were like the tigers at the Oakland zoo, or the wolves he watched on television on Mutual of Omaha's Wild Kingdom as a boy.

Ray's dad told him it was always better to be the diner than the dinner. Ray decided early he would not become a grass-eater. He would become a meat-eater.

But this morning, in his haste to exploit the golden opportunity of her unexpected solitude on the road, Ray screwed up. He'd failed to heed his father's words and acted like a grass-eater when he fixated on her. Certainly not like a predatory meat-eater.

He'd rammed her car, and before the slut had time to recover from the impact, he rendered her senseless with the Nova stun gun. It worked just like the brochure promised.

Then all hell broke loose. He was dragging the whore to his car when he was tackled. He didn't even see the guy, because he was blinded by the elation he felt at having the slut practically fall into his lap. And by his burgeoning arousal. As he'd dragged her along, helpless to stop him, Ray could feel himself become erect beneath the coveralls. Another grass-eater quality: distraction. Before he knew it, Ray was thrown to the ground.

The stun gun didn't work too well on the young blond man; one of the leads must have snagged on the sleeve of his jacket, blunting the charge. It only dropped him to his knees. That's when Ray made his worst mistake.

Ray should have stepped back, drawn his pistol, and executed the son of a bitch when he had the chance. But he didn't; he instinctively tried to use the stun gun again, and the guy was too fast. He blocked the Nova and punched Ray in the crotch.

Ray had never before experienced such pain. Lights danced before his eyes and he was surprised he didn't pass out. He dropped the stun gun and staggered back. He could barely breathe, and his balls felt as if they would erupt like the volcanoes depicted in the National Geographic magazines in his mother's bathroom.

But Ray didn't fall. He went to his knees, like his opponent, but didn't go down. Ray was proud of that. If he had, it would have been all over; the big blond guy would have had him.

Through the blinding pain, Ray reached for his pistol. He almost had it out when the blond dude pulled a gun of his own. As they simultaneously rose to their feet, his adversary fired first and shot him square in the chest.

The bullet's impact initially hurt less than he thought it would, a lot less than the punch in the groin. The body armor really worked. The bullet struck the metallic trauma plate in the center of the vest, knocking Ray back a step. The most pronounced effect of the gunshot was that it snapped Ray out of the agonizing sluggishness created by the groin punch. He raised his pistol and returned fire as the blond guy missed with a second shot. Ray emptied the entire magazine of nine-millimeter bullets in a matter of seconds. Unfortunately, by then the bastard had taken cover behind the slut's smashed car. Which was all right with Ray; he used the time to limp to his car and make his getaway.

It had been a very close call. Ray knew his anxiousness to grab the whore was what had nearly cost him his life. He'd gotten greedy and lost his focus. He'd let himself become distracted. Now he was going to have to change the plan and the timetable to implement it.

Haste makes waste.

Who was the blond guy? A cop assigned to protect her? Ray doubted it. If he'd been part of a protection detail, he would have been better prepared and wouldn't have been alone.

An off-duty cop who happened to pass by at the time of the crash and witness the attempted kidnapping? Possible. But if he was an off-duty cop, wouldn't he have drawn his gun and yelled "freeze" or "police" or something similar?

The guy sure looked like a cop. Ray's mind struggled to find the answer. A boyfriend?

A possibility Ray couldn't ignore. Who else but a boyfriend would follow the slut like that?

Ray made up his mind to check into that likelihood. He knew that intelligence was his most effective weapon. He learned that from one of the many books he'd read over the years as a member of the military-book-of-the-month-club.

Ray's breathing was finally beginning to calm from the argument with his mother. He tried to let himself drift off to sleep, despite the throbbing in his scrotum and chest. Although the bullet that struck his chest didn't seem to hurt at the time, when Ray got home and doffed the armor, he found a large raised welt over a deep bruise and discovered it hurt to inhale or exhale deeply.

Ray nodded off, comforting himself, as he often did, with memories of Sissy. He remembered the night she put him to bed with a glass of milk and promised to buy him a new baseball glove at the end of the summer.

The last thought in Ray's head before sleep finally took him was the memory of Sissy's breasts, winking at him through the dim light in his father's garage.

CHAPTER 17

"What in the hell is he doing here?" Paige demanded.

"Mister Farrell is working for me," her father answered.

"Doing what, exactly?"

"Consulting."

"It would figure you two would be acquainted," she said. "You both share the same ethics. Or lack thereof."

"I'll take that as a compliment," Farrell said.

Paige glared at him. "What's your story, Sergeant Wendt? Were you aware this felon was working for Dad?"

"Alleged felon," Farrell corrected her. "I was never charged with any crime." She ignored him.

"I just found out about Mister Farrell's involvement myself," Wendt told her. "Believe me, I was as surprised as you."

"I'll bet," she said, returning her ire to her father. "What the hell were you thinking?"

"That I didn't want my daughter dead."

Paige eyed Farrell. "That guy who intervened today; I knew I'd seen him before, I just couldn't place him. He was with you in federal court last year, wasn't he? He was your accomplice during your multistate crime spree?"

"My partner, you mean," Farrell corrected her again. "And you're welcome."

"For what?" she challenged.

121

"For saving your life," the Judge said. "Regardless of how you feel about hiring Mister Farrell, the irrefutable fact remains, if I had not, you wouldn't be standing here now berating us."

Paige looked to Sergeant Wendt to refute her father's claim. Wendt looked at his shoes.

She turned to her father. "You had me followed?" There were both disbelief and outrage in her voice.

"Yes," Farrell answered for Judge Callen. "It was all I could do at this point in the investigation." He met her gaze evenly. "I don't regret it."

"Nor do I," Callen said. "Like it or not, you owe your safety, and quite probably your life, to Mister Farrell's astute judgment and proactive intervention."

"Where were the police all this time a lunatic was stalking me and a private investigator was following me?" Paige asked Wendt.

"Getting permission," Farrell answered before Wendt could speak. Wendt looked up from his feet and grunted his admission that Farrell was right.

Paige looked from Wendt, to Farrell, to her father. Her eyes flashed for a moment, and the truth of Farrell's words settled in. She exhaled a long breath, ran her hands over her battered face and through her damp hair, and slumped down in what had been Farrell's seat across from her father. Farrell went back to the bar and began making a drink.

"What a week," she said to no one in particular.

"It could be worse," her father reminded her.

"I suppose so." The exhaustion was beginning to overtake her. "You could have told me you had someone following me," she said to her father.

"If I had," he said, "you'd have asked me who it was. If I'd told you, you'd have thrown a fit."

"And you would have been unconsciously looking over your shoulder, which would have potentially compromised the tail and endangered you," Farrell added over his shoulder.

"I still don't like it," she said.

"Here," Farrell returned from the bar and handed Paige a drink. "It'll do you good."

"I don't normally drink," she said, but accepted the glass.

"This is hardly a normal day," her father said softly. Paige nodded and took a gulp of bourbon, wincing as it burned down her throat.

"Don't let me interrupt your conversation," Paige said after catching her breath. "I believe when I entered you were talking about motive."

"Perhaps this is a discussion best left for a time when you're feeling better," the Judge said.

"You mean a time when I'm not around to hear you discussing me," she countered. "No thanks, Dad; if it's all right with you, I'll stay and listen for myself." She gestured to the trio. "Please, go on with your debate about my stalker's motive. I'd like to know what you three criminal experts have come up with."

"We were only speculating," Wendt said, "about motive."

"Don't let me stop you. That's really the heart of this case, isn't it? Motive? The reason why this asshole is targeting me? I'm dying to hear your theories." She jutted her abraded chin at Farrell. "You had the floor when I came in, Mister Private Investigator."

"Paige," the Judge said, "this can wait for a time when you're not so tired."

"You mean not so argumentative, don't you?" Judge Callen tapped his hand on his cane in exasperation.

"Very well, Ms Callen," Farrell said. "The way I see it, you need to hear this discussion anyway because you more than anyone might be able to lend insight into the stalker's motive."

"I'm listening," she said, setting down her drink and folding her hands on her lap.

Farrell took a sip of his bourbon before continuing. "This guy could have any number of motives. We narrow the possible motives by eliminating the least likely ones. Hopefully, that process leads us to our suspect's motive."

"And to him," Wendt said.

"The first motive we can eliminate is a random act. We can take that one off the list for obvious reasons."

"You lost me already," Judge Callen said. "What 'obvious reasons'?"

"This motive would mean Ms Callen was targeted by the suspect at random," Farrell said. "He saw her at the bus stop, or jogging, or somewhere else without any previous direct connection to her. It doesn't fit this guy's profile. Everything that's happened so far indicates a very personal motive."

"I agree," Wendt said.

"How do you arrive at this conclusion?" Judge Callen asked.

"If this stalker simply wanted to rape and murder Ms Callen," Farrell said, "he could have done it at the beach yesterday morning. He had her isolated and alone. But he didn't. He took pains to let her know he was coming back. He wants to prolong it." He looked at Paige. "He wants her to suffer. That's not random; that's personal."

"OK," Paige said. "The random motive is eliminated."

"That's a good thing," Farrell said. "Frankly, if this guy selected you at random, we'd be in the worst shape possible. There would be virtually no way to know how he selected you as a victim. In that case, all we could do is to wait until he strikes and hope to catch him in the act."

"Which is what Mister Farrell's foresight saved you from this morning," the Judge said.

"I haven't forgotten," Paige said, pointing to her battered face.

"The second possible motive is Ms Callen's personal life. An old boyfriend who can't let go, a rebuked suitor, an unrequited romance, that sort of thing."

"I hate to disappoint you, but I don't have the most active social life. Or a history of stormy relationships."

"I wish you did," Wendt said.

"You'd prefer the case to have a romance angle?"

"In a way, yes," the sergeant said. "Personal motives are the easiest to flesh out. They're also the most common motives for stalkers. You sure there's no one from your past, even the distant past, who might harbor a fixation on you?"

"What about Chad?" Judge Callen asked. "He was certainly upset about the way things turned out between you two."

"Who's Chad?" Wendt asked.

Paige's scowled at her father. "That was almost three years ago, Dad. And it couldn't be Chad. He's over six feet tall. The guy who attacked me is five-foot-ten at most. And I'd know if I saw those gnarly yellow teeth before."

"Chad could have put someone up to it," Farrell said. "Hired the stalker. It's been done before. Who's Chad?"

"Chad was engaged to Paige," the Judge answered for her. "She broke it off."

"Much to your dismay," Paige said. She turned to Farrell and Wendt. "Chad and I met in law school. We dated exclusively for a couple of years. We were engaged to get married."

"Why didn't you?" Farrell asked.

"My mother died the week before the wedding," Paige said, looking down.

"I'm sorry for your loss," Farrell said. "But I have to ask: how did Chad take your breaking off the engagement?"

"Not well," Judge Callen said.

"Mom's death wasn't unexpected, but it threw a wrench in the timetable Chad's family had planned for our very elaborate wedding. They wanted a big one with all the trimmings. His family owns a law firm in the city, and Chad expected me to mourn Mom and get on with marrying him so he could get busy working on a full partnership at his dad's firm. Apparently, I disrupted their schedule." She smiled slightly. "It was a blessing in disguise. Better to learn your spouse is a jerk before tying the knot."

"That's a lesson I had to learn twice," Farrell said.

"Me too." Wendt chuckled without mirth. "I'm on my third wife; an occupational hazard."

"You ever hear from Chad since?"

"Yeah," said Paige. "I got an invitation to his wedding last summer, if you can believe it. I didn't go."

"Doesn't mean he isn't our guy," Wendt said. "Or that somebody else you may have dated or refused to date isn't our suspect."

"You're on the wrong track. I don't think my stalker's motive originates from my personal life," Paige said.

"You'd know better than anyone," Farrell said. "But we still have to check every possibility."

"I get it. What's another possible motive?"

"Your work," Farrell said. "You don't exactly have an occupation where enemies are a rarity."

"This third category for a motive is where I believe we'll find our man," Wendt said.

"You've been a deputy DA for what, about five years?" Farrell asked.

"That's right," Paige said. "I got hired by the district attorney's office when I graduated law school."

"Very impressive," Farrell said, casting a suspicious glance at Judge Callen. "Doesn't hurt to have relatives in high places."

"I resent that," Paige sat up, her eyes flaring. "I'll have you know I was hired by the district attorney's office on the merit of my application and exemplary law school credentials, no matter what anybody thinks about cronyism and my father's influence."

"And I'll have you know, Ms Callen," Farrell said, "I am not a murderer or felon, no matter what you said about me in federal court."

"Who's going to believe that?"

"I would ask you the same question," Farrell said. "Getting hired at the DA's office in the same county where your father is the senior superior court judge, straight out of law school, without your father's influence; who's going to believe that?"

Paige started to retort but couldn't. Judge Callen looked into his drink. Sergeant Wendt noticed the ceiling.

"Let's get back to your job," Farrell continued. "Five years as a prosecuting attorney is a long time to be making people unhappy."

"Who said I make people unhappy? I do my job well."

Farrell cued Wendt by taking a drink.

"Open your eyes," Wendt told her. "Everybody hates deputy DAs. Victims hate you because they blame you for allowing the criminals who victimize them to get off. Suspects hate you because you put them away. Jurors and witnesses hate you because you inconvenience them; you keep them from their jobs and families in endless courtroom maneuvers. And cops hate DAs, maybe most of all, because you sit on your bureaucratic butts in an office and plea-bargain away the collars they risk their butts on the street to bring in, and then have to go out and face the same crooks again after you let them off." Wendt grinned. "Hell, Paige, it would be a lot easier to find someone that liked you." He put up his hands. "Because you're a deputy DA, I mean," he quickly added.

"Thanks for clarifying that," Paige said.

"This motive creates the largest suspect pool," Farrell said. "As a result, it's going to be the most difficult to sift through. Anybody come to mind that fits this profile? A crook who threatened you? A disgruntled victim?"

"Nobody off the top of my head," Paige said. "I get a lot of threats. Every decent deputy DA I know does."

"Any specific threats stand out?" Farrell asked her.

"Not really," Paige said. "They're part of the territory. I don't take most of them seriously." Farrell looked to Sergeant Wendt.

"I've already got two detectives, along with a couple of DA's inspectors who offered to help out, down at the courthouse scouring through Paige's old case files. They're looking for anyone remotely matching the suspect's description." Wendt looked around the room. "It's going to take a while. And even if we find the guy somewhere in Paige's previous cases, how will we know?"

A long minute of silence followed. Farrell lit another unfiltered Camel. Paige wrinkled her nose but said nothing.

"If you'll permit me," Judge Callen said, "I want to sum up the possible motives as I understand them so far."

"Be my guest," Wendt said.

"The first motive, you said, would be the person stalking Paige targeted her at random, correct?"

"That's right."

"The second motive would originate from Paige's personal or social life, like an ex-boyfriend?"

"Right again," Wendt confirmed. "And the third motive would be a suspect emanating from Paige's occupation as a deputy district attorney."

"I see," Judge Callen said. "That's a wide range of possibilities."

"There's a fourth possibility," Farrell proclaimed, exhaling smoke.

"A fourth motive?" Wendt asked. "I guess you know something I don't."

"Hardly a first," Farrell mumbled around his cigarette.

"What would the fourth motive be?" Judge Callen asked.

"You," Farrell said.

CHAPTER 18

"You're kidding." Paige said to Farrell. "I'm the one getting stalked and attacked, and you think the suspect is going after Dad?" She gave her father a sour look. "Some ace detective you hired."

"I don't see it," Wendt agreed with Paige. "The Judge is a much softer target than Paige. If this guy was gunning for him, why attack her? Why not go straight for him? He could have had the Judge any time he wanted and with a lot less effort than it took to go after her." He made no effort to conceal his contempt for Farrell's premise. "What you say makes no sense. The Judge is retired, he's almost always at home, usually alone, and not very ambulatory. No offense–"

"None taken," Callen said, although a frown started at the corners of his mouth.

"If he was after the Judge, why go to all the trouble of messing with Paige?" Wendt continued. "Besides, we don't even know this guy is aware of who Paige's father is." He shook his head. "Not to mention, there's also the 'whore' and 'slut' thing. The suspect has called Paige those specific names repeatedly: on the beach, when he phoned her at work, when he spray-painted them on her walls, and in the note he left on her car. Those are sexually derogatory terms men use against women, Mister Farrell. I think you're reaching. This guy isn't after the Judge; he's got radar lock on Paige. You're dead wrong."

"I'd like to hear Mister Farrell out," the Judge said.

"Maybe I'm wrong," Farrell conceded. "I've been wrong before. But what better way to hurt a man than through his children? For a detective, you perpetually ignore the obvious truth that this stalker isn't simply trying to injure or kill Ms Callen. If that was his goal, he could have done that any time he wanted. He used a real pistol this morning; why the toy gun yesterday? And when he broke into her condo, why not wait inside and attack and kidnap her when she returned, if that was his intent, instead of torching the place and making a play for her later on the road?"

"Who knows why a psycho does what he does?" the police sergeant said. "The guy's a whack job; we may never know what his motive is. And as far as the Judge being his target, I think you're off base."

Farrell took a drag and exhaled through his nose. "You're looking at what's happening to Paige as a series of individual crimes, directed at her. What if they're not?"

"What else would you call them?"

"A crusade. Not a series of single acts against Paige, but instead a campaign of terror aimed at her father, using Paige as the means."

"That's ridiculous," Paige blurted. But Farrell could see the wheels of doubt beginning to turn behind her eyes. The Judge's, too.

"Maybe the suspect's objective all along," Farrell suggested, "isn't primarily Paige? Maybe she's the secondary target, and everything that's been done to her so far is intended to terrorize him?" Farrell looked at the other faces in the room. "Maybe the motive is something in the Judge's history and not hers?"

"Seeing as how you're full of maybes," Wendt said, "I've got a 'maybe' notion of my own. Maybe you're getting paid by the hour to dazzle the Judge with your investigative prowess; maybe paid a lot. Good for you. Maybe this unsubstantiated idea about the Judge being the stalker's target is your way of feeding an already worried parent a lot of malarkey about him being the reason his daughter's getting stalked so he'll keep paying your extravagant fees?"

"That sounds like a reasonable theory to me," Paige said.

"At least as reasonable as blaming Judge Callen for his daughter's troubles," Wendt said.

"If insulting me would lead you to the perp," Farrell said, "he'd already be locked up."

"I'm sorry if you feel I'm insulting you, Mister Farrell. But I've got better things to do than entertain your harebrained theories."

"You're absolutely certain," Farrell said, "that you can exclude the Judge as the primary target?"

"Technically, until I nail this creep, I can't exclude anyone," Wendt admitted, "including the Easter Bunny. But that doesn't mean I'm going to start chasing rabbits because you see colored eggs."

"If you say so. How about you, Your Honor? You think I'm chasing my tail looking into your possible enemies?"

"I don't know," Callen said. "I've certainly made a few over the years." Wendt shot Farrell a scornful glance.

"What I know," Wendt said, "is that I've got work to do, and it's not getting done while I'm here listening to this nonsense." He turned to Paige. "I can't tell you what to do," he said, "but you may want to lay low here at your father's for a while."

"Where else am I going to go?"

"After what happened today, with the suspect getting shot, I don't think we're going to hear from him for a while.

He's probably licking his wounds somewhere. You should be safe here at the Judge's home."

"Should be?" Paige said.

"I'll have patrol officers drive by at irregular intervals and check the house."

"I didn't know the suspect was shot," Farrell said.

"There's a lot you don't know, Mister Farrell."

Farrell's face hardened. "I'm getting a little tired of you taking your incompetence out on me," he said.

"Are you planning on doing something about it?"

"You'll be the first to know."

"Gentleman," the Judge intervened. "This doesn't get us anywhere. Mister Farrell's associate shot the suspect, you say?"

Wendt nodded. "That's what witnesses are telling us. Your sidekick, the one who shot him, isn't cooperating. He's invoked his right to remain silent. Without any of the information he can provide, all we can do is collect witness statements and alert local hospitals to look out for someone with a gunshot wound meeting the suspect's general description."

"Is my partner being charged?"

"Yeah. Possession of a loaded and concealed handgun without a permit, and reckless discharge of a firearm within the city limits."

"What a bogus pile of bullshit," Farrell spat. "He used that gun to save Ms Callen's life, and you're going to charge him?"

"He broke the law," Paige said matter-of-factly. "Why wouldn't he be charged?"

Farrell turned to the Judge.

"If you'll contact the Alameda County sheriff's office," Callen began, "you'll find a permit to carry a concealed firearm in the name of Kevin Kearns was issued yesterday under the sheriff's signature."

"You've known his name all along," Wendt accused the Judge.

"Of course," Callen said. "I always know the names of my clients."

"You're representing him?"

"That is correct," Judge Callen said. "Why so surprised? I may be a retired judge, Sergeant, but I still have the ability to practice law. And I advise all my clients to invoke their Fifth Amendment right to remain silent while in police custody until I can personally meet with them."

"I don't believe it," Wendt said. "You're actually interfering with the investigation."

"I don't see it that way," Callen said. Paige stood up.

"You all make me sick," she said. "Playing your little games and changing the rules when it suits you. Meanwhile, I'm counting the hours until a madman ends my life." She looked at Judge Callen. "You know what, Dad?" she said. "There are times I'm ashamed to admit you're my father."

Her words stung the old judge. Paige turned and started to walk from the study.

"That's far enough," Farrell called out, grabbing her by the elbow and tossing his cigarette into the remains of his drink in the same motion. "You're not going anywhere." Paige's eyes widened. He steered her back to her chair. "Sit your ass down." She was too stunned by his unexpected action to do anything but comply.

"Now just a minute–" Wendt took a step forward.

"One word out of you," Farrell cut him off, "and she won't be the only person in this room wearing a black eye." Wendt halted.

"Young lady," Farrell began, "you had no call to say that to your father. None at all." He leaned down until his face was inches from hers. "You might be Miss High-and-Mighty Deputy District Attorney today, but this man used to change your diapers. If it wasn't for him doing something unorthodox he knew you'd disapprove of and despise him for, you'd be in the trunk of a car right now." Farrell's face got tight. "Or in a shallow grave."

Paige looked up at him with her mouth agape. Farrell stood back up.

"Your father did what any good parent would do: whatever it takes to protect his child. And he did it knowing full well you'd hate him for it. Maybe someday, if you become a parent, you'll understand that. Loving your child so much that you're willing to risk them turning on you just to do what's best for them." He looked down at her. "Whether they're mature enough to appreciate it or not."

Farrell pointed his thumb at Wendt. "The sergeant here is doing his best. He's a good man working under a mountain of red tape. I know; I used to toil under that mountain myself. You think he didn't want to have you tailed?" Farrell looked at Wendt, who gave him a weak smile. "He did. He was in the process of assembling a protection detail. But for bureaucratic reasons beyond his control, it didn't happen. Your father knew this, and instead of sitting idly on his hands, he seized the initiative and took the necessary steps to ensure your safety."

Farrell put his hands on his hips. "And there's one other person you might reconsider dumping your puritanical disdain on. My friend and partner, who is currently rotting in a municipal jail cell. This young man's only crime was damn near getting killed keeping you from that same fate. And you want him charged with two rinky-dink misdemeanor crimes related to the very gun he used to save your ungrateful ass? If you were my daughter, I'd turn you over my knee."

Paige stood up from her chair. Her face lost all its color. "You can go to hell," she told Farrell. She looked from him, to Sergeant Wendt, and finally to her father. "All of you."

"Paige–" her father pleaded.

"I'm going to lie down," she cut him off. She walked from the study.

Farrell retrieved another cigarette. The Judge's face slackened. Wendt broke the silence.

"That was quite a speech," he commented. "Thanks for saying what I wanted to but couldn't."

"Maybe I should run for public office?" Farrell said, lighting his smoke.

"I'm sorry," was all the Judge could say. "She's always viewed everything in very black-and-white terms, like her mother. To her, the law and rules in general are the glue which hold her world together. If anything," he went on, looking at the floor, "it became more pronounced after my wife's death."

"There's no need to apologize. I probably shouldn't have been so hard on her," Farrell said. "The kid's had a rough couple of days." He exhaled smoke. "But she's the victim now; she's on the other side of the fence. She's learning the hard way that the rules, and the system, aren't necessarily going to keep her safe."

"I agree with you," Wendt said. "But I'm part of that system. I can't say it."

Farrell gave Wendt a conciliatory nod. "We'll get this guy, Sergeant." He turned to the Judge. "We're not going to let anything happen to your daughter."

"My name is Randy," Wendt said, extending his hand. Farrell shook it. "What do you say we go get your partner out of cold storage?" Wendt now faced the Judge. "That is, if his attorney here will permit us to finally obtain his statement so we can release him?"

"No charges?" Judge Callen asked.

"No charges," Wendt affirmed.

"Have my client call me when you get to the station," Callen said. "I'll advise him to cooperate. Then he's all yours."

"Thanks for the drink, Your Honor," Farrell said. "I'll be in touch." He and Wendt headed for the door. As they left, Farrell looked back and saw the Judge sitting forlorn with his drink.

"Do you really think the suspect's motive might originate with the Judge and not his daughter?" Wendt asked once they were outside.

"Hell, I don't know," Farrell said. "I'm flying by the seat of my pants."

"So you've got no plan? Just wait for this asshole to strike again?"

"Didn't say that," Farrell said.

CHAPTER 19

"Hi, Kevin," Farrell said. "Nice to see you."

"I wish I could say the same," Kearns said.

Kearns was being escorted by Sergeant Wendt through the front doors of the Alameda Police Department headquarters on Oak Street. He had his coat over one arm, bags under both eyes, and a scowl on his face.

"Sorry about your stay in the hoosegow," Farrell said.

"You should be. I wasn't back working with you even one full day and I find myself in a fight, a shoot-out, and locked in jail. Again. It's just like old times, Bob." Kearns ran his hands through his short hair and looked up at the sky. "What the hell was I thinking?"

"Come on." Farrell put his arm around Kearns' shoulder. "You'll feel better after a meal and some rest."

"I doubt it," Kearns said. "But if you're buying, I'm hungry. It's been over twenty-four hours since I've had anything to eat. Or sleep."

Several uniformed police officers passed by the trio entering or exiting the police administration building. All gave sharp glances at Farrell and Kearns. Wendt saw them; Farrell and Kearns paid them no mind.

"I'd think about moving along pretty soon," Wendt said. "You two aren't exactly popular around here."

"We're going," Farrell said to Wendt. He handed the police

sergeant one of his business cards. "Let's stay connected, Randy. I don't expect you to lay out the red carpet, but we stand a better chance of keeping the Judge's daughter safe and bagging the guy trying to do her harm if we don't butt heads." Sergeant Wendt responded by digging out one of his own business cards and extending it to Farrell.

"You might want to reconsider giving him your card," Kearns said. Wendt looked puzzled.

"Never mind." Farrell elbowed Kearns. Farrell and Wendt exchanged cards and a handshake.

Just as they were shaking hands, the front door of the police department burst open and two men strode forcefully down the steps towards them. One was in uniform, the other in plainclothes. Both cops' hot eyes were locked on Farrell.

"Who's your friend, Randy?" the taller uniformed cop demanded. He was well over six feet in height and overweight, and had his dyed black hair swept over his bald spot. He looked to be in his early thirties. He also had the bleary eyes of a regular, heavy drinker. The name tag on his uniform read "McCord". The plainclothes detective with him was about the same age, much shorter, and just as fat.

"Take it easy," Wendt told the newcomers. "They were just leaving."

"You take it easy," McCord said.

"Bob Farrell," Farrell said. He stuck out his hand and grinned. "Nice to meet you."

"I know who the fuck you are," McCord spat, refusing the offered hand. "You're lucky I don't kick your ass right now." He wheeled on Wendt. "What the fuck is he doing here?"

"None of your business," Wendt told him.

"Winning friends again, I see," Kearns said. Farrell shrugged.

"Do all your cops threaten citizens while in uniform?" Farrell inquired, his eyes laughing. Wendt sent Farrell a dirty look.

"It sure as hell is my business," McCord said to Wendt, ignoring Farrell's question. "I heard he was skulking about," he told the sergeant. He turned to Farrell. "You got a lot of nerve showing your face around here."

"Have we met?" Farrell asked him innocently.

"No, we haven't," McCord snarled. "But you met my brother. A year ago Christmas, you tried to kill him with his own shotgun."

Farrell's eyes jettisoned their mirth. "No, I didn't. That's not what happened. You weren't there. If I tried to kill your brother, Officer McCord, he'd be playing a harp right now."

McCord started to lunge at Farrell. Wendt and Kearns stepped between them. The plainclothes officer stood by with his fists clenched.

"I was there," the plainclothes cop blurted. "And I didn't forget you pointed a gun at me." He sent what he thought was a fierce glare at Farrell, diminished by his cherubic face and doughboy physique. "Maybe I'll return the favor sometime."

"Be careful what you wish for," Farrell admonished. "Last time we met, I didn't pull the trigger. Next time, you might not be so lucky."

"You threatening me?" plainclothes challenged.

"Not threatening anybody," Farrell explained, his voice calm. "But if you break leather on me, be ready to meet the coroner."

"Fuck you, asshole!"

"There's a quick-witted comeback," Farrell drawled to Kearns.

"Swell company you keep, Sergeant," McCord said, using Wendt's title instead of his name. The meaning wasn't lost on Farrell.

"Last warning, Officer," Wendt said, returning the formality. "You want to end up an ex-cop, like your brother, stick around. You want to keep what's left of your career intact, you'll turn your butt one hundred and eighty degrees and get the hell out of here."

"Let's beat it, Joe," the plainclothes officer said. He faced Farrell. "The air stinks around here."

McCord glared at Wendt but let the plainclothes officer lead him away by the arm. A few steps away, he turned back and pointed a fleshy finger at Farrell.

"This ain't over," he said. "And that goes double for your fuckhead sidekick."

"It was a pleasure meeting you, Officer McCord," Farrell said. McCord stormed off, muttering obscenities under his breath. Kearns wiggled his fingers in a goodbye.

Wendt shook his head. "You two are a couple of real comedians. Laugh now, but you'd better not screw around in Alameda," he advised. "McCord holds a grudge. And he's got friends."

"You let him carry a gun?" Farrell asked.

"He's actually a pretty good cop, believe it or not," Wendt said. "His brother was one of the officers you jacked last year out on Bay Farm Island. His friend in the suit was the other."

"I figured that part out already," Farrell said. "He's a detective?"

"No. He's on modified duty; a worker's compensation claim. He's off street duty and working in the records division. Says he has a back injury."

"You don't sound convinced," Farrell said.

"What do I know?" Wendt said. "Could be he's malingering. It happens. That's for the docs and shrinks to figure out."

"Sounds like Officer McCord is the one who needs to talk to a shrink," Kearns said. "He's wound a little tight, if you ask me."

"McCord's brother didn't take kindly to being held hostage and having you disarm him," Wendt told Farrell. "He was already a drunk, and his marriage was on the rocks. That event was the straw that broke the camel's back. Within a couple of months of meeting you, he was fired for repeatedly being intoxicated on duty."

"And now his big, fat, gun-wielding, grudge-holding brother blames you," Kearns said, making an OK sign with his fingers. "Nicely done, Bob."

"If there was another way, I'd have used it," Farrell said.

"Don't sweat it too much," Wendt said. "Frankly, McCord's brother was eventually going to get fired anyway; you just accelerated the process."

"I did thirty years with San Francisco PD," Farrell noted. "I'd be lying if I said I hadn't seen it before."

"Me, too," Wendt agreed. "In any case, it's water under the bridge."

"Apparently not for Officer McCord," Kearns said.

"Give me a call, will you," Wendt said, "before implementing any more of your schemes involving Deputy District Attorney Paige Callen? Especially if they're going to occur on this island?"

"I'll stay connected," Farrell told him. "When do I get my gun back?"

"Not anytime soon, I'm afraid. Mister Kearns here may have put a bullet from it into our suspect. We have to keep it for evidence purposes, even though he's not getting charged."

"Fair enough." Wendt left the two men and returned into the department.

"Let's get some chow," Farrell said.

"Can we stop by my place first? It's only a block away. I want to grab a quick shower and a change of clothes. I smell like jail funk."

"Sure," Farrell agreed. They walked to Farrell's Oldsmobile and drove the block to Kearns' apartment on Park Street. But when Kearns led them to the exterior door leading upstairs to the apartments he found his key no longer fit the lock. He was about to go into the bar and locate the owner, Johnny Costanza when the gruff Italian-American came out to meet him.

"Hi, Johnny," Kearns said. "I was just coming to find you. For some reason, I'm locked out."

"Sorry, Kevin," Costanza said. "I have to evict you."

"What for? I'm paid until the end of the month."

Costanza handed Kearns a roll of cash. "I know. Here's your refund. I already packed all your stuff. It's boxed up in my office."

"What gives?" Kearns demanded. "Why are you putting me on the street?"

"Were the Alameda cops here today?" Farrell interjected. Kearns looked quizzically at Farrell and then back at Costanza. The tavern owner looked down and slowly nodded.

"Jesus Christ," Kearns said. "So while I'm locked up in their jail, the Alameda cops toss my room? Is that what you're telling me?"

Costanza nodded again.

"And they 'advised' you to kick Kevin out, didn't they?" Farrell asked.

"What can I do?" Costanza pleaded. "I run a legal place; you know that. But to the cops, it don't matter. They want to shut me down, they shut me down. They can have the Department of Alcoholic Beverage Control, or the county Health Department, find any reason they want." He put his hand on Kearns' arm. "I got to run a business in this town, you know? I got a family, Kevin. I go against the cops, I'm out of business. I'm sorry."

"Forget it, Johnny," Kearns said, deflated. "It isn't your fault."

"I threw in a couple hundred extra bucks for you keeping the room so clean," Costanza said. "No hard feelings, huh?"

Kearns examined the roll of cash he was given by Costanza. "I appreciate the thought, Johnny, but I pay my own freight." He peeled off several bills and stuck them in the pocket of his former landlord's shirt. "Where's my stuff?"

"Follow me."

Kearns and Farrell were led into an office by Costanza, who left them alone and returned to the bar. Two cardboard boxes were stacked on the floor. Kearns opened them and found his meager collection of clothes, toiletries, and possessions loosely piled inside. He sifted through until he found a pair of combat boots.

"Going hiking?" Farrell asked. Kearns ignored him and thrust his arm inside one of the boots. A moment later, he came out with the thick envelope of cash given to him by Farrell the night before.

"Well played, Kevin," Farrell whistled. "Seems I've taught you a thing or two after all."

Kearns stuffed the envelope into his jacket. "At least the bush-league cops in this town didn't find this. I'm sure if they had, it would be gone." He shook his head and looked up at Farrell.

"Don't say it," Farrell said.

"Say what?"

"That I'm bad luck. That's what you're thinking, isn't it?"

"Less than twenty-four hours ago, I agreed to work a job with you. In that time, I've almost been killed, locked up in jail, and now I'm evicted from my apartment and out on the street. What would you call it, Bob?"

"A minor setback," Farrell said. "Can I at least buy you a meal?"

"Why not," Kearns said. "I've got nowhere else to go."

They went into the bar. Farrell ordered a double bourbon, and Kearns a draft beer. Farrell told the grill staff to throw a couple of burgers on. The tavern was thinning out after the lunch hour, and Farrell selected a secluded table near the back.

"So, tell me about this morning," Farrell said, lighting a cigarette.

"Not much to tell," Kearns answered. "I followed her out of the condominium complex and west across the island. She was driving a metallic-blue Saab convertible with the top up." He took a sip of beer. "I'd forgotten how easy on the eyes she was."

"She's a looker, all right," Farrell said. "I just came from a meeting with her at her father's house. Little banged up, but she could easily stroll the catwalk."

"Still got the attitude?"

"Does she ever," Farrell acknowledged. "She was extremely pissed off her father hired us. Furious might be a better word for it."

"She shouldn't be," Kearns grunted. "Wasn't for you and me, she'd be in a dungeon somewhere. This guy means business, Bob."

"Tell me about him," Farrell said, exhaling smoke.

"He's got balls, that's for sure. Rammed her off the road in broad daylight. Got out of his car and went after her like the fucking Terminator. Not a big guy; he was wearing coveralls and a ski mask. Gloves, too. He was dragging her to his car when I entered the picture."

"How'd it go down?"

"He had a stun gun, or Taser, whatever they call it. Didn't see it until he nailed me. Felt like I'd pissed on an electric fence. Almost took me out." Kearns drained some more beer. "I gave him a nut-shot on the way down. It rocked him enough that he must have figured it was time to go lethal. He went for a pistol." He looked over his glass at Farrell. "I was faster." Kearns drained his beer in a long gulp and held up his glass. "You're still buying, right?"

"Sure," Farrell said quietly. A waitress came and took Kearns' glass. When she had left, Farrell said, "I'm glad he didn't get you, Kevin."

"You're glad? It wasn't for his lack of trying," Kearns said. "He let loose an entire magazine at me from a high-capacity semiautomatic pistol. Maybe a Beretta or a Glock; must have been fifteen or twenty rounds." Kearns grinned tightly. "Some of the citizens witnessing it must have thought they were in Beirut."

"But you got some shots of your own off, right?"

Kearns leaned across the table. "Damn straight. Hit him right in the ten-ring with that horse-pistol you gave me. It knocked him back a step, but that's all." He tapped the tabletop for emphasis. "This guy was wearing body armor. He had on a ballistic vest under his coveralls."

The waitress returned with a fresh beer. Neither man spoke until she'd left. Kearns took another big gulp of beer before continuing.

"Who is this guy, Bob? A stun gun? Body armor? A military-grade pistol? You told me this deputy DA gal had a stalker, but I didn't expect him to be another Vernon Slocum. She's a good-looking woman, so I figured it was probably a lovesick ex-flame or a co-worker with an obsession; maybe even a gang-banger she sent away who got released from prison. But this guy? He's something altogether different. He's put some righteous effort into his program. This is personal for him."

"You're right, Kevin; this guy has put a lot of work into his stalking. Which means he isn't going to give up."

"Whoever he is," Kearns said, "he's got a serious hard-on for that deputy DA"

"Or her father," Farrell said, taking a drink.

"Her father? You think this lunatic is going after the girl to get to her father?"

"Don't know," Farrell said truthfully. He tamped out his cigarette in a green-and-yellow Oakland Athletics ashtray. "The cops think I'm off target, but I've got a hunch there may be something to it. The Honorable Judge 'Iron Gene' Callen made a lot of heavy-duty enemies during his time on the bench. He sent up Hell's Angels, Black Panthers, and everything in between. And when you got sentenced by Iron Gene, you got the whole tamale. He put more people on death row than any other superior court judge in Northern California. The word 'leniency' wasn't in his vocabulary."

"Kind of a stretch, ain't it?"

"That's what the cops think," Farrell said.

"How would we even begin to know where to look for the guy if he's from the Judge's past?" Kearns offered.

"Damned good question, Kevin."

"So, what's the plan?" Kearns asked. "I assume you have one?"

"I do," Farrell said. "But I'm not sure you're going to like it."

"When have I ever liked one of your plans, Bob?"

"Good point."

"What about Deputy District Attorney Callen? Is she going to like the plan?"

"She doesn't know about it yet. Neither does the Judge."

"And when she finds out?" Kearns asked.

"She's going to hate it," Farrell said.

CHAPTER 20

Ray slept most of the afternoon. When he awoke, his head was throbbing, his testicles were still sore, and his ribs were so painful, he had difficulty sitting up. When he got to the bathroom, he found the vomitus he had so generously deposited across the floor earlier now in full aromatic bloom. The odor nearly caused him to vomit again.

Ray cleaned up the mess and took a hot shower. When he finished, he felt much better. He washed down some crackers with aspirin and Pepto-Bismol and got to work; he was anxious to get on with his plan. He was also fueled with rage over his failure this morning and wasn't about to waste it.

Ray slicked back his hair, glued on his false mustache with spirit gum, and donned his only suit. He made sure to put on his dented body armor underneath the clean white shirt. He reloaded his 9mm Glock, careful to put on surgical gloves before handling the weapon or cartridges, and added a small flashlight to his side pocket. In the opposite pocket he put his set of guitar strings, several more pairs of surgical gloves, and a thick pair of leather work gloves. When he left the house, he could hear his mother watching Roseanne upstairs, undoubtedly with a full glass of vodka in her hand.

Ray drove to the Bay Area Rapid Transit station on Fruitvale Avenue and stole a Ford. It was easy to gain entry into the parked car with the slim-Jim he had fashioned from a flat hacksaw blade. He learned how to make it from a mail-order pamphlet on improvised tools and weapons that could be fashioned from common household objects.

The car Ray chose was a dull-gray 1985 Fairmont. He'd taken it from the BART parking lot because the car's owner would likely not report it stolen for hours. He drove the car for several blocks, then stopped and removed the license plates. He also affixed a magnetic citizens-band radio antenna to the roof of the car. The vehicle now looked like what Ray hoped was a typical unmarked police sedan.

Swigging Pepto-Bismol in his stolen Ford on the drive to High Street, Ray went over his plan again in his mind. He knew his key advantages were initiative and relentlessness, and he was glad he'd forced himself out of bed and into action. He suspected the authorities would be expecting him to lay low after the botched kidnapping attempt in Alameda earlier in the day. That's what most stalkers would do, but not Ray.

Ray located the house he was seeking and parked directly in front. He learned of the home and formulated his plan, after meticulously reading the address book taken from Paige Callen's condominium. The book was proving to be a gold mine.

The house was a small-framed, single-story dwelling situated on High Street in Oakland. Like most homes on the block, the house sported burglar bars on the windows and a reinforced steel gate in place of a screen door. The East Oakland neighborhood surrounding the house was not an environment where Caucasian men in suits were commonplace, unless you counted the police detectives who regularly frequented the area, visiting crime scenes.

Ray exhaled a final stream of smoke and tossed his cigarette out through the open car window. He glanced at the digital readout on his watch; it read 9.27pm. He removed the surgical rubber gloves from his hands and placed them into his pocket. Straightening his tie and covering the door handle with his handkerchief, he got out of the car and strolled confidently across the sidewalk to the house. He made certain to grind out the discarded cigarette butt with the heel of his highly polished shoe.

Ray knew that as a white guy in a suit in this neighborhood, at this time of the evening, he would attract attention unless he was a cop. The residents here would most likely hide from or ignore a police officer. This was exactly what Ray was counting on. Ignoring the furtive glances from sidewalk loiterers, he strode purposefully up the walk and rang the doorbell.

After a moment, the door opened but the security gate remained shut. A short, plump, middle-aged Mexican woman stood in the doorway, a cautious look on her face. She was wiping her hands on her apron.

"Missus Reyes?" Ray asked. The woman nodded.

"I'm Detective Evans from the Alameda Police Department," Ray announced, lowering his voice. He briefly flashed a wallet containing a silver, seven-pointed Alameda Police star and laminated identification card. Ray had constructed the star out of a soup can lid, carefully cut, stamped, and polished using his modeler's skills. He'd learned how to make the ID card, which contained a Polaroid photo of him in his false mustache, from a mail-order book on fraudulent documents. "I understand you are employed by Judge Callen at his home in Alameda?" He stashed the wallet a moment after flashing it.

She nodded again. "Who is it?" a man's voice, thick with a Hispanic accent, called out from the interior.

"I'm very sorry to bother you at this late hour," Ray said sincerely, "but this is about the recent attacks on the Judge's daughter. It's rather important I speak with you. May I come in?"

A heavyset, dark-skinned man almost as short as Mrs Reyes came into view. He was wearing jeans and a plaid work shirt. His thick hands held a beer and a newspaper.

"It's the police," she told her husband. "He wants to talk to me about what happened to Paige."

"What do you want to know?" Mr Reyes said.

"Well, sir, I have a few questions I'd like to ask your wife. I'd rather the neighbors didn't hear what I have to say; it's confidential. Do you mind if I come in?"

"OK, come on in. But make it fast; the A's game is on. They're playing the Red Sox in Boston."

"I'm an Athletics fan myself," Ray said pleasantly. "Looks like they got the American League West already locked up."

"Let's hope it stays that way," Reyes said.

"I'll be brief." Ray smiled. "The last thing I want to do is keep you from the game." Mrs Reyes nodded at her husband and he opened the reinforced door. "Thank you," Ray said.

"Ask your questions," Mr Reyes ordered once Ray was inside and the door was closed. Ray made a flourish of taking out a notebook and pen before starting. He wasn't invited into the house any farther than the hallway inside the door.

"You're the housekeeper at the Callen home, is that correct?" Ray began.

"Yes. Both of them."

"Both of them?"

"That's right. I help out at the Judge's house three times a week and I clean his daughter's once a week. But her place burned today."

"She's worked for Judge Callen over twenty years," Mr Reyes chimed in proudly. Ray nodded studiously and made an exaggerated gesture of writing in his notebook.

"You have keys to the house?"

"Yes," she answered. "Both of them. Why do you ask?"

"Yeah," Mr Reyes asked. "Why do you want to know that?"

"Folks," Ray said, "it's just a routine precaution. We need to interview anyone who has access to the Judge's home: gardener, plumber, exterminator, anyone who has a key. You wouldn't want the Judge's house to burn down like his daughter's, would you?"

Mrs Reyes shook her head. Ray went on.

"And you know the access code to the alarm on the Judge's house?"

"Of course. I have to go in and out, and the Judge can no longer walk very well. His leg does not permit him to move around easily. To answer the door is very difficult for him."

"Of course," Ray said. "I understand. What is the access code?" He was careful to keep his gaze focused on his notebook.

"Why do you need to know?" Mrs Reyes eyed Ray suspiciously. "Why don't you get the alarm code from Judge Callen?"

"It's like this," Ray lied. "We need to change the alarm access code to be on the safe side. But to do this, we need everyone who has the old code to verify it so we know exactly who has permission to enter the Judge's house. Also, the alarm company won't change the old code without knowing how many people currently have it."

"I don't know," Mrs Reyes bit her lip. "It seems if the Judge wanted the police to have the code to his house, he would have given it himself."

"This has to be done quickly and quietly," Ray said sternly, "and as soon as possible. The Judge is already asleep. If you'd like to disturb him at this hour with a phone call and ask him if it's all right for you to give the police who are trying to protect him and his property the alarm code, be my guest."

Mrs Reyes' hesitation was obvious. Ray merely smiled, but he nervously wondered if she was going to call his bluff and refuse his request. Then her husband spoke up.

"Give the detective what he asks. He is a police officer, for heaven's sake. Do you want the Judge to be angry with you?"

She looked at her husband, shrugged, and then back at Ray. "The code is four, zero, three, one. When you go inside the front or back door, there is a box on the wall. You must push in the number within ten seconds or–"

"I know how an alarm system works," Ray said. He wrote the code in his notebook. "May I see your key to the Judge's house?"

"My key? What for?"

"Will you just give the man what he asks?" Mr Reyes said. He made no effort to contain his exasperation. He wanted the intrusion over, the policeman gone, and to return to the baseball game. Mrs Reyes turned and went into the house, muttering under her breath in Spanish. She returned a moment later, rummaging through her purse. She held up a set of keys for Ray's inspection.

"This one is for the front door and this one for the back," she said, singling out two keys for his inspection.

"Excellent," Ray exclaimed. "You've been very helpful." He noted the location of the keys on Mrs Reyes' ring. "I only have one more question."

Mr Reyes couldn't hide his relief any more than his irritation.

"We're concerned that the man who is stalking the Judge and his daughter–"

"He's after the Judge, too?" Mrs Reyes cried out, fear overtaking her features.

"We don't believe the Judge is any danger," Ray calmed her, mentally kicking himself for his slip of the tongue. "We just want to cover all the bases."

Mrs Reyes crossed herself. "You had me scared for a second, Officer."

"You said you only had one more question?" Mr Reyes tapped his newspaper against his leg.

"Yes." Ray turned to Mrs Reyes. "If the Judge's daughter were to go and hide somewhere, where would she go?"

"Why not ask her?" Mrs Reyes said. "I don't know where Paige would go."

"How about her boyfriend's place?"

"What boyfriend? Paige has no boyfriend that I know of. I can tell you, though, it would please her father greatly if she was to meet a young man and settle down. But I know of no boyfriend, and this is a thing I would know."

"She has no place she would go to be safe? No relatives or friends she could hide out with for a while?"

"You said one more question," Mr Reyes reminded Ray.

Ray was thinking of the address book in his pocket and how many entries it had written inside. It would take forever to eliminate them.

Mrs Reyes rubbed her chin. "There is one place. It's in Napa, in the wine country. She has an aunt who lives there. Paige used to spend her summers there as a child. I believe she would go to her aunt if she had to hide." She nodded to herself. "Yes, I'm positive. It's a big house among the vineyards. Very isolated. And very beautiful."

"Oh, I forgot," Ray said. "I have one more question." He looked apologetically at Mr Reyes. "I'm so sorry."

"Of course you do," Mr Reyes said through gritted teeth. "Go ahead."

"Is there anyone else in the house?"

"No," Mrs Reyes replied, puzzled at the question. "Our children are grown up and have moved away. There is only us."

Ray folded his notebook and returned it to his pocket.

"Thank you both very much," he said. "You'll never know how helpful you've been."

"May I have one of your business cards, Detective Evans?" Mrs Reyes asked. "I will see the Judge tomorrow. If he is uncomfortable with anything I have told you, I would like him to be able to call you."

"Certainly," Ray said. But when he reached into his pocket he came out with his thick leather work gloves instead of a business card. He donned them while the Reyes looked on.

"It's cold out tonight," Ray commented when he saw the quizzical expressions on their faces.

"It's actually pretty warm," Mr Reyes contradicted.

"So it is," Ray said.

He brought his knee up into Mr Reyes' groin. The older man doubled over and fell to his knees, dropping his beer and newspaper. In almost the same motion, Ray whirled and struck the horrified Mrs Reyes savagely under the nose, upward, with the heel of his hand. It was exactly the technique illustrated in FM 21-150, the World War II–era US Army field manual entitled Unarmed Defense for the American Soldier. It had been a Military Book Club Book of the Month selection. Mrs Reyes dropped to the floor, instantly unconscious. Blood streamed from her shattered nose.

While Mrs Reyes lay inert, Ray kicked her husband in the face several times, also rendering him unconscious. The effort caused Ray's still-tender genitals and bruised ribs considerable pain, but in his excitement he barely felt it. Mr Reyes lay motionless, face-down on the floor next to his wife.

Ray went right to work. He took a guitar string from his pocket and looped it over Mr Reyes' head. Once it was in place around his neck, he looped it once more. He took an end of the guitar string in each hand, placed a knee in Mr Reyes' back, and pulled with all the force he could muster.

Mr Reyes lurched convulsively, suddenly awake, and tried to grab the razor-like wire digging into his throat. Blood seeped from the seam created by the wire and his eyes bulged. He appeared to gasp but no sound came.

Ray pulled for more than a minute, amazed at the strength of the older man as he fought for his life. He bucked and thrashed like a horse in a rodeo. But with Ray's weight on his back and the wire noose around his neck, the outcome was inevitable. With an explosive burst of escaping air, the wire tore through Mr Reyes' windpipe and discharged his lungs'lungs' captive cargo. He released his final breath and lay still. An out-of-breath Ray was careful to avoid the expanding pool of blood beneath the body as he stood up.

To avoid the lake of blood, Ray walked around Mr Reyes in a wide circle to reach his wife. He dragged her by the feet until she was well clear of the growing stain. Ray extracted another guitar string from his pocket, since the first was irretrievably embedded in Mr Reyes' throat. He repeated the double-loop procedure around her neck in the same fashion he had done with her spouse. Then he repeated the tug-of-war with her neck. A minute later, she too was dead. Unlike her husband, Mrs Reyes never woke up to struggle. Her lifeblood joined her spouse's on the floor.

Ray again carefully backed away from the body to avoid soiling his shoes with blood. He peeled off the surprisingly bloodless leather gloves and replaced them with a set of surgical rubber gloves from his pocket. He turned the leather work gloves inside out and put them back into his pocket as well.

He retrieved Mrs Reyes' dropped purse and removed the key ring. Ray took only the two keys to the Callen home and returned the ring to the purse. Then he opened the front door and exited the house, making sure he locked the steel gate before pulling it shut behind him.

Ray lit a cigarette and strode casually to his faux police car. He got in, fired up the stolen Ford, and drove back to Fruitvale Avenue. He abandoned the car a block from the BART station and walked back into the parking lot where he'd left his Hyundai.

Whistling jauntily, Ray drove back over the Miller Sweeney Bridge towards home.

CHAPTER 21

Paige Callen awoke to the sound of her own stifled scream and the agony of deep, painful cramps in her calves and legs. She was bathed in a cold sweat, and the blankets covering her were twisted around her body.

She sat up in bed, wincing in discomfort, and pointed her toes to ease the aching muscles. Within a few seconds, the muscle cramps subsided. She blinked and rubbed her eyes to dispel the remnants of the nightmare that had shaken her from her slumber.

Paige could only vaguely remember the dream; fleeting scenes of sudden violence and a claustrophobic sensation. She swept her hair from her damp forehead and got out of bed.

She switched on the light in the bathroom. After blinking as the stark fluorescent glow evaporated the darkness, she stared into the mirror and grimaced at the image looking back at her.

He left eye was blacker than ever. She parted her hair to examine the bald patch and stitches. The abrasions on her brow and the tip of her nose had scabbed, and she took solace knowing they were superficial enough to heal within a day or two. She splashed water on her face, slipped into a thick robe, and went downstairs for something to abate the dryness in her mouth.

As Paige descended the staircase, she noticed a light emanating from the partially opened door of her father's study. She peered in to find her father, also clad in a bathrobe, seated at his desk. He was wearing his reading glasses and seemed to be looking intently at something concealed from her view. She opened the door and stepped inside.

At the sound of Paige's entry, the Judge looked up, startled, and hastily secreted something into the open top drawer of his desk. Paige glanced at the grandfather clock across the room. Its ornate, polished brass hands read 3.11am.

"Dad, do you know what time it is?"

"I do. What are you doing up?"

"I just asked you the same question," she said. The Judge removed his glasses and leaned back in his chair.

"I'm an old man. I fall asleep at odd hours of the day and find myself wide awake at equally odd hours of the night. What's your excuse?"

"I couldn't sleep. Thought I'd get a glass of juice from the kitchen. You want anything?"

"I'll have whatever you're having."

Paige disappeared. Within a couple of minutes, she returned to the study with two glasses of orange juice. She handed one to her father and sat down on the plush couch opposite his desk.

"Bad dreams?" he asked after taking a sip.

"No," she said. "What makes you think that?"

"You're a lousy liar, Paige," the Judge smiled. "Always have been. That could be fatal for an attorney."

Before Paige could retort, a blinding bright white light filled the room from outside. After a moment, the light faded and was gone. Paige started to get up to check the window.

"Just a patrol unit spotlighting the house," the Judge remarked. "Letting us know it's out there."

"Your doing?" she asked, settling back into her seat.

"Sergeant Wendt's. Standard procedure for extra attention by the sector patrol officer assigned to this beat."

Neither spoke for several long minutes. Paige broke the silence.

"Dad," she began tentatively, "I guess I owe you an apology for the way I bit your head off today. It wasn't appropriate to do in front of strangers."

"Those strangers are doing everything within their power to protect you."

"Sergeant Wendt, perhaps," she said. "But that Farrell character? He's not a cop; he's a crook. I don't trust him as far as I could throw him."

"You don't know him."

"The hell I don't," she said. "I reviewed the prosecution packet on him and his just-as-crooked partner. When they walked away free and clear after all that they did, I had to stand there and watch it happen. Don't tell me that I don't know him."

"Do you know why he and his partner weren't prosecuted?"

"Some sort of shady deal Farrell brokered with the Feds, I assume."

"You assume because you don't know," the Judge said. "For your information, I do."

"Of course you do. You always know the dirty little secrets." Paige looked skeptically at her father. "It's how you control people. How you always get them to do what you want them to do."

"This is about your mother, isn't it?"

Paige shrugged. "I don't want to fight with you," she said, without refuting his statement. She instinctively knew that she could no more defend herself against her father's clever sparring today than she could as a child. She took a slow breath and resigned herself not to get sucked into his game.

"It's me you have a problem with, isn't it?"

Paige folded her arms across her chest. "It's what you do. And who you do it with. People like that Farrell creep."

"Bob Farrell had the foresight to plan for a contingency the police did not foresee," Judge Callen said. "I don't want to think about what would have happened to you if I hadn't retained him and he hadn't deployed his associate to protect you."

"That's what I mean," Paige said. "Just because you think you know what's best for me doesn't give you the right to make decisions about my life. And just because this Farrell jerk made a sound call, once, doesn't change who he is or what he's done. He's a wrong man, Dad. End of discussion."

"We'll have to agree to disagree on that," Callen said.

"We will."

The Judge stared at his knuckles. Paige drank her orange juice.

"What shall we talk about?" he finally said.

"Whatever you like," she said.

"Fair enough. How about discussing you going away for a while?"

"You never let up." She shook her head. "Forget it; I'm not running away from this."

"Who says you'd be running away? Take a vacation. Go visit your aunt in the wine country. You haven't seen her in years, and you know she'd love to have you. You always loved the ranch so much as a child. Why not go?"

"You know why not: I'm staying until this thing gets resolved."

"Its resolution could be your death," he said.

"Getting a bit melodramatic, aren't we?" she taunted. As soon as she spoke, she regretted it.

"Are we?" Callen countered. "I'd call being stalked, assaulted, having your house burned, and nearly getting abducted fairly dramatic, wouldn't you?"

"We aren't in court; I'm not going to play word games with you. Lay off."

The Judge opened his hands. "How can I 'lay off'? You're my daughter. I'm your father. I don't want to see you hurt. And I'm not convinced you're aware of the seriousness of the situation you're in."

Paige rolled her eyes. "Of course I'm aware of how serious the situation is." She pointed to her face for emphasis. "But I'm a big girl now. And I don't want you interfering in my life. You can't continue to make decisions about me without my say-so. It's got to stop."

"You're willing to risk harm and go unprotected because you don't like the company I keep? Because you think I'm breaking the rules?" The Judge pointed a finger at his daughter. "You think the man in the ski mask isn't breaking the rules? Hell, Paige, he's making them up as he goes along. You can't take those kinds of chances with your life."

Paige stood up. "I'm not Mom," she said softly. "You're not going to run my life. We both know how that ended up, don't we?"

Her voice, though muted, vibrated with suppressed emotion. With each word she spoke, the Judge seemed to diminish in stature.

"I was only trying—"

"Then stop," she commanded, cutting him off. "Just stop. I'm going to handle this in a legal and appropriate manner. Without bending the rules. That's final."

The Judge nodded. His lower lip was trembling ever so slightly, and the makings of a tear began to form in the corner of one eye.

Paige sighed. "Dad, I didn't mean to–"

"It's all right," he said, his turn to cut her off. "Why don't you go to bed? It's been a long day."

She began to reply, then thought better of it. She walked over to where her father sat dejectedly at his desk and put her arms around his shoulders. She briefly laid her cheek against his forehead. Two swollen drops of water ebbed down his weathered face. He irritably brushed them aside.

"Oh, Dad," she said.

"Forgive me," he said. "Blubbering like a schoolgirl. Must be another sign of old age."

"I've got to get some sleep," she said. "I've got a busy day tomorrow."

"You're not thinking of going in to work?"

"Don't start up again," she said. "Good night." She walked out of the study.

Once Paige had gone, the Judge wiped his eyes on the sleeve of his robe and replaced his glasses. He returned his attention to the contents of the desk drawer he'd hastily closed when Paige had entered.

From the drawer he removed an elaborately engraved nickel-plated revolver. It was a Smith & Wesson Model 10, with the old-style, four-inch tapered barrel. The handgun had been a gift from one-time Alameda County Sheriff Tom Madigan. Judge Callen carefully opened the cylinder and inserted six .38 Special cartridges. He tucked the revolver into his waistband and wrapped his robe around it.

The Judge spent the remaining hours until dawn examining the second object he'd removed from the top drawer of his desk. It was a framed black-and-white photograph. The picture depicted a little blond-haired girl and a tall, distinguished-looking man in judge's robes. They were both smiling and holding hands.

CHAPTER 22

It was well after noon by the time Paige reached her office. She'd awakened feeling exhausted and disjointed, and found her usually chipper father in the kitchen, morose and un-talkative. Mrs Reyes had not arrived yet, which was unlike her, and the Judge was grumpy as a result. He was a man of routines. He barely noticed her kiss to his forehead as she grabbed a cup of coffee and headed out the door. She was forced to again borrow her father's Mercedes-Benz sedan, since her Saab had been totaled in the previous day's collision.

She spent the remainder of the hectic morning meeting with insurance appraisers and contractors, obtaining estimates and commissioning repairs to her damaged condominium. Once she'd accomplished these tasks and ensured that work had begun, she loaded the car with enough of her smoke-scented clothing to tide her over until the repairs were completed and she could return. She would deal with the insurance claim on her wrecked car tomorrow.

Paige parked the Mercedes in her designated spot at the courthouse and took a moment to scribble a note explaining that the car belonged to Judge Callen, so it wouldn't be towed away by a hyper-conscientious parking technician.

Standing on the steps of the courthouse as she approached was Deputy District Attorney C. Timothy Potter. He was smoking a Benson & Hedges menthol and ogling the female passersby as they strolled past on their way to the Park Street business district and its many shops, restaurants, and cafes. At his feet was a collection of discarded fast-food wrappers that contained the remnants of substances that left corresponding stains on the lapels of his expensive suit. On seeing Paige approach, Potter ground out his cigarette and patted down his thinning hair. Grinning to himself, he ducked inside the courthouse lobby and hid around the corner behind the door. He was certain she hadn't seen him. The lobby was almost devoid of people, since the lunch hour was in full swing.

As Paige entered, elbowing the courthouse door open, Potter leaped out from behind her and yelled. "Boo!" A gleeful smirk spread across his features.

In a gasping twitch, Paige whirled to face him, her briefcase falling to the floor. Her arms involuntarily lifted to cover her head and face. Unable even to scream, her face had gone ashen white and tremors racked her entire body.

"Paige, it's OK," Potter stammered, realizing how terrified she was. A sick look replaced his laughing expression. "Take it easy; it was only a joke."

"You fucking bastard," she cursed, waiting for the trembling to subside. She was shaking so hard, her shoulders hurt.

"Don't be so uptight," he said. "Jeez, it was just a little gag. Lighten up." He began to straighten his tie.

Paige reached out a fist and slammed it into his face. Potter's head went back and his eyes momentarily crossed. He reached up with both hands and covered his bleeding nose.

"You hit me," he exclaimed in astonishment. "You actually hit me." He lowered his hands to examine the blood on them.

Paige was actually somewhat astonished herself. She

stared at her own fist, not convinced she had actually done the hitting. Her skinned knuckles wouldn't lie.

"You fucking bitch," she heard Potter say. "I'm going to have you arrested."

At Potter's indignant threat, the volcano of tension, fear, and exhaustion that had been building to a fever pitch within Paige during the past two days erupted. She looked slowly at her bloodied fist, then at Potter's pudgy face, and back to her fist. Her tremors vanished and she felt strangely calm. Potter's voice seemed like it was being projected to her ears through a mile-long tunnel.

"You're finished; I'm going to sue your ass."

Paige hit him again. This time, instead of an instinctive reflex punch, she coiled her arm back and put everything she had into it. She aimed for and struck Potter's already-bleeding nose dead-center. Potter fell straight down to the ground on his butt. The trickle of blood that had been ebbing from his nostrils became a river.

Potter shook his head. A small group of onlookers began to gather.

"I don't fucking believe it." he said, shaking his head. "The fucking bitch hit me again."

"Who are you calling a bitch?" he heard her say. When he looked up, she kicked him in the stomach. He rolled over on his side and began to retch.

Paige sensed she was creating a spectacle but didn't care. She knew she should be appalled but was not. As she stood in the lobby of the hall of justice with a black eye, a bruised face, and skinned knuckles, beating the crap out of a fat county lawyer, she realized she felt better at that moment than at any time in the last two days. But as fast as the euphoria of release came, it went. With her rage gone, Paige found her chest heaving, her eyes watering, and was almost unable to stand on legs of rubber.

The giant bulk of Charlie White appeared. He pushed through the growing crowd and took Paige gently around the shoulders. He began to lead her to her office.

"Oh, Charlie," Paige began to sob, a flood of emotion suddenly pouring forth. "He scared me. He scared me so bad. I don't know what came over me." Tears streamed from her eyes.

"It's all right, honey," Charlie cooed. "Let's get you into your office."

At the office door, Charlie and Paige were met by Carmen, the secretary she shared with Potter. Carmen's eyes went wide.

"What—"

"Never mind," Charlie cut her off. "Take Paige into her office, get her some water, and don't let nobody in. Nobody; you got it? And take the phone off the hook."

Carmen had been employed by the DA's office long enough to know better than to argue with Charlie. Once Charlie released the shaken Paige to Carmen's care, he returned to the lobby.

Potter had risen to his hands and knees and was finishing what appeared to be a lengthy puking session. He lolled his head from side to side, repeating the words "fucking bitch", and occasionally punctuated his declarations with spit. Most of the onlookers had left; the odor and image of Potter's ejected fast-food meal was more than enough incentive to drive them away. Charlie walked around the widening pool of gastric fluids and retrieved Paige's dropped briefcase.

"I see we had chili dogs for lunch," the bailiff chuckled.

"Go to hell," Potter retorted.

"I warned you to leave her alone," Charlie said, "but you were too stupid to listen. Well, now you learned."

"Fuck you, White," Potter groaned, rising unsteadily to his feet. "I'm pressing charges. You can tell her that."

"What the hell happened?"

White and Potter looked up to see Sergeant Wendt enter through the main doors. "Christ, Charlie," Wendt asked. "What did you do?"

"I didn't do it," White said, "but I wish I did." He gave Potter a contemptuous stare. "If I'd done it, the sorry bastard would be in the hospital instead of choking up his chowder."

"Deputy District Attorney Paige Callen assaulted me," Potter announced. "I want her arrested for battery. It was a totally unprovoked attack."

"You're kidding? Paige Callen did that?" He pointed to Potter's bashed and bloodied nose.

"Absolutely," Potter insisted. "I just told you I want her arrested. Under California law, as a sworn police officer, you cannot refuse to accept my citizen's arrest. I want her arrested. Now."

"I know how to do my job," Wendt said. "I don't need the likes of a barf-covered Perry Mason to tell me how. Until I talk to Ms Callen, nobody gets arrested."

"She's in her office," White spoke up.

"C'mon, Charlie," Wendt said. "Let's go see her." They headed for the deputy district attorney's office.

"Wait a minute," Potter said. "Don't you want to get my side of the story first? I'm the victim."

"I already know your side of the story," Wendt answered him over his shoulder. "I'm a detective, remember? You got the shit beat out of you by a pretty young blonde. Case closed." White guffawed.

Once in the DA's office, the police sergeant and the bailiff found a more-composed Paige Callen at the water dispenser, gulping down aspirin. She gave them a weak smile when she saw them.

"Hi, Randy," she greeted. "How's your day going? Mine's going swell."

"Hi back," he said. "Funny thing happened on the way to your office. I was coming to check on your well-being and update you on the progress of the investigation. When I arrived, I found a short fat dude who looks a lot like your co-worker on all fours in the lobby, hurling his guts out. Looks like he went one very short round with Mike Tyson. You wouldn't know anything about that, would you?"

"Cut the baloney," Paige said. "He jumped out at me from behind; some kind of joke, I guess. Startled the hell out of me. I don't know what came over me. As soon as I saw him laughing, I saw red. I'm sorry."

"Don't apologize to me," Wendt said. "I'm not the one who got thumped."

"Actually," she said, "I'm not sorry at all. It felt good."

"It may not feel good for long," Wendt told her. "Deputy District Attorney Potter wants me to arrest you." Charlie White nodded in affirmation.

"You're kidding."

"I wish I was. Potter's insisting. And he knows I can't refuse his citizen's arrest."

Paige plopped heavily into her chair. White set her briefcase gently on her desk. "That's just great," she said. "This has been the worst week of my life." She rubbed her brow. "And it's only Wednesday."

Potter entered the office, wiping his mouth with a handkerchief and glaring at Paige.

"Happy with yourself, Miss Smartass?" he asked.

Charlie White started toward him. Wendt quickly got between the bailiff and attorney.

"Watch your mouth, shithead," White growled. "One more word like that out of you and there ain't gonna be enough cops on this planet to save your sorry ass."

"You heard that, Sergeant; he threatened me."

"Shut up," Wendt said to Potter, struggling to keep the

much-larger bailiff at bay.

"You can't tell me to shut up in my own office. I have a right to—"

"Shut your mouth!" Wendt said again. "Another word out of you and I'm going to let Charlie loose."

Potter remained silent, fuming. Wendt stepped back from Charlie, satisfied for the moment that no more violence was imminent. He looked from one deputy DA to the other.

"I don't know what happened here today, but I think we should all forget it."

"I'm not forgetting anything," Potter said. "I want her arrested."

"It sounds to me like you brought the incident upon yourself," Wendt said. "Ms Callen said you jumped out at her with the specific intent to scare her."

"Maybe so," Potter conceded. "But I didn't assault her. I didn't even touch her."

"No, you merely jumped out to put a fright into a woman who has been the victim of potentially lethal assaults twice within the past two days." He stared at Potter in disdain. "Apparently, you thought tormenting her would be good for a laugh. It's not only immature, it's cruel. But it backfired, and the laugh was on you. And now you want me to arrest Ms Callen for reflexively responding to the panic that you created." Wendt shook his head. "I don't think that's grounds for a battery arrest."

"I don't give damn what you think," Potter said. "I want her arrested. By law, you can't refuse. If you do, Sergeant, you are guilty of a crime. And believe me, I will prosecute you for it. Arrest her."

Wendt was about to reply to Potter when Paige silenced him with a wave of her hand. "He's right, Randy," she said. "You have to arrest me if he insists. Let's get it over with so I can go home. I don't feel so well."

"I think there may be grounds for an arrest of Mr Potter here for attempted battery on you, Paige. If you thought you were about to be assaulted–"

"Save your breath," she interrupted him. She stood up from behind her desk. "I'm not going to sink to his level. Let him file his charges if he wants. Let him sue if he wants. Maybe it'll make him feel like a man."

"Arrest her," Potter insisted.

Wendt glowered at Potter, who smiled smugly in return. "Whatever you say, Counselor," he said. "But for the record, you're a piece of shit."

"I'll be reporting your comments to your chief of police."

"You do that," Wendt said. He directed his next comments to Paige. "Come on, Ms Callen. I'll drive you to the station and book you myself. Since battery is only a misdemeanor, I'll have you out within the hour on a citation."

"Wait a minute," Potter said. He removed his stained jacket. "I'm not going to be made out to be the bad guy in this."

"The shoe fits," Wendt said.

"I'm the victim here. And even though I've been brutalized by Paige–"

"Ms Callen," she corrected him,"

"I'm not entirely without mercy," Potter said.

"What's your point?" Wendt asked.

"I'm just saying," Potter went on, taking a seat behind his own desk, "maybe this whole unfortunate arrest could be avoided?"

"Quit posturing," Wendt said. "If you've got something to say, say it. Otherwise, I've got to get Ms Callen to the station and get her booked per your citizen's arrest."

"I am not without consideration for Ms Callen's plight," he said.

"Is that why you tried to scare the daylights out of her?" Charlie White asked.

"I'll ignore that remark," Potter said loftily. "All I'm saying is that perhaps I could be persuaded to drop the charges if an appropriate apology were presented."

"What the hell does that mean?" Wendt asked.

"It means," Potter answered, "that an apology from Ms Callen would go a long way to persuading me to drop the charges."

"You're saying that if I apologize to you, you'll drop the charges?" Paige asked.

"I didn't say that."

Wendt's patience was evaporating. "Quit playing your grammar-school games and spit it out, you insufferable little prick. What do you want?"

"I believe," Potter said slowly, turning his gaze from the sergeant to Paige, "that an apology might be an appropriate start of compensation for the injuries I suffered today."

"What kind of compensation do you want?" Paige asked, no effort to disguise the disgust she felt.

"As you can plainly see, my medical expenses will be significant. And this suit you ruined cost over a thousand dollars. Your father is loaded; you can afford it."

"I'm not giving you a dime."

"Then the charges stand." He turned to Wendt. "Sergeant, do your duty."

"When I first met you," Wendt said to Potter, "I gave you the benefit of the doubt. I didn't want to judge you on your appearance. I figured you couldn't be as slimy as you looked. I was wrong."

"I don't give a damn what you think of me, Sergeant."

"You're filth," Bailiff Charlie White said. His fists were clenched. "Fucking filth."

"That goes double for you, Bailiff," Potter retorted.

Paige grabbed her purse. "Let's get going, Randy," she said. "I want to be home as soon as possible after I get booked."

"You'd rather get arrested and go to jail, which will probably result in your termination with the district attorney's office, than swallow your pride, apologize, and pay me an appropriate compensation for my pain and suffering?" Potter asked, gloating.

"No," Paige corrected him. "That's not it. If I was sorry, I'd apologize. But I'm not sorry. I enjoyed seeing you wallowing on the floor in a puddle of your own puke. It was an image I'll always treasure. I should have taken a picture."

Potter's face drooped; anger flashed over his features.

"And as far as paying you is concerned, I won't give you a penny. I'd rather write a check to the criminal who's stalking me. You're an insect, Chaz," she said. "You can go to straight to hell."

"You'll be sorry," he said.

"You already are. I'll see you in court."

CHAPTER 23

The sounds of the Mamas and the Papas drifted across the room to where Ray Cowell sat working at his drafting table. He was carefully painting the undercarriage of a partially assembled Corsair fighter/bomber. Radio station KOIT, San Francisco's "Lite Rock, Less Talk" station, was his go-to music for modeling work because it played fewer commercials and more of the softer tunes he preferred when modeling.

It was early afternoon, but Ray was still wearing his pajamas. He'd phoned his boss at the shipyard and told him not only was he not coming in today, he would be taking the next two weeks off on vacation. His supervisor was livid but could do nothing. Ray had been working for Maersk for well over ten years, had never used a sick day, and had accrued many weeks of unused vacation leave. He was a diligent, valued, and loyal employee, and knew his use of personal time could not be refused.

Ray felt calm. He always felt at peace when in his room and assembling his models, but felt especially tranquil today. The pain in his testicles and ribs had improved significantly overnight, and he felt relaxed and confident, almost elated.

Whenever he worked on his model aircraft, his mind drifted back to when he was a child. To the time when his mom was pretty and his dad would tousle his hair and give him pretend haymakers to the chin. In those days, during good weather, he would be outside playing catch with his dad or teaching Skipper tricks. But during the rainy season, he and his dad would build airplane models in the basement.

In those days, the basement was not his room. The basement was a damp, musty storage area, and Ray's mom would make them go down there to build models because of the glue and paint fumes. Ray and his dad cleaned up the basement and put in a table. When the family bought new furniture upstairs, the basement inherited the old sofa and some worn chairs. Ray's dad installed lighting and better ventilation, and soon the basement was like a special clubhouse where only he and his dad were members. It got to where Ray enjoyed the rainy days as much as the sunny ones. And although Ray's mom always said she hated "the dungeon", she would come down when Ray and his dad were building models and bring sandwiches or cookies. His father even painted a sign on the outside of the basement door, in dripping-blood letters like The Munsters, which read "The Dungeon".

Sometimes they would build model cars or boats, but Ray's favorites were the military aircraft. While building these, Ray's father would tell him spellbinding stories of his days fighting the hated communists in Korea. Ray would listen in rapt attention as his father told hair-raising tales of midnight patrols, desperate ambushes, and bloody bayonet charges.

Those days were precious and short. During the winter rainy season, Ray would excitedly count the days until the weekend. He and his father were regulars at the hobby shop on Park Street, and Ray couldn't wait until Saturday arrived to begin building the newest military aircraft from the pages of the Revell catalogue.

Ray's father was skillful with his hands and taught Ray to pay strict attention to detail when constructing his models. He showed Ray how to use a brush and how to blacken the plastic around the engines with a cigarette lighter and Styrofoam. He reminded his son that in wartime, attention to detail was extremely important and could be the difference between life and death.

He told Ray about the time a fellow soldier forgot to take the loose coins out of his pocket while on a patrol, which resulted in his death in a withering hail of gunfire when the enemy heard the jangling sound.

"Attention to detail," his father would always tell him. "It's the difference between how a boy does a job and how a man does a job." Ray would nod in agreement.

"Do you know how you get attention to detail, Ray?" he would ask.

"Planning," Ray would answer on cue. "By planning."

"Right," his dad would affirm as Ray proudly beamed. "Planning is the key. What a good soldier you would have been. Those commies wouldn't have fooled you, Ray."

Ray sighed, set down the uncompleted Corsair, and lit a cigarette. Sometimes his longing for those times was so powerful it hurt. Sometimes he fantasized about building a time machine and going back to the Alameda of his youth. Back to when his pretty mother tucked him into his bed upstairs in the house and kissed him goodnight. When the television was black-and-white, and shows like The Outer Limits and The Addams Family filled his evenings.

He exhaled smoke and grunted, casting his momentary lapse into nostalgia aside. He could never go back and he knew it. His idyllic childhood had been ripped from him, not gradually through the natural progression of growing up, but in the swift passing of one terrible summer.

All that Ray had endured since that fateful summer was a painful blur. The remainder of his youth was spent watching his life disintegrate, piece by piece. At school he was a bullied loner and outcast, with only his books for friends. At home he stood mute witness to his mother's transformation from the angel of his childhood to a pathetic drunk, dependent on the debasing consolation of strangers and the solace of the bottle. Soon, Ray began to spend all his time in the basement, even the nights when his mother wasn't upstairs entertaining an endless string of faceless men. Her intoxicated laughter and the animal sounds emanating from his mother's bedroom permeated the basement refuge where Ray spent sleepless nights with only his tears for comfort.

As always, the tranquility Ray experienced building models in the solitude of his basement room wasn't to last. His mind inevitably began to give way to reminiscence of the losses he had suffered. A lifetime of losses.

His failed military career, the only glimmer of hope in an otherwise bleak future. A chance to pursue his love of both electronics and aviation. Gone.

His brief engagement. To Ray, this loss mattered the least, but it was nonetheless a loss. He'd met Maritay, a Filipina co-worker, several years after beginning work as a shipping clerk. Like him, she was a lonely, quiet recluse. She was neither attractive nor pleasant, and looking back, Ray wondered if he'd initiated the relationship merely to discover if he was capable of one. After several weeks of awkward dating and clumsy sexual encounters, he asked her to move in with him, upstairs in his mother's house.

It was a mistake. As the weeks went by, Maritay spent increasing time hanging out with his mother upstairs while he continued to retreat to the comfort of his beloved dungeon each evening. The basement was the only unchanged remnant of Ray's childhood, and he was reluctant to abandon it. It was his fortress of solitude, like in the Superman comics he read as a youth.

Arguments ensued. Frustrated at what she perceived as Ray's neglect, Maritay would call him a "mama's boy" and try to follow him when he retreated to the basement. Ray would ignore her.

One day, a month after Maritay had moved into the house, Ray came home from work to find the lock on the dungeon forced open. He dashed inside to find Maritay and his mother, drunk as usual, digging through his closet. His military periodicals and pornographic magazines were scattered on the floor, his drafting table was upset, and an under-construction scale model of Doolittle's B-25 had toppled to the ground.

"So, this is what you do down here," Maritay sneered in her thick accent. "Play with toys and jerk off?" Maritay's fleshy face and the slackened face of his mother leered at him in contempt and triumph.

"You had no right to come down here," he said, his own face contorting with barely suppressed rage. "This is not your place."

"What are you afraid of?" Maritay taunted, holding up a copy of Hustler. "That we'll find something we're not supposed to?"

Maritay received a fist in the mouth for an answer. Before she could fall, Ray hit her in the stomach. Maritay collapsed to the floor, the wind knocked out of her. His mother shrieked and dropped the glass of vodka she was holding loosely in one hand. She started for the stairs that led up to the kitchen. She didn't make it.

Ray leaped over the scattered pile of magazines and grabbed the back of his mother's hair. Scooping up the nearest magazine, a copy of The American Rifleman, he slapped his mother in the back of the head.

"No, Raymond," she howled.

Ray released his hold on his mother and used both hands to roll the publication into a baton. Then he smacked her across the head again, this time with the rolled-up magazine. His mother fell to her knees and put her arms over her head.

"You fucking bitch," he hissed, as he began to slap his mother repeatedly in the face and head with the makeshift club. "I... expected... this... from... Maritay." Ray punctuated every word with a strike. "But... you... know... better... than... to... come... down... here."

"No, Raymond," she pleaded. "It was Maritay! She made me! It was her idea!"

He continued to whack his mother until she gave up trying to defend herself against the blows and fell back blubbering to the floor. Ray struck her one more time across the face.

"Get up, you drunk piece of shit, and get the fuck out. If you ever come down here again, I'll kill you. I swear it. Get out."

Ray's mother crawled up the kitchen stairs on her hands and knees, sobbing and wailing. When she had gone, he turned to Maritay, who was gasping for breath on the basement floor. He dropped the rolled-up magazine and searched the drafting table until he found what he was looking for; his X-acto knife.

Ray pounced on Maritay. He clamped a hand over her mouth. Maritay's eyes widened when she saw the scalpel-like tool in Ray's grasp.

With Maritay's arms pinned to her sides beneath him and his weight preventing her escape, Ray pressed the triangular blade of the X-acto knife against one of her eyelids. She instantly froze.

"Listen to me carefully, you whore," he said softly. "Get your things and get the fuck out. If I ever see you again, I'll kill you. No one will ever find your body, no one. Do you understand, slut?"

She nodded faintly, conscious of the razor poised over her eye. Ray stood up. Maritay scrambled to her feet and ran up the stairs.

Ray spent the rest of the evening putting his room back in order. He half expected the police to arrive and arrest him, but they never did. He slept well that night. When he awoke, he found Maritay gone.

When he arrived at work the next morning, he learned that Maritay had phoned in her resignation. She left no reason for quitting and no forwarding address. Ray never heard from her again.

On the way home from the shipyard that night, Ray stopped at Big B Lumber in Oakland and purchased lumber, wood screws, and two stout locks. He reinforced the doorjambs of the kitchen and outside basement doors, and installed the two heavy-duty locks.

Ray's mother avoided speaking to him for a couple of weeks after Maritay's departure but eventually returned to her nagging self. Neither he nor his mother ever mentioned Maritay again, and in a short time it was as if she had never existed.

But to Ray it was another loss, an easier one to adjust to than his other losses, but a loss nonetheless. He became even more reclusive after Maritay and never again attempted to initiate a relationship with a woman not inhabiting the pages of his pornographic magazines.

Over time, Ray began to gradually realize that the common denominator in his troubled life had always been women. It was a girl who lured his father to his demise, and a woman who shattered his dream of a career in military aviation. Even his mother had betrayed him. Perhaps all women were whores, like his father said that night years ago in the garage.

Maybe they were all sluts.

The Judge didn't see it that way. He didn't know what it was like to lose things.

To a whore. A slut.

Ray would teach him.

Ray had waited a long time to show the Judge what it was like to lose things.

He ground out his cigarette and ended his reverie. It was getting late and he had much to do in preparation for tomorrow. He got up from the drafting table and went to the closet.

Ray retrieved his army duffel bag and started to remove the contents, spreading them out on the floor for inspection.

"Planning," Ray whispered to himself. "Planning is the key."

CHAPTER 24

Bob Farrell entered his apartment, a half-smoked cigarette dangling from his lips. He was carrying a bundle under his arm. Kevin Kearns sat on Farrell's living room sofa, eyeing the older man disdainfully.

"Hi, Kevin," Farrell greeted him, setting down his parcel on the kitchen table. "Brought you something," he said, unwrapping the package. Inside were a Remington Rand government model 1911A1 .45 caliber pistol, a scabbard, a couple of spare magazines, and a box of fifty .45 caliber cartridges. "Just like the one you used in the army, I'll bet. Certainly as old; borrowed it from a friend."

"You have friends?" Kearns asked.

"Hilarious," Farrell said. He kept his coat on. San Francisco, even in early summer, was cold in the morning. "When I left this morning, you were sawing logs. How was the couch?"

"Better than a park bench," Kevin said.

"Glad you slept well. We have a busy day ahead of us." Farrell glanced at his watch. "We have to be in Alameda to meet with Judge Callen at noon. We'd better get going." He tamped out his cigarette in an ashtray.

Kearns made no effort to get up. He continued to look steadily at Farrell.

"What's eating you?" Farrell asked, finally noticing Kearns' sour face.

"Why didn't you tell me Jennifer was in town?"

Farrell sighed and his shoulders slumped. "How'd you find out?"

"She called when you were out. Left a message on your machine."

Farrell looked at his feet and patted down his combover. "I'm sorry I didn't tell you, Kevin. I didn't want to hurt your feelings."

"How long has she been here?"

"She flew in from Omaha a couple of days ago," Farrell admitted.

"And you didn't want me to know? Thanks, Bob; thanks a lot." He stood up.

"It's not what you think–"

"What am I supposed to think?" Kearns cut him off. "That I'm not good enough to see your daughter? Apparently, that's what you think."

"You're wrong."

"Am I? I know exactly what you think I'm good for. I'm good enough to almost get killed covering your ass halfway across the country, searching for Vernon Slocum. And I'm good enough to step in the line of fire guarding that sanctimonious bitch of a DA so you can play your PI games and bilk her father. But meeting up with your daughter, who I haven't seen in almost a year? That, evidently, I'm not good enough for." Kearns' face reddened.

"Take it easy, will you?" Farrell said. "You're mistaken."

"Sure, Bob. I'll take it, all right," he said, his voice rising. "That's what I'm good for, taking it. Taking your lies and getting used."

Kearns headed for the door. Farrell stepped in front of him, showing his palms. "Kevin, you don't even have a place to go."

"Thanks to you," Kearns reminded him. "Another one of the many benefits of being Bob Farrell's friend: homelessness."

Kearns started forward again; Farrell put his hands on the younger man's chest.

"Wait a minute," Farrell implored.

"What for? More of your bullshit?"

"Will you calm your redneck butt down and hear me out? Please?"

Kearns didn't answer him but didn't move. He folded his arms across his chest.

"The reason I didn't tell you Jennifer was in town is because she asked me not to," Farrell said solemnly.

"I don't believe you," Kearns said. "Jennifer wouldn't do that."

"It's the truth."

"Why?" Kearns challenged. "Why would Jennifer tell you to do that?"

Farrell rubbed his eyes with both hands. "Because she didn't come alone."

"Huh?"

"You heard me; Jen didn't come alone. She brought her fiancé."

"Fiancé?" Kearns deflated. His arms dropped.

"That's right; Jennifer is engaged."

"When?"

"I only found out myself about a week ago. I wasn't supposed to know, but my ex-wife called to gloat because Jen told her first; Ann never could keep a secret. I guess she already met with Jen and her boyfriend and gave her approval. Jen flew out here from Omaha, ostensibly to announce her engagement to me."

"Where is she?"

"She and her beau are staying at the Westin in Millbrae, near the airport."

"Together? In the same hotel room?"

"I'm afraid so, Kevin," Farrell said. "That's what engaged couples do in the twentieth century. It's called premarital sex. You should try it sometime. Would do you good."

Kearns ignored Farrell's sarcasm. He felt like he'd been punched in the stomach. He ran a hand through his hair. "So Jennifer's engaged," he whistled. "Who's the lucky guy?"

"I only met him once, when I picked them up at the airport a few days ago. He's one of Jen's fellow students at Creighton Law School. Looks like one of the Kennedys. Probably just as crooked."

"A lawyer." Kearns shook his head. "She's going to marry a fucking lawyer. That's perfect."

Farrell put his arm on Kearns' shoulder. "I should have told you. I'm sorry."

"Forget it," Kearns said. "I was an idiot to think I stood a chance."

"Consider yourself lucky," Farrell soothed. "She's my daughter, remember? If you two had gotten together, you would have eventually killed each other."

"That's a load of crap and you know it. Your daughter was there for us, both of us. When it mattered, too. Jennifer stuck her neck out to get me out of jail in Omaha, covered my escape from the Feds at the hospital, and the first face I saw when I woke up in intensive care in California was hers." He looked at Farrell. "Jen's all right, Bob; she's solid. I just hope her fiancé knows it."

"I guess he'll find out," Farrell said.

Kearns managed a strained smile. "I'm sorry for what I said a minute ago. That stuff about you using me and being a liar. It was out of line."

"Don't mention it," Farrell said loftily. "Most of it's true." He grinned at Kearns.

Kearns couldn't help but grin back. "Fuck you," he said.

"You should have seen your face when I told you," Farrell chuckled. "I thought you were going to piss your pants." He busted out laughing. "Last time I saw puppy eyes like that was at the animal shelter. I thought for a second I might have to give you a hug."

"Then I surely would have killed you."

"I'd kill myself," Farrell said.

"I was pretty pathetic, wasn't I?" Kearns confessed.

"You said it, not me. Come on, let's get on the road. We've got work to do."

"What makes you so sure I'm still on board with this bodyguard detail?"

"Hell, Kevin," Farrell said, grabbing the .45 and shoving Kearns out the door, "what else have you got to do?"

"You have a point," Kearns conceded.

"Besides," Farrell went on, "this stalker thing has the potential to put a lot of money in your pocket. Mine, too. And if we play our cards right, you'll get an appointment to the sheriff's department. That's plenty of incentive from where I sit. All we have to do keep the Judge's daughter safe and bag the asshole trying to hurt her."

"And not get killed in the process," Kearns pointed out.

"There's that," Farrell admitted.

CHAPTER 25

"I was asking myself how this day could get any worse," Paige said to Sergeant Wendt. He parked his unmarked police sedan behind the burgundy-colored Oldsmobile resting in front of her father's house. She pointed her chin at Farrell's car. "I have my answer; Farrell's here."

"Farrell works for your father," Wendt reminded her. "He has a right to consult with his boss."

"I need to get a hotel," she said, shaking her head.

"Not a good idea," Wendt told her. "You need to stay where you can be seen."

"You mean by someone other than my stalker?" she said.

"Not funny," Wendt said. He opened the car door for her and they walked into the house. Paige let them in with her key.

"I wonder where Mrs Reyes is?" Paige remarked as she and Wendt entered. "I haven't seen her for a couple of days."

"Maybe she's taken ill?" Wendt suggested. "Or on vacation?"

"I'll have to ask Dad," Paige said, leading them into the study. When they walked in, two of the three men in the room stood up; her father remained seated.

"Good afternoon, Ms Callen," Farrell said. He was holding a drink and a lit cigarette.

"Mister Farrell," she greeted him frostily. Wendt nodded his acknowledgment.

"Randy," Farrell saluted with his glass. He turned back to Paige, motioning with his drink toward the man standing next to him. "I believe you've met my partner, Kevin Kearns?"

Kearns met her gaze. "We've met twice before," she said. "Once in federal court—"

"And again when he saved your life," Farrell finished for her.

Paige's features hardened. She approached Kearns. "I suppose I should thank you," she said coolly.

"Don't put yourself out," Kearns said.

Paige was about to retort when Judge Callen interceded. "I'm glad you're both here," he said. "We were discussing strategy."

"How kind of you," Paige said icily.

The Judge dismissed his daughter's sarcasm and continued. "Mister Farrell has a plan that I think is worthy of consideration."

"I'm all ears," Paige said. "Particularly since his plan presumably involves me."

"The floor is yours," Callen said to Farrell. Paige, Wendt, and Kearns took seats. Farrell remained standing.

"The way I see it, we have two problems," he began, after first taking a drink and a long drag from his smoke. "First and foremost, we have to protect Ms Callen. The second priority is to identify and stop her attacker."

"We know this already," Paige said.

Farrell ignored her and went on. "The hard reality is, at this time we don't have a clue on his identity and motive, do we, Randy?"

"I'm afraid not," Wendt conceded. "We've got detectives and DA's inspectors working around the clock, going through Paige's previous prosecution case files, but so far nothing stands out. The only sample of his handwriting we have is from the spray-painted wall at Paige's condo, and our handwriting expert says there's been no similar handwriting matches in any of the documents in her files. None of the forensic evidence is producing any leads, either. The stolen car was clean as a whistle. The paper and envelope used in the note he left on her car were common drugstore stock, and the typewriter he used is a Smith Corona; only about a zillion of those in circulation. The typewriter is just like his gun; once we find it, it'll be easy to match up, but without it, we've got zilch."

"The plain truth is the investigation is stalled," Farrell said. "That's no reflection on Sergeant Wendt or his department; that's just the way it is." Wendt reluctantly nodded his assent. "Since we can't prevent what we don't know, that leaves us only one option: nail this guy in the act." He looked at Paige. "This obviously poses significant risks."

"You don't say," Paige said.

"Especially if he's a kamikaze," Farrell said. "If this guy doesn't care if he gets caught, or if he's willing to die to get her, he's going to be all the harder to stop."

"What does that mean?" Paige asked. "A kamikaze?"

"It means," Wendt answered for Farrell, "certain types of stalkers are kamikazes; they're so determined to nail their targets, they don't care if they get apprehended or killed in the process. Some actually seek death. They're happy to go up in flames as long as they can take the object of their obsession with them. Lots of these whack jobs shoot themselves after killing their victims; they're called murder-suicides. Others try to get the cops to do it for them; a suicide-by-cop.I'm sure you've seen it before."

Paige nodded. "Don't prosecute many of them," she admitted. "Usually nobody left to prosecute."

"I'm not sure if your stalker fits that profile," Farrell said. "He's gone to a lot of trouble to keep from getting caught so far. Fact is, we simply don't know at this point. Unfortunately, his self-preservation instinct might only be temporary."

"Temporary?" the Judge asked.

"Yes. Motivated for now only by a desire to prolong your daughter's suffering. If and when he reaches the end of his deranged program, he may be willing to sacrifice himself to take her out. I've seen it before."

"Me too," Wendt said. "Kamikaze."

"So Paige is essentially at the mercy of a homicidal lunatic's insane agenda?" Callen said.

"Correct," Farrell said. "And thus far, we're also entirely at the mercy of his schedule. We don't know when or where he's going to strike."

"We could put Paige in a safe house," Wendt suggested. "At least for a while."

"For how long?" Farrell asked. "It's expensive, can't be maintained forever, and all the stalker has to do is wait it out. Ms Callen can't stay underground for long, not and have anything close to a normal life. The stalker obviously knows all about her, certainly enough to have hit her at home on his terms. All he has to do, if she goes underground, is go underground himself. He'll surface when she does and go after her all over again. Time is on his side, not ours."

"What can we do?" Judge Callen said.

Farrell paused to drain his bourbon and inhale some more of his cigarette. "We can offer the stalker incentive to strike on our terms. Divert his energy to another target. It might expose him, draw him out."

"How do we do that?"

Farrell looked down at Paige. "A boyfriend."

"What?" she sat up.

"That's right. A boyfriend."

"That's ridiculous; I don't have a boyfriend," she said. "I'm not dating anyone right now. I haven't in some time."

"There's a mystery for you," Kearns said under his breath. Paige jerked her head at him sharply. Wendt suppressed a grin.

"I'm confused," Callen said. "What's a boyfriend going to do for us?"

"Put the stalker off his game," Farrell said. "Throw a wrench in his plans. Shake up his timetable."

"How?"

"Think about it," Farrell said. "This stalker knew where Ms Callen works, her schedule, where she lives; even what type of alarm she uses at her condominium, right, Randy?"

"That's right," the sergeant agreed. "He's done his homework."

"If she suddenly emerges with a boyfriend, especially one that appears to be a long-established relationship, our friend the stalker is going to be puzzled, maybe even a little pissed off. He's going to wonder how he didn't know about their relationship. How he missed it. And his next logical move—"

"—Is to find out as much as he can about the boyfriend," Sergeant Wendt finished. "Maybe try to hurt her by going after him."

"That's my thinking," Farrell said. "It's a long shot, but it's all we've got right now."

"It's actually not a bad idea," Wendt said, looking from Farrell to the Judge. "Giving the stalker another potential target would at least double our chances of luring him out."

"I agree," Judge Callen said. "And given the lack of other alternatives, I concur that Mr Farrell's suggestion, at least for the time being, is our best chance to snare this maniac."

Paige clapped her hands, an artificial smile on her face. "I'm delighted you're all in agreement. There're two problems, however, that you geniuses haven't thought of:

one, as I already noted, I don't have a boyfriend." Her phony smile vanished. "And two, there's no way in hell I'm going along with your idiotic plan."

She turned her icy gaze to her father. "I realize you can't control your impulse to manipulate me, but this takes the cake."

"Paige," the Judge said, "we're only trying to do what's best to catch this criminal. If you have a better idea, we'd love to hear it."

"Here's my idea," Paige said to her father. "How about you quit trying to run my life?" She pointed her finger next at Farrell. "How about you stay away from me?" Her stare lighted on Wendt. "And how about you get busy and catch this son of a bitch? Isn't that supposed to be your job?"

"What about me?" Kearns asked innocently.

"You can go to hell," she told him. She got up and stormed out of the study.

"I'll get right on it," Kearns said as she walked away.

All four men looked at each other and shrugged. "She had a rough morning," Wendt finally explained, breaking the silence. "She got put on administrative leave by the district attorney."

"What for?" Farrell asked.

"She punched out her office partner yesterday," he told them. "Guy's a real asshole. He jumped out at her and yelled 'Boo!' Thought it would be good for a laugh."

"What a shitty thing to do," Farrell said. "Doesn't he know what she's been through?" He ground out the remains of his cigarette in the marble ashtray.

"He does," Wendt said. "Which made it all the more thoughtless. Paige overreacted, of course, and punched him in the nose."

"That can happen," Farrell said, "when people get startled. Reflex action; self-defense."

"That's true," Wendt agreed. "But kicking him when he was down on the ground puking isn't. He's pressing charges."

"Uh-oh," Farrell groaned.

"Not to worry," Judge Callen said. "I've got a call into the DA and I've already referred Paige to a friend of mine who is a top-drawer criminal defense attorney. She's got an appointment scheduled with him this afternoon in Oakland. Sergeant Wendt has kindly offered to escort her. I'm certain this assault and battery incident will get resolved quickly."

"With your juice, I'm sure it will," Farrell said. "But it's trouble your poor daughter doesn't need right now."

"I'll say," Wendt concurred.

"Probably just as well," Farrell said, lighting another unfiltered Camel and heading back to the Judge's wet bar to refresh his bourbon. "If she doesn't go to work, it's one less place her stalker can attack her. Makes our lives a little easier."

"It certainly wouldn't hurt for Paige to keep a low profile for a while," Wendt agreed.

Paige reentered the study. The hostility had dissipated from her demeanor.

"I want to apologize," she said. "To each of you. I realize you're trying to do what you think is in my best interests. I shouldn't have reacted the way I did." She sighed. "This stalker thing and this trouble at work make me feel like I've lost control over every facet of my life. When I walked in and heard you discussing my case, it set me off. I know that's no excuse." She blew a lock of hair from over her black eye. "It's been a difficult week."

"So we heard," Farrell said. "If you'd like, I can have a talk with this jerk who's pressing charges against you. I can be very persuasive."

"I'll vouch for that," Kearns chimed in.

"No, thank you," Paige said quickly. "That won't be necessary. I did it, so I'll face it. I take responsibility for my actions."

"An honorable trait," Farrell said. "Your stock rises."

Paige smiled weakly.

"Will you at least consider Mr Farrell's plan?" Judge Callen asked her, returning the subject to the previous topic. "I realize it's something you don't want to do. But if it has even the slightest chance of helping Sergeant Wendt catch this madman, don't you think we ought to give it a try?"

"I'll think about it," Paige relented, too tired to argue further. "But even if I agreed to the charade, where am I going to find a pretend-boyfriend?"

"That's easy," Farrell announced, pointing at Kearns with his now-refilled bourbon. "Paige; meet Prince Charming."

"Oh, fuck," said Paige.

"Ditto," Kearns said.

CHAPTER 26

Ray strode purposefully across the residential yards, the tools on his belt flapping against his waist as he walked. It was a little after three in the afternoon, and the quiet Dayton Avenue cul-de-sac was devoid of vehicle or pedestrian traffic.

Ray was wearing a Pacific Gas and Electric work shirt over jeans and boots. A San Francisco Giants baseball cap topped his head, dark sunglasses covered his eyes, and his upper lip was adorned once again with a spirit-gummed theatrical mustache. Finishing the ensemble was a wide leather tool belt, complete with a flashlight and what appeared to be a walkie-talkie but was in reality a handheld police/fire scanner.

He was also wearing translucent latex gloves, invisible to all but the closest observer. Except there were no close observers; Ray had seen to that.

He'd been monitoring the house from inside the bed of a stolen pickup truck for several hours, hidden comfortably inside the vehicle's camper shell. The truck was parked at the intersection of Dayton Avenue and Grand Street, half a block from Judge Callen's home. Ray watched as black-and-white Alameda police cars rolled lazily by every hour or so. He also saw two men leave the Judge's place and get into a burgundy-colored Oldsmobile and drive away. Both looked like cops, but from his distance, he couldn't make out anything but their basic features. Shortly after the Olds left, Ray saw who he believed was the slut and another man leave the house and get into an unmarked Ford sedan and drive away.

Ray forced himself to wait another five minutes in case either of the vehicles returned, and got out of the truck. He checked his appearance in the side mirror and began to walk through the neighborhood. He made his way from property to property toward the Callen mansion, checking each house's gas meter along the way. He even made notes on a small clipboard on his belt. The fourth house he reached was the Callen home.

Ray went directly through the Callens' rear gate and made a pretense of checking the gas meter. Then he walked around to the rear yard. Taking a key from his pocket, he inserted it into the rear patio door. As expected, the key worked.

As he turned the key, he glanced at his wrist. Scrawled there, above the latex glove, was the alarm code: 4-0-3-1. Like the key, it was obtained from the late Mrs Reyes. Ray knew after opening the door he had ten seconds to enter the alarm code to prevent the alarm from activating. He gently twisted the key to minimize the sound of the lock's tumblers and opened the door. He saw the blinking green light on the alarm panel directly across from him. The green light meant the alarm was not activated, and that he hadn't needed the alarm code after all. It also meant someone was home, as he hoped.

Ray stepped inside, leaving the door slightly open, in case he needed to make a hasty exit. He removed his sunglasses and pocketed them. Then, he drew his 9mm Glock from under his shirt.

The patio door he had just entered led through a laundry room into the kitchen. The floor was tiled, and Ray padded softly and slowly to dampen the sound of his footsteps. Soon, he was through the kitchen and on plush carpet. Now able to move more rapidly, he navigated the hallway toward the house's interior.

Ray reached a set of French doors and peered inside. There, seated with his back to the doors, sat Judge Callen. Ray ducked quickly away.

After peering cautiously for several long seconds, Ray relaxed. It was apparent the elderly Judge was asleep at his desk, slumped in an expensive-looking leather chair, in what appeared to be a study. He passed the study and swept the rest of the house, room by room. Though confident the Judge was alone in the big house, Ray had to be sure. Attention to detail, that was paramount. Within minutes, he'd ensured there were no other occupants besides the Judge in the big mansion. He returned to the study.

The Judge was snoring peacefully, his chin on his chest, his reading glasses still on his nose. His hands were folded over his rising and falling stomach. Next to him on the desk was a mostly full glass of amber liquid.

Ray lit a cigarette. He picked up the glass and tossed its contents in the Judge's face.

"Wake up, Your Honor," he said, as Judge Callen sputtered to wakefulness. "Court is now in session."

The Judge shook his head to clear the liquid from his vision. He looked up at Ray, his eyes widening. He quickly reached under his sweater.

The Judge's sudden movement surprised Ray, who reflexively leaped forward and slammed the slide of his pistol against Callen's head. The old man toppled to the floor, blood flowing from a gash over his forehead. He sprawled out and lay still.

Ray leaned down and rolled the unconscious man over. There, in his hands, was a nickel-plated revolver.

Ray let out a long, smoky breath. That had been close. Sometimes, even with the best planning and attention to detail, things went awry. The old bastard certainly surprised him. Who'd have expected the retired old codger to be wearing a gun, safe and snug in his own study in the middle of the afternoon? Ray put the gun up on the desk.

Ray was disappointed. He wanted to tell the Judge what he was going to do to his daughter. He wanted the Judge to hear what was in store for her. He wanted to see the Judge's face when he learned what awaited his only child.

He looked down at the old man. The pool of blood from his head was growing, but he could still see the rise and fall of his chest. Ray suspected he might hemorrhage to death within the hour, but he couldn't wait that long; he had to be sure.

Ray put out his cigarette and pocketed the butt. He replaced his pistol in his waistband and removed a guitar string and his extra-thick leather work gloves from another pocket. He donned the gloves and was looping the guitar string around the Judge's neck when the doorbell rang.

He jerked upright from where he'd been leaning over the Judge. The doorbell rang again and again, and between rings there was an insistent knocking. Drawing his pistol, Ray raced from the study to a front window. He carefully parted the curtains and glanced outside.

Parked in the driveway was a cherry-red Porsche. Standing on the porch, he presumed, was the Porsche's owner.

The man was short, much shorter than Ray's own five feet ten, and wearing a double-breasted pin-striped suit. He had on Italian loafers with no socks, and he had thinning hair which looked to be dyed. The most striking thing about the man, however, was the two black eyes he was sporting, along with a strip of surgical tape over his nose.

Ray waited long minutes for the man to go away, but he wouldn't. Despite getting no response to his incessant doorbell-ringing and door-pounding, the man continued to do it. He tried the door handle several times between knocks and rings, and Ray was certain the man would have entered if the door was unlocked. He reasoned the man must be a regular visitor or perhaps was expected by the Judge. A relative? The whore's boyfriend?

Ray gritted his teeth and swore under his breath. He'd discounted the possibility of a boyfriend during the months of preplanning and surveillance he'd conducted, but now wondered if he'd missed something. He'd found no indication of a man in her life. But then, he was surprised, outraged, and almost killed by the sandy-haired man who came to her aid. Now here was another man in the picture, the man currently on her father's doorstep. Ray nervously wondered what other surprises he hadn't anticipated awaited him.

Finally, after what seemed like hours, the man left the porch. But to Ray's chagrin, he didn't return to his car. Instead, he walked through the side gate towards the rear of the house, the same route Ray had entered. Ray suddenly remembered he'd left the rear door ajar.

Cursing, Ray sprinted from the front of the expansive house, down the hall, past the study, through the kitchen to the laundry room. He reached the rear door just as it swung open.

A startled C. Timothy Potter looked up when he saw Ray. Ray barely had time to put both gloved hands, and his pistol, behind his back as Potter entered.

"Who're you?" Potter demanded indignantly.

"Uh," Ray stammered, out of breath and momentarily taken aback by Potter's bold arrival. "I'm... uh... here to read the meter. There's nobody home."

"If there's nobody home, how'd you get in? And why didn't you answer the door? I've been knocking for ten minutes."

"There's a gas leak," Ray lied. "Doing some repair work."

"Where's the Judge?" Potter asked. "Where's Paige?"

"They're... uh... gone for the day. Due to the gas leak."

"This doesn't seem right," Potter said. His eyes narrowed as he stepped forward and scrutinized Ray. "Is that a fake mustache?" He puffed out his chest. "I think I need to see some identification."

"Identify this," Ray said. He brought out the Glock and placed the barrel against Potter's forehead.

Potter's eyes widened and his jaw dropped as Ray fired. The deputy DA's head snapped back as the 9mm slug tore through his skull. He crumpled to the floor.

At the sound of the shot, a dog began to bark in one of the adjacent yards. Ray looked over his shoulder, back into the house's interior, and was about to return to the study when a man's voice, emanating from the adjacent yard, stopped him.

"...was that? Sounded like a damned cannon going off."

Ray looked in the direction of the voice and saw a bald man in Bermuda shorts and sandals staring directly at him through a gap in the backyard hedges. Potter's inert body was clearly visible at his feet. His and the neighbor's eyes met, and an instant later, the man was scurrying off, no doubt to alert the police.

Ray needed no further urging. He ran from the rear of the house toward the truck he'd parked at the end of Dayton Avenue, as front doors opened and people stared. He still had the pistol in his hand.

It seemed like miles to the truck. Ray jumped in, stashed his pistol, and began to frantically twist the filed-down master key he'd left jammed in the ignition. On the third twist, the engine fired up and he screeched out of the neighborhood, heading south toward the beach.

In less than a minute, he was on Shoreline Drive. He parked along the bike path that ran parallel to the beach and turned off the engine. He rapidly stripped off his cap, leather work gloves, PG&E shirt, and mustache, as well as his trousers and boots. He was wearing a green Oakland A's T-shirt and athletic shorts underneath. He kept the latex gloves on. Ray slipped on a pair of tennis shoes and stuffed his tool belt, clothing, and boots into a small knapsack, which he put on. He clipped the police scanner to his shorts and inserted the earpiece into his ear.

Ray then nonchalantly got out of the truck and opened the rear camper hatch. He extracted a bicycle from the bed of the truck and walked it across Shoreline Drive to the bike path. He mounted the bike and forced himself to pedal slowly along the waterline, making a point to study the panoramic view of the San Francisco skyline looming over the Bay. He saw several police cruisers pass him as they raced toward the direction of the Callen home. As he pedaled, he switched on the police scanner. He blended in easily with the other bicyclists, pedestrians, joggers, and skaters populating the beachfront path.

By the time Ray heard the dispatcher's voice on the scanner, broadcasting the description of the truck, he was halfway home, cursing his bungled opportunity.

CHAPTER 27

Bob Farrell brought his Oldsmobile to a halt in the Alameda hospital parking lot farther from the EMERGENCY entrance than he preferred. The lot was already packed with marked and unmarked police cars. He tossed his cigarette to the pavement and made his way into the facility.

Farrell had dropped off Kearns at a car rental agency after leaving Judge Callen's house with instructions to rent a vehicle. They agreed to meet for dinner later to discuss their next move. Kearns wanted to get a haircut and go to the Davis Street shooting range in San Leandro to test-fire the .45 pistol Farrell had acquired for him. Shortly after leaving Kearns, Farrell heard Judge Callen's address broadcast over the police scanner in his car as the location of a possible homicide.

Farrell raced to the Callen home on Dayton Avenue. An ambulance was pulling out, lights flashing and sirens blaring. He parked a block away and approached on foot. There were neighbors milling in the vicinity, and several uniformed cops scurried busily about. He noticed a red Porsche in the driveway. A cop was putting up crime scene tape around the property. One of the officers in the yard was McCord.

"The fuck are you doing here, asshole?" McCord demanded when he saw Farrell.

"Is the Judge all right?"

"This is a police matter, Mister Private Investigator. You ain't a cop. This is also a crime scene. So get the fuck out of here."

"I'm Judge Callen's friend. And I'm not in your crime scene, Officer McCord," Farrell said, gesturing to the yellow tape and his location outside of it. "I only want to know if the Judge is all right."

"Fuck you," McCord said.

Several neighbors overheard the exchange between Farrell and McCord. A very elderly woman approached Farrell, giving the uniformed cop a disapproving glare.

"The ambulance took Gene away," she said. "He looked bad, but he was alive."

"Thank you," Farrell said to her. She stuck her tongue out at McCord and returned to her own yard. Farrell turned to walk back toward his car.

"We ain't finished," McCord called after him.

"Speak for yourself," Farrell said over his shoulder. Halfway to his car, he stopped. He returned to the woman who had informed him of the Judge's condition. McCord watched this in disdain.

"My name's Bob Farrell," he introduced himself. "As you heard, I'm a friend of Judge Callen's. I was wondering if I could go into your side yard and get a glimpse into Judge Callen's property from your fence?"

The woman smiled. "Won't that piss off that rude policeman with the foul mouth?"

"I'm certain it will," he said.

"Then help yourself." Farrell nodded his thanks and headed for her side yard gate.

"Where do you think you're going?" McCord called out. Farrell ignored him. He navigated the expansive side yard and went directly to the fence adjoining the Callen property. He peered over the fence into Judge Callen's rear yard.

He saw a plainclothes detective and two uniformed cops standing over the body of a man which lay half in the open back door. The corpse was Caucasian, fat, and wearing a suit. One of the shoes was off, revealing a bare foot. It was also wearing an exit wound in the back of the head.

Farrell saw McCord storming into Callen's backyard from the front, scanning the fence line for him. When he saw Farrell, McCord came straight toward him.

"I told you to get the fuck out of here," McCord said.

"We were in the Callen's front yard when you told me that," Farrell smiled pleasantly. "I did what you asked. Do I look like I'm in your crime scene now?"

"Don't fuck with me."

"If I decide to fuck with you, Officer McCord, you'll be the first to know."

Farrell abruptly turned his back on McCord and walked toward the front of the property.

When he emerged from the side yard, the elderly woman who had invited him onto her property greeted him. She was talking to two other elderly neighbors in hushed whispers.

"Is it true there's a dead guy in Gene's backyard?" she asked eagerly.

"Yep," Farrell told her. "Deader than Caesar."

McCord suddenly emerged from the Callens' backyard, brushing off the arm of a fellow officer who tried to hold him back. He stomped straight for Farrell.

"Would you mind sticking around a moment?" Farrell asked the trio of neighbors. "I may need witnesses." The elderly woman nodded.

McCord walked up, fuming, and wordlessly reached out to grab Farrell's collar. His face was a mask of fury. Farrell ducked under the much larger man's arm, and McCord lunged past him. Off balance, McCord stumbled, pivoted, and turned to go after Farrell again.

"That's enough," Farrell said. He swept his always-unbuttoned suit coat aside, putting his hand over, but not touching, the Smith & Wesson .38 on his hip. As an honorably retired peace officer, Farrell was legally allowed to carry a concealed firearm. And like most retired cops with his tenure, he would have sooner left his apartment without his trousers than his revolver.

"You're way out of line, Officer. That badge and uniform aren't a license to assault me. Try to put your hands on me again and you'll need your gun," he said.

McCord stood seething, his large belly and chest rising from the exertion of racing twice through the Callen's substantial yard. His pallor was beet red.

The same cop who tried to contain McCord before approached and took his arm again.

"Jesus Christ, Joe," he said to McCord. "What the hell are you doing? People are watching. You want to get fired?"

Farrell didn't flinch. Finally, McCord let his partner pull him away.

"This ain't over," he told Farrell, pointing a finger. Farrell said nothing in reply, allowing his hand to fall to his side and his jacket to once again drape over his weapon.

"That police officer has anger issues," the elderly woman said. "He shouldn't be allowed to have a gun."

"I'd have to agree with you there," Farrell said, lighting a cigarette. He thanked the woman and returned to his car. Moments later, he arrived at the hospital, only five blocks away.

When Farrell entered the emergency room, he found Sergeant Randy Wendt talking with a physician. There was a uniformed cop busily scrawling on his clipboard. When Wendt saw Farrell, he nodded an acknowledgement.

"Hello again, Randy," Farrell greeted him as the physician broke off his conversation with the sergeant and returned to his duties. "Long time, no see."

"It's been what, a couple of hours?"

"This guy works fast," Farrell said. "He must have been watching the house and saw us leave."

"I was thinking the same thing," Wendt said. "The son of a bitch is relentless. He doesn't let up."

"How's the Judge?" Farrell asked.

"Lucky as hell to be alive," Wendt told him. "Looks like our stalking suspect got into the house and attacked him. We found Iron Gene on the floor of his study with a cracked noggin and a wire around his throat."

"Not to be ungrateful, but why isn't he dead?"

"Looks like the suspect was interrupted in the act."

"By the stiff on the rear patio?"

Wendt's eyebrows lifted. "How'd you know about that?"

"I'm a detective, remember? Who is he? Or should I say, who was he?"

"Deputy District Attorney Charles Timothy Potter," Wendt said. "If you can believe it."

"Paige's office partner? The schmuck who's pressing charges against her?"

"The one and only," Wendt said. "Can't say I'm heartbroken over his demise."

"At least that lets Paige off the hook for the assault," Farrell said. "That's some good news. But the bad news is that our stalker has graduated to murder."

"He certainly has," Wendt said. "Even before he clipped Potter."

"What do you mean?"

"On a hunch, I sent a detective to Oakland this morning to check on Mrs Reyes, the Callen's part-time housekeeper. She didn't show up for work, and Paige was worried."

"I've got a bad feeling about what you're going to tell me," Farrell grimaced.

"Go with it. Oakland PD now has a double homicide to add to their already-overflowing murder caseload. Mrs Reyes and her husband were found garroted in their home. Been dead twenty-four to thirty-six hours."

"Wire garrote? Like Judge Callen?"

"You guessed it," Wendt confirmed.

"How did our suspect even know where Judge Callen's housekeeper lives?"

"Don't know," Wendt said. "We know this guy does his homework, and he's very thorough; he could have followed the housekeeper home some evening after she left the Judge's house for all we know. Paige is pretty broken up about it. Feels responsible."

"Poor kid. Where was she when all this went down today?"

"With me. I drove her into Oakland to consult with an attorney on the assault charges against her. I didn't want to leave her alone, in case this nut tried again. We were just leaving when I got the radio call. She's in with her dad."

"What's his condition?"

"They're admitting him to intensive care as we speak. I'm not sure if that's a good sign or a bad sign. I was going there now."

"I'll join you," Farrell said. The two men headed for the elevators. The intensive care unit was located on the third floor.

"I don't suppose there were any witnesses today?" Farrell asked, as the elevator doors swooshed shut.

"Surprisingly, yes, for all the good they'll do us. A couple of the Judge's neighbors are retired busybodies," Wendt said. "Spend a lot of time sticking their noses into other people's business."

"I met a few of them," Farrell said. "We should all have such neighbors."

"Apparently, the suspect was dressed like a gas meter reader. One of the neighbors saw him enter the block, thought nothing of it until she saw him a few minutes later running away with a gun in his hand. Nobody got a good-enough look to identify him if they saw him again; old eyes and too far away."

"A vehicle?"

"Found abandoned at the beach a little while ago. Stolen out of Oakland last night. It'll probably be as devoid of prints and evidence as the last stolen car he dumped."

Wendt and Farrell exited the elevator. A uniformed officer stood outside a door to one of the rooms. Wendt nodded to him and they entered. Paige was seated by her father's bed, her eyes puffy from crying. She looked up at them briefly, then back to her father. There were a nurse and a man in surgical scrubs in the room as well.

Judge Callen was conscious. His head was bandaged and he was wearing a neck brace. He had an oxygen tube inserted into his nose and an intravenous line in his right arm. It was his face, however, that was the most unsettling.

The right side of the Judge's face was slack, as if made of putty. His right eyelid drooped almost shut, and the corner of his mouth on that side curled downward in a rubbery frown, saliva pooling in the corner. His eyes, however, were as bright as ever, and they flashed in recognition when he saw Farrell and Wendt come in.

The physician was speaking with Paige but doing so loudly enough for the Judge to hear also.

"The blow to your father's head induced what amounts to a mild stroke, Ms Callen," he said.

"What does that mean?"

"It means the right side of his body is paralyzed. We have him on steroids to reduce brain swelling, and his vitals are strong, which is a good sign. Barring unforeseen consequences, he should make it. As far as permanent damage, it's too early to determine. It's entirely possible the partial paralysis is a temporary condition, and he may make a full recovery. We'll know within the next twenty-four hours. But he needs rest now, and as much as you want to be with him, I'm afraid you'll have to leave." The physician looked around the room at all of them. "That goes for everybody."

"Ferl," the Judge said, his face straining with effort.

"What, Dad?" Paige put her ear over her father's mouth to hear him better.

"Ferl," he repeated, his face reddening.

"He wants to talk with you, Bob," Wendt said.

"I'm right here, Your Honor," Farrell said, stepping closer.

"I can't allow this," the physician said. "He's becoming worked up. I don't want him to compromise his recovery."

"Lone," Judge Callen forced out. "Ferl... lone."

The Judge's meaning was clear. He wanted to speak with Farrell privately.

"I'm going to have to insist this conversation be postponed until another time," the doctor announced. "He's becoming agitated–"

"No," the Judge said again, cutting the doctor off. "Ferl... lone."

"Let the Judge speak," Wendt said. He faced the doctor. "Three people are dead, there's been an attempt on the Judge's life, and two attempts on his daughter, who is still in the killer's crosshairs. We need to hear what he has to say, and he wants to say it to Farrell."

"All right," the physician conceded. "Five minutes, no more."

"Thanks, Doc," Wendt said. "Everybody out but Farrell," he announced to the room.

"I'm not going anywhere," Paige said firmly. "Anything my father has to say I can hear too."

The Judge's face reddened further. "Lone," he said again. "Out." His body trembled from the effort to speak.

"I'm not going anywhere," Paige repeated defiantly.

Wendt took her by the shoulders. "I'm not going to stand here and watch your father kill himself trying to prove he's more stubborn than his daughter. If he wants to speak with Farrell alone, that's his right. You're going to leave this room with me, this instant, or I'm going to drag you out."

Paige shrugged herself out of Wendt's grip, glared at Farrell, and stormed out. The doctor, nurse, and then Wendt followed her. "Five minutes," the doctor reiterated as he closed the door behind him. "No more." Farrell nodded.

Once they were alone, the Judge forced a twisted smile. Farrell spoke first.

"I've seen you look better," Farrell smiled. "What's on your mind?"

The Judge took a deep breath, preparing for the exertion of speaking. "Rotect... Aige," he finally got out. He blurted his daughter's name with such force, Farrell thought he would pass out. "On't... let... him... get... her," he gasped.

Farrell put his hand on the Judge's shoulder. "Count on it," he said.

"Apa," Callen continued, veins distending on his forehead. "Ranch." He paused for another breath. "Napa... safe there."

"OK," Farrell told him. "You want Paige at the ranch, wherever that is, that's where she'll go, whether she wants to or not. Kevin's on the way as we speak. I'll have him escort her there. From here on out, he won't let your daughter out of his sight." The Judge seemed comforted upon hearing this, but his eyes posed a question.

"Don't worry," Farrell told the Judge. "Kevin's young, but he's tough. He was a grunt in the army and a deputy sheriff back in Iowa; he's seen action. And I can personally attest to his fortitude. The hardheaded redneck doesn't have the word 'quit' in his vocabulary. He won't let anything happen to Paige. You can be sure of that."

"On't... care... what... it... costs," Judge Callen said.

"I sure as hell do," Farrell joked. "But we can talk about money when you're feeling better. Right now, you've got to rest and I've got to earn my pay."

The Judge's eyes burned at Farrell. "Get... him," he said. "Fore... he... gets... Aige."

"You can count on that, too."

CHAPTER 28

Paige sat in the passenger seat of the rented Jeep Cherokee and stared out the window with her arms folded across her chest. In the driver's seat was Kevin Kearns. He kept his eyes on the road, occasionally glancing over to verify if Paige was still deliberately indifferent to his presence. It was after sundown and they were driving on Highway 12 toward Napa Valley.

Kearns arrived at the hospital and met Farrell and Paige in the hallway outside Judge Callen's room in the intensive care unit. Paige did not appear particularly pleased to see Farrell. He was discussing the Judge's wishes with Paige when Wendt returned from consulting with the uniformed police officer posted as Callen's guard.

"I said I'd go, didn't I?" Paige said.

"Where are you going?" Wendt asked her, having overheard only a fragment of their conversation as he approached.

"Apparently, I'm going to visit the wine country," Paige said, rolling her eyes and jerking a thumb towards Kearns, "with Galahad here."

"So that's what the Judge wanted from you," Wendt said to Farrell. "For you to take his daughter out of harm's way." The sergeant tuned to Paige. "That's a good idea; I'm glad you're finally listening to reason. You should have bugged out two days ago."

213

"That's what Dad wanted; I guess he's getting his way. Again. As usual."

"He's only thinking of your safety," Farrell offered.

"All right," she growled. "It's bad enough I have to leave with my father quite possibly on his deathbed, but you two can spare me the sermon."

"When are you leaving?" Wendt asked, not wanting to arouse Paige further.

"Right now," Farrell answered for her. "You need to get anything?"

"What's to get?" Paige asked sarcastically. "Everything I own is either burned or wrecked. Even if I wanted anything from my father's house, it's a crime scene; the police won't let me in."

"I'm afraid not," Wendt agreed. "Our evidence technicians are going to be there for some time."

"You got everything you need?" Farrell asked Kearns.

"Yeah; and plenty of cash to buy what I don't. Thanks."

"I'll need a phone number," Wendt chimed in to Paige. "I want to be able to reach you. There's no telling how long you'll be gone."

"It won't be very long," Paige said. "I promised Dad I'd leave for a while, but I didn't say anything about the duration of my involuntary exile."

"Quit playing games," Wendt scolded her, unable to conceal the irritation creeping into his voice. "Haven't you figured out this guy coming after you isn't screwing around? Three people are dead, your father was almost killed, and there's nothing to indicate he's going to stop until he gets you. Have you forgotten you're his primary target?"

"Get with the program for once, will you?" Farrell joined in. "Can't you see that short of surrounding you with a SWAT team twenty-four hours a day, which the Alameda police department doesn't have the resources to do, Randy can't protect you? If you insist on staying, all you're going to do is give your stalker more opportunity to take you out. Your father knows this; why don't you?"

"I'm worried about Dad," she said. "I need to be with him right now."

"No, you don't," Farrell said. "Your father's safe." He tilted his head toward the uniformed cop down the hall. "He's protected here; you're not. He wants you out of danger. You saw yourself how agitated he got after arguing with you. If it puts him at ease, knowing you're safely away from here, he'll rest better and heal faster. Think of him."

"In that respect, I have to agree with you; Dad'll blow a gasket if he thinks I'm in jeopardy. I made a promise to go away; I'll keep it. I'm just not pleased about it."

"You're not alone. None of us are pleased with the situation right now," Farrell said.

"We won't be happy until this guy is nailed and jailed," Wendt said. "Now go to the wine country, visit your family, and try to relax. You can call me every day if you want. I'll keep you up to speed on the investigation. Who knows, maybe we'll get a break? In any case, with you gone, the Judge will rest easier knowing you're safe. And we can devote our energy to catching this freak without worrying about protecting you."

Paige nodded. "All right, I'm going." She looked up at Kearns. "Do I have to go with him?"

"The Judge is paying Kevin to protect you," Farrell said. "He already pulled your ass out of the grease once already. Or did you forget?"

"I didn't forget," she said. "I just don't like it, that's all."

"You don't like it?" Kearns echoed.

"Could you try to not be difficult for once?" Farrell asked her. "Please? If not for your own safety, then for your father's sake?"

"I agreed to go, didn't I?" she said. She pointed a finger a Kearns. "Don't even think about bossing me around," she admonished him.

"Give it a rest," he said. "I got roped into this, same as you."

Paige held her tongue and headed for the elevators. Kearns shrugged and followed after her.

An hour later, they were passing through the vineyards of the Napa Valley. Paige hadn't spoken a word, nor looked in Kearns' direction, the entire journey. Ten miles south of Napa, Kearns broke the silence.

"Your aunt lives in Napa?" She ignored the question. "I seem to recall your father mentioning a ranch. Is the ranch in Napa, or somewhere outside the city limits?"

Again Paige ignored him. He let out a long sigh.

"Ms Callen, you're eventually going to have to speak to me."

"Why?"

"For directions, if nothing else."

"When you see the exit for highway 121, take it north," she said. "I'll direct you from there."

"Thank you."

"You're welcome."

They drove on in silence. Once through the sleepy town, Paige gave curt instructions until they veered off on a private dirt road approximately fifteen miles north of Napa. A half mile in, the road began to climb steeply. Kearns went up a sharp grade another five minutes, past a seemingly endless sea of planted grapes, until the Jeep crested the hill. In the basin below, surrounded by oak trees, the lights of a house twinkled at them.

"This is it," she announced as Kearns eased the Jeep past a wrought-iron-topped brick gate and onto a large circular stone driveway.

"Doesn't anybody in the Callen family live in a regular house?" Kearns remarked, taking in the property. Paige didn't answer. She got out of the car and headed up a stone path to the house. He stepped out of the car after her but stopped at the driver's door.

The large, elaborate two-story structure was comprised of stone, and like many of the wineries and homes in Napa Valley, had an almost medieval appearance. Kearns could see two structures on each side of the home, one of which he surmised was a guest cottage by its size and proximity to the main house. The other building was as big as the house and set much farther back; a barn or storage facility, he thought.

A porch light came on and Kearns looked up to see Paige greeted by a tall, handsome woman who looked to be in her mid-fifties, and who bore a noticeable resemblance to Judge Callen. She was wearing jeans and a sweater. Paige and the woman embraced.

"Aunt Elsa," he heard Paige say. He thought he sensed emotion in her voice.

"It's wonderful to see you," the woman said. "Even under the circumstances. It's been too long."

"I know," Paige said. "I've been so busy with work, and–"

"Never mind," Elsa told her, stepping back from their embrace. "You're here now." She put her arm around Paige's shoulders. "C'mon, let's get you inside."

The two women started to enter the house, arm in arm, leaving Kearns standing awkwardly beside the Jeep. He was about to clear his throat when the woman turned around.

"Good grief, how rude of me," she said, leaving Paige in the doorway and approaching Kearns. "Paige, you didn't introduce me to your gentleman friend."

"He's neither a gentleman nor my friend," she answered from behind her aunt. "And he was just leaving."

"I'm Kevin Kearns," he said, disregarding Paige's comment and accepting Elsa's outstretched hand. She had a strong handshake and her palm was thick with calluses of someone who works outside with their hands. She also had striking blue eyes, like Paige. Kearns liked her immediately.

"Elsa Callen," she introduced herself. "It's good to meet you. You're leaving?"

"Yes," Paige interjected. "He was just leaving. Isn't that right, Mr Kearns?"

"That wasn't the deal and you know it," he said.

"Deal?" Elsa asked, looking from Kearns to Paige. "What deal?"

"You brought me to Napa. Your job is done. You can be on your way now."

"No dice," Kearns said flatly. "My partner made your father a promise; I'm here to keep it for him."

"Hold on a minute," Elsa said, puzzled. "Before anybody stays or goes, I think I should know what's going on."

"There's nothing to talk about," Paige said. "He's not staying; that's final."

Elsa looked to Kearns. "What's this about?"

"I'm being paid by Judge Callen to physically protect Paige. I'm not leaving her side, at least not until I get the word from the Judge or my partner. For the record, I'm no happier about it than she is, but that's how it stands."

"Is this true, Paige?" Paige's silence and scowl were her answer.

"I see," Elsa said, biting her lip. "Gene isn't a man to be trifled with. He may be my brother, but I wouldn't cross him." She turned back to Kearns. "It looks like you'll be staying."

"I'm sorry for the inconvenience," he said.

"It's no bother." She smiled, showing a lot of white teeth. She scratched her chin. "I've already made up one of the guest rooms for Paige. You're welcome to the couch tonight; I'll make up another room for you tomorrow."

"Thank you kindly," Kearns told her, "but I'm sure my presence under the same roof would upset Ms Callen. I'll sleep in the car, if you don't mind."

"The guest cottage!" Elsa exclaimed, snapping her fingers. "It's been so long since it's been used, I almost forgot about it. You're welcome to stay there, Mr Kearns, if you don't mind the chill. It's a bit musty inside, but if we open the windows, it'll air out in no time. It has its own bathroom and shower. A kitchenette, too."

"That will be fine. And my name is Kevin."

Elsa took a moment to appraise him. "So it is, Kevin," she finally said. "Help yourself; the cottage is unlocked."

"Thank you. May I ask a question or two about the property?"

"Fire away."

"Is this road the only way in?"

"It is, unless you don't mind a three- or four-mile overland hike."

"Do you have an alarm system?"

"Sure do; want to see it?" Elsa put two fingers into her mouth and whistled. Seconds later, a huge yellow Labrador came bounding from the house. He flew past Paige and into the yard.

"Kevin, meet Cody; my alarm system." Cody ran up to Kearns, his tail wagging furiously. Kearns knelt and rubbed the dog's neck and ears.

"That's my Cody," Elsa chuckled. "Part roommate, part child, part alarm system, and full time pain in the ass."

"He's beautiful," Kearns said, grinning. He stood up. "With your permission, I'll be turning in. It's been a long day. Thank you for your hospitality, Ms Callen. It was nice to meet you."

"It's Elsa," she corrected him. "And those questions you asked just now; do you think Paige's stalker would actually follow her all the way out here?"

"We don't know much about him," Kearns said, "except that he's a very determined individual. Goodnight, Elsa."

Kearns headed for the guest cottage with Cody following behind him. Elsa watched them disappear into the darkness. After Kearns left, she mounted the steps and gave her niece a reassuring hug. Paige, too, had been staring after Kearns as he left, a fact which did not go unnoticed.

"I like him," Elsa said. "He's seems like a fine young man. He has honest eyes. Good-looking fellow, too."

"Christ, Aunt Elsa; you've known him all of five minutes."

"Some things you just know," she observed. "Let's get you settled in."

CHAPTER 29

"Thanks for meeting me for a drink," Sergeant Wendt said to Farrell. He took a seat across from Wendt at a secluded booth in the back of the tavern where until only a few days ago, Kevin Kearns had resided upstairs above the bar. It was a little after ten in the evening.

"No problem," Farrell said. "I'm always thirsty."

"It's not like I have anything better to do," the Alameda police sergeant grumbled. "I have a fresh murder, an open stalking investigation, and an attempted murder against one of the island's wealthiest, most prominent, and politically connected citizens to solve; it's the perfect time to kick back and relax with a cold one."

"Sounds like you need a drink more than me," Farrell smiled. He lit a cigarette and motioned for the waitress. She started towards their table but was intercepted by her boss, Johnny Costanza, who sauntered over.

"Double bourbon over ice," Farrell told him. Costanza gave Farrell a nod of recognition and turned to Wendt. "Usual, Randy?"

"Sure, but make it light on the vodka; I'll be back at work later tonight." Costanza left for the bar.

"It's a bad sign when the bartender knows your poison without having to order," Farrell said. "It's a worse sign when he knows your name."

"This place is an unofficial cop hangout," Wendt explained, "since it's only a block from the station."

"Convenient," Farrell said.

"I used to be a regular after my second divorce and before I remarried; now, not so much." Wendt leaned back in his chair.

"I'm glad you reached out," Farrell said. "We need to compare notes. There's also something I wanted to discuss with you I couldn't back at the hospital."

"Not many notes to compare. The investigation's become a full-blown clusterfuck. I spent the rest of the afternoon after I left you at the hospital getting my ass chewed by the chief, as if this crime wave was my fault. He summoned an emergency meeting with the district attorney, and together they're doing their best to make my life a living hell."

"That's what bureaucrats and politicians do," Farrell said.

"I don't blame them, actually. It's a pretty heavy-duty crime for this little island, and it's generating heat. We have a young, attractive, female deputy DA who's being stalked, her father, a retired superior court judge, was almost killed, and a deputy DA who's DOA, all within the same week and the week ain't over. It's like a fucking made-for-TV movie. And you'd better believe the press is all over it. That's why I wanted to meet with you; I had to get out of the station or I was going to shoot somebody."

"I thought it was the pleasure of my company."

"Fat chance," Wendt said. "And it gets worse. Tomorrow, they're going to start up a task force."

"A task force?"

"You were SFPD; you know the drill. Assemble an all-star team of detectives from the department, the sheriff's office, and the DA's inspector's office, and throw as many resources as possible at the case. Put out a daily press conference. Makes the public feel like a lot is being done."

"Most of the investigative task forces I worked on," Farrell said, "were a smokescreen designed to kick up dust and send a message to the public that no expense was being spared to solve the crime. Sometimes they worked, but usually the task force was really only about damage control and repairing the department's battered reputation, mitigating liability and spreading the blame when things went to shit. You ever notice when a case is successfully resolved by a task force, every department on the team wants to claim the win, but when it goes bellyup, the task force provides each player with somebody else to point the finger of blame at?"

"It's no different in this instance," Wendt said. "What makes it worse is that we're no closer to identifying the stalker than we were on Monday morning. I don't think a task force is going to change that."

Johnny Costanza returned with their drinks. "Kevin find a place to live yet?" Costanza asked, setting the drinks down on the table. He gave Wendt a disapproving glance. Wendt accepted his drink without acknowledging the bar owner.

"Kevin's doing all right," Farrell said. "He doesn't harbor you any ill will; he knows it was out of your hands."

"Sure as hell was," Costanza said, sending another glimpse Wendt's way before heading back to the bar."

"Let's talk about another topic," Wendt said. "This Callen thing gives me a headache. You said you had something else on your mind?"

"How well do you know Officer McCord?"

"Not very well," Wendt said, downing some vodka and orange juice. "Came on the force about ten years behind me. Charismatic guy; real popular with the newer recruits. Tips a few."

"You don't socialize with him?"

"No," Wendt answered. "It's a small department; everybody knows everybody. But no, we don't swing in the same circles. Why do you ask?"

"I stopped by the crime scene at Judge's Callen's today before I met you at the hospital." Farrell exhaled a long plume of smoke. "Ran into the friendly and courteous Officer McCord."

"How did that turn out?"

"He assaulted me," Farrell said evenly. "In front of a half dozen witnesses, several of whom were cops. One of them had to pull him off."

"Joe McCord is a very large guy," Wendt said. "You're lucky he didn't hurt you."

"He's lucky I didn't kill him," Farrell said.

Wendt's eyes darkened. "So why ask me about it? I already told you what McCord's problem with you is. Your beef is with him, not me."

Farrell sipped bourbon. "Thought I could do you both a favor," he said.

"How's that?"

"I understand that McCord's got a hard-on for me. And I definitely get that he has a problem controlling his temper. I don't intend to file an internal affairs complaint against him; at least, not yet. That ain't my style; I don't pitch accusations against fellow cops. But I'm done getting threatened and way past done getting assaulted."

"OK, Bob; I still don't see how this is my problem."

"You're a violent crimes detective, aren't you?"

"You know I am."

"Then it is your problem. You're the guy who's going to have to clean up the mess if McCord doesn't steer clear of me. Just because I'm not looking for trouble doesn't mean I'm not prepared for it. You can tell him I'll let today go; this one's on the house. But the next time he decides to get stupid with me, he'd better be ready to go all the way to the hospital or the morgue."

"I'll pass it along," Wendt said dryly.

"I appreciate it," Farrell said, finishing his drink. He stood up, ground out his cigarette in the ashtray, and dropped a couple of bills on the table.

"So what's your next move, Sherlock?" Wendt asked.

"I'll let you know when I do," Farrell told him. He waved a goodbye and walked out of the bar.

Farrell strolled to his Oldsmobile and got in. He pulled out and proceeded on Park Street until he reached the bridge into Oakland. He was halfway across when the blue-and-white flashing lights lit up his rearview mirror. Farrell traversed the bridge, then pulled directly into the middle of the parking lot of Nikko's Café and stopped. Nikko's, a twenty-four-hour eatery situated on the border between Oakland and Alameda and only a block away from the on-ramp to the Nimitz Freeway, always had a few Oakland PD and CHP cars parked in its generous lot.

Farrell extracted his Retired San Francisco police department inspector's badge and put both hands on the steering wheel with the badge in plain view. He waited for the cop to approach.

"Evening, Officer," Farrell said when the cop reached his driver's side door.

"Step out of the car," a voice commanded.

"Aren't you going to ask for my license and registration first?" Farrell asked.

"Step out of the car."

"I'm a retired cop and I'm lawfully armed," Farrell announced loud enough for anyone in the vicinity to hear. A group of café patrons and loiterers watched the traffic stop with rapt attention. Several cars were blocked from leaving the lot by the traffic stop, forcing their drivers to act as involuntary witnesses.

"Step out of the car; I'm not going to ask you again."

Farrell complied. He reached through his open driver's window and unlatched the door from the outside, never putting either of his hands out of sight even for a second. He got out, stood up, and kept both his hands well above his elbows, his gold badge glinting in the flashing lights of the police car.

The cop was young, with a crew cut and a cherubic, sneering face. He had his right hand on the butt of his revolver at his side.

"Don't you even want to see my identification?" Farrell asked with a smile.

"I know who you are," came the curt reply.

"Why am I being pulled over?"

"You were weaving in the lane back there," the cop answered.

"No, I wasn't," Farrell said.

The officer's sneer became more pronounced. "How much have you had to drink tonight?"

"One drink," Farrell said. "Not enough to be DUI, even in Alameda."

"We'll see about that."

"Where's Officer McCord?"

"What?"

"You heard me," Farrell asked loudly. "Officer McCord; you know, the guy who put you up to following me from the bar and pulling me over?"

Just then, a tall African-American Oakland police officer walked out of Nikko's to cover the Alameda cop.

"Code four," the Alameda officer said over his shoulder, extending four fingers of one hand. The tall African-American nodded and began to reenter the café.

"Code eight!" yelled Farrell. The Oakland cop whirled around.

"It's OK," the Alameda cop said. "I'm cool. Code four."

"It's not code four," Farrell called out, holding up his badge. "And it's not cool. I'm a retired San Francisco police inspector and I'm being unlawfully rousted by this police officer. He says I'm drunk driving and I'm sober as a judge."

The Oakland cop stopped mid-stride. The Alameda cop put his hand out. "It's OK," he insisted. "I'm code four."

"I told him I'm armed," Farrell shouted. "How the hell can it be code four if only one officer has an armed man detained and he's refusing cover?"

The Oakland cop said something inaudible into his portable transceiver. Seconds later, another Oakland cop emerged from Nikko's. This cop was older, Caucasian, and had a potbelly and sergeant's stripes on his sleeves. Together they approached Farrell and the Alameda officer who'd pulled him over.

"What do you got?" the sergeant asked the Alameda cop.

"Possible DUI," the cop said hesitantly.

"Bullshit," Farrell said. "This is bogus." He held out his badge case, which also contained his Retired SFPD identification. The sergeant accepted it and looked it over. Then he looked over Farrell, paying particular attention to his eyes. One of the cars blocked in by Farrell's car began to honk. Soon, other car horns began to join in.

"What was the probable cause for the stop?" the sergeant asked.

"He was weaving in the lane," was the nervous answer.

"That's also bullshit," Farrell said. "He followed me from a bar on Park Street."

"You been drinking?" the sergeant asked Farrell.

"Just one. And I was having it with an Alameda Police sergeant named Wendt who can vouch for me."

The Oakland sergeant turned back to the Alameda cop.

"He doesn't look lit up to me. Why haven't you started your field sobriety tests?"

"I was waiting for my cover officer," the cop stammered.

"Then why did you wave me off?" the African-American cop asked.

"Because this is nothing more than a roust," Farrell answered for him.

"Why would the Alameda cops be rousting a retired SFPD guy?" the sergeant inquired, looking from Farrell to the Alameda cop.

"It's a long story. The short version is because I'm a private investigator working a case in Alameda and there're a few cops that aren't happy about it."

"He's drunk driving," the Alameda officer insisted hotly. It was getting hard to hear with the honking of the horns.

"There's a CHP car in the Nikko's lot," Farrell pointed out. "That means there's a chippie inside Nikko's. They have portable Breathalyzer devices. I'd be glad to take a breath test right now."

"That won't be necessary," the Oakland sergeant said. He handed Farrell back his badge and ID case. "You're free to go, Inspector," he said.

"Thank you, Sergeant," Farrell said.

"How long you been wearing a badge?" the sergeant asked the Alameda officer.

"Three years."

"You act like it was three minutes. Ain't you been taught that you don't jack up cops, or retired cops, or cops' families? It's one of those rules you won't find in your general orders handbook but that everybody wearing a badge knows." He shook his head in disgust. "Get the hell out of here," he told the young cop. He glared at Farrell. "Both of you. You've taken up enough of my lunch hour." He and the African-American cop returned to the restaurant.

Farrell pocketed his badge and headed to his car.

"You skated this time," the Alameda cop bellowed over the cacophony of car horns. "You'd better watch your back."

"Give McCord a message from me," Farrell said. "Tell him this just got personal."

CHAPTER 30

At the sound of knocking on the cottage door, Kearns jumped up from where he'd been doing pushups on the floor and slipped into his trousers. He opened the door to find Elsa Callen standing there.

"Good morning, Kevin," she said. "I figured you'd be up. I hope I'm not disturbing you?" She noticed the jagged network of scarring across his muscular abdomen and chest.

"Not at all," he said. "Been up since dawn. Please come in."

"Nope," she said with a smile. "I came to invite you over to the house for breakfast. You look like a fella who can put away a solid meal in the morning."

"That's very kind of you," he said.

"I'll be in the kitchen," she said over her shoulder as she turned and headed back to the house. "Back door's unlocked."

Kearns slipped on his socks and shoes and put on a sweater over a T-shirt. While he was certain the afternoon would be sunny and hot once the fog burned off, he'd discovered Napa Valley mornings are damp and chilly. He took a moment to slip the .45 into his waistband over his right hip and pocket a spare magazine before leaving the guest cottage for the main house.

Kearns was greeted at the rear kitchen door by Cody, who met him with ears down and tail wagging. He gave the big yellow Labrador a scratch behind the ears and a hug. "Help yourself to coffee," he heard Elsa's voice from inside.

Kearns entered a kitchen the size of a military chow hall. The inviting aroma of freshly brewed coffee assailed his nostrils. He followed the scent to a large stainless steel pot on a ten-burner stove. In the center of a large oak table was a plate of sweet rolls.

Elsa Callen appeared from within a walk-in pantry carrying a fifty-pound bag of puppy chow. Kearns rushed to take the bag from her. Cody's tail wagged furiously. "Let me get that," he said.

"Don't trouble yourself," Elsa waved him off. "Been doing this every day for years. Keeps me young." She tilted the bag into a large ceramic bowl, and before it was filled, Cody's nose was buried in the dish.

"Cody hasn't been a puppy for a couple of years," she explained, "but you'd never know it." She returned the bag to the pantry. "What'll it be?" she asked when she emerged. "Eggs? Pancakes? You name it, I've got it."

"You're too kind." Kearns smiled, putting up his hand. "Just coffee, please, and the pleasure of your company."

"You're a charmer, you are," Elsa chuckled. She retrieved two mugs from a cupboard and poured two doses of steaming java. "Cream or sugar?"

"Neither."

"Good for you; that's the way men should drink coffee." She sat on a stool in the nook and motioned for Kearns to sit as well.

"Is Paige up?" he asked, taking a tentative sip and sitting down.

"No, and I didn't want to wake her. She looked exhausted when you two arrived. I could hear her tossing and turning all night."

"She's been through a lot this week, that's for sure."

"Do you mind if I ask you a few questions?" Elsa asked, looking at Kearns over the rim of her mug.

"Of course not; I'm the intruder here. Ask away."

"I couldn't help but notice you two weren't hitting it off too well," she began. "I realize it's none of my business, and I apologize if I'm prying, but I'd like to know what's going on between you and my niece? Is there anything more between you other than merely protecting her?"

"Valid question," Kearns said. "No apology necessary. We are not an item, if that's what you mean. In fact, Paige would find the notion pretty amusing, if not actually insulting."

"I'm confused; if she's reluctant to be protected by you, why did she consent to it?"

"It might save you some fishing if I just told you what's going on," he offered.

Elsa smiled. "It would at that."

"I'm here essentially for the same reason Paige is and just as reluctantly; I got convinced to come against my wishes. In Paige's case, it was her father who coerced her here. In my case, my partner hoodwinked me into the trip, on Judge Callen's say-so. She's here to lay low; I'm here to see nobody hurts her. It's that simple."

"Are you a police officer? You look like one."

"I was once. Now I work as a private investigator."

"And you couldn't refuse this assignment?" Elsa asked.

"I'm not in a position right now to refuse work," Kearns admitted.

Elsa took this in, looking into her coffee. After a moment she looked back up at Kearns. "Well," she said, "for what it's worth I'm glad you're here, even if Paige isn't. You look like a guy who can take care of himself. And it sounds like Paige is in serious danger."

"You'd never know it by watching her," he said. "She seems more incensed at having her work schedule disrupted than she does about having a homicidal stalker hunting her."

"You're wrong there," Elsa corrected him. "Paige is a Callen, and like her father, has an iron will; it's genetic. Her frosty exterior is a result of the way she was raised; it's practically her heritage. But I know her and she's scared. She's terrified from the top of her head to the tip of her toes; don't you believe otherwise."

"Are you sure we're talking about the same person?" Kearns asked.

"Don't let Paige's icy front fool you," Elsa said. "I remember the little blonde girl who spent every summer here riding horses and romping in the sun. Under that shell is the sweetest, most adorable person you'd ever want to meet."

"That's certainly a revelation," Kearns said, shaking his head. "I've heard her called some things, and 'sweet' wasn't on the list."

"That's from trying to be like her father. She's spent her whole life trying to impress the sanctimonious bastard, and all it's gotten her is a degree from the school of hard knocks. Underneath that hard-ass armor coating she puts up is a scared kid who's still grieving her mother's death. She portrays herself as a tough cookie, all right, but there's a soft center inside; don't you doubt it."

"What about you?" he inquired. "I sense none of the famous Callen chill in your bones, if you don't mind me saying so."

"I don't mind; that's an easy one to answer. Growing up, my big brother was always the serious one and I the carefree simpleton. He wanted wealth and power and all I ever wanted was a home and family."

"You've surely done all right in that regard," Kearns said. "This place is beautiful."

"I know. Shameful, aren't I? I love the place. Fell in love with it almost forty years ago when I first laid eyes on it, and the love affair never ended. We sold the interest in the winery a few years before my husband passed away. This has been my home since I was a newlywed."

"And Paige spent all her summers here?"

"Since she was old enough to walk. Her parents had a pretty stormy relationship. She ended up here for a variety of reasons, not all pretty ones."

"Is this so terrible a place for a kid to spend the summer?"

"Not at all," Elsa said. "We loved having her, especially my son, Mark. Paige was like a baby sister to him. But even a small child senses things. She knew her parents were having troubles and why she was here instead of home with them. It's a tough thing for a child to have to deal with."

"You mentioned you have a son; is he still close to Paige?"

"No. He died of leukemia when he was sixteen."

"I'm sorry," Kearns said. "I didn't mean to hit a nerve."

"You didn't," Elsa reassured. "I'm at peace with it."

Before either could speak again, Cody let out a short bark and raised his head towards the hallway. An instant later, Paige walked in, rubbing sleep from her eyes. She was wearing an oversized flannel shirt, and her long legs ended in bare feet. She frowned when she saw Kearns.

"Good morning," Elsa said. "Join us for breakfast?"

"No, thanks," Paige answered grumpily. "I just lost my appetite."

Kearns winked at Elsa and stood up. "That's my cue; thanks for the coffee."

Elsa stood also. "My pleasure. I enjoyed our talk."

Kearns headed for the kitchen door but stopped before

reaching it. "Is there anything either of you need from town?" he asked. "I need to get some clothes and toiletries; thought I'd make a run into Napa."

"I certainly do need a few things, but you're not getting them for me," Paige said.

"I have to do some grocery shopping myself," Elsa said, "now that I have guests. I noticed you two vagabonds didn't arrive with much more than the clothes on your backs last night. We could hit some clothing stores and get lunch in town, make a day of it. How does that sound?"

"It would be lovely," Paige said, "if we could go without him tagging along."

"No dice," Kearns said. "I made a promise, and I intend to–"

"I know, I know," Paige cut him off, sighing. "Duty, honor, country. The almighty Judge Eugene Callen wouldn't have it any other way."

"You don't have to be such a grumpy bear," Elsa admonished her. "What you need is a little breakfast to brighten your perspective. How about blueberry pancakes?"

A smile started at the corners of Paige's mouth. "You know they're my favorite."

"How about you, Kevin? Sure I can't interest you in some blueberry pancakes?"

"I'm going to get a shower," he said. "Thank you again for the coffee." He gave Paige a stern look. "And please don't leave for town without me."

"We wouldn't dream of it," Elsa assured him. Paige harrumphed.

As soon as Kearns was gone, Paige plopped heavily onto the stool he had vacated. She stretched and yawned. Her black eye was beginning to fade, and the abrasion on her nose was almost healed. Elsa began the makings of pancakes.

"I don't know why you're being so damned friendly to him," Paige complained.

"And I don't know why you're being so unfriendly. He seems like a fine young man. He has excellent manners and he's very easy to talk to."

"He's a thug, Aunt Elsa. He's as crooked as they come, like all of Dad's cronies."

"I find that hard to believe," Elsa said, cracking eggs. "I like to think I'm a fair judge of character. I get a good read from him."

"Hah," Paige scoffed. "You don't know him like I do. He and his even more crooked partner chased halfway around the country last year, searching for a fugitive and breaking every law they could along the way. They were practically on the FBI's 10 Most Wanted list."

"What did the fugitive do?"

Paige paused before answering. "He was a serial child killer," she said.

"Did they catch him?"

"Yes," she admitted.

"It would seem Kevin and his partner are pretty good at what they do," Elsa commented. "That's the kind of person I want protecting you."

"He broke the law. I'm supposed to condone that?"

"I'm sure he had his reasons."

"You always did see the good in people," Paige said.

Elsa set down the bowl of pancake batter and faced her niece. "Do you know what your problem is?" she asked. She didn't wait for an answer. "Your problem is that you always see the bad. And on top of it all, you have such a black-and-white outlook on things. Life isn't black and white; things aren't always either good or bad. Usually in life, things are kind of gray. A lot of good people do bad things, Paige. And occasionally, some bad ones do some good. Kevin Kearns may have done some things you don't approve of, but he's here looking out for you."

Elsa's brow furrowed. "Despite your lack of gratitude."

"Aunt Elsa," Page countered, "I'm not nine years old. I don't need a babysitter or a bodyguard. And if I did, I sure wouldn't choose him."

Elsa pointed a pancake-batter-covered wooden spoon at her niece. "Wake up, girl. Your father is in the hospital right now, nearly done in by the madman who's after you. And from what I understand, you could have been killed yourself a time or two recently. You're in serious danger. And when you're in danger, you shouldn't be so particular about who's in your corner."

Paige jumped up from her seat, her eyes flashing. "Who told you about what happened to me?"

Elsa's eyebrows lifted in puzzlement. "Didn't your father tell you? He called yesterday morning to let me know you were going to be coming out to the ranch. He explained all about the attack on the beach and how your condo got burned up." She looked up at her niece, who stood fuming over her. "He also told me how Kevin Kearns nearly got killed saving your life." Her eyes met Paige's. "He said Kevin was a good man and that he would protect you. After meeting Kevin in person, I agree with my brother."

"Wait a minute," Paige declared angrily. "Dad tried to talk me into coming up here the day before yesterday and I declined. We got into an argument over it, in fact. You're telling me he called you yesterday morning and informed you I was coming?"

"Of course; I assumed you knew."

"That smug bastard," Paige said. "He took it for granted he'd get me to come even after I refused. He even went so far as to call you on the phone and announce my arrival. And this was before the attempt on his life." Her jaw clenched. "That melodramatic sickbed routine at the hospital was probably an act. I don't believe it."

"Why do you act so surprised?" Elsa said. "When has your father not gotten his way, especially when it concerns you?"

Paige slumped back into her seat and put her chin in her hands. "It's like a bad dream I can't wake up from," she said in a deadpan voice, her anger dissipated. "Some whacko is out to kill me, I'm shackled with this jerk Kearns, and my own father dances me around on strings like a marionette."

"You poor thing," Elsa soothed, stroking Paige's hair. "Try not to worry. Everything will work out; I know it will. Let me get your pancakes ready."

"Aunt Elsa," Paige looked up, a weary smile spreading across her face. "You're a sweetheart, but frankly I don't think blueberry pancakes are going to help."

"Could they hurt?"

CHAPTER 31

At 10am, the temperature had already breached the nineties. Elsa and Kearns were sitting on the porch, waiting for Paige. Cody was languishing at their feet. The front door opened and shut, and Paige emerged from the house shielding her eyes from the bright sunlight. She was clad in an oversized T-shirt, a pair of cut-off shorts, and faded Keds sneakers. Her hair was combed down, giving her a girlish appearance.

Kearns stood up as Paige strode past.

"What are you looking at?" she asked indignantly. "Haven't you ever seen a woman before?"

"Lighten up, Paige," Elsa said. "You're going to ruin a perfectly nice day before it even begins. And you look adorable."

Paige's face scrunched. "I wish you would refrain from saying things like that in front of him."

"Excuse us a moment," Kearns said to Elsa, as he firmly took Paige by the arm and led her to the opposite side of the porch.

Paige angrily allowed herself to be dragged off, not wanting a confrontation to occur in front of her aunt. Once they were out of Elsa's view, she jerked her arm from Kearns' grasp.

"Keep your paws off," she snapped.

"It's time we had a talk," he said.

"I should say so," she said. "If you think—"

"Shut up," he cut her off.

"What did you just say to me?"

"You heard me; shut up. I'm going to speak now. If you don't like it, tough shit."

Paige's face reddened, but she crossed her arms and held her tongue.

"I realize you don't like me. And that you don't want me here. Your inability to keep from expressing your displeasure at my presence speaks volumes about your maturity."

Paige started to retort but Kearns silenced her with a wave of his hand. "I'm not finished, Counselor; you'll get your chance to cross-examine." He lowered his hand. "As I was saying, you don't like me; I don't much like being around you, either. But that's the situation we're in. Stomping your foot and pouting doesn't change things."

"So?"

"So I'm proposing a truce. I'm not saying you have to like me, or even be nice to me. Just stop being such a spoiled brat. Be civil. Would that be so damned difficult?"

"If I don't?"

"Then you don't," Kearns said. "And your stay here becomes harder than it has to be. The hard way or the harder way; it's your choice."

"For how long?"

"Who knows?" Kearns answered. "At least until your father gets out of the hospital. In the meantime, all you have to do is sit by the pool and relax. You can't do any good back in Alameda except draw the stalker to you and your father. And you said yourself you had some vacation coming. Where are you going to go, anyway? It's not safe at either your father's house or your condominium. Why not make the best of it? I promise to do my part to avoid annoying you. What do you say?" He extended his hand.

Paige's expression of defiance softened and she uncrossed her arms. "I must admit, you can be persuasive when you want to be, Mister Kearns. Apparently, you've put some thought into our dilemma."

"And you thought I was just another pretty face."

"I'll ignore that last remark," she said without humor. But her voice and her demeanor had lost their venom. She took his hand tentatively and shook it. "Deal," she said.

"Deal," he echoed. "And my name is Kevin."

They returned to the front of the house to an expectant Elsa. Kearns opened the Jeep's doors for the two women, and a forlorn Cody stared at the trio mournfully as they clambered in without him.

"We'll be back before sundown," she informed the Labrador as the Jeep pulled away from the house.

Elsa assumed the role of tour guide during the ride into Napa, showing off points of interest and naming the wineries as they passed them. When they reached town, she directed Kearns to a shopping center.

"We'll get our dry goods first," Elsa announced, "and our groceries last. Paige and I are going to look for clothes; if you want to avoid the girlie shopping, we can meet you later."

"Sorry, Elsa," Kearns said, "but I'm going to stay with Paige."

Paige started to scowl again but checked herself and said nothing in protest. Kearns followed dutifully behind them as they entered the various stores on their spree. Elsa seemed delighted to be with her niece and doted on Paige as they shopped. Within an hour, Kearns was relegated to carrying their purchases and loaded down with packages and bags like a golf caddy.

At a sportswear outlet, Paige again departed for the dressing room. Elsa nudged Kearns.

"My niece is a pretty thing, wouldn't you say?"

"I hadn't noticed."

"Tell me, Kevin, are you married?"

"No, ma'am," he replied, suppressing a smile. "Why?"

"Just curious," she said. She left him to go across the store to examine shoes, leaving him standing alone outside the women's dressing room.

A moment later, Paige emerged from the dressing room, walking backwards to admire herself in the mirror. She was wearing a brightly-colored sundress that featured a plunging neckline and was short enough to display her outstanding legs.

Not realizing her aunt had departed, she said over her shoulder, "What do you think? Too racy?"

"Not at all," Kearns said.

At the sound of his voice, Paige whirled, blushing. Her eyes flashed in anger. "I thought you were my aunt."

"You're mistaken."

Elsa reappeared. "Honey," she exclaimed, "that dress was made for you! You should get it."

"Apparently Mr Kearns... er... Kevin, shares your opinion."

"You have good taste," Elsa told him with a laugh. "Funny; you don't look like a man who keeps abreast of ladies' fashion."

He grinned, holding up two crossed fingers. "Are you kidding? Me and Calvin Klein are like this."

Even Paige couldn't suppress her laugh.

"What do you say we take a break and get some lunch?" Elsa suggested.

"Good idea," Paige said. "I'm famished. Give me a minute to get out of this dress."

"No, you don't," Elsa said. "You look perfect just the way you are. You're leaving that on."

"You should trust your aunt," Kearns said.

Paige looked from Elsa to Kearns and blushed again, this time deeper than before. Kearns thought he detected a faint smile grace her features. To his surprise, she didn't protest, and they left the shop with her still wearing the new dress.

After depositing their purchases in the Jeep, Elsa, Paige, and Kearns ended up in one of the many sidewalk cafes adorning downtown Napa. Elsa ordered a glass of white wine, Paige a margarita, and Kearns a draft beer.

"The first order of business after lunch," Elsa declared to Kearns after they'd placed their orders and sent the waiter off, "is to get you some new clothes."

"Hold on a minute," he protested. "I only need a few items. My clothes are fine."

"For a vagrant," Elsa said.

"If I have to endure Aunt Elsa's shopping fetish," Paige pointed out, "so do you."

After dining, Kearns found himself dragged from shop to shop. He was forced to try on multiple items of clothing and parade out of the dressing room for the women's snickering approval.

"He's a very handsome young man," Elsa mentioned to Paige when Kearns had once again returned to the fitting room. "He's so muscular and athletic-looking."

Paige wrinkled her nose at her aunt. "That'll be enough of that," she cautioned. "You're about as subtle as a flaming arrow. I'm on to your little games; cease and desist right now."

"But you agree he's handsome?"

"If it will shut you up on the topic, yes, I'll agree; he's not a bad-looking guy."

"Why, thank you," Kearns chirped from behind Paige. He winked at Elsa, who began to laugh.

"You weren't supposed to hear that," Paige howled, glaring hotly at her aunt. Kearns stifled a chuckle.

"Can we go now?" Paige demanded, ignoring the laughter.

CHAPTER 32

Ray left at sundown, ensuring he had a full tank of gas in his Hyundai before departing. His mother watched from the window as he loaded the car with everything he would need for his big weekend. He didn't acknowledge her before he drove off.

Earlier in the afternoon, he'd called the Alameda County district attorney's office from a pay phone and asked to speak with Deputy DA Paige Callen. Ray identified himself to the secretary who answered as one of the contractors who was conducting repairs on her fire-damaged condominium. He claimed he needed her signature on a materials order to continue work. The secretary informed him Ms Callen would be both out of the office and out of town for at least the following two weeks. He asked the secretary for Ms Callen's phone number and was curtly told she could not divulge that information. He asked where she was vacationing, and was again advised that was also information not to be divulged. Ray thanked her and hung up.

He returned home and thumbed through Paige's address book. Under the heading Aunt Elsa - ranch, he noted the rural route address in Napa. Pulling out a map of California, he verified the location as north of Yountville on highway 29, approximately halfway between Napa and St Helena.

Ray used the remainder of the afternoon before departing to take a nap. He wasn't going to leave until nightfall and wanted to be as rested as possible for the journey ahead.

This time, there would be no mistakes.

CHAPTER 33

The sun was barely above the San Francisco skyline by the time Farrell guided his Olds down into the parking garage under his Lombard Street apartment. Not that it mattered; it had been a typical San Francisco summer day, overcast, foggy, and cold. He'd spent the morning in his apartment, chain-smoking and phoning in favors from colleagues who were still on the force and still had access to computerized databases. The Bay Area law enforcement community was a close-knit one, even between different departments within the region, and Farrell was counting on the fact that there was always somebody in one department who knew somebody from every other and who knew all the gossip. Turned out he wasn't wrong.

He spent the afternoon visiting two different cities in the East Bay. He took his work camera with him, an expensive 35mm Nikon with a telephoto lens, and ended up getting lucky and taking more pictures than he anticipated. First, he drove to Pinole, and then to Antioch, both blue-collar suburbs east of San Pablo Bay. As evening wore on, a satisfied Farrell waded through the heavy commuter traffic back into the city. He stopped at a pharmacy on Van Ness that offered overnight film developing and dropped off the two rolls of 35mm he'd shot during the day. When he finally pulled his car into his designated stall in the underground garage of his apartment building, he was tired, hungry, and needed a drink.

Farrell climbed wearily out of his car and stretched. His watch read a little after 7pm. He still had time to get a shower and a cold drink, and make a check-in call to Kearns at the phone number Paige Callen had given him for her aunt's ranch in Napa before meeting Jennifer and her fiancé for a late dinner.

Farrell was locking his car when he caught the flash of movement out of the corner of his eye. He dropped the keys, pivoted, swept aside his trench coat and jacket, and almost had his hand on his Smith & Wesson .38 when the first blow landed. It was more than a fist and struck him on the side of his head with enough force to light fireworks in his eyes and rubberize his legs. He kept his feet, but only because the impact sent him careening into his own parked car.

He could vaguely discern the outline of a very large man looming in front of him, and felt his leaden fingers tug on the wooden grips of his revolver. He fought to bring the weapon clear of its holster and to bear on his assailant.

Farrell's gun never left the holster. Another hammering blow, also from an object harder than a fist, hit him in the kidney from the opposite direction. This one was paralyzing, and Farrell's body convulsed. He slid down the side of his Oldsmobile to his knees, where he remained for only an instant before the first attacker struck him in the head again.

He toppled to the concrete, fighting to remain conscious. He was on his back and unable to move. He couldn't feel his arms or legs, and when his vision came back into focus, he saw two pairs of boots in front of his face. He looked groggily up towards their owners.

Above him stood two men, one of whom he recognized. It was the short, fat plainclothes cop who'd accosted him on the steps of the Alameda Police Department along with Officer McCord, the one who was working in records due to an alleged back injury. He was carrying a sawed-off baseball bat. Next to him stood a very tall, slovenly, stoop-shouldered man whose resemblance to McCord was unmistakable. In one of his hands was a black leather sap. With his empty hand he reached down and removed Farrell's revolver from his belt.

"Former Alameda Police Officer McCord, I presume," Farrell said woozily. The horizon was tilting and he struggled to keep from passing out.

"That's right, motherfucker," a deep voice, thick with fury, replied. "How's it feel to be on the other end?"

"Peachy," Farrell slurred. He was kicked in the stomach for his answer.

"Does that feel peachy?"

Farrell curled into a fetal position, agony rippling through his torso. It was a full minute before he was able to speak again.

"Where's your brother?" he sputtered. "You know, the one who still has a job?"

This time, the kick came from the short cop and walloped into Farrell's upper back.

"I thought you were on modified duty," Farrell coughed when he could again talk. "Wouldn't want you to strain your back."

"My back's just fine."

"So I see. Last time I saw you two knuckleheads, it was at the end of your own shotgun."

"We didn't forget."

"Got twenty years on each of you, and you still come two-on-one with bats and blackjacks. You really are a couple of pussies. Should have known by how easy you gave up your sidearms."

The short cop moved in, raising his cut-down bat, but McCord stopped his arm. Farrell began struggling to his knees. McCord let him.

"You're one to talk," McCord said. "Pulling a shotgun on us; pretty fucking cowardly."

"I did what I did to save a little girl," Farrell said. "I'm not sorry. You two knew the score. You're trained cops and were both armed; you didn't like what was going down, you could have made a move."

"And you'd have cut us down with the scattergun," McCord said. "Some choice."

"I didn't, though, did I?" Farrell leaned on his car and got shakily to his feet. He kept one arm posted on his car's hood, the other held tight against his stomach.

"No," the short cop agreed. "You didn't shoot. Bet you're wishing now you did."

"You're wrong," Farrell corrected him, his breath gradually returning, enabling him to speak in a semi-normal tone. He tried to stand fully erect but the pain in his gut wouldn't let him. "I don't shoot cops; I'm one of the good guys. Hell, I even returned your revolvers."

"Listen to this guy," the short cop sneered to McCord. "He thinks he did us a favor."

"Some favor," McCord chided. "We were laughingstocks. We got suspended for losing our guns. Guys didn't want to work a beat with us."

"Everybody makes mistakes," Farrell said, looking from one of his assailants to the other. His head, though throbbing in anguish, was beginning to clear. "Yours didn't have to be a career-ender. That was your choice, not mine."

"The hell it was. You fucked up my whole life."

"Shit happens to all of us, McCord," Farrell said. "We don't always get to deal the cards; we only get to play them. Your hand didn't have to mean dealing yourself out of a job; you did that all on your own. If it makes you feel better blaming me for your failure, so be it. But I'm done getting fucked with by you, your dim-witted brother, and your half-witted sidekick here."

"Oh, yeah?" McCord said. "You think I'm the one fucking with you?"

"Damn straight. You've already beat the hell out of me; what more do you want? Do I have to listen to your whining, too?"

"Do something about it," McCord challenged. "Call your buddies at SFPD if you still have any. Only thing is" – he showed his yellow teeth – "me and Tommy here have about fifteen Alameda cops who'll swear we're playing poker at a bachelor party in El Cerrito right now."

"Then what are you two assholes waiting for? If you're going to make a move, do it. You've got my gun; use it if you have the balls. Otherwise, get the hell out of here and leave me alone."

"Get him, making demands," the pudgy cop cackled.

"How about you play these cards?" McCord said, his jaw setting. He threw a savage uppercut into Farrell's stomach. Farrell gasped and again slowly slid down the body of his car. This time, however, instead of facing the parked auto, he kept his back to the chassis. He sat down heavily, both hands clasped against his middle. He leaned his back against the tire and tucked his feet under him cross-legged style. His hands dropped between his legs as he let out an exhausted breath, apparently no longer possessing the strength to hold them against his pummeled midsection.

"How do you like that?" Tommy the fat, disability-claiming cop asked, leering over him.

"No more than you're going to like this," Farrell answered, producing the Beretta .25 semi-auto from his ankle holster. From his position seated on the ground, the natural place to aim the pistol was directly at Tommy's crotch.

It was instantly obvious to McCord and Tommy that Farrell had goaded them into slugging him into a sitting position where he could cross his feet under him and access the pistol strapped to his ankle.

Tommy the Alameda cop froze. His jowly face slackened and his eyes widened.

McCord didn't freeze. He instinctively raised his sap to thump Farrell once again in the cranium.

Farrell swung the pistol around and fired. Since McCord was also standing over him, opposite Tommy, the Beretta's barrel naturally gravitated towards his groin as well. At the sharp crack of the .25 caliber semi-auto's discharge, McCord half shrieked, half gasped, dropped the blackjack, and fell to the ground, both hands squeezing his groin. Farrell immediately snapped the pistol back to cover Tommy, who hadn't moved.

"Drop the bat," Farrell commanded. Tommy opened his hand and the bat clattered to the concrete of the parking garage.

Farrell struggled excruciatingly to his feet, pulling himself up via the side mirror of his own car. With his gun hand, he covered Tommy.

"Kneel down," he said once he was standing. Tommy complied. "Interlock your fingers over your head and cross your ankles." Again, Tommy complied. "If you even think about moving, I'll shoot you in the face."

"Please—"

"Shut up," Farrell cut him off. He walked shakily over to where McCord lay writhing, blood seeping between his fingers and staining his trousers. McCord's face was ash white. He looked up at Farrell, unable to speak.

Farrell leaned over McCord, still keeping his Beretta trained on Tommy, and patted him down until he retrieved his old black .38. After ensuring the ex-cop had no more weapons, including on his ankles, he pocketed the Beretta and switched the Smith & Wesson snub to his gun hand. He tugged McCord's wallet from his hip pocket.

He walked over to Tommy, who was crying. Stepping behind him, he placed the muzzle of his revolver against the back of his head. He felt Tommy's body stiffen. With his left hand, he reached around and patted down the kneeling cop. He removed a stainless steel Smith & Wesson .38 from his waistband and found no other weapons on him. He pocketed the gun. He found Tommy's wallet and took it.

Farrell walked around Tommy to a location between the two men where he could see and cover them both. McCord rolled from side to side, his fingers locked on his crotch, emitting animal-like sounds from somewhere in his throat. Tommy was openly sobbing but kept his hands clasped over his head as Farrell had told him.

Farrell reached inside his coat with his left hand and extracted his well-worn flask. Flipping open the cap expertly with one thumb, he put the container to his lips and took a swig that drained half its contents in one long gulp.

He then capped and replaced it, all the while keeping his revolver loosely poised at a place midway between his two captives. This time, when his left hand emerged from his coat, it came out with one of his unfiltered Camels and his battered Zippo. He lit the cigarette and took in a long drag.

"Seems like we've been here before," Farrell finally said. Tommy was biting his lip to quell his sobs.

He set the two wallets in the hood of his car. Still covering the pair with his revolver, he rifled through them with his free hand until he produced their driver's licenses.

"Way I see it, Officer Thomas Lerner," he said, reading from their IDs, "and Former Officer Dennis McCord, I've got three choices." His voice was tight with the pain he was experiencing in his head, gut, and back.

"First choice is to do what you two douchebags already think me capable of: shoot you both dead right now, throw your sorry asses in my shiny Oldsmobile, and dump you in the San Francisco Bay." He took another drag on his smoke. "I'd love to hear what your alibi pals in El Cerrito would have to say when your bodies washed up in Oakland. My alibi is a retired superior court judge.

"Second choice," Farrell continued, "is to open my car door and lean on the horn until somebody in one of the apartments upstairs comes down to investigate. They'll call the SFPD, and you two dickheads will get arrested. I've got enough marks on my body to correspond to the baseball bat and blackjack you so thoughtfully brought. You probably wouldn't do much jail time, Officer Lerner, but your police career would be over, just like your friend McCord's here. A felony conviction, disgrace, and the loss of your pension probably wouldn't do your marriage and health much good. And after the beating you threw down on me with that cut-down bat, your back-injury disability claim would look a lot like worker's compensation fraud." He exhaled smoke. "That's a felony, too." Tommy looked at the ground, afraid to meet Farrell's eyes.

"But there's a third choice," Farrell said, mostly to Lerner, since he wasn't even sure McCord was able to comprehend what he was saying. "You get up, take McCord out of here, and get him to a hospital. You could make up whatever story you wanted about how he ended up with a hole in his gonads. Cleaning your guns, Russian roulette, whatever. Then you get him to rehab and go on with your miserable lives. And count your lucky stars that

I'm one of the good guys, like I already told you."

Lerner looked up at Farrell, incredulous.

"I could have shot you both a Christmas ago and I didn't; I'm not going to shoot you now. Stand up."

Lerner rose tentatively to his feet. "Get him out of my sight," Farrell ordered, pointing to supine McCord.

Lerner scurried over to McCord and pulled him to his feet. He draped one of the larger man's arms over his shoulders. They both started for the entrance to the garage in a wobbly four-legged gait. Farrell stepped in front of them. Both men's eyes met Farrell's, McCord's in pain and Lerner's in fear.

"I won't forget what you did to me tonight," Farrell said, around the cigarette in his mouth. "You came to my home, ambushed me, and beat me down on my own doorstep. It won't happen again."

He spit out his cigarette and pressed the two-inch barrel of his Smith & Wesson Bodyguard slowly against first McCord's and then Lerner's foreheads. On the shorter man's brow, he thumbed back the Bodyguard's shrouded hammer with an audible click. Lerner squeezed his eyes shut, squirting tears out. McCord just looked down.

After a moment, Farrell withdrew the revolver, lowering the hammer.

"That's twice I've had you two numbskulls at the muzzle of a gun, and twice I've spared you. Three strikes and you're out. If either one of you dickheads ever crosses my path again, so help me God, I will end your lives. Do you understand?"

Lerner bobbed his head repeatedly, McCord almost imperceptibly.

Farrell took out Lerner's .38, extracted the cartridges, and stuffed the unloaded weapon back into the Alameda cop's pocket. He did the same with their wallets but kept the IDs.

Farrell held up their licenses in front of their eyes before putting them into his own pocket with a flourish. His eyes hardened. "I know where your families sleep. Think it over."

"You'll get no more trouble from us," Lerner said.

"I guarantee it," Farrell said. "Beat it."

CHAPTER 34

The day's fierce heat was beginning to break as the sun started to dip below the hills overlooking Elsa Callen's Napa Valley home. Kearns was on the expansive rear patio with Elsa, attending to the chicken, potatoes, and sweet corn sizzling on the barbecue. He was clad in a too-new-smelling, crème-colored short-sleeved shirt with a small alligator embroidered on the front, new khaki shorts, and new running shoes. He felt like a mannequin and said so.

Elsa was seated at a patio table nearby, enjoying a glass of white wine and the onset of evening. She had accepted Kearns' offer to prepare dinner. Cody lay at her feet.

After concluding their clothes shopping, Elsa, Paige, and Kearns stopped at a supermarket and loaded the Jeep with groceries. Despite Elsa's protests, Kearns insisted on paying and on a box of doggie snacks for Cody.

By the time the trio arrived home and unloaded their purchases, it was nearing dinner time. Paige excused herself to phone Alameda and check on her father. Kearns poured Elsa a glass of wine, opened a Bass Ale for himself, and busied himself slicing and prepping the chicken in a marinade he concocted with store-bought barbecue sauce, to which he added salt, pepper, and brown sugar. Elsa made a fresh green salad, despite Kearns' insistence she was to relax. She also mixed a pitcher of margarita, telling Kearns she happened to know Paige was partial to the beverage. He wrapped the potatoes and corn in aluminum foil, and he and Elsa retreated to the patio to fire up the grill. Cody stood at Kearns' feet the entire time he was in the kitchen and dutifully followed them both outside. Slipping Cody the occasional doggie treat when Elsa wasn't looking may have had something to do with it.

"He likes you," Elsa remarked, nodding at Cody. "He doesn't always take to newcomers."

"I've always hit it off with children and animals," Kearns said. "It's everybody else I have trouble with."

"I find that hard to believe, especially with your gourmet cooking skills."

"I'm no gourmet. I claim the skills of a bachelor, nothing more."

"You've never been married?"

"Nope. Not even close."

"I'm sorry," Elsa said. "I'm prying again. Remember I said to tell me to mind my own business anytime you want."

"I'm a stranger in your home, so you have a right to know who I am. I'll tell you anything you'd like to know."

Elsa sipped wine. "You're not from California, are you?"

"Nope," Kearns said again. "Born and raised in Iowa."

"I should have guessed by your manners, if not by your accent. Is your family still back in the Midwest?"

"Don't have any," Kearns said, arranging items on the grill. "All I ever had was my mom, and she died while I was in the army."

"I'm sorry to hear that. What brought you to California?"

"That's a long story. It's also not a pretty one. Better save that for after we eat; I don't want to kill your appetite."

"I couldn't help noticing the gun on your hip. Do you always carry one?"

Kearns instinctively patted his waist to ensure his shirttail was covering the weapon.

"Don't worry," Elsa assured him. "It's not obvious. I caught a glimpse of it when you were trying on clothes today. I'm sure no one else saw it."

"By 'no one else' you mean Paige?" Elsa nodded. "To answer your question," he said, "no, I don't usually carry a gun. In my current circumstances, I feel it's better to be prepared."

"I wasn't criticizing. My husband had several guns and did a lot of hunting around here. Do you hunt?"

For a moment, Kearns eyes took on a faraway look. "Yeah, I've done some hunting in my time," he said finally.

"What kind?"

"Big game," he said, flipping the chicken. "The two-legged kind."

Elsa pondered this. "You don't hunt animals?"

"Naw," Kearns admitted. "Not that I have anything against it. Did some hunting growing up. Nowadays, I try not to kill anything that isn't trying to kill me."

Kearns set aside his tongs and refilled Elsa's glass. "How do you know I want another glass?" she impishly asked.

"How could you refuse?" he smiled back. Elsa laughed.

"It's refreshing talking with you," she said. "As much as I enjoy my solitude out here, I cherish good conversation."

"I've never been much of a conversationalist."

"Nonsense; you're a natural. Besides, you were ambushed. My husband was a quiet man, like you, and over the years, I grew very skilled at drawing words out of him. You never had a chance."

"You are skilled," Kearns said. "I think I've said more to you in the past day than to anyone else in the past year. If I was ambushed, it was a pleasant trap."

"I'm flattered."

"Do you mind if I ask you a question?"

"I should mind?" Elsa gasped in feigned outrage. "After all the prying I've done?"

"I was curious about your last name; why do you retain your family title?"

"Two reasons," she said. "I was years ahead of my time in thinking a woman needn't relinquish her family name to her husband, and because I married a guy named Elkenfeldt. Can you imagine going through life with a name like Elsa Elkenfeldt? People would have suspected me of being a fugitive Nazi war criminal."

Kearns' head rocked back in laughter. "You've got a point."

"I wonder how Paige is doing." she asked. "She's been on the phone for over an hour."

"Hopefully, it's good news."

As if reading their thoughts, the rear door opened and Paige emerged. She strode wordlessly past Elsa and Kearns and slumped heavily in one of the plush patio chairs. Cody wandered over and nuzzled her with his wet nose. She rubbed his neck. She also let out a long breath and ran both hands through her hair. As she did this, the shaved spot and stitches over her left ear became visible. She kneaded her temples and made no effort to speak.

"Well," Elsa said gently, "are you going to leave us in suspense?"

Paige looked up at her aunt. "I don't mean to be rude; I suddenly have a doozy of a headache."

Kearns silently left the patio and went inside. He returned a moment later with a glass of water and the pitcher of margarita. He set down the pitcher and handed Paige the water and two aspirin.

"The whole glass," he ordered, dropping the aspirin into her open palm. She complied. When she set her empty water glass on the table, he filled it with margarita.

"Thank you." She took a sip. "This is a little stiff." She winced at Kearns.

"So are you," Elsa said. "Blame me; I'm the bartender. So, what's the news with Gene?"

"Apparently, Dad's doing a lot better," she began. "He's still in intensive care but only because Sergeant Wendt can better protect him from there. I spoke with Dad's physician."

"What's his prognosis?"

"Good. There's still some mild paralysis, but it's improving dramatically. His memory and mental function seem as good as ever. Basically, the medical people think he'll make a full recovery."

"That's great news," Kearns said.

"It surely is," Elsa agreed.

"The doctor said he still needs a lot of undisturbed rest. He told me to stay away. He's under the impression that my presence upsets Dad." Her eyes began to well up.

"Your father only wants you safe," Kearns said softly. "It's not that he doesn't want you there."

"I just want to be there with him," Paige said, emotion heavy in her voice. "I know we haven't been close since Mom died, but now, with the possibility of losing him... I..."

Paige's voice cracked and two swollen tears slid down the sides of her face. Elsa went to her, knelt, and put her arms around her niece.

"Don't feel badly," she soothed. "Whatever might have come between you and your father doesn't matter now. All that matters is that you have each other and you love each other."

"Oh, Aunt Elsa," Paige sobbed, burying her face in her aunt's arms. "I haven't been much of a daughter."

Kearns sensed it was time to get another beer from the refrigerator inside the house, even though he'd brought a spare with him.

"Enough of that talk," he heard Elsa say as he walked away. "You have all the time in the world to tell Gene how you feel. Everything is going to be fine."

Kearns retrieved a cold Bass Ale from the refrigerator and drained most of it while watching Elsa and Paige through the kitchen window. They remained in an embrace for many minutes, and he waited as long as he could before loudly opening the rear door. Any longer and the chicken roasting on the barbecue would burn. He went straight to the grill, averting his eyes to the stone patio floor.

At his arrival, Elsa and Paige stood up. Both were wiping their eyes. Paige avoided looking at Kearns.

"Soup's on," Kearns announced, louder and more cheerfully than necessary. Elsa and Paige retrieved the salad and dinnerware from inside while he rescued the food from the grill.

Kearns seated Elsa and Paige. He topped off Elsa's wineglass and refilled Paige's margarita before serving the salad. Then he lit the two candles on the table, as the sun had fully submerged below the brown hills, taking the daylight with it. He heaped the plates with baked potatoes covered in shredded cheese, roasted sweet corn, and finally, golden chicken breasts dripping in sauce.

Once both women were served, he took his seat. Paige was looking at her plate and didn't see Elsa wink at Kearns and mouth a silent "Thank you". When Paige finally looked up, a self-conscious smile adorning her features, Elsa raised her glass.

"Here's to the chef," Elsa said. "And an evening to remember."

"An evening to remember," Paige echoed. The faint "tink of three glasses reverberated into the night.

CHAPTER 35

Elsa Callen entered the kitchen from the rear patio and approached Kearns. He had just finished the dishes from dinner and was sitting down at the kitchen table. Cody was at his heels and a fresh beer was in his hand.

He'd left the women alone on the patio after dinner. More than an hour passed as Elsa and Paige chatted away in the enveloping darkness. He and Cody did the post-dining chores; Kearns mostly doing the dishes, and Cody mostly eating doggie snacks and rubbing against his leg.

"Want to see something?" Elsa asked him.

His curiosity aroused, Kearns followed Elsa outside to the patio.

"Angelic, wouldn't you say?" she said in a hushed tone, nodding her chin at Paige.

Paige was slumped in her chair, her knees tucked under her dress. Her cheek rested on top of her knees and her eyes were closed. The gradual rise and fall of her chest was her only movement.

"She's dead asleep," Elsa said. "She looks like she did as a child."

"It's probably the margaritas," Kearns said.

He was forced to agree with Elsa's assessment of her appearance. With her long blond hair cascading over her tan legs, her pretty, slack face, and her mouth parted slightly in sleep, Paige did indeed appear both childlike and angelic.

"It's not the liquor," Elsa corrected, "though it may have helped. Haven't you noticed a change in her since you arrived?"

"Actually, I have," Kearns admitted. "She seems to be calmer, more relaxed. I hardly believe it's the same Paige Callen."

"She lives too stressful a life," Elsa said. "Lord knows she had a stressful childhood. But whenever she came here to the ranch, she was always able to shed her worries and just be herself. I see it happening again now."

"Seeing is believing," Kearns said. "And I've certainly seen a change in Paige. She hasn't called me a foul name all day."

"And you thought I was crazy when I told you how sweet she is."

He laughed. "I'll confess to that, but you have to give me some credit; you don't get to see how she acts away from here. She's a real ballbuster."

"Of course she is," Elsa said. "She's a Callen. I already told you; it's her legacy."

Neither spoke for several minutes. Kearns looked up at the countless stars brightly winking overhead.

"I couldn't stand to live in a metropolitan area; can't see the stars for the haze. I'd go insane," Elsa finally said.

"I grew up in the country," he said. "I know what you mean." Silence again prevailed for several minutes.

Elsa quietly cleared her throat, breaking the silence. "I didn't ask you out here to gaze at the stars, Hercules. We need to get Paige upstairs."

"Meaning I do the heavy work?"

"Absolutely; somebody has to be the brains of the outfit."

Kearns laughed again, leaned down, scooped Paige into his arms, and stood up. She murmured but did not awaken. Elsa led him into the house.

"She too heavy for you?" Elsa whispered with a hint of challenge.

"Are you kidding?" he whispered back. "I was just about to climb the Empire State Building and start swatting airplanes out of the sky."

"Don't let me stop you," Elsa chuckled.

Once they mounted the stairs, Elsa opened a door and they entered a beautifully decorated bedroom. Kearns approached the bed and set Paige gently down as Elsa peeled back the covers.

"Thank you, Kevin. I'm sure Paige will thank you herself in the morning."

"I wouldn't bother telling her about this," he disagreed. "She's not that relaxed."

Kearns took a moment to glance at Paige's peaceful features before leaving Elsa to undress her and finish tucking her into bed. As he descended the stairs, he found Cody at the bottom, staring up at him wistfully.

"All right," he said to the Labrador. "Enough with the concentration-camp eyes. I'll get you a treat."

Cody wagged his tail and led the way into the kitchen and to the cabinet where he'd seen Kearns earlier deposit the treats.

Kearns left an ecstatic Cody munching on a biscuit and strolled through the house. It was the first time he'd been beyond the kitchen since his arrival.

The house was elegantly but not ostentatiously furnished. He went from room to room taking in the décor. In one room were an elaborate series of bookshelves, laden with books, and a bulky desk. On the desktop were several framed photographs. He recognized Elsa. As he surmised, she was stunning in her youth. With her in some of the photos was a tall, outdoorsy-looking man and a young boy whose features were marked with traits of both parents.

Elsa's husband and son Mark, no doubt. There were also a few pictures of Paige in various stages of childhood. He was examining an array of shotguns in a handcrafted gun cabinet when he sensed movement behind him.

"Quite an arsenal, wouldn't you say?" Elsa asked.

"I was just admiring your home," he said. "I hope you don't mind."

"Not at all," Elsa assured him.

He continued to examine the weapons. "Do you know how to shoot?"

"My husband taught me a long time ago, but it's been many years since I have. Why?"

Kearns scratched his jaw. "It's good to have a contingency plan, that's all. I only brought a handgun. Good for close-range work but leaves a lot to be desired in open country."

"I haven't forgotten why you're here, Kevin. You're welcome to use any of these guns if you think they'll help keep Paige safe."

"I appreciate it."

"Do you think Paige's stalker could find her all the way out here?"

"Who knows?" He shrugged. "Stranger things have happened. In any case, it's better to be prepared."

"Given what Paige and her father have endured these past few days, I would say that's a prudent philosophy. Do what you think is best."

"Thank you."

"Well," she said, yawning, "I'm going to bed myself. Thanks for a wonderful dinner. And for carrying Paige upstairs. Without you here, I'd have had to wake her up, and I get the impression Paige hasn't been getting much sleep lately."

"It was my pleasure."

Elsa went for the stairs. Before she reached them, she turned and faced Kearns again.

"Kevin," she said tentatively, "do you think the police are going to catch this guy?"

He took a while to answer. He contemplated placating her, but one look at Elsa's strong, honest features put that thought to rest.

"No," he answered her at last. "He's too good."

"What do we do? Nothing?"

"I didn't say that."

Elsa squinted at him, tilting her head. "Gene was right about you," she finally said. "He may be a lot of things, but I will say this: my brother is an excellent judge of character. I'm glad you're here."

"So am I. Goodnight, Elsa."

CHAPTER 36

Bob Farrell lay in the tub, barely able to move. He had an ice-filled towel against the side of his head and a lit cigarette in his mouth. He also had a fifth of Kentucky bourbon at hand without the cumbersome middleman of a glass.

It had been a little over an hour since he'd staggered up the stairs to his apartment, leaning heavily on the railing at each step. Once inside, he undressed, an operation that normally took a moment but tonight took many minutes. Each time he moved his arms, the muscles in his abdomen cried out in agony, and the act of getting his shirt off required a bourbon break. After disrobing, he checked himself in the bathroom mirror. In addition to the jagged hatchet scar running down his shoulder and the circular sphincter gunshot scar dotting his chest, both remnants of his final encounter with Vernon Slocum, he noticed the beginnings of bruises on his sides and back. He turned on the bathtub spigot and headed to the toilet. When he relieved himself, he was not surprised to find his urine pink.

He gingerly checked himself and was comforted to discover no apparent broken bones. He was lucky and knew it; if the weighted leather sap had struck him in the front of his head instead of the side, he'd have orbital fractures around his eye. That none of his ribs were cracked was another gift he thanked his lucky stars for.

After dragging the telephone by its extended cord into the bathroom, Farrell slid into the tub of steaming water and lit a smoke. It was another ten minutes before he mustered the strength to phone Jennifer at her hotel and tell her he would be unable to meet her and her fiancé for dinner. He'd planned to call Kearns at the Napa ranch where he was guarding Paige Callen, but the number was on a folded piece of paper in his wallet, and he didn't have the energy to climb out of the bath and retrieve it from his trousers.

Farrell's eyelids were beginning to droop when the phone's ringing startled him to wakefulness. He picked up by the third ring.

"Farrell," he answered wearily.

"Bob, I can't believe what you just did to our daughter," came the shrill voice of his ex-wife, Ann, through the receiver. Though divorced since Jenny's junior year in high school, she never missed an opportunity to berate him.

"What are you talking about?"

"You know damned well what I'm talking about. Jennifer just called. She's upset because you're standing her up. She came all the way out here from Omaha to present her fiancé and–"

"I'm not in a position to entertain tonight," he cut her off.

"Drunk again?"

He held the receiver away from his ear, took a drag on his smoke, and then a long pull on the bottle. He finally put the receiver again to his ear.

"No, but I'm working on it," he said. "If it's any of your business."

"You're breaking her heart; do you know that?" Ann asked.

"She's not a child, Ann. Jen's a twenty-four year-old law student; she'll understand. Believe me, I didn't want to stand her up. It was a particularly rough day at work, and I'm in no condition. I'll make it up to her."

"You've been saying that for years," she nagged.

"I'm also not in the mood for any of your crap," he said. "What do you want?"

"I want you to know how disappointed and angry I am at the way you're treating Jennifer," she said.

"Point taken. Why do you care so much whether I have dinner with Jen and her crummy boyfriend or not?" As soon as he asked the question, the answer hit him.

"I don't," she weakly replied.

"You were going to be there too, weren't you?" Farrell accused. "At dinner tonight? That's why you're so pissed off about me not showing up. It wasn't Jennifer who's upset over my bailing out; it's you."

The silence over the phone confirmed his presumption.

"Well?" he demanded.

"What do you expect me to say?" she huffed. "I thought for once, just once, on the occasion of your only daughter's engagement, we could be together as a family and be civil to one another. Is that so bad?"

"Yes, Ann, it is. I don't like you, and you hate me. We're divorced, remember? We don't get along. Being together with you under any circumstances is not my idea of a pleasant evening. And bushwhacking me at dinner is not something I suspect Jenny had anything to do with; that idea's got your fingerprints all over it." He shook his head, sending shock waves of pain throbbing through his skull. "And to think I was actually feeling guilty about stiffing Jennifer."

The sounds of Ann as she began crying emanated from the telephone. Farrell rolled his eyes.

"Ann, I really don't need this," he said.

"You don't even know what today is, do you?" she sobbed. "You have no idea."

"Yes, I do," he said. "It's Friday. It's also the day I got the shit kicked out of me."

"It's our silver anniversary," she cried. "We got married twenty-five years ago today."

Farrell's shoulders slumped and his jaw dropped. He stared at the receiver in disbelief.

"That's why you wanted to have us all together tonight?" Farrell asked incredulously. "Even though we can't stand each other? Because it's our wedding anniversary?"

Truth is, he had no idea it was their anniversary. He didn't remember their wedding date, especially since divorcing her.

"I thought it would be... special... for Jennifer to announce her engagement on our anniversary," she bawled.

"That's the craziest thing I ever heard," Farrell bellowed into the phone. "Our marriage was a disaster. And you want our daughter to launch her engagement on our anniversary? Are you nuts? That's like shooting off fireworks to commemorate Hiroshima."

Weeping was all he heard in reply.

"Ann," he said, softening his tone. "Don't cry. I didn't mean to–"

"You'll never understand," she cut him off. "Men never appreciate the significance of an anniversary. It doesn't matter that our marriage fell apart; it began because we loved each other. The anniversary is supposed to honor the beginning, not the end." She cried some more. "You never did understand."

"Ann–"

"Goodnight," she said, still wailing. "Enjoy your booze." The line clicked dead.

"Don't mind if I do," he said, reaching for the bottle.

CHAPTER 37

Paige stretched her stiff muscles, her body aching and disjointed. She'd arisen early, her head thick from alcohol consumption the night before. She splashed water on her face, tied her hair in a ponytail, and laced on her running shoes. Then she crept quietly downstairs and out through the rear door.

The morning dew was heavy on the ground, but she sensed the day would be another scorcher. After executing a series of limbering exercises, she set the timer on her digital wristwatch and set off.

It felt good to be running again for the first time in over five days. She passed the long dirt road that served as a driveway and was ascending a path leading up the hill when she sensed motion behind her. Breaking stride long enough to glance over her shoulder, she saw Kevin Kearns behind her in the distance. Cody was at his heels. He was running to overtake her.

Kearns was shirtless and clad in running shorts and shoes. Paige didn't slow down, instead continuing her ascent with a steadily increasing stride. To her surprise, within a few minutes he caught up with her. Cody galloped alongside.

"Whoa, there," he breathlessly called as he approached. "You run one helluva pace."

"If you don't want to be on stage with the big girls," she replied without looking back, "stay in the dressing room."

"Mind if we join you?"

"Would you leave if I did?"

"Nope."

They ran together in silence over the brown hills. Paige occasionally looked over to see how Kearns was managing and was mildly impressed. She'd deliberately stepped up the pace once he cruised up to her, hoping for the satisfaction of watching him suffer keeping up. If he was suffering, he didn't show it.

She knew Kearns possessed the muscular physique of a regular weightlifter, but didn't expect him to exhibit the stamina of a consistent runner as well. She also noticed the scars. Paige knew she was setting a blistering pace, but he showed no signs of slacking off. In fact, he was smiling.

"I realize you're trying to run me into the ground," he said, finally breaking the silence. "If I concede that you're tougher than me, will you take it a little easier?"

She nodded, slowing her pace. "I get a little competitive sometimes."

"So I noticed."

Several more minutes passed in silence. The sun crested the horizon, and with it the temperature rose noticeably. The trio ran up and down the rolling knolls, their feet pounding on the uneven terrain. The vineyards surrounding her aunt's home below them, shrouded in mist burning off with the sun's arrival, created a magnificent view. Kearns said so.

"It's spectacular, isn't it?"

"Are you trying to make small talk?"

"I guess I am. Bothering you?"

"Considering I came out here to be alone, you could say that."

"What a difference a hangover makes," he joshed to Cody, rubbing the dog's neck. "She was splendid company last night, and this morning she's back to being the Wicked Witch of the West." Cody's tongue lolled as if in agreement.

"Speaking of last night," she said, "I found myself in bed this morning with no recollection of how I arrived and without my clothes. You wouldn't have had anything to do with that, would you?"

"Now I know why she's in such a charming mood, Cody old boy," he chuckled. "She thinks I molested her."

"I didn't say that."

"You didn't have to; you were thinking it."

"I was not. I—"

"Take it easy," he interrupted her. "I carried you upstairs. Your aunt undressed you."

"You better not have undressed me," she said.

"I was only teasing you," he grinned, "because it's so easy to do."

Paige stopped suddenly and put her hands on her hips. Her face was flushed, her breathing was heavy, and she wore a look of exasperation.

"What do you mean by that?"

"Just what I said," he answered, coming to a stop alongside her. He too was slightly out of breath from their run. "It's easy to poke fun at you because you're so damned serious about everything. You've should laugh once in a while. For such a beautiful woman, you sure are a sourpuss."

"What did you call me?"

Kearns walked up to her, his own hands on his hips, and looked directly into her eyes. Cody eyed them both. "I said you're a sourpuss."

"Before that?"

"I said you're a beautiful woman."

Paige wanted to avert her eyes but for some reason couldn't. The moment was laden. She felt uncomfortable but, strangely, didn't want the moment to end. She felt out of control; an unfamiliar and unpleasant feeling to her. She swallowed and looked down at her watch.

"I guess we'd better start heading back–"

Her sentence was cut off by Kearns' kiss. Though taken by surprise, to her astonishment, she did not pull back. She felt his strong hands cup the sides of her face, and his lips pressed deeply into hers.

Paige opened her eyes, not remembering when she had closed them. She put her palms against his chest and pushed, feeling the heat and power of his body. She turned her head, sensing his reluctance to separate and feeling some of her own. Kearns stepped back.

As soon as they parted, Paige looked down. Cody looked up at her, panting. Kearns appraised her evenly.

"I wish that hadn't happened," she told the Labrador.

"I would apologize," he said, "but I'm not sorry."

"I am," she said.

With that, and without looking back at him, she whirled and began to retrace their route at a full run.

"Paige! Wait!"

Kearns started to run after her, Cody again at his heels, but slackened his pace when he realized she was sprinting. He contented himself to jog along behind her at a distance, keeping her in view.

"It was only a kiss," he said to Cody, lengthening his stride.

Paige, Kearns, and Cody ran back to the house. They were oblivious to the watchful eyes above them, concealed within the foliage surrounding a fallen oak. There, under the cover of the scrub overlooking the valley, a silent observer kept vigil.

CHAPTER 38

Ray Cowell was careful to keep both hands cupped over the lenses of the binoculars to prevent a reflection from the glass. He'd learned that technique from reading the Marine Corps Scout/Sniper Training Manual.

He'd been overlooking the ranch since before dawn from a vantage point high on the ridge above the basin. Ray saw Paige, Kearns, and Cody leave the house and begin their winding ascent of the hills. He was easily able to keep them in view without divulging his hideaway.

Ray was elated. He wasn't sure the slut would even be at the address in rural Napa, despite what the housekeeper had told him, until he saw her familiar features outside at first light.

Ray's car was parked on a remote fire trail a little more than a mile from the entrance leading to the Callen ranch, where it was both hidden and accessible. He left his vehicle covered in burlap strips and tree branches, in the manner he'd seen armored vehicles camouflaged from view in military history books. A casual observer couldn't detect the car from the main road, and someone specifically looking would have to be almost upon the Hyundai to discover it.

After stashing his car, Ray had hiked several miles around the far side of the hills behind the ranch and begun his climb to the crest of the hill overlooking it. He'd brought a powerful flashlight along for the nighttime hike, but with an almost full moon found he hadn't needed it.

Ray was dressed in military fatigues. He wore green-and-black jungle boots on his feet, and a boonie hat adorned his head. His duffel bag had been carefully packed but was heavier than he'd anticipated. He'd been forced to stop many times during the early-morning trek to catch his breath and adjust the shoulder straps, which were cutting into his collarbones, along with his father's M1 carbine. He was a heavy smoker, he was unaccustomed to physical exertion, his bruised chest was still sore, and he hadn't anticipated how difficult walking through the woods would be under the burden of his gear. He panted heavily and his legs felt like they were made of lead.

Ray had thoroughly reconnoitered the area via car before embarking on foot, and was comforted to learn the ranch's nearest neighbor was over six miles away. He had concocted a story about hunting in case he encountered anyone but realized that scenario was unlikely due to the seclusion of the Callen property.

He located the perfect place an hour before dawn. It was in the tangle of a giant downed oak tree and overlooked the ranch. The tree and the overgrown brush surrounding it were just over a thousand yards from the rear patio, easily within viewing range using his high-powered Zeiss binoculars. The spot offered superb concealment.

Ray began unpacking his things and setting up his observation post, not expecting any activity at the house for several hours. He was delighted to observe the whore, true to her routine, emerge from the dwelling at first light. He was less delighted to see the muscular man and dog emerge several minutes later and follow her. He couldn't be certain but was almost sure the man was the one who intervened on the slut's behalf the day he tried to take her.

He remembered how the housekeeper scoffed at the theory of the slut having a boyfriend. If he wasn't a boyfriend, who was he? A bodyguard? That possibility concerned Ray.

He planned to observe and gather intelligence today. He knew from his father's lessons and a book he read on the origins of the Office of Strategic Services, the most important weapon in any soldier's arsenal was intelligence. How well you knew your enemy could be the difference between victory and defeat.

Nonetheless, Ray felt ready for what lay ahead. He fantasized he was fighting in Korea alongside his father. The weight of the carbine felt reassuring, and he was certain if his dad could see him now, he would be proud.

Ray badly wanted a cigarette but resisted the impulse to light one. He remembered reading that the Viet Cong could smell American tobacco in the sterile jungle environment at a distance of several hundred yards.

He watched through the binoculars as the slut and her friend jogged steadily up the hill, the yellow dog trailing behind them. Every part of him had been waiting, almost living, for what would soon transpire.

Ray was aware his previous acts had been childish and amateur, not the actions of a professional. He'd planned poorly and executed those plans impulsively. He'd let himself become excited. He'd made mistakes. He would not make mistakes again.

He flashed his nicotine-stained teeth in a feral grin when he looked through the binoculars and saw them kiss. So much for the "no boyfriend" theory. He laughed as they turned around and ran back the way they came.

"Run along home, whore," he said aloud, as he watched them depart. "Get in a fuck while you can. Make it a good one, though; it'll be your last."

He set aside his binoculars and unfolded a camouflage-colored tarpaulin to use as shade. He wasn't particularly tired; it was a byproduct of the residual adrenaline left over from his early-morning exertion, but he knew he had to rest. Soon, the heat would set in and make sleep difficult. He wanted to be as fresh and ready as possible; it was going to be a busy night.

Tomorrow would be even busier.

CHAPTER 39

Kearns sat outside on the rear patio, enjoying breakfast with Elsa. Cody was munching on his own breakfast underneath Kearns' chair.

When they returned from their morning run, Elsa was already in the kitchen. Paige passed her wordlessly, ignoring her aunt's hearty, "Good morning".

Kearns smiled a greeting and went to the cottage for a shave and shower. Twenty minutes later, he was on the patio, where Elsa was laying out breakfast with Cody dutifully at her side. When Kearns arrived, Cody trotted up.

"How does breakfast sound?" Elsa greeted him.

"Marvelous," he said, kneeling down and giving Cody a vigorous hug. "I'm starved."

"How was your jog?"

"Could have been better."

"I figured. The black cloud over Paige's head was a clue."

They sat down together and Elsa poured Kearns a tall glass of orange juice. "You know," he said, nodding his thanks, "sometimes I think I could screw up a cannonball."

"Don't give it another thought," she consoled him. "Paige will be fine by this afternoon. Be patient; I told you this place has a positive effect on her. She'll come around. Besides, it's too beautiful a day to spoil with a sour attitude, even for her."

"Maybe not; I really stepped on my dick this time." He winced. "Pardon the expression," he added, an embarrassed look on his face.

Elsa tossed her head back and laughed. "No need to apologize," she said. "It was one of my husband's favorite sayings. Only, he would say 'I stepped on my dick with hobnailed boots'. I'm not offended."

"Paige sure was," he said, buttering a slice of toast.

"Whatever happened between you two will blow over," Elsa assured him.

"I doubt it; I kissed her."

"You don't say," Elsa said, her eyebrows lifting. "Worse things could happen to a pretty girl."

"I should have known better."

"Oh, phooey. I'm sure if you did it, it was the right thing to do. Damned if that's not just what she needs. A little kissing now and then never hurt anybody."

"You think so?"

"I do. I've known Paige all her life, remember? She always tried so hard to be such a straight little arrow to please that heartless father of hers."

"I've met the Judge," Kearns said. "I never thought of him as heartless."

"You weren't his only daughter. He was tough on her." She sipped coffee. "When you're a little girl, all you want is for your father to put you on his knee and tell you how precious you are. But there was none of that mushy stuff in Gene Callen's home, no, sir. He was as stiff at home as he was on the bench. It's what eventually drove his wife away."

"You mentioned marital troubles before."

"That's right," Elsa continued. "But I don't blame Gene entirely. Claire was a big girl when they met, and she knew what she was getting into when she married him. I may have already mentioned Gene is an excellent judge of character; it's one of his many strong points. He knew his wife was more than a match for him. But his weakest point, and it's a flaw he's passed on to his child, is his inability to express his feelings. Oh, he knows the right things to say, all right, but when it comes to actually relating to people, especially those he cares about, he's all thumbs, always has been."

"Is that why Paige is so cold-shouldered most of the time?"

"Of course. Like her father, she'd rather diminish the importance of a relationship than admit she needs it. And just like her father, she's driven by a fierce self-reliance as a result."

"Basically, you're telling me she's shy?"

Elsa laughed again. "Kevin, you have a way of eloquently simplifying things."

"Just a guess," he said.

"I'd call it an accurate guess. For goodness' sake, she's twenty-eight years old, yet she acts like a bashful schoolgirl when a classmate shows interest. Not a lot of men show interest, I'm willing to wager."

"You kidding? Paige is beautiful."

"She is, but she's guarded. Standoffish. Most guys aren't looking to work that hard in their relationships; Paige is high maintenance. And she can be very intimidating, even for an attorney."

"I suppose I'm too dense to be intimidated," he said.

"One of your strong points," Elsa said.

"In any case," he exhaled, "I was out of line. I shouldn't have kissed her. It's probably why she hasn't come out to join us for breakfast."

"Nonsense. She's on the phone with a police officer from Alameda. I heard them conversing as I was coming out."

"Sergeant Wendt?"

"I didn't catch the name. In the meantime, have some eggs and sausage; for a guy your size, you eat like a mouse."

Kearns accepted a loaded plate. "I should mention," he said, "that I took the liberty of borrowing one of the shotguns. I have it out in the cottage where I can get to it. I hope you don't mind."

"Of course I don't mind. I just pray you won't need it."

"I'll drink to that," he said, raising his glass of orange juice.

The sliding glass door opened and Paige walked out, squinting in the sun. Kearns stood as she approached the table and did not resume his chair until she was seated. Though she nodded as he pulled out her chair for her, she did not meet his eyes.

"What's the news from Alameda?" Elsa wasted no time asking.

"Dad's doing a lot better. They're going to move him out of the intensive care unit. Sergeant Wendt said he'll still be under guard, at least for now. I'll be able to speak with him later this afternoon."

"Any progress in the investigation?"

Paige shook her head. A long silence ensued.

"Let me give you the day's itinerary," Elsa announced, ending the awkward quiet. "On the agenda today is nothing, absolutely nothing. You two are going to sit by the pool and keep Cody company. And you're going to relax; that's an order."

"Sounds like heaven to me," Kearns said. Paige nodded imperceptibly.

"Get your suits on. I'll clean up. The rest of the day is for taking it easy."

After breakfast, Paige and Kearns retired to their respective rooms to change as their host had ordered. When Kearns emerged, he found two towels, two glasses, and a large pitcher of ice water with lemon slices on the table nearest the pool. He'd brought his own towel with the .45 tucked discreetly inside.

Kearns was arranging two deck chairs by the pool when Paige came out. She boldly walked across the patio, but he could sense how self-conscious she was in her swimsuit. She needn't have been.

Paige was wearing a modest white two-piece, which displayed her magnificent legs to perfection. Kearns felt a tightness in his throat as he tried not to stare, and was grateful for the Ray-Ban sunglasses he wore and their ability to conceal his scrutiny. Her long blond hair was pinned up, revealing the shaved patch and stitches, but also showcasing her neckline and shoulders. Her firm breasts rode above a hard, flat, and tiny waistline.

Elsa reappeared with a bowl of sliced fruit and several books.

"Aren't you going to join us?" Kearns asked.

"At my age, the sun isn't very kind. I'll be inside in my favorite chair doing the same thing you two are doing. If you want anything from the kitchen, give a shout."

"Don't you have anything more contemporary?" Paige said, examining the books. There were copies of Cooper's The Deerslayer, Wells' The Island of Doctor Moreau, and Hemingway's The Sun Also Rises.

"The classics are always contemporary," Elsa reminded her niece. "That's why they're classics."

"I love H.G. Wells," Kearns said eagerly. "Haven't read any of his stuff since I was a kid. It's perfect; thank you."

"Ta-ta." Elsa waved, returning to the house.

Once she left, Kearns and Paige settled into their chairs. Paige napped and Kearns read. Neither spoke a word as morning faded into the afternoon. Every hour on the hour after noon, Elsa would return to the pool from the kitchen with a beer for Kearns and a margarita for Paige.

Occasionally, Paige or Kearns would take a dip in the pool to cool off; the temperature was over one hundred degrees Fahrenheit. During the times Paige was in the water, Kearns found it particularly difficult to concentrate on the chapter he was supposed to be reading. She glided across the pool, her strokes smooth and effortless. He noticed she was careful not to get her stitches wet. He also noticed her glancing at him a time or two when it was his turn for a dunk.

The combination of sun, relaxation, and alcohol had a tranquil effect. By late afternoon, Kearns felt his eyes growing heavy. When he turned to look at Paige lying next to him, he realized she was fast asleep. He checked his watch; it read after 5 o'clock.

Kearns stood up, yawned and stretched, and for the second time in as many days scooped Paige gently into his arms. She gave no indication of waking up, and he could tell by the depth of her rhythmic breathing she wouldn't be waking anytime soon. He padded noiselessly in his bare feet into the house.

Elsa sat up from her chair as Kearns strode past. She lowered her reading glasses, her eyes flashing mirth.

"I see all the relaxation was too much for her," she said.

"Me, too," he whispered. "I'm going to grab a nap myself as soon as I put her to bed."

"What about dinner?"

"Can we make it a late one? The sun and booze tend to kill the appetite."

"That sounds ideal."

Elsa preceded him upstairs and opened the door to Paige's room. Kearns placed Paige carefully on the bed. Elsa kissed her on the forehead, and they left her to slumber.

"If you don't mind," he said once they were downstairs, "wake me when Paige wakes up, would you? We could have dinner then. I'll cook."

"You cooked last night. I hardly ever get to cook for anyone but Cody, so it'll be my pleasure. Enjoy your nap."

Kearns retrieved his book on the way to the cottage in case he awoke before Paige. Cody obediently trotted after him.

"You sure are a good fellow," he told the Labrador, who followed him inside. He left the door ajar in case the dog wanted out.

Leaning against door was a shotgun. It was a 12-gauge Remington model 870 Wingmaster with a twenty-six-inch ventilated-rib barrel. It wore the scars of many seasons' hard use but had been lovingly cared for. Kearns envisioned Elsa's husband squatting in a duck blind, waiting for game birds to take flight. He wondered if he'd ever hunted with his son Mark before his untimely death.

Kearns loaded the shotgun's tubular magazine to capacity with four 00 buckshot shells, leaving the chamber empty and the safety off. The government .45 he slid under the pillow of the bed. He stripped off his shorts and slid under the covers, looking forward to the bliss of sleep. Cody, uninvited but nevertheless welcome, hopped up on the bed and lay at his feet.

When Kearns awoke, it was dark. He sat up with a start. Cody was gone, and the cottage door was wide open. He sensed a presence in the room. With his heart pounding, he guided his right hand under the pillow and over the grip of the pistol resting there. He peered into the darkness, waiting for his eyes to adjust to the dim light.

When his eyes finally focused, he relaxed. Standing inside the doorway, silhouetted by the moonlight, stood Paige. With the light behind her, her face was shadowed and he couldn't make out her expression. She was wearing a short robe and standing motionless.

"Paige," he began. "What–"

"I thought about this morning," she said, quieting him. Her voice was almost inaudible, even in the hushed silence of the cottage. She approached the bed. Throwing back her shoulders, she let the robe slip off. Beneath it she wore nothing.

Kearns blinked, unsure of what he was seeing. The moon's illumination danced across her features, lending Paige an almost otherworldly glow. Her hair was down and her face, now visible, was calm.

Wordlessly, she peeled back the covers and climbed into bed. Kearns could feel the heat emanating from her body. She placed her hands on his shoulders, and he let her push him back down. Paige leaned over him and pressed her lips against his.

Still in shock, it was several seconds before he responded. Paige's body was hard and hot, her lips and tongue a moist inferno. There was a barely subdued urgency in her embrace. It was as if Paige had been suppressing an uncontrollable need and suddenly unleashed it. Kearns put his hand on the small of her back, lifted, and turned his body around hers, placing her underneath him. Their mouths melted further. She reacted with fervor, arching her back, leaning into him.

Much later, when the wave subsided and both lay out of breath and entwined in each other's sweat-soaked limbs, she snuggled against him. A long time passed with nothing spoken.

"You must think I'm crazy," she finally said.

"Not at all. I think you're enchanting."

"Enchanting?" She propped herself on one elbow to face him. Her eyes were wide in disbelief. "You've got to be kidding."

He smiled. "I know it sounds corny–"

"I'll say."

"–but the term applies."

Kearns thought she was going to argue with him, but instead, Paige resumed her snuggling position. She ran her hand over the scars on his chest and abdomen.

"These are from the child killer Vernon Slocum, aren't they?"

"Yes."

"He almost killed you, didn't he?"

"Yes."

"Why did you go after him? Why didn't you let the police handle it?"

"It was mine to do."

"What made it your responsibility?"

"These aren't the only scars he left me," Kearns said, touching her hand on his chest.

"I'm not sure why I came here," she said, as if an explanation was necessary.

"Wasn't that you wanted to enough?"

"It's out of character for me."

"Only because it's been a long time since you let your guard down and relaxed. Is that so terrible?"

Another long silence came on. Eventually, Paige broke it. "You took a big chance today, kissing me," she said into his neck.

"I couldn't help myself; I like you."

"I think I'm starting to like you too, Kevin."

"Starting?" he mocked. "When will you know for sure?"

"Maybe tomorrow morning," she said mischievously, climbing on top of him.

Afterward, she fell asleep in his arms. Not long after Paige succumbed to slumber, Kearns drifted into sleep as well. He awoke to Paige's cries and found her in the throes of a nightmare. Her fists were clenched and her body drenched in cold sweat.

He held her tightly and swept the matted hair from her eyes. The nightmare abated. She never woke up, and soon fell back into undisturbed sleep.

Kearns did not fall back asleep, electing to remain awake and stand vigil against her nightmares.

CHAPTER 40

Ray Cowell was not a happy camper.

The last twenty-four hours had passed in agonizing slowness. His body hurt more and his mood darkened with each passing minute. He craved a cigarette so badly, he physically ached. The previous day was the longest stretch he'd gone without smoking since he'd picked up the habit in his fifteenth year.

He'd almost allowed himself the pleasure of a cigarette once or twice, but each time he did, the faint scent of chlorine from the pool below would waft by. Ray decided not to risk the distinct smell of burning tobacco divulging his presence.

What Ray presumed would be a relaxing day of observation and preparation had instead become a miserable period of almost unbearable torment. The sun had poured down on him mercilessly all yesterday, baking his body, soaking him in sweat, and magnifying his craving for a smoke exponentially. His makeshift campsite/observation post, composed of a sleeping bag and camouflaged tarpaulin, had provided shade but no protection from the blistering heat.

Ray emptied his only canteen by early afternoon and cursed himself for not bringing more water. He presumed one canteen would be more than enough. He hadn't anticipated how thirsty he would become lying immobile in the heat of the Napa Valley. And the salty snacks he'd brought along, crackers and beef jerky, which he gobbled incessantly since he couldn't smoke, heightened his thirst even more.

The fatigues he wore were hot and restrictive. When his overheating skin could bear them no longer and he shed them, he found the fleas and mosquitoes more than willing to feast on his exposed flesh. Even the fleeting pleasure of masturbation, which he indulged in as he watched the slut frolic at the pool, was no consolation and left his throat and mouth dryer than ever.

Ray had, during the eye-opening past twenty-four hours, become acutely aware of the disparity between reading military texts and actually carrying out the maneuvers described in them.

His generally poor physical condition didn't make matters any easier. Ray's thin body was flaccid from his sedentary lifestyle and chronic lack of exercise, and his two-pack-a-day cigarette habit augmented this weakness. The uphill hike through the woods from his car to his vantage point over the Callen property the previous morning, under the weight of his loaded duffel bag, left his legs trembling and his breath coming in gasps.

The night, though somewhat cooler, had passed no more quickly. While he welcomed the sun's departure and the decline in temperature it brought, Ray did not receive the increased insect activity with the same eagerness. He spent a fitful night slapping at his face and neck and again cursing himself, this time for not having the foresight to anticipate a need for mosquito netting.

By the time the sun began to crest the horizon, Ray was a mess. His muscles were stiff and cramped from lying motionless for so long, his skin was a mass of insect bites and stings, and his throat was as dry and scratchy as the weeds covering the dusty hillside below him. And his lack of sleep for nearly thirty-six hours sparked a steadily rising tide of fury along with his mounting exhaustion.

Ray squinted through his binoculars, his jaw clenching behind cracked lips. He grunted in satisfaction as he watched the whore and her boyfriend jog away from the ranch, taking the same route as yesterday. He was beginning to think they were never going to leave.

He checked his watch. He'd timed their run the day before, which lasted just under fifty-five minutes. He had plenty of time. He waited until they rounded the first turn and were out of sight to make his move.

Ray got shakily to his feet, his muscles screaming in protest. He felt light-headed and blinked several times to clear the cobwebs from his brain. He put on a pair of gloves and picked up his carbine, which he stared at in disgust. Once again, he became irritated at his lack of foresight and failure to give attention to detail its proper place in his planning.

Ray had replaced the standard stock of the M1 some weeks before, modifying it with a pistol grip and sling for concealment under his coat. At the time, he thought the modification quite clever, ideal for an urban environment where carrying a rifle around grabbed attention. But out here, in the country, he would much rather have had the full-length stock in place where he could shoulder the weapon for an aimed shot if needed. As it was, the carbine's accuracy was greatly diminished by the fact that it could now only be fired like a pistol.

He pulled back the bolt of the M1 carbine and let it ride forward to chamber the first cartridge. It had a thirty-round magazine in place. He was also armed with his 9mm Glock pistol in a holster at his waist and a hunting knife. Ray looked around at the remainder of his gear scattered in the makeshift hide.

The original plan called for Ray to pack all his gear back into the duffel bag, shoulder it, and take it with him down the hill. There, he could discard the bag before entering the house. Once his mission was completed, he would take one of the cars, possibly the new-looking Jeep the slut had arrived in, load his duffel bag into it, and drive himself back to where he'd stashed his own car.

But as he stood up on shaky feet to ready himself for the final phase of his plan, his body weak from lack of water and sleep, and the previous day's torturous vigil, he decided to amend his plan. Ray realized he didn't have the strength to carry the duffel down the hill and still maintain the necessary energy needed for what lay ahead. He elected to leave his gear on the hilltop; he could always retrieve it later after he'd eaten and drunk from the kitchen below. He put on his hat, crouched low, and began to descend the slope toward the house.

His plan was quite simple. With the slut and her boyfriend gone, Ray would enter the house and deal with the old woman quickly and quietly. Then he would wait in ambush for the lovebirds to return and take them by surprise. That had been the original plan; how things were supposed to have unfolded at the Judge's house in Alameda. But then the idiot in the Porsche had showed up and ruined everything. As a result of that unforeseeable occurrence, Ray hadn't been able to finish the Judge and was lucky to make his escape. Sometimes, even the most careful plans could go awry, Ray had discovered.

Nothing was going to go awry today, because Ray was taking no chances. He planned to cut the boyfriend down first, using the carbine, since by then, noise would no longer be a consideration. Then he would deal with the whore.

That would take a while.

Ray felt his groin tighten at the thought of being in the house alone with the slut, with no one to intervene and all the time he wanted. Images of her begging helplessly flooded over him, and he shuddered in anticipation of what was to come. She was going to make up for yesterday.

For all his yesterdays.

Ray covered ground rapidly, getting a second wind. His anticipation triggered an adrenaline jolt, and he found himself picking up his pace. Within minutes, he was at the edge of the patio, and the cool blue water of the pool reminded him of his burning thirst. He resisted the urge to stop and take a drink, as the open ground between the patio and the back of the house was easily visible to anyone looking out through the rear windows. He remembered the woman was an early riser and had breakfast ready when the slut returned from her jog the morning before.

Ray tiptoed across the stone patio and put his back to the wall adjacent to the sliding-glass rear door. The door was open. He could hear movement from inside as well as music.

He took a moment to glance at his watch. He'd used twelve minutes to descend the hill. Ray was well within his preplanned time parameters for setting up in the house before the slut and her boyfriend returned. He peered around the doorframe into the home's interior.

The kitchen came into view. He could see the woman's back as she faced the stove. She was wearing a long flowered robe and slippers, and her hair was down past her shoulders. The smell of bacon cooking made Ray's mouth water. The serene sounds of classical music emanated from somewhere within.

Ray slung the carbine over his shoulder by its web sling and drew his knife. He held it low, with the blade facing out, as illustrated in William E. Fairbairn's Scientific Self-

Defence. The distance between him and the old woman was perhaps twenty feet. He entered the kitchen as quietly as he could.

Ray moved deliberately, willing her not to turn around. His heart was racing, and he was gripping the knife handle so tightly, his hand was cramping. He had only to pass a series of waist-high cabinets and he would reach her. Three or four steps at most, no more.

He was almost upon her when all hell broke loose.

The big yellow Labrador leaped at his midsection, a snarling juggernaut of animal ferocity. Ray screamed and tried to back up, but the dog was already on him. He staggered rearward as he felt canine teeth sink deep into his left thigh. The dog must have been curled up on the other side of the cabinets, hidden from sight at the woman's feet.

The woman whirled on him. Ray was on one knee, slashing at the dog with his knife, trying to fend off the furious attack with his other forearm. He could see his own blood on his arm and leg. He felt the knife sink into the animal's flesh, but the dog gave no quarter. It continued to growl and chomp, the onslaught of its jaws savage and relentless.

He released the knife and began fumbling for his pistol. The Labrador shook its head back and forth with Ray's forearm locked in its mouth, spraying droplets of blood throughout the kitchen.

While struggling desperately with the dog, Ray forgot about the woman until it was almost too late. He saw her swing the pan at his head and ducked at the last instant. As a result, he avoided the impact of the cast-iron cudgel, but instead had the left side of his face and neck drenched in sizzling grease.

Ray howled in anguish as the blazing hot liquid burned into his skin. The pain was overwhelming and he fell back to the floor. His brain was momentarily numbed from shock and his vision blurred. His body still reflexively thrashed against the marauding dog.

Ray was vaguely aware of clearing the pistol from its holster and raising it up. He fired as fast as he could, convulsive jerks of the trigger that emptied his pistol of all eighteen rounds in a matter of seconds.

Suddenly, all was quiet. Ray became conscious of his own labored breathing and struggled to sit up. The Labrador lay motionless across his legs. He had to squirm to get from beneath the animal.

The old woman was lying face down and not moving. Blood leaked from her head and created a small pool on the floor. Ray pulled himself up by the cabinets. He could barely stand. He assessed the damage to his body.

His thigh was bleeding badly, and his fatigue trousers were soaked in his blood from crotch to knee. His left arm was in no better condition; the sleeve of his camouflaged shirt was shredded and torn away. The flesh underneath was a jagged series of gaping wounds. Both thigh and arm throbbed in agony.

His face, however, produced a pain level making his other injuries pale in comparison. He gingerly raised a hand to his left cheek. What he felt there evinced a guttural sob.

His ear was shriveled and tender, and he couldn't find his eyebrow over his left eye. The flesh surrounding his jaw and neck was moist and tacky, and deposited a glistening combination of fluid and cooked skin on the fingers of his gloved hand.

The dog! How could he have forgotten the dog? He'd seen the animal yesterday, trailing along behind the slut's boyfriend as they completed their early-morning jog. Yet he'd failed to notice the animal's absence this morning, when he'd observed them again jog merrily up the trail at first light.

How could he have been so careless? How could he have made such a mistake? It must have been the lack of sleep, or the sun, or the thirst, or the bugs, or not smoking, or being too eager to execute his plan. In any case, it didn't matter now. He'd been stupid, blind, and clumsy, and his mistake had cost him the mission. He had no choice but to abort. He would be lucky to get away before the whore and her boyfriend returned. He certainly knew he was in no shape to deal with him again.

He looked once more at his watch. He had to scrape the blood away with his right hand to read the dial. He didn't know how much time he had before they returned. Ray hadn't planned on having to resort to his pistol to take out the old woman. It was a certainty the whore and her consort had heard the barrage of gunshots.

He momentarily pondered searching the house for the keys to the Jeep outside and fleeing in that vehicle, but quickly discarded the idea. Ray hadn't brought his auto-theft tools with him, and now knew he hadn't long before the duo either returned or summoned the police. Searching the large house for car keys he may never find was now out of the question. He knew he had to make his escape, and fast, before the wounds to his arm and leg rendered him immobile.

He picked up his knife, reshouldered the carbine, and limped out the way he'd entered, through the rear sliding door.

Ray left an easily discernible blood trail behind him as he staggered along as fast as his excruciatingly wounded leg would allow. He bit his lip to stifle his cries of pain as he hobbled across the patio. He felt weak and nauseous and fought the urge to vomit, knowing the act would weaken him further. He knew it would be much shorter to climb the steep hill and go past his observation post and directly to the fire road where he stashed his car. With his badly damaged leg impeding his gait, however, he was forced to take the well-worn cow-path, an indirect but level route.

As Ray headed for the trail, he passed the two cars in the driveway.

CHAPTER 41

Kearns suddenly stopped running and grabbed Paige's arm. They'd been on the trail a little more than fifteen minutes.

"What's the big idea?"

"Shut up," he snapped, holding up his hand to signal silence. "Don't you hear it?"

"Hear what?"

"Listen."

She did. When she held her breath, she made out faint popping sounds in the distance. They sounded to her like firecrackers. Within seconds of starting, they ceased.

"Gunshots," he announced, his voice tense. "Pistol caliber."

"Are you sure?"

"Positive; those are gunshots."

"Aunt Elsa! We've got to get back–"

Kearns grabbed her around the waist as she turned and started to run. She struggled to free herself from his grasp. "Let go of me!"

"Don't be a fool," he said, restraining her. She stopped struggling and faced him.

"We can't stay here and do nothing," she said, her eyes showing the first signs of panic.

"We won't. But running into an ambush won't do your aunt any good. We've got to get help."

She nodded and forced herself to calm down. She realized Kearns was right.

"Paige, you're going to have to go for help."

"How?"

He looked around. "We're several miles east of the highway we came in on. If you run west, opposite the direction of the sun, you'll hit the road eventually. Hail a motorist and get to a phone. Call the sheriff's office and get them out to your aunt's place with everything they've got."

"What about you?"

"I'm going back to the house to see what I can do."

"I'll go with you. I can–"

"No," he insisted. "There's no time for debate. Go get help. It's the only way."

She gave Kearns a last look, squeezed his arm, and took off at a sprint. He turned and headed back the way they'd come at a full run.

Kearns had been a regular runner for years. He knew his pace and his limitations. He pushed hard, breathing through his nose and lengthening his stride over the uneven terrain. He realized he had to reach the ranch, and fast, but he also had to have some juice left in his tank when he arrived. He didn't know what he was going to find when he got there.

Paige sprinted hard. The calf-high grass nipped at her ankles. She struggled to maintain even respiration, the fear in her heart affecting her lungs and forcing her to gulp in air. Images from the past week flashed through her mind as she ran. She tried not to revisit them, needing all her concentration to avoid falling down or twisting an ankle on the rocky hillside. The harder she ran, the more relentlessly the fear fought for purchase in her consciousness.

She remembered jogging last Monday, and the unexpected and savage blow that sent her sprawling into the sand. She recalled the raspy voice of her tormentor when he phoned her at work. She recollected the foul epithets sprayed in orange paint on the walls of her burned-out condominium.

Paige remembered the helpless, defeated sensation of having her stunned and immobilized body dragged across the pavement to her captor's waiting car. She could almost hear the deafening gunshots as Kearns exchanged gunfire with her kidnapper.

The image of her father lying battered in the intensive care unit, tubes running into his nose and arms, danced in her mind. She ran on.

Minutes passed like days. Kearns heard several more gunshots, perhaps five or ten, in a steady, rhythmic succession. These shots were louder than the ones he'd detected earlier, and his military-trained ear told him they were the reports of a semiautomatic rifle-caliber weapon. Two gunmen, or one gunman with two guns? Neither scenario was pleasant. His heart sank, but he ran on, more determined than ever.

Soon, he realized he was climbing the last hill before the final descent onto the Callen property. He crested the hill and descended rapidly, then slowed to a walk, crouching low. Up ahead, less than a hundred yards in the distance, lay the house. He scanned the vicinity for signs of a vehicle besides his Jeep and Elsa's Volvo station wagon, but saw nothing. He duck-walked as far as he dared and then slid to his belly and high-crawled the remaining twenty yards to the guest cottage. He could see the rear patio doors of the main house standing open.

He squinted up at the surrounding hills. It had been several years since his army days, the last time he'd scanned the ground above him for hidden snipers. He could smell the odor of burnt gunpowder heavy in the air.

Kearns wasted no more time. A skilled man with a rifle

would have made quick work of him already. If Elsa was injured inside the house, he was wasting minutes that could mean the difference between life and death. He got up and sprinted around the front of the cottage and dashed through the open door, his fists clenched to deal with a potential threat inside.

The cottage was empty. He grabbed the shotgun, racked the slide action, and stuck another shell into the magazine. He peered out through the door, willing his breathing to calm down.

Kearns didn't hesitate. He rushed from the cottage toward the rear patio door, aiming toward the interior. He noticed the blood trail leading away from the house but kept his focus and the Remington on potential threats ahead. He stopped at the entrance and put his back to the wall. After scanning behind him to see if someone had crept up, he ducked his head inside for a quick look.

The scene that met his view was a grisly one. The kitchen was a maelstrom of splattered blood and shell casings. More than a dozen bullet holes dotted the cabinets, stove, and refrigerator, leaving shattered remnants of food containers and glassware throughout. Lying on the floor, facedown, was Elsa Callen. Cody lay unmoving at her feet.

Still directing the shotgun in front of him, Kearns gritted his teeth and went inside. He stepped over Cody's inert form to reach Elsa.

Elsa was warm and her chest was moving. He carefully rolled her over, and to his relief, she awoke and sat up. He checked her injuries. Her eyes were unfocused, she had a grazing gunshot wound to her hip and a nasty gash on her forehead, but thankfully seemed otherwise unhurt. He noticed there was a large cast-iron skillet on the ground next to where she fell. It had a crater in the center from a bullet's impact and was still hot to the touch.

"Kevin–"

"Sit quiet," Kearns said softly. The wound on her head wasn't severe but, like all head wounds, bled badly. He reached up on the counter and retrieved a kitchen towel and pressed it against the injury.

"Where is he?" he asked.

"I don't know," she answered, her coherence returning. "I think he ran out." She took the towel from him and held it against her head. "I'll manage; check on Cody, will you?"

He went to the dog. Cody had a gunshot wound through his flank and several lacerations along his neck and shoulders. He also had a lot of blood around his muzzle, and Kearns could tell it wasn't his. The Labrador had taken a bite out of someone, presumably the shooter. The dog whimpered in recognition of Kearns.

"It's all right, old scout," he consoled the dog, patting his head. "You did what you could. Help's on the way." Cody tried to lick his hand.

Kearns stood up and grabbed the kitchen phone. Elsa reached out her hand.

"Give it to me; I can phone for help." Her eyes met his. "Cody took a piece of him, and I tossed a pan full of boiling grease in his face. He's hurt bad."

"That iron pan probably saved your life," he said, noticing the nine-millimeter casings strewn about the floor. He surmised one of the bullets struck the pan as Elsa was wielding it, and the impact sent the skillet careening into her own head.

"Kevin," Elsa said, her voice as hard as her eyes. "There's only one road out of here."

Kearns got her meaning and nodded. He handed Elsa the phone and wordlessly turned and left the kitchen.

He tracked the blood trail out of the house, across the patio, over the stone walk, past the pool, and to a path leading up the hillside. The path led in the opposite direction of the one he and Paige ran each morning, toward the main road.

Kearns was about to head back to the cottage to retrieve the car keys to the Jeep when he noticed that all four tires on the vehicle, and those on Elsa's Volvo, were flat. The second wave of gunshots he'd heard was undoubtedly the suspect shooting out the tires to prevent being followed. He cursed under his breath.

Kearns checked his watch, biting his lip. Nineteen minutes had passed since he and Paige first heard the shots. He knew shooting out the tires could only mean one thing: the suspect believed he could be overtaken by a vehicle on the only road off the Callen property leading to the main highway. That meant the suspect's car was probably somewhere near the main road, possibly on the county fire road he'd seen when driving in. He presumed the suspect hiked in over the hills on foot; that's the way Kearns would have done it.

Kearns could easily see the blood left by the wounded stalker on the dusty path. He started to follow the crimson trail but then abruptly stopped. It occurred to him if he avoided the winding path and instead climbed the steep grade directly in a line toward where the path merged with the road, he might be able to cut the gunman off. It would mean running a long way uphill, but he wasn't wounded like his adversary, who was apparently limited to the flat, well-worn path out of necessity.

It was worth a try. Kearns took off at a full sprint, running with all his might. He was grateful his muscles were already warm, but the awkward weight of the shotgun interfered with his stride. He knew holding anything in reserve now would be pointless if he was going to reach the fire road in time to catch his opponent. His legs pumped furiously up the steep hill, sticks and brambles tearing at his shins. He spent the next five minutes toiling up the grade.

By the time he crested the hill, his taxed lungs were on fire and his legs were trembling. His breath was coming in labored gasps, and several times during the ascent, he had to use the butt of the shotgun to break a forward tumble. After fifty yards of relatively flat ground at the top, he began his descent.

Once again, he spared nothing. Going downhill was much easier, and he hoped to make up for lost time. He had to focus intently on his footing, knowing the likelihood of injury from a fall was much greater with the increased speed of his reckless, full-speed plunge down the grade.

Ahead, vague in the expanse below, Kearns could make out the tracing of the fire road. And he could just discern the outline of a vehicle. The car's silhouette became more pronounced as he watched a man, an ant in the distance, stripping off what appeared to be brush camouflage.

Kearns' heart thumped in his chest. His arms were lead stumps and his legs felt like anchors. He knew he was nearing exhaustion but willed himself to push on. He remembered his shotgun training at the Iowa Law Enforcement Academy in Fort Dodge and knew the reliable effective range of the 00 buckshot in his shotgun was no more than twenty-five yards. He hoped the longer twenty-six-inch barrel of the Wingmaster he was carrying, as opposed to the twenty-inch police models he'd trained with, might provide a bit more range. By his estimation he had several hundred yards to go to even have a chance at nailing the suspect.

He ran on.

As Kearns rapidly closed the distance, he could see that the vehicle was a blue-colored compact sedan. The man standing next to it was Caucasian and wearing camouflage military fatigues. By the stiff manner in which he moved, Kearns could tell he was in a great deal of pain. He was fumbling with a brown cloth and some branches he'd placed on top of the car to hide it. The car was parked near a small grove of trees, and if Kearns hadn't seen the man peeling off the vehicle's disguise, he never would have spotted it. He was a little more than one hundred yards away, and beginning to fear the man would hear his footfalls.

When Kearns was almost completely down the slope, he entered a flat plain of waist-high grass. All the suspect had to do was look up; Kearns was completely in the open.

Kearns thought about ducking beneath the grass and sneaking up on the suspect but quickly discarded that idea when he saw the man open the driver's door of his car, remove his hat, and toss it inside. In another few seconds, he'd start the engine and drive away. There was no time for any tactic other than a straight-on charge. He still had thirty or forty yards to go before he was in shotgun range. He was now close enough to notice the man was balding. Kearns put everything he had left into his sprint.

At thirty yards, the suspect must have sensed the motion of Kearns' approach. He suddenly looked up, recognition widening his eyes. He swung a carbine up from a sling and aimed it at Kearns.

Kearns dove, allowing his considerable momentum to carry him forward as he tucked his head and shoulders and rolled. He executed a sideways combat roll in the manner he'd been taught in basic training. An instant later, the sharp reports of rifle fire echoed across the plain.

He began to crawl forward, hoping his movement would not disturb the tall grass and give away his position. He felt and heard the shots whistling overhead, interspersed with the occasional crack and whine of a bullet impacting rock. Kearns knew the military carbine couldn't have more than a thirty-round magazine, but it felt like a hundred bullets screamed toward him.

The sounds of shooting stopped; replaced by the sound of an automobile engine starting up. Kearns knew it was now or never.

He leaped to his feet and shouldered the Remington. He fired his first shot as the blue sedan began to move, putting the bead sight slightly ahead of the vehicle's windshield. He was at the farthest possible effective range of the nine approximately .30 caliber balls contained in each twelve-gauge shell.

The car picked up speed, heading for the main road. Kearns pumped the shotgun as fast as he could and sent the remaining four 00 buck rounds in the direction of the retreating blue sedan. The dirt kicked up by the wildly spinning tires clouded his view and he was forced to watch in defeat as the vehicle vanished from sight, apparently unhindered by the fusillade of buckshot.

Kearns dropped the shotgun and went to his knees. He put his head in his hands. He hadn't gotten close enough to the car to obtain the license plate number or more than a cursory description of the man driving it.

He remained in that position for several minutes, waiting for his breath to return. He could hear sirens faintly in the distance and surmised Paige had been successful in her effort to summon help.

Kearns finally got up and retrieved the shotgun. He walked the thirty yards to where the car had been stashed in hopes of finding something the suspect had discarded. All he found were tire tracks and sheets of burlap covered in grass and sticks. Upon examining the improvised vehicle camouflage, Kearns couldn't help but be reminded of his own military training. Was the suspect a vet? He'd have to discuss that possibility with Farrell.

Kearns began to trudge back the way he'd come and then stopped. Standing at the place where the suspect had his car deposited, and looking at the sun for bearing, he realized that neither the well-worn path the suspect had used to make his getaway nor his own overland route was the most direct course to Elsa's property. A second hill, adjacent to the one he'd just surmounted, was the simplest means. He could see now, from the perspective of where the suspect's car was stashed, the stalker chose the smaller hill for his escape, even though it was a greater distance. He presumed the stalker took the more level path back to his car due to his injuries.

Kearns elected to follow the other route back to Elsa's ranch, the one he suspected the stalker originally used. As he walked, he contemplated what he knew of the suspect. He was discouraged to conclude, despite the day's encounter, that he knew little more than before.

He knew the stalker was smart. He planned his acts with cunning and care. But he made mistakes. He must not have anticipated that Elsa and Cody would put up a fight.

The mist was finally burning off, and with the sun's arrival came heat. Kearns plodded up the hill, spent from his exertion and the energy vacuum created in the wake of adrenaline release. The shotgun felt heavy in his hands. He was almost to the top of the hill overlooking Elsa's property. He could see a large downed tree surrounded by scrub foliage.

When he reached the summit, he was surprised to find a small clearing within the remains of the fallen oak tree. In the center of the clearing was a camouflage tarpaulin draped over some bushes to form a makeshift tent. There was a sleeping bag beneath it. There were also a faded olive drab US Army duffel bag and the remnants of potato chips, crackers, and assorted snack wrappers lying about.

Kearns squatted down over the sleeping bag and from that vantage point discovered a bird's-eye view of the Callen ranch below. Clearly, the stalker had been here observing. But for how long?

Kearns dumped out the contents of the duffel bag. He found an empty canteen, still in its canvas cover, a GI L-shaped flashlight complete with a red lens, an expensive pair of military-grade Swiss binoculars, and several thirty-round magazines for an M1 carbine, loaded with standard full-metal-jacket "hardball" ammunition. There were also a bayonet and a scabbard for the M1 and a mostly eaten bag of beef jerky, along with an empty box of saltine crackers. None of the items would have been conducive to latent fingerprints, and Kearns remembered being told that even the battery inside the stun gun the suspect left at the scene of the attempted kidnapping had been wiped clean. He doubted these articles would be any different.

Kearns picked up the binoculars and looked down at the house below. There were two sheriff's cars and an ambulance in the driveway, and he could see Paige standing outside talking to the paramedics as Elsa was being treated.

Kearns dropped the binoculars and picked up the duffel bag. He knew from his own military experience that stenciled on the bag would be the name of the person who was originally issued the item. Sure enough, on the side in faded block letters was the name Pascoe, Arnold R., along with a pre-Social Security-era military serial number. He picked up the sleeping bag next.

The sleeping bag was a mummy-shaped US Army cold-weather model. Like the duffel bag, its once-green color was faded to an almost tan hue. Inside the bag, at the top of the cocoon where the lining began, was the standard white US Government label the military affixed to everything made of cloth it issued.

Kearns, again from his own army experience, knew that soldiers typically hand-marked their sleeping bags with their own names to distinguish them from the countless other identical bags in their unit. The faded but still-legible handwritten name on the label read A.R. Pascoe.

Used army sleeping bags and duffel bags were items that could be purchased at any one of thousands of military surplus stores across America. They could even be ordered by mail and delivered to your home. But many troops kept their rucksacks, duffel bags, and sleeping bags after finishing their tours; Kearns had kept those items himself. The fact that both the sleeping bag and the duffel belonged to the same owner made their acquisition at a surplus outlet highly unlikely.

He scratched his head. It seemed implausible that the killer would make so glaring an error as to leave traceable items lying around, especially in light of the considerable effort he had expended thus far to ensure his identity was not compromised. Farrell had told him even the 9mm bullet casings found at the attempted kidnapping scene, and inside the Judge's house, were devoid of fingerprints.

Maybe the suspect hadn't intended to leave the items? Perhaps he'd expected to return to his improvised watchtower and retrieve them? What if his hasty retreat, brought about by his unforeseen injuries, had precluded him from going back the way he came and recovering the tools he'd brought to assist him in his psychotic game of cat-and-mouse?

Kearns pondered a moment, came up with an idea. He arrived at his choice by asking himself, "What would Bob Farrell do?"

Using the bayonet, Kearns cut away the portions of the duffel and the sleeping bag label that contained the names. Then he wiped the binoculars and bayonet with the sleeping bag to eliminate the possibility of his own fingerprints. He tucked the identifying tags into his shoe.

Taking a deep breath, he picked up the shotgun and began descending the hill toward Elsa Callen's house.

CHAPTER 42

When Kearns came down the hill, he was accosted by the sheriff's deputies at gunpoint. He was ordered to drop his shotgun and lie face down on the ground. He got handcuffed before they would accept either his or Paige's explanation of who he was. He understood why and didn't complain.

Once the deputies were convinced Kearns wasn't a criminal, he was able to give them a general description of the suspect, his vehicle, and the direction he was going when last seen. It wasn't much.

He learned that Paige had reached the highway and flagged down a passing motorist. The motorist was a San Francisco businessman who, along with his wife, was getting an early start on touring the wineries. They drove Paige to a convenience store where she was able to phone the sheriff's department, identifying herself as an Alameda County deputy district attorney. Minutes later, Elsa's call was also received by the sheriff's department. Two deputies picked Paige up and drove to Elsa's house, with lights and siren, where they made her remain in the backseat while they entered her aunt's home with revolvers drawn. It was a tense few minutes for Paige until the deputies emerged. When they came out with Elsa leaning on their arms, injured but alive, Paige's worst fears went unrealized. She cried in relief.

Elsa was taken by ambulance to the Kaiser Hospital in Napa for treatment and Cody was driven to a veterinary hospital. Elsa repeatedly had to assure Paige it wasn't her fault, as she was loaded into the ambulance. Paige hugged her aunt and promised to meet her at the hospital later.

Soon more deputies arrived, some of them detectives. Not long afterward, a crime scene wagon rolled up and disembarked a crew of technicians who began to process Elsa's kitchen for evidence. Kearns watched as they took samples of the suspect's blood from the patio and inside the house; Kearns ruefully wished he'd left it all.

The deputies wouldn't let Paige and Kearns speak with each other until they had taken their statements separately. Kearns retreated to the cottage with a detective, giving Paige a weak smile and a wave as he went. She remained with two other detectives and gave her own statement, including a synopsis of the events that had transpired in Alameda during the past week, the reason for her being in Napa in the first place. She listened impatiently as one of the deputy sergeants called Sergeant Wendt to verify her story.

Once Kearns gave his statement, he was asked to walk a deputy and a crime scene technician back over the steep hills behind Elsa's property to reenact his pursuit and gun battle with the suspect. It would be the fourth time he would mount the steep hills overlooking the Callen property within a couple of hours, and he was running out of gas. He asked permission to get a snack from inside the house, in the pantry, which was separate from the kitchen, promising not to disturb the crime scene. The deputy consented and let him enter the house through the front door as he waited outside.

Once inside, Kearns headed not for the pantry as he had told the deputy, but into the study belonging to Elsa's deceased husband. There he picked up the phone and dialed Bob Farrell's apartment, hoping his partner was still home. He checked his watch; it was almost 11 o'clock in the morning.

"Farrell," the creaky voice over the line greeted him. Kearns could only wonder how many unfiltered Camel cigarettes and bourbon-laced coffees his partner had consumed for breakfast.

"Bob; it's Kevin," he said urgently.

"Sorry I didn't call you last night," Farrell began, "I was–"

"Shut up, will you? I haven't got much time. The place is crawling with cops."

"Cops?" Farrell's voice perked up.

"Yeah. Paige's stalker showed up this morning. Attacked the house after Paige and I left for a jog. Shot the place up–"

"Paige's aunt?" he interrupted.

"She was injured, but she's OK. Listen, I found a makeshift observation post in the woods where the suspect must have been watching the house. He left some gear stashed there. I found a name on two of the items: a military sleeping bag and duffel bag. It was the same name."

"Why would he leave something with his name on it?" Farrell asked incredulously.

"I don't believe he intended to. His plan got changed after he got mauled by a Labrador retriever and burned with a frying pan full of cooking grease. Got a pencil?"

"I do; go ahead."

"The last name is Pascoe, the first name is Arnold. Middle initial is R." Kearns spelled out Pascoe for him.

"Anybody else know about this?"

"Nope; I covered my tracks."

"Well played," Farrell said. "You're starting to think like a true detective."

"I don't want the cops to bag this jerk before I get my hands on him. I'm beginning to take getting shot at personally."

"We'll get him, Kevin," Farrell assured him. "And before the cops do. That's why we get paid the big bucks."

"I don't care about the money," Kearns said. "I want my mitts around his neck."

"You and me both."

"I've got to go," Kearns said. "I'll call you back as soon as I can."

"Before you go, I have to ask," Farrell said, "any idea how this guy knew Paige was in Napa?"

"Don't know. But he sure seems to know her every move."

"He sure does."

"One more thing, Bob; he's hurt. Pretty bad, I think. He left a lot of blood at the scene. For what it's worth."

"Hopefully, it means he'll be out of commission for a while."

"Not this guy; he never quits." Kearns hung up and raced to the pantry. He grabbed a container of orange juice and an apple, then ran to the front door. He slowed to a nonchalant walk as he exited the house.

CHAPTER 43

It was early afternoon by the time Bob Farrell hobbled into the Alameda hospital. His banged-up body was stiff and sore, and he still couldn't stand fully upright. He sported an ugly purple bruise on the side of his jaw and neck.

He'd spent a busy hour on the phone after Kearns called him from Napa. It was Sunday, and most of Farrell's former cronies still employed by SFPD had enough seniority to be off on weekends. He telephoned virtually every contact he still had at the San Francisco Police Department until he finally found an acquaintance to help him. The only person he could cajole into scanning the records for the name "Arnold R. Pascoe" came up empty. There were plenty of Pascoes in the Department of Motor Vehicles and criminal databases, all right, but nobody with the first name Arnold who matched the suspect's general description and profile.

He showered, dressed, and wheeled his Oldsmobile through the city traffic over the Bay Bridge to Alameda.

When he arrived at the Alameda hospital, he was encouraged by the Judge's transfer from the intensive care unit into a regular room. A bored-looking, uniformed Alameda policeman recognized Farrell and motioned him into the Judge's hospital room after briefly glancing up from his magazine. The Judge looked up when Farrell walked in.

"Hello, Bob," the Judge said. He had only a hint of the

impaired speech he'd developed in the wake of the attack several days previous. His face no longer seemed paralyzed, and he appeared rested and alert. The remains of his lunch sat on a tray next to the bed, and he was sipping a glass of 7UP through a straw. If he noticed Farrell's battered condition, he didn't mention it.

"You look well, Your Honor," Farrell said, shaking his hand. He found Judge Callen's handshake firm. "I see they've got you on solid food; that's a good sign."

"The doctors are telling me I'll make a full recovery. I'm almost there now. I'm getting released this afternoon."

"Glad to hear it."

"Any news from your partner?" the Judge asked. "Or Paige?"

"That's why I'm here. Her stalker paid a visit to your sister's home in Napa this morning."

"Is Paige—"

"Take it easy; she's fine. Your sister sustained some injury, but she's going to be OK. Kevin shooed him off, but the bastard got away."

"Tell me what happened."

Farrell shook his head. "No offense, but I don't know the details and there's no time. I didn't come here to report what happened in Napa. I need your help. Kevin came up with a solid lead, and I need to move on it."

"What can I do?"

"Does the name Arnold Pascoe mean anything to you?"

The Judge canted his head. "Seems to ring a bell, but I can't place it. Why?"

"The name's connected to our man. I have a hunch it's a name that may not be found in any of the current computer records."

"I sat on the bench in Alameda County for over forty years, Bob. A lot of people came and went. My memory isn't what it used to be, even before the knock on my head."

"Can you think of anybody who might know?"

Callen snapped his fingers. "Deputy Charlie White. He was my bailiff. He's still working at the courthouse; he's been there as long as I have. He's an institution. Should have retired years ago but won't. Has no family. Just shows up at court every day, like the rising of the sun. Old Charlie has a memory like an elephant. If this Pascoe fellow is anyone connected to me or Paige through the courts, Charlie would remember."

"How do I reach Deputy White?"

"He lives in town. An apartment off Buena Vista Avenue, I believe. Hand me the phone and I'll call the duty district attorney's inspector; he can give me White's address and phone number."

Farrell brought the phone over to Callen's bed. The Judge paused before he dialed. "You still carrying that flask of Kentucky bourbon around with you?"

"I am," Farrell answered. "You sure it's a good idea in your condition?"

"I'll forget you said that," Judge Callen said, holding out his glass of 7UP.

CHAPTER 44

Ray Cowell lay on the couch in agony, waiting for a knock on the door.

The pain in his left arm was barely tolerable, in his left leg significantly worse, and in the left side of his face and neck excruciating. He rocked his body back and forth, his fists and teeth clenched. Every few seconds, he slammed his good arm into the wall over his head and cursed. It had been a disastrous two days.

Ray drove back to the Bay Area from Napa in record time. As he drove, his mind reeled from the catastrophic outcome of what he'd thought were well-laid plans. As a result of his carelessness, he went from what was supposed to be a triumphant victory to almost being killed at the hands of a feral dog and a crazy old woman. Instead of reveling in the slut's final, glorious suffering, he'd been forced to retreat for his life. He'd fled in wounded terror, leaving his gear behind.

He still didn't know what propelled him around the hills and back to his car. All he could remember was staggering blindly to the vehicle, dizzy with pain and shock.

The whore's boyfriend nearly caught him. When Ray looked up and saw him sprinting down the hill, shirtless and covered in dust, his heart almost stopped. The son of a bitch looked like Tarzan, had a shotgun in his hands, and was tearing up the ground between them like a marauding tiger. The expression on his face, even at a distance, told Ray that taking prisoners wasn't the young man's intention.

Ray saw him just in time. He opened up with the M1 carbine, and when the boyfriend was forced to hit the dirt, he used the time to get into his car and make his escape. It had been close. His blue Hyundai now sported a number of 00 buckshot holes in its body and a spider-webbed windshield, courtesy of the man's return fire.

As Ray sped back to the Bay Area, blood seeped from his shirt and trousers and soaked the seat of his car. He was oddly grateful for the pain, because it kept him from blacking out. He spent most of the drive back frantically checking his rearview mirror.

By the time Ray tucked his compact sedan safely into his garage, he was almost unable to stand. He wanted to pass out, but the searing pain of his injuries again kept him from drifting into that welcome abyss.

Once inside his basement, he wasted no time. He went directly to the bathroom and stripped off his shredded camouflage fatigues in the tub. A nauseous Ray examined his wounds in the mirror.

The first thing Ray noticed was his face. The left side, stretching from his temple to his neckline, was a pulpy mass of raised blisters and welts. His eyebrow was gone, and his left ear was a tacky, raised blob of flesh. The pain was immense, and when he risked a touch, the pressure from his hand in some spots sent waves of torture rippling through his head; in other spots, he felt nothing at all. According to the military first aid manuals he'd read, that meant the burns he sustained were somewhere between second and third degree.

He looked at his left arm. There were several deep puncture wounds on opposite sides of his forearm. He had no trouble moving his wrist, which meant no tendon or ligament damage. But the wounds were gaping and had only stopped bleeding profusely within the past half hour.

His left thigh was dotted with similar wounds. The aching sensation deep in the leg indicated extensive muscle damage. These wounds, like the holes in his arm, had only just stopped bleeding.

Ray knew he was lucky. The dog bites, like most animal bites, would require no stitches. He knew the way to treat puncture wounds was to thoroughly disinfect them, cleanse them regularly, and leave them open to drain.

But Ray also knew from his military field medical guide that the germs from the animal's mouth would be embedded to the depth of the bite and could be expected to go septic almost immediately.

Ray hobbled from the bathroom and retrieved a phone number from a roster of all Maersk employees he'd obtained at work. He dialed the number, and the phone was picked up by the second ring.

"Security," a gruff voice answered.

"I want to speak with Jimmy Chavez," Ray said, trying to keep normality in his voice.

After a brief wait, another voice came on the line.

"Chavez," said the voice.

"Jimmy, it's me, Ray. I've got a serious problem."

"Where you been? I ain't seen you around for days," Chavez said.

"I've been on vacation," Ray said, struggling to keep the anguish from his tone. "I need your help. I'll pay."

"That depends on the kind of help you need," Chavez said.

James "Jimmy" Chavez was a part-time security guard at the Port of Oakland shipyards. He was also a full-time crook. If you needed something and were unwilling to pay

SEAN LYNCH   323

full retail price, especially if you weren't overly concerned with the temperature of the item, Jimmy Chavez was your man.

Ray knew he sold marijuana and methamphetamines and just about any other drug you could think of to the longshoremen at the shipyards, and that his part-time security gig was not his primary source of income. The security guard job merely gave him access to the dock workers who were the main purchasers of his illicit wares.

"I need medical supplies. Painkillers. Antibiotics."

"I get it," Chavez chuckled. "You've been on vacation partying and caught yourself some drippy-dick. Gotta watch out for that funky pussy, Ray-Ray. That shit will make your junk shrivel up and fall off. What's the matter; too embarrassed to go to the free clinic yourself?"

"I'm hurting, Jimmy. I've got money. You going to help me or not?"

"Relax," Chavez told him. "I ain't proud; I been to the clinic lots of times. But it'll cost you."

"I'll pay you three hundred bucks over whatever the stuff costs."

"Shit, Ray; you must really be hurting. Deal."

"You got a pencil to write this stuff down?" Ray asked him.

Ray gave him a list of items, most of which he was reading directly from one of his first aid manuals. He had to speak slowly and spell a lot of the words for Jimmy, which infuriated him. The list included Vicodin, Betadine, prescription-strength antibiotics, prescription-strength antibiotic ointment, hydrogen peroxide, and gauze.

"This must be a serious case of VD you got, Ray," Chavez commented when he finished reciting his shopping list. "Five rolls of gauze? What you gonna do? Wrap up your dick like the mummy?"

"Just bring it," Ray said. He told Chavez where he wanted the stuff delivered. "Get here within the hour and there's an extra fifty in it for you."

"I'm almost there," Chavez said, hanging up.

Ray staggered to the couch and collapsed. His head was swimming and he thought for a moment he was going to throw up. Above him, the model aircraft suspended from the ceiling swooped and dived.

He'd made too many mistakes. Despite his planning and his best efforts at making his father proud, Ray knew he'd fucked everything up. Leaving his gear back in Napa was the final straw; that mistake that would unravel everything. Game over.

As he waited for Chavez to deliver the medicine, he thought about his father and how much he missed him. The aching he felt for his lost childhood rivaled the shrieking pain in his body. How he wished he was back in those days, the days before he became Ray Cowell.

Before the summer of 1964.

CHAPTER 45

The apartment door opened before Farrell knocked. Standing before him in the doorway was a giant.

"You Farrell?"

"I am."

"Come on in," the giant motioned, stepping aside. "The Judge said you'd be coming over."

Farrell entered an apartment with no sign a woman had ever graced it. The walls were adorned with sports posters and pictures of cars. Beer cans, dirty dishes, and soiled laundry lay scattered over worn furniture. A Sam Browne gun belt, complete with a revolver, lay on the coffee table in the middle of the room. There were also a pair of boots and a tin of polish next to the gun. The air was thick with cigar smoke.

"I'm Charlie White," the giant said in his booming voice. He was clad in a Hawaiian shirt with a multicolored stain on the front, and had a day's gray stubble on his chin. A cigar smoldered in one corner of his mouth like it had been pounded in with a sledgehammer. He looked to be somewhere in the range of fifteen years older than Farrell, close to the Judge's age. White stuck out a paw that completely encircled Farrell's hand when he shook it. He pointed to a chair at the kitchen table.

"You want a drink?" he asked Farrell.

"Always," came the reply. "What do you have?"

"Name it," White commanded.

"Bourbon over ice, if you please."

"You work for Judge Callen?" he began, pulling a bottle of Wild Turkey from a cupboard.

"I do. I'm a private investigator. Judge Callen hired me to find the man who's stalking his daughter."

"Callen's a good man," White said. "The best. Old school. Known him forever. Work with his daughter Paige at the courthouse." His brow furrowed. "You were a cop, weren't you?"

"Almost thirty years at SFPD," Farrell told him.

"What are you going to do if you find this creep?" White asked. "Arrest him?"

"Not likely." White seemed satisfied with the answer. "You mind if I smoke?"

"Knock yourself out," White told him.

Farrell lit an unfiltered Camel with his battered Zippo and exhaled a long stream of smoke.

"What can I do to help?" He poured two triple shots over ice and sat down at the table opposite Farrell.

Farrell raised his glass; White did the same. "Does the name Arnold R. Pascoe mean anything to you, Deputy White?"

White let bourbon roll around his mouth a moment before answering. "It does," he finally said. "Real nasty blast from the past."

"Tell me about it."

CHAPTER 46

The summer of 1964 would always remain etched in Ray's memory. The images of that fateful season faded little with the passage of time.

Ray was eight years old, and it was the summer his mother began working at the gift shop on Park Street to bring in extra money. It was the summer before he became Raymond Cowell.

It was the summer of Sissy Levine.

That summer, Ray's dad began working longer hours at the naval supply depot. He also began to spend more evenings away from home with his co-workers. Though he always found time to toss the baseball with Ray or thrill him with exciting stories of fighting the communists in Korea, he was drinking more, and not just his customary Budweiser after work. On more than one occasion, Ray would go into the garage and find his father, bleary-eyed and slack-jawed, with an empty bottle at his feet.

He remembered those episodes very well, because it was during such times his father would yell at his mother. Sometimes he would even hit her. Ray would hide in his room and cover his ears. Eventually, his mother would come in and convince him that everything was all right. By then, his father was usually gone and might not be home again for several days.

When he returned, his dad was his old chipper self and would bring small presents for Ray and his mom. Once he brought Ray an authentic San Francisco Giants baseball cap.

That summer was also when Ray's mom began hiring Sissy to babysit him on the nights she worked late at the gift shop. At first, Ray was insulted that at eight years old, his mother thought he still needed a babysitter. But Sissy, who was fifteen years old, let him stay up past his bedtime to watch The Twilight Zone.

Sissy's real name was Cecelia Levine, and her family lived down the block on Pacific Avenue. Sissy had long, dark hair and had to wear a retainer on her teeth at night, which looked like a horse's bridle to Ray. Sometimes after she put him to bed, she would take one of his dad's Chesterfields and smoke it in the backyard after she thought Ray was asleep.

Ray would sit up in bed and peer at Sissy through his window. She would lounge in the backyard, and he would watch her silhouette outlined against the white garage wall as she puffed away on his father's cigarette. Sometimes, one of the neighborhood boys would come over and the two of them would go into the garage.

When this occurred, Ray would creep in his pajamas out the back door to the far side of the garage. By climbing on the garbage cans stationed there, he could look in through the window above his father's workbench. Through a kaleidoscope of Stanley handcrafted tools, he could spy on Sissy and her visitor in the semidarkness of the garage's interior.

Ray watched as the boy kissed Sissy and put his hand under her shirt. She would moan and rub against him. The first time Ray witnessed this, he was shocked to learn she wasn't even wearing her retainer. He stared, fascinated, as they kissed with their tongues and the boy rubbed Sissy's chest.

For some reason, Ray would get short of breath while observing Sissy and her friend and start to feel warm and tingly all over. He knew Sissy's chest wasn't big like his mother's, but the boy didn't seem to mind. Every so often, the boy would try to touch Sissy between her legs, but she would push his hand away, even though it appeared she didn't want him to stop. It was very confusing.

The garage meetings between Sissy and her visitor usually ended with her announcing that Ray's parents would be home soon. Not only was that her guest's cue to exit but Ray's as well. When hearing those familiar words from Sissy, he would quietly climb down from the garbage cans and resume his place in bed.

One hot July night, however, the routine changed dramatically. Ray was, as usual, perched atop the garbage cans and peeking intently through the garage window. This was the tenth or eleventh time he'd observed Sissy in the garage, and for some reason unknown to him, he never found it boring, even though she and her visitor always did the same thing. He found when watching his babysitter, he experienced tightness between his own legs and a pounding in his chest not entirely caused by his fear of getting caught.

This particular night, Sissy seemed more daring. Not only did she let the boy rub under her shirt, but she took it off! Ray gasped through the steamed-up window, riveted by what he saw. She was wearing a bra, but not like his mom's, which he sometimes saw when she left the bathroom in a hurry. Sissy's bra showed more of her skin. A lot more.

As the boy began to rub Sissy's chest, she shrugged her shoulders and the bra slipped off. Sissy was half naked!

Ray's legs started trembling; the tightness between them had reached a fever pitch. Suddenly, Ray was flat on his back, the crash of the garbage cans exploding in his ears.

Before Ray could get to his feet, the boy who only seconds before had been rubbing Sissy's bare chest was holding him by the scruff of his pajamas, a fist poised over his face like a dragon.

Just as Ray thought he was about to die at the hands of Sissy's visitor, Sissy herself came running out of the garage. Her shirt was now on but her bra was sticking partially out of one hip pocket.

Sissy yelled at the boy, whom she called Teddy, and tugged at this arm. After a moment, he released Ray, calling him "a little pervert". He stormed off.

Once Teddy left, Sissy seemed strangely calm. Ray expected her to yell at him and threaten to tell his parents. Instead, she helped him to his feet and put him to bed.

Still shaking from his ordeal, Ray lay in bed with the covers up to his chin as Sissy brought him a glass of milk. In hushed tones, she told him she supposed he'd been watching her for a long time. He nodded. Sipping his milk, Ray noticed how pretty Sissy was, maybe even as pretty as his mother, even though her chest was smaller.

Sissy explained that what he'd seen wasn't bad, but if his parents found out she'd been in the garage with a boy, she'd get into trouble and wouldn't be allowed to babysit him anymore. And then he wouldn't get to watch Rick Jason and Vic Morrow in Combat! or go beyond the boundaries of imagination in The Twilight Zone. She told Ray if he promised to keep what he saw a secret, she would buy him a new baseball glove with some of her babysitting money at the end of the summer.

Ray finished his milk and promised not to tell a soul. His heart burst with pride that someone as mature as a fifteen year-old would entrust him with so important a secret. Sissy kissed him on the forehead and left.

The events of that July evening seemed spectacular to Ray until an occurrence less than a week later made them seem inconsequential by comparison.

As usual, his father was out with his co-workers. His mother was working the late shift at the shop. Sissy was babysitting and had just put him to bed. Moments later, from his open window, he again heard Sissy greeting her backyard visitor. Ray resisted the impulse to spy on her, because the memory of his last disastrous jaunt was still fresh in his mind.

Ray tried to sleep. He wondered if Sissy would take her bra off again, or if the last time was a special occasion. As his eight year-old brain pondered the status of Sissy's brassiere, a terrible sound reached his ears. Footsteps, heavy and slow. His father!

Ray heard the garage door swing open and the sound of his dad's indignant voice. His angry words spilled through his open window.

"...out of here, you little bastard. I catch you on my property again, I'll kick your ass up to your eyebrows. Beat it." The sounds of lighter, faster footsteps echoed and faded. Then Ray heard the garage door close.

Ray couldn't resist. The drama about to unfold in the garage was too exciting to miss. Would his father yell at Sissy? Spank her? Forbid her from babysitting him any longer?

Like a cat, Ray was out the back door and on his garbage-can perch, shivering with anticipation. But when his eyes crept over the rim of the window, what he saw puzzled him.

Sissy was seated on the garage floor where Ray had seen her many times in the past. She was covering her bare chest with her sweater and crying. His father stood over her, looking down. He had a nearly empty pint of bourbon in his hand and an expression on his face Ray had never seen before.

Ray could hear what he was saying, even though his speech was fuzzy.

"…a slut. That's what you are. A whore. A goddamned whore. Am I paying you fifty cents an hour to fuck boys in my garage? Is that what I'm paying you for?"

His father was using words Ray didn't understand. Sissy cried harder.

Suddenly, his father reached out and snatched the sweater away from her. She stopped crying, and a shocked look adorned her face.

"What's wrong, slut? Can't I see your tits? You'll let some punk kid paw at your boobs but won't let a real man take a look?"

Ray watched in a combination of fascination and horror as his father unfastened his trousers and took out his thing. Sissy started to scoot away, but his dad followed her and cornered her against his workbench.

Ray was hypnotized, his heart pounding as never before. His father's thing was standing up as if it had a will of its own.

Sissy started to scream, but before any sound left her lips, his father smothered her mouth with her own sweater. He dropped his bottle and it shattered. He pinned Sissy, who was struggling terrifically, against the bench. With one hand still covering her mouth, he forced his other hand under her skirt and pulled off her underpants.

Ray was beginning to feel frightened. His father was obviously very upset with what he'd caught Sissy doing in the garage with her friend and punishing her severely. The look of pain and terror on her face scared him. Ray became afraid of what his father might do to him if he learned about his spying; maybe his father would punish him in the same way?

The thought of his father's thing, coming after him like it was going after Sissy, made Ray wish he'd never gotten out of bed. Now it was too late. If he tried to climb down now, his father would surely hear him. His only hope was to wait until his dad was done punishing Sissy, and sneak back into his room when his father left the garage.

His father was on top of Sissy and shoving his stomach over hers with tremendous force. Ray could hear her muffled screams through the sweater over her mouth. Ray decided the punishment must be very painful indeed.

Finally, his father stopped pushing and stood up. He was sweaty and breathing hard.

To Ray's horror, he saw his father's thing covered in blood. Sissy lay sobbing on the garage floor. His father threw her sweater and underpants at her in disgust.

"Fucking slut," he heard his father say. "You ever tell anybody about this, and I'll say I caught you in here with one of your boyfriends. Who do you think people will believe?"

His father left the garage, pulling up his trousers.

Sissy got up, still crying hysterically. Ray noticed that she also had blood between her legs and on her stomach.

Ray panicked. If his father went into his bedroom to check on him and found him gone, Ray would experience his father's punishment firsthand. Forgetting the need for silence, Ray leaped from the garbage cans, ran straight for the back door, and was in his bed with the covers over his head when he heard his father enter through the front door.

Sissy never babysat again. After that night, his father stopped staying out late and came home right after work each day, eliminating the need for a babysitter. In a surprisingly short time, Ray's eight year-old attention span pushed the horrific punishment his father inflicted on Sissy into the recesses of his mind. At least for a while. He did remember the words his father used, and vowed to someday learn the meaning of "fuck" and "whore" and "slut".

Once, Ray saw Sissy. Though her family lived only a block away, it seemed that since her punishment, she avoided the part of Pacific Avenue where Ray's family resided.

It was a month after she last babysat him when Ray saw Sissy at McKinley Park. He waved to her, but when she saw him, she got up and walked away. Her eyes seemed sad. Ray felt sorry for her, remembering the incident with his father in the garage.

But one Saturday, not long after summer ended and school began, Sissy came to the house. Ray was outside bouncing a tennis ball against the garage with Skipper when she arrived. Ignoring him, Sissy walked up to the front door and knocked. His father answered the door in his undershirt.

All Ray heard Sissy say before his father motioned her inside was that she knew his mother was at work. His father wouldn't look at her directly. They went inside and Ray's dad closed the door.

Ray continued to bounce the tennis ball for the better part of an hour before Sissy emerged. He heard his father say he'd pick her up later and that everything would be all right. Sissy only nodded, a sullen look on her face. It looked to Ray like she'd been crying.

Ray never saw her again.

That night, Ray's father drank more than usual. He left after dinner in the car, which was rare, since he normally walked to one of the bars on Park Street only a few blocks away. He came home early, too. Early enough that Ray was still up and watching TV. When he entered the house, he had a peculiar look on his face, the same expression Ray had seen him wear the night he punished Sissy.

The next day, exciting things happened in the neighborhood. Alameda policemen, resplendent in their tan uniforms and caps, went door to door. It wasn't until they came to his house he found out why.

Listening from behind a chair, Ray heard a tall policeman ask his parents if they'd seen Sissy. Actually, he called her Cecelia Levine, but Ray knew Sissy was only her nickname. She'd been missing since the night before, and her parents were frantic. Ray's mom told the policeman they hadn't seen Sissy in weeks, and Ray's dad bobbed his head in agreement with his wife's statement.

Ray would never forget the next time he saw the tan uniforms of the Alameda police. It was after supper, only a couple of days after the first policeman came to their house to ask about Sissy. His dad was in the garage, drinking alone instead of with his co-workers. Ray was on the porch with Skipper.

A big black and white police car skidded to a halt in front of their house. As Skipper began to bark, two cops piled out with their revolvers drawn. Another police car pulled up abruptly behind the first and two more Alameda cops got out, also with their guns in hand.

To his amazement, one of the cops ran right past him to his front door. Two others ran to the rear of the house, and the fourth to the garage.

"Police," the cop shouted, pounding on his parents' front door. "Open up! We have a warrant!"

Ray couldn't believe what he was witnessing. It was just like on Dragnet.

Just as his mother opened the door, a loud voice called out from the garage.

"He's in here! I got him!" The other cops raced to the garage.

When the policemen came out, Ray couldn't believe his eyes. His father was in handcuffs and being roughly dragged to one of the police cars. His head was down.

Ray's hysterical mom ran to the cops, declaring her outrage and demanding to know why her husband was being abused in such a fashion.

Ray would never forget what the policeman told his mother that fateful evening. He told her that Ray's father was being arrested for the murder of Cecelia Levine.

Ray's world would never be the same.

Over the next few days, cops and reporters came and went. People would come to stare at them, many not from the neighborhood. Soon, his mother started going to meet with men at the courthouse on Central Avenue. She took Ray with her, dressed in his Sunday best, but left him outside in the hallway when she went in to talk. Sometimes, she came out crying.

At school, Ray was bullied and beaten. Gradually, he learned things. Some things he overheard, other things he learned from the court documents and newspaper clippings his mother left on the kitchen table. But the final, awful truth would only be revealed weeks later when Ray went to the courthouse each day for the trial.

Ray told his mom he didn't like to go to the courthouse because he didn't like to see his father handcuffed. But his mother insisted on taking him, telling him it was very important. The lawyers told her it was good for the jury to see Ray and his mother so they knew he was a family man; it might bring sympathy. Sympathy might mean mercy.

It was in that awful courthouse that eight year-old Raymond Pascoe learned the truth about his father and came of age. It was just before Christmas, 1964.

Ray learned the strangled body of Cecelia Levine had been discovered two days after her disappearance by a sanitation worker at the Alameda dump, or Mount Trashmore, as it was nicknamed by the locals.

During the homicide investigation, Alameda police detectives discovered that Cecelia Levine, like countless teenaged girls, kept a diary. In that journal, along with accounts of her first kiss and her rendezvous with her boyfriend while babysitting at the Pascoe household, was a heartrending account of her rape at the hands of Ray's father, Arnold Pascoe. Also of her discovery six weeks later that she was pregnant.

The prosecuting attorney read the journal to the jury, page by tragic page. Desperate to keep the news from her parents, and with nowhere else to turn, Cecelia had approached her rapist for the necessary funds to finance an abortion. Cecelia's diary entries chronicled her despair and, in one particularly tortured entry, her contemplation of suicide. The journal's final entry, dated the day of her disappearance, contained a jubilant announcement that her assailant was not only going to pay for the abortion but drive her to a clinic in Oakland to undergo the procedure.

Ray watched a parade of witnesses corroborate Cecelia's journal. He even heard Teddy, the boy who visited Sissy in the garage, testify to the truth of her journal entries.

Ray learned things. He learned that Cecelia was in fact going to have a baby at the time of her death, and the blood type of the unborn fetus, whatever that was, matched his father. He learned tire tracks at the landfill matched the family car. He learned that fibers from Cecelia's sweater were found in the garage.

But the most damning evidence came from the accused himself. In a drunken stupor on the night of his arrest, Ray's father made incriminating statements that mortified the jury and sealed his fate.

"Fucking whore," he called Sissy. "Slut." Those were his father's words, repeated for the jury by the cops who'd heard his father utter them the night of his arrest.

Ray told no one of what he'd witnessed between his father and Sissy. He kept what he knew locked inside him. He felt sorry for Sissy because she was dead. But he felt sorry for his father, too, and couldn't understand why everyone seemed to hate him.

Of course his father had to punish Sissy. Didn't they understand? She was a whore and a slut; that's what his father had said. But in the end, it didn't matter. Ray's idyllic life was over.

Ray could no longer play outside. His mother kept him indoors to prevent him from hearing what people yelled as they drove by. But Ray heard anyway.

The only good thing Ray remembered from those terrible days at the courthouse was the pretty blonde girl. She was about kindergarten age, and each day at lunchtime, while the courtroom was empty, the little girl would come with her mother. The massive bailiff would lift her up to the huge desk where the judge sat.

Ray and his mother always remained inside the courtroom, while everyone else, even his father's lawyers, went out to dine during the noontime break. He would watch as the girl handed the judge, a tall man with blond hair who walked with a limp, a brown paper bag containing deviled eggs or sandwiches or fruit. It reminded him of the times when he and his dad were building airplane models in the basement, and his mother would bring them down sandwiches and cookies. The little girl had freckles. She was very pretty.

She was obviously the judge's daughter, and the way he doted on her made Ray think of the times his father threw the baseball with him and rubbed his head, or wrestled with him in the backyard.

Ray learned the little blonde girl's name. He heard her father say it almost every day of the trial during lunchtime.

Her name was Paige.

Soon, the trial was over. On the last day, Ray's mother dressed him extra carefully and told him that today, of all days, it was important he look his best. As Ray stood in his now-familiar spot in the courtroom, his mother squeezed his hand so tightly it hurt.

The judge told his father to stand up. When he did, the judge spoke. Ray would never forget the words he said.

"Arnold Roy Pascoe, you have been fairly tried and duly convicted by a jury of your peers for the crime of rape and two counts of murder in the first degree. Do you have anything to say before I pass sentence?"

Ray would see his father's defeated expression in his nightmares for years to come.

"I got nothing to say."

"Very well. You are hereby sentenced to the maximum penalty the law allows me to levy for the heinous crimes you have committed. You will be remanded forthwith to the correctional facility at San Quentin, and at a time yet to be determined, you will be put to death. I will not ask God to have mercy on your soul, praying instead He direct that sentiment to the family of the child, and unborn child, you mercilessly destroyed." The sound of the gavel echoed like a gunshot.

The last image Ray Pascoe saw of his dad was when the bailiff led him away in chains. His father wouldn't look him in the eye.

As the crowd bleated and flashbulbs popped, Ray must have fainted. The next thing he remembered was being in his mother's arms outside the courthouse as she pushed her way through the throngs to the car.

After that, Ray's life became a waking nightmare. Without the financial resources to move away, his mother changed their names back to her maiden name, Cowell. It was the end of Ray's childhood.

Arnold Pascoe sent almost daily letters to his family from his new home on San Quentin's infamous death row, but Ray's mother never opened them. She tore them up and threw them away. In time, the letters stopped coming.

But death by lethal inhalation was not to be for Arnold Roy Pascoe. Fortunately for him, the last person to die in the gas chamber in the State of California, Aaron Mitchell, was put to death in April of 1967. San Quentin's "Green Room" went vacant as the Supreme Court examined the constitutionality of the death sentence. Arnold Pascoe and one hundred and ninety-two other death row inmates were subsequently integrated into the general prison population in 1972.

Ray, by then in his teens, worked long hours delivering newspapers, repairing electronics, and enduring the daily hell that had become his existence. Within a few years, the beatings and taunting stopped, replaced by sidelong glances and hushed whispers.

In June of 1973, just before Ray's seventeenth birthday, word came to the Cowells that Arnold R. Pascoe had become a statistic. He had become one of the more than two dozen inmates murdered behind the walls of San Quentin that year. The Department of Corrections official who showed up at the house to notify Ray's mother was met with drunken laughter. The official turned over Arnold Pascoe's few personal effects to Ray; his mother was too intoxicated to sign for them. Only one of his father's meager prison possessions he kept.

A faded black-and-white photograph of a small, smiling boy and his father.

CHAPTER 47

Kearns spent the hour after he hung up from Farrell hiking in the hills with sheriff's personnel. He led them to the observation post overlooking the property and to the gear the suspect had left there. The evidence technician photographed everything in place, and then he and the deputy carefully began examining the items with latex-gloved hands. Kearns said nothing when the deputy held up the sleeping bag and duffel and perused the cut-out patches of cloth where the names had been.

"This guy didn't take chances," the deputy remarked, poking a finger through the hole in the duffel bag where Kearns removed the name tag. "We'll probably find some of his hair inside the bag, but without a body to match it up to, we're out of luck."

Next, Kearns led them along the route he pursued the suspect and to the place where the suspect stashed his car. They recovered the burlap vehicle camouflage. They also found Kearns' ejected shotgun shells, as well as a lot of expended .30 carbine casings from the suspect's weapon.

"Looks like it went down just like you said," the deputy observed, standing up.

"I wasn't lying," Kearns said.

"Didn't say you was. You know how it is; we gotta verify your story."

342

"I know."

Thankfully, they were spared the long hike back. The deputy called someone on his handheld transceiver and within a few minutes, a sheriff's patrol car came cruising up the fire road. Kearns and the deputy rode back; the evidence technician remained to make a plaster casting of the tire tracks left by the suspect's vehicle.

When they returned to Elsa's house, the crime scene technicians were done inside her kitchen and were outside packing up their gear. Paige was inside cleaning up. At Kearns' request, the deputy had his dispatcher phone the Napa office of the car rental agency he'd rented the Jeep from to report the damage to the tires. The deputy also had his dispatcher phone a tire outlet in Napa to come and replace the tires on Elsa's Volvo. The sheriff's department wanted to keep the tires from Elsa's car as well as from the Jeep for evidence. It was by then early afternoon.

Kearns excused himself and entered the kitchen. He began picking up debris and glass alongside Paige.

"Are you OK?"

She nodded, looking around at the carnage. "This is all my fault."

"You can't blame yourself," he said.

"Can't I? If I hadn't come here, none of this would have happened. Aunt Elsa took me in and almost got killed for her hospitality."

"What about this psycho who's after you? You don't think he had something to do with it?"

Paige turned to face him. "Of course he did. But it was Dad, and Sergeant Wendt, and you and your partner who convinced me to come. I was stupid enough to do it, and I dragged the killer along with me. But Aunt Elsa was the one who paid for it." She turned away.

"It's not your fault," he said to her back. "It isn't."

She said nothing in reply. It took a moment for Kearns to realize she wasn't speaking because she was silently crying. Her shoulders slumped and tears rolled down her cheeks. He was reminded of what Elsa had told him about how the ranch melted away Paige's armor to reveal the innocence of the girl inside.

He stepped closer and put his hands on her shoulders. Her crying became more pronounced. He turned Paige around and pulled her into his chest. Instead of resisting, which he half expected, she melted into him and buried her face in his neck. Minutes passed.

A deputy poked his head in the rear door, started to say something, but backed out when he saw Kearns' expression. Within a few minutes, Paige had composed herself and stepped back from Kearns. As she did, she looked into his eyes.

"Go upstairs and take a hot bath," Kearns told her. "Get yourself cleaned up and changed. I'll see the deputies off. Then I'll finish cleaning up the kitchen. Pretty soon, the car will be fixed and we can go get Elsa and Cody."

"OK," she said. She started to walk away. Paige suddenly turned, leaned forward, and kissed Kearns tenderly on the lips. "Thank you," she said. She went upstairs. He took a deep breath and watched her go.

Once the sheriff's deputies had left, Kearns finished cleaning up the kitchen. He made sure to wipe all the blood from the cabinets and walls, and mopped the floor with ammonia.

As he was finishing, two vehicles drove up. One was a truck from a tire store, and the other was a large tow truck. The two occupants of the tow truck busied themselves with changing the tires to Elsa's Volvo, using the winch to lift first one end of the station wagon and then the other. He paid the tow truck crew out of the money he'd gotten from Farrell. When that was done, they repeated the procedure with the rented Jeep. Kearns signed some papers and within an hour, they were done and gone.

He next went into the guest cottage and emerged a half hour later, shaved and showered. Kearns was wearing jeans, boots, and a T-shirt; a jacket was slung over his shoulder. It would be twenty degrees colder in the Bay Area than in Napa Valley. His .45 was tucked in his waistband under the shirt. He packed his remaining things in the Jeep. By the time he took out the garbage and ensured the cottage, Elsa's Volvo, and the house were locked up, Paige was coming downstairs with her hair in a ponytail and dressed for travel.

"Let's go," he greeted her, extending his hand.

"OK," she said, taking it.

Thirty minutes later, they met Elsa in the emergency room of the Kaiser Hospital in Napa. She was still wearing her bloody bathrobe but looked remarkably healthy given what she'd been through. Her head was bandaged and she had a slight limp, but she seemed her usual vibrant self. A sheriff's deputy was wrapping up her statement.

"Elsa," Paige ran to her. They embraced. "I'm so sorry."

"What do you have to be sorry for, girl?"

"This is all my fault. If I hadn't—"

"I don't want to hear that kind of talk," Elsa cut her off. "Not a word. This wasn't anybody's fault except that lunatic who's after you." Paige nodded and they embraced again. For a moment, both looked like they were going to cry. Kearns stared at his shoes.

"Where's Cody?" Elsa asked the deputy.

"Dog's at the Napa Valley Veterinary Hospital," he said. He provided directions.

Elsa signed herself out of the hospital and twenty minutes later, they had Cody in the back seat of the Jeep and were on the way back to her house. The veterinarian who treated Cody told them the dog received over forty stitches and had a bullet pass through and through his flank but would make a full recovery. Kearns paid the vet, using most of the remaining cash he'd been given by Farrell, leaving him with less than a hundred dollars. Once in the Jeep, a groggy Cody nuzzled against Elsa and fell asleep. An IV bag hung from the coat hook, its translucent tube ending under a piece of tape on one of the Lab's forelegs.

"So, what's the plan now?" Elsa asked when they were in the car.

"I've got to get back," Kearns said. "My partner and I have work to do."

"To catch this madman?"

"Something like that."

"What about you, Paige?"

"I'm going with him."

"Wouldn't it be safer for you to stay out here at the ranch with me and Cody? Surely you don't think after what happened today, the stalker will be coming back to Napa anytime soon?"

"Your aunt's got a point," Kearns said. "You'd probably be safer here than in Alameda."

"Maybe," Paige said. "But I've got to go back. I can't run from this; I see that now. And I can't expose anyone else to it by being around me. Look what happened to Dad, Mrs Reyes, my co-worker, and now Aunt Elsa? All because they were connected to me." She placed a hand on Kearns' arm. "This is mine; I've got to see this through to the end." She looked directly at Kearns. "Like you and Vernon Slocum."

Kearns nodded his assent.

When they arrived back at Elsa's house, Kearns carried Cody inside and put him into his doggie bed. He removed the empty IV fluid bag as he was instructed by the veterinarian and left the dog's antibiotics on the kitchen table. Paige helped Elsa inside.

"You two get going," Elsa insisted. "I'll be all right. But I expect a phone call from you every day."

"Of course," Paige said, her eyes watering again. "I love you, Aunt Elsa."

"You know I love you, too," she answered, taking her niece's face in both hands. "Why don't you come and live here permanently? At least take a few months off and rest. You know money isn't an issue with either Gene or I. Come stay here with me."

"I can't," Paige said. "My life is back in Alameda."

"Your life is killing you, honey. You can make a new one here."

"I can't," Paige said again.

"Will you at least think about it?" Elsa pressed.

"OK," Paige relented, to placate her aunt. "I'll give it some thought."

"May I use your phone?" Kearns asked.

"Of course. Use the one in the study."

Kearns left Paige and her aunt to continue their conversation. He retreated to the study and closed the door, then grabbed the phone and dialed Farrell's apartment. To his relief, Farrell picked up.

"Kevin," Farrell answered. "I'm glad to hear your voice. I've been waiting for your call."

"Sorry it took so long. It's been a busy afternoon."

"You ain't the only one who's been busy. How soon can you get here?"

Kearns checked his watch; it was 6.37pm. "If I push it, under an hour."

"Push it; we've got work to do."

"You got a line on our stalker?"

"Maybe. Meet me at the Judge's house as soon as you can."

"On my way."

Kearns ended the call and returned to the women. "We have to get on the road," he announced. He faced Elsa.

"I'm sorry for what happened here, and the trouble we brought into your home."

"Nonsense," she said, looking at her niece. "If you can't count on family when you're in trouble, what good are they?" Elsa looked back to Kearns. "I truly enjoyed meeting you, Kevin," she said. She gave Paige a wink. "I hope to see you again."

"Thank you for your hospitality," he said, extending his hand. "It was an honor to meet you."

"Put that handshake away," Elsa ordered, grabbing Kearns in a bear hug. He smiled awkwardly.

"Take good care of my niece," she ordered him. Her eyes twinkled when she stepped away. "Though I suspect you already have."

Kearns' complexion reddened. He thought he detected a faint smile on Paige's features.

CHAPTER 48

Ray sat on the couch, smoking a cigarette and waiting for the taxi to arrive. His preparations were completed. He was ready. It was time.

Jimmy Chavez had arrived as promised, and with all the things Ray requested. Ray wouldn't let him in, instead making the exchange from behind the partially open exterior basement door.

In addition, he asked Chavez if he had anything that would help him stay awake. "A pick-me-up," Ray had said.

For an additional thirty dollars, Chavez sold Ray a small quantity of methamphetamine; "crank," he called it. He told Ray if he snorted it, he'd feel like running a marathon.

After Chavez left, Ray popped several painkillers and antibiotics, and began the excruciating task of cleansing and bandaging his wounds. Sitting in his bathtub, he rinsed his wounds with Betadine and hydrogen peroxide. After that he showered, washing off the dried blood and Napa Valley dirt from his body. By the time he finished his shower, the painkillers were beginning to kick in, and the agonizing pain from his injuries, as well as the itch and sting of his many insect bites, began to fade to a dull ache. He vaguely remembered he hadn't slept, eaten, or drunk anything for well over twenty-four hours.

When Ray got out of the bathroom, he took several more painkillers and snorted the entire amount of meth. He'd never used an illegal drug before and didn't know what to expect. Blood instantly rushed to his head and he felt a tingle all over his body. Soon, he not only didn't feel much pain but felt pretty good. Refreshed, he slathered antibiotic ointment over his burned face and neck and into the many punctures in his left forearm and thigh. He was wrapping his wounds with gauze when things went haywire.

All of a sudden, his head became woozy and he felt extremely dizzy. He fell back to the couch. The room spun around him.

Ray didn't know how long he sat slumped on the sofa. He couldn't tell if he was awake or asleep. He thought he was asleep, because he saw things that he sometimes dreamed about, but when he looked around, he found himself seemingly wide awake in his basement room. He was confused. He sat on his couch and was dive-bombed by the model aircraft swirling above him. Spectral images danced before his eyes.

Ray saw his mother, her red hair shining in the sun. She smiled at him, looking young and beautiful, and beckoned him to wash up for supper. He saw Skipper, running along Pacific Avenue, his ears back and his tail wagging. He saw his father, squeezing his bicep and telling Ray he would grow up to be a major leaguer. His father looked tall and strong and smelled like Aqua Velva.

Ray also saw Sissy, her bright eyes laughing. She was holding a checkerboard and telling him OK, one more game before bedtime.

Ray reached out to touch Sissy and fell off the couch. He blacked out; he didn't know for how long. When he awoke and his vision returned, he found himself lying on the floor among his magazines and books. He looked up and the ghostly images reappeared. But these were darker, more sinister apparitions.

He saw his mother again, but this time she was old and drunk and fat, and smelling of vodka. Her cackling laugh pierced his ears. He saw Skipper under the ground, worms crawling from his empty eye sockets, his once-sleek coat eaten by insects. He saw his father, his face contorted, spittle pooled at the corner of his mouth. His aftershave aroma had vanished, exchanged for the stale odor of cigarettes and whiskey. He stood bow-legged, his trousers around his ankles, staring down at Sissy.

And Ray saw Sissy under the ground like Skipper. But there were no worms eating her eyes. Instead, Sissy's eyes were open and staring out from the blackness of her grave. Her eyes bored into him and her mouth began to move. She was saying Ray's name, but no words came out. Sissy's face was gray and her lips were black. She was moving, clawing her way through piles of garbage, struggling to get out...

Another image replaced Sissy. In this one, Ray was in the courtroom, looking up at the monolith of the judge's bench. Ray saw himself at eight years old.

He saw himself pull away from his mother and rush up to the bench. He felt his small fists pound on the wooden wall before him. He saw himself pleading, insisting the judge was wrong and that his dad couldn't be a killer. He told the judge his dad built model airplanes, and could whistle like a sparrow, and was helping him get his merit badge in woodcraft.

Ray saw the judge nod to the huge bailiff, who came and tried to take him back to his mother. Ray thrashed in the bailiff's arms, begging, saying, "You can't take my dad away; I love him."

Raw saw the impassive judge look down at the struggling boy who was him. Ray heard himself yell in his eight year-old voice, "I'll get you! I swear I'll get you!"

Ray sat up screaming, the sound of his own childlike voice echoing in his brain. The images vanished. Once again, he was alone in his familiar basement. Within a moment, his head cleared, and he stood up. Epiphany flooded over him.

The revelation struck him like a lightning bolt. Something forgotten had returned to him. Ray realized the vision wasn't merely a dream; it was a message. And within that message was his destiny.

He put on a pair of shorts and went upstairs. His mother was asleep in her chair in front of the television and didn't even know he'd come up. In the kitchen, under the sink, he retrieved several of her empty vodka bottles.

Back downstairs in his basement, he filled the bottles with a mixture of gasoline and kerosene taken from an old camping stove. Then he tore up several Styrofoam cups into small chunks and stuffed them into each bottle. He finished by cutting a towel into strips, soaking them in lighter fluid, and taping one strip along the side of each bottle. Ensuring the caps were secured tightly, he stuffed the bottles into his gym bag.

Ray reloaded the magazine to his Glock and several more magazines to the M1 carbine to replenish the ones he'd been forced to leave in his observation post in Napa. Two of the thirty-round carbine magazines he connected end to end with electrical tape. This time, Ray didn't concern himself with wearing gloves to ensure the bullets were devoid of his fingerprints.

Next, he dressed, choosing the suit he wore when he disguised himself as an Alameda police detective. He put on his dented ballistic vest under the dress shirt. Once dressed, he slung the M1 carbine over his right shoulder and put on a long trench coat over it. He slung his gym bag across his left shoulder and checked his appearance in the mirror. Except for his scarred face, he looked like a traveling businessman on the way to the airport.

Then Ray went upstairs and said goodbye to his mother.

A few minutes later, he came back downstairs, out of breath, and phoned a local cab company. He sat down again on the sofa to smoke and wait.

Lighting a cigarette in the dark, Ray never felt so calm. He understood now. Everything had happened for a reason.

What Ray believed were failures were not; they were his destiny. A legacy passed on from his father. It was fighting against that inevitability that had destroyed his life. He realized now that all the pain and trauma he had suffered were caused by his reluctance to honor his true purpose and accept his fate.

A lifetime of bitterness was dispelled. A crushing weight was lifted. His anger and self-loathing dissipated. Ray had come to know, in the agony of a fever dream, his final truth.

Ray was overcome with gratitude. If his life had ended that fateful summer, the summer of Sissy Levine, he would have never known. He would have never appreciated the value of his childhood. The idyllic bliss of being embraced by the rapture of each splendid day he would have taken for granted, as all children do.

It was clear now. The ordeal of growing up, his abysmal loneliness, was a gift. Ray's failures and defeats and shattered dreams had served a grand design.

Ray had come to a higher understanding. He could release the shame. He didn't have to be Raymond Cowell anymore.

He was Ray Pascoe. His father's son.

A yellow taxi pulled to a stop in front of the house Ray grew up in. A horn honked twice.

Destiny was calling.

CHAPTER 49

By the time Paige and Kearns arrived at her father's house, the sun hadn't quite fallen below the horizon, but the dense fog had rolled in, bringing darkness early. A black-and-white Alameda police cruiser sat in front of the house, its lone occupant writing a report. Bob Farrell's blood-red Oldsmobile was parked across the street.

Farrell opened the door to let them in. He gave Kearns a hearty handshake.

"Good to see you," Farrell said. "The Judge is waiting. Come on in."

Paige nodded a silent greeting to Farrell and walked past him into the house. Kearns lingered.

"What the hell happened to you?" Kearns asked after Paige left, noting the dark bruise on his partner's neck and jaw.

"Couple of Alameda cops threw me a blanket party," he said. "I'll tell you about it later. Right now, we've got work to do."

They entered the study and found Paige hugging her father, who was seated in his familiar high-backed leather chair in the study with a blanket over his lap. He beamed when he saw his daughter. Deputy Charlie White stood in one corner, an unlit cigar clenched in his teeth. He was clad in a dress shirt and slacks, and a large revolver was visible on his hip.

Paige stood when they entered, and the Judge motioned Kearns over. He approached and shook the older man's hand.

"Good to see you're feeling better," Kearns offered.

"Thank you for keeping my daughter safe," he said solemnly. "That's twice you've almost been killed protecting her. I won't forget it."

"I wish I could have done more, Your Honor." He looked at Paige, who blushed slightly. "She's worth it."

The Judge looked from Kearns to his daughter, his eyebrows lifting ever so slightly. This didn't go unnoticed by Farrell.

Judge Callen made introductions. Kearns shook the bailiff's immense hand.

"With your permission," Farrell spoke up, "my partner and I have urgent business to attend to. If you'll excuse us?"

"Of course. Good hunting and good luck."

"Where are you going?" Paige asked.

"We have something to run down," Farrell answered before Kearns could. "We'll be back soon."

Paige escorted them to the door. "Don't go anywhere," Kearns told her, "and keep the doors locked. There's a uniform outside and Deputy White in here. You'll be safe until I get back."

"Be careful, will you?" Kearns nodded. She leaned up and kissed him lightly on the lips, aware that Farrell was watching.

"Let's go, Romeo." Farrell nudged him, rolling his eyes. Once they walked out, Kearns waited until he heard the front door locks click before he accompanied Farrell to his car.

"I underestimated the power of your redneck charm," Farrell said, unlocking his car's doors. "You work fast. When you left for Napa, Paige wouldn't have pissed on you if you were on fire; now she's kissing you goodbye."

"Give me a break," Kearns said. "Where we going, anyway?"

Farrell let him change the subject. "House on Pacific Avenue. Ironically, it's only a couple of blocks from the police station." He fired up the Oldsmobile's engine.

"Who lives there?"

"Arnold R. Pascoe used to," Farrell said. "Take a look." He handed Kearns a sheaf of photocopied newspaper clippings. Kearns flipped on the map light and began to read. The first one was from the Oakland Tribune and headlined with "Alameda Man Arrested in Child-Slaying". It was dated September 1964.

"After you gave me the name, I spent the afternoon at the library. Got some useful stuff there, but the real dope I got from Deputy Charlie White. That dinosaur is an encyclopedia of Alameda County criminals dating back before Christ was a corporal." Farrell wheeled the car north on Grand Street.

"White knows who Arnold Pascoe is?"

"He does." Farrell lit a cigarette. "I'll give you the condensed version because we're pressed for time. Arnold Pascoe was convicted of the rape and murder of his son's babysitter, here in Alameda, back in 1964."

Kearns skimmed the articles. "It's says here Judge Eugene Callen presided over the trial."

"Correct. He also sentenced Pascoe to death after he was convicted."

Kearns continued to read. "So it does. But it doesn't figure; this Pascoe guy would be in his late fifties by now. He can't be our stalker."

"No, he can't," Farrell agreed. "He died in prison in the early Seventies. But his son is alive. Still lives in the same house to this day. Changed his name from Pascoe to Cowell."

"You're kidding. You think our stalker is Pascoe's son?"

"Looks that way," Farrell said. "His driver's license puts him at about the right age, and he fits the description."

"You think revenge is the motive? For his old man being sentenced by Judge Callen in 1964?".

"Appears so," Farrell said. "Payback for the man who took his father from him."

"I don't get it," Kearns said. "Why now? Why wait so long? If what you're telling me is true, this Pascoe kid could have nailed the Judge anytime."

"Keep reading," Farrell prompted. "There's an article in there that I think answers your questions. It's an Alameda Times-Star piece. It contains references to what Pascoe told the Alameda cops on the night he was arrested."

"Here it is," Kearns said. He held the article up to the light. "Says here when Pascoe was asked why he did it, he told the cops it was because his victim was a 'whore' and a 'slut'." He looked over at Farrell. "Those are the same two words written on the wall of Paige's condominium."

"Exactly. And the same two words written in the note left on her car, and the names Paige was called when the suspect phoned her at work. Believe in coincidence? I don't."

"Jesus," Kearns whistled. "But that still doesn't answer the question of why now?"

"Look at the date of Arnold Pascoe's arrest," Farrell told him.

Kearns returned to the original article. "September 14th, 1964," he said. "So?"

Farrell exhaled smoke. "What was the date of the first attack on Paige? On the beach?"

"It was last Monday."

"You mean Monday, September 18th?" Farrell said with a smirk.

"Holy shit," Kearns said. "It's an anniversary."

"A silver anniversary," Farrell noted. "My ex-wife recently reminded me that men don't usually appreciate anniversaries."

"Maybe she should meet Paige's stalker," Kearns said.

Farrell turned east on Pacific Avenue. After few blocks, he pulled over and shut off the engine.

"Address is halfway up the block on the left," he told Kearns, putting out his smoke in the ashtray. He opened the glove box and removed a flashlight. Then he drew his Smith & Wesson revolver, opened the cylinder, and ensured the weapon was fully charged with five rounds. Kearns followed his lead, press-checking his .45 to verify a loaded chamber. He had two spare magazines in his back pocket.

"How do you want to play this?" Kearns asked.

"We'll let ourselves in and make ourselves at home," Farrell told him, holding up a small leather case. "My lock picks from my days as a burglary inspector."

"What if he's inside? Don't forget this guy has an M1 carbine and a bulletproof vest," Kearns said.

"You got a better plan?"

"We could call the Alameda cops?" he suggested, knowing how Farrell would react.

"To hell with those bush-league assholes," Farrell said. "They have to play by the rules; we don't."

"Let's do it," Kearns said.

They got out of the car and quietly closed the doors without slamming them. Bootlegging their guns, Farrell and Kearns crossed the street and walked past several residences until they stood in front of a run-down house with a sinking roof and decaying yard.

Farrell approached the door, staying off to the side. His flashlight was in his left hand, his revolver in his right.

"Cover the basement door," Farrell cautioned.

Kearns positioned himself at the corner of the house, where he could cover the exterior basement door and the garage door and still keep his eye on Farrell. He held his pistol in both hands at low ready, flicking the safety down and off.

Farrell holstered his revolver, switched on his flashlight, and tucked it under his arm. He reached into his coat and came out with his lock picks. Within a minute, Kearns saw him gently turn the door handle. He pocketed his lock picks, switched off the light, and again drew his revolver, motioning for Kearns to join him on the porch.

"You're pretty good at that," Kearns whispered to him.

"All burglary detectives worth a damn are," Farrell whispered back. "You ready?"

Kearns nodded. Farrell opened the door and they went in, the older man making entry first.

The interior was dark, the only illumination coming from the flicker of a television in a room up ahead. The house smelled musty, and the faint odor of spoiled food emanated from the kitchen.

The house was small, and Farrell and Kearns moved quickly from room to room, leading with their guns. They passed through a narrow hallway and peered around the corner into the main room. An overweight, gray-haired woman was sprawled in a recliner with her back to them, a bottle of vodka and a glass resting on the carpet at her feet. The television was tuned to Doogie Howser, M.D.

Farrell lowered his gun and moved closer.

"Hello," he said softly, not wanting to alarm the woman. She didn't respond. He moved even closer. "Excuse me," he called out, afraid she'd wake up startled from her slumber, terrified by the two strangers in her home. She remained unmoving. Farrell walked between the woman and the television to visually announce his presence. Once he did, he realized the woman would never be startled again. He waved Kearns over.

Kearns stepped forward and saw what Farrell had already seen. A large kitchen knife was buried in the woman's chest. Her eyes were closed, her mouth was slack, and her hands remained lifeless at her sides. If it weren't for the blade impaled in her breast, she could have been asleep. Farrell touched her bare arm.

"Dead an hour at most," he said. He turned her hands over. "No defensive wounds; by the looks of it, she got stuck while sleeping."

Kearns tapped the vodka bottle with his toe. "There are worse ways to go."

"Let's check the rest of the house. He might still be here."

Farrell and Kearns swept the small house from room to room, their pistols gripped tightly, expecting him around every corner. They found no one. The last room they checked was the kitchen. Kearns pointed to the door leading down into the basement. Farrell pointed to the heavy-duty locks.

"Work your magic," Kearns said.

Once again, Farrell withdrew his lock picks. This time, Kearns held the flashlight for him. It took a little longer because the locks were newer than the ones on the front door, but within a few minutes, the former SFPD inspector had them open. Kearns led them down the stairs with Farrell's flashlight and his pistol leading the way.

At the bottom of the stairs, Kearns found a light switch and elbowed it on. There was nobody inside the tiny basement apartment.

What they did find when the lights came on was a bonanza. Perhaps a hundred beautifully crafted model airplanes hung suspended from the ceiling. The floor was littered with military magazines and books. A sofa rested in one corner and a large drafting table in the other. Farrell went into the small bathroom.

"Check this out." Kearns held up several empty cardboard ammunition boxes he found on the floor; their labels listed the contents as 9mm and .30 caliber.

"Kevin, come here and take a look at this," Farrell countered. Kearns stuck his head into the bathroom and saw the tub full of bloody towels, shredded, blood-soaked military fatigues, and bloodstained gauze. The sink contained several half-empty bottles of pills: antibiotics and painkillers.

"Any more doubts?" Farrell asked Kearns.

"None. Where do you suppose he is?"

"I wish I knew."

"You think he'll be back?"

"I doubt it," Farrell said. "Not after saying goodbye to his mom with a butcher knife."

Farrell walked out of the bathroom. He scanned the room, his eyes finally lighting on the drafting table. The only two items on the table were an address book and a single model airplane. The plane was resting on top of the book. It was as if they were specifically left out on display to be found. He lifted the airplane, picked up the address book, and opened it.

Farrell flipped through the pages. "This belongs to Paige Callen."

"He must have taken it from her condo," Kearns said. "She hasn't been home since the fire. Probably doesn't even know it's missing."

"This is how he found her housekeeper in Oakland," Farrell stated.

"And her aunt's ranch in Napa."

Farrell handed the address book to Kearns. "She feels bad enough already. First chance you get, put it back in her condo; she doesn't need to know."

Kearns accepted the book and pocketed it. "Thanks, Bob."

"Forget it."

Farrell looked down at the lone model airplane grounded on the drafting table. He picked it up and examined it. It was the only model aircraft in the basement that wasn't hanging by filament from the ceiling as if in flight. He turned it over, wondering why that particular airplane was selected out of all the others to rest on Paige's address book, and why a model plane even needed to sit atop the address book at all. The remains of the filament it had been hanging from was freshly cut and still attached to the fuselage.

Kearns watched his partner scrutinize the toy plane. Farrell's face suddenly lit up in revelation.

"Shit," Farrell cursed.

"What is it?"

"A Mitsubishi Zero," Farrell proclaimed, tossing the model plane to the ground. "Come on, let's go." He headed for the stairs at a run.

"What's so special about an old Japanese airplane?" Kearns asked, puzzled. He raced up the stairs on Farrell's heels.

"It's the weapon of the kamikaze," Farrell shouted over his shoulder.

"Oh, fuck," Kearns said.

CHAPTER 50

Kearns and Farrell could see the smoke and flames as the Oldsmobile skidded to a stop on Dayton Avenue. The source was the Judge's mansion. Several neighbors were standing on their porches and in their front yards, their mouths agape. Some were crying and pointing to the police car still parked in front of the Callen home. The black-and-white cruiser's driver's side door was standing open, and a uniformed cop lay partially inside the car and partially on the street.

When Farrell and Kearns jumped out of the Olds, their guns in hand, they could hear the faint wailing of multiple sirens beginning in the distance. They ran over to the police car. Kearns covered the house with his pistol while Farrell knelt and checked the downed officer's vital signs.

There weren't any. Officer Joe McCord was dead from multiple gunshot wounds. The military rounds of the M1 carbine had punched through his ballistic vest like a hot knife through soft butter. McCord's lifeless eyes stared up at the sky. His revolver was still in its holster.

"Not even an asshole like McCord deserved to get it this way," Farrell said, standing up. "Never even had a chance to clear leather."

Sporadic gunshots could be heard from inside the house, the rapid report of a semi-auto rifle interspersed with the sounds of a large-caliber handgun.

"We have to go in now," Kearns said, gripping Farrell's shoulder. "We can't wait."

"I know."

Farrell reached into the patrol car and unlatched the Remington police shotgun from its vertical dashboard mount. He also took McCord's revolver from its scabbard and handed it to Kearns.

"I'll go in the front," Kearns announced, accepting the cop's gun and stuffing it into his waistband. "You go in the back. We'll meet the bastard in the middle."

Farrell patted his partner on the shoulder and winked.

"See you inside," he said, and took off.

Kearns ran to the front door. He didn't bother to check if it was locked. He kicked it open, splintering the jamb, and went in.

Intense heat met him. Shadows flickered with the flames, which were dancing across the curtains, walls, and carpets. Kearns looked down the hallway and saw the mountain of Deputy Charlie White lying on the floor ahead. Kearns moved forward, covering the corners with his .45. He stepped on numerous expended .30 caliber casings as he advanced.

Charlie was dead, his huge torso riddled with bullet holes. His revolver lay near his hand; the legendary lawman hadn't gone down without a fight. Kearns moved on, the fire raging around him.

In the study, Kearns found Paige and the Judge. They were across the spacious room. The Judge was on the ground, dazedly looking up at the man standing over them. Paige was sprawled across her father, shielding him with her body. It appeared Paige had retreated there, dragging her father in an attempt to take refuge behind the big mahogany desk when confronted by her stalker.

"Out of the way, slut," the man said, "or I'll shoot through you."

He was wearing a long coat and leather gloves, and holding a cut-down M1 carbine in his right hand. In his left was a Molotov cocktail with the improvised fuse already lit. His back was to Kearns.

Kearns knew with Paige and her father on the ground and the gunman standing up, he'd never get a better shot. Paige's eyes unconsciously transferred from the gunman to Kearns. The stalker saw them move.

He spun, bringing up the carbine. Kearns let loose, emptying the magazine of his pistol into the gunman's chest. The impact of eight .45 slugs sent the man, who was of slight build, stumbling backward and careening to the ground. He landed on his butt, his back against the bookshelves. He fired the carbine one-handed as he came to rest, sending a rapid-fire volley in Kearns' direction. The Molotov cocktail fell into his lap without breaking.

Kearns dropped to the floor as bullets slammed into the walls around him. He realized as the carbine continued its barrage that his adversary was again wearing body armor. He discarded the empty .45 and drew the dead cop's revolver from his belt.

Kearns lay on his stomach and brought up the wheelgun in a two-handed, prone-supported firing position straight out of the police academy manual. He thumbed the hammer back. He felt Farrell's presence above him, the shotgun in his hands.

The stalker's carbine had run dry. He released it and drew a black pistol from his own waistband. Instead of aiming it at Kearns and Farrell, however, he swiveled the handgun ninety degrees to point the weapon at Paige and her father. The man's eyes were raging with merciless wrath. A skeletal leer adorned his burn-scarred features, lending him a demonic appearance in the radiance of the surrounding fire.

"Fucking slut," he screamed. Paige cringed, awaiting the bullet.

Farrell and Kearns both fired.

Kearns emptied his revolver, the .357 magnum bucking in his hands. Farrell fired all four shotgun rounds, pumping the action as fast as he could. One of their rounds struck the Molotov cocktail, instantly igniting the homemade napalm inside and engulfing Raymond Cowell/Ray Pascoe in an exploding fireball. The wall of books behind him was consumed by the firebomb.

Kearns pushed himself to his feet as Farrell dropped the shotgun. They ran to Paige. Farrell grabbed her by the arm and Kearns picked up the Judge in a fireman's carry. They scurried out of the study as Ray Pascoe was immolated. He thrashed and twitched, his maniacal shrieks reverberating in their ears as they fled.

The house's interior was fully engulfed; the Molotov cocktails had done their job. Flames licked at them as they raced down the hallway, past the body of Charlie White, and through the front door.

They were met by firefighters and police officers.

"Anybody else still inside?" a firefighter asked. He had to yell to be heard over the roar of the fire and the engines of the numerous emergency vehicles that filled the street.

"Nobody alive," Farrell told him.

A firefighter led them across the yard and out to the street where an ambulance waited. Kearns shrugged the Judge off his shoulders and onto a waiting gurney. An oxygen mask was placed over his nose and mouth. The Judge was still conscious. He squeezed Kearns' arm in gratitude. Kearns gave him a thumbs-up and a weak smile. The ambulance drove away, its siren screeching.

Paige went into his arms, trembling and sobbing. Kearns held her and watched the fire digest her father's house.

Farrell extracted his flask and took a long drink. After he replaced his flask, he lit a cigarette and looked over at his partner. Kearns met his eyes.

"Not a bad day's work," Farrell said, exhaling smoke.

"For a part-time detective," Kearns said.

CHAPTER 51

Sergeant Randy Wendt walked out of the house, tucking in his shirt. His hair was disheveled and his suit coat and tie were slung over the crook of his arm. He didn't see Farrell walk up behind him. Farrell had a manila envelope in his left hand, and his right was tucked inside the pocket of his raincoat.

"Good morning, Sergeant Wendt," he exclaimed loudly.

Startled, Wendt turned around.

"Bob Farrell," he said with a grunt. His eyes darted briefly back to the house. "What the fuck do you want?"

"Not very friendly today, are we?"

"Why should I be? I've got a dead cop on my hands, thanks to you."

"How is that my fault?"

"If you and your idiot sidekick had called us when you first learned who Ray Cowell was, maybe McCord would still be alive."

"That's bullshit and you know it," Farrell said. "Don't blame me for your incompetence. It isn't my fault we discovered his identity first. Besides, if we'd called the cops, you'd have pissed away days building probable cause, writing warrants, and getting permission from bureaucrats. Paige Callen and her father would be dead alongside McCord and Deputy White."

"What do you care? You got paid, didn't you?"

"I did," Farrell gloated. "Handsomely, too. I could buy a small Caribbean island with what the Judge paid me."

Wendt glared at Farrell. "I'm busy," he said. "I've got things to do. McCord's funeral is tomorrow."

"The funeral is at Saint Joseph's Basilica in Alameda, isn't it?"

"Don't tell me you plan on attending?" Wendt said. "There was no love lost between you and McCord."

"That depends on you," Farrell said.

"On me?"

"Here you go, Sergeant." He handed Wendt the manila envelope. "I brought you a present."

"What's this?"

"You weren't being honest with me," Farrell said as Wendt accepted the envelope. "You told me you didn't know Officer McCord very well. I believe you said, 'We don't swing in the same circles'. You lied to me, Sergeant Wendt."

"Says who?"

"Says the facts; I checked. I'm a detective, remember?"

"You don't know shit," Wendt challenged. But his eyes looked worried.

"I know you were his primary training officer and the best man at his wedding."

"Big fucking deal. I trained a lot of new recruits. And you know yourself cops get married and divorced like other people buy cars. I've been the best man at so many weddings, I could be ordained."

"I know some other things, too," Farrell went on. "I know you were the one who strong-armed Kevin Kearns' landlord into evicting him. And I know it was you who set me up for the stomping I took in the garage at my apartment in San Francisco. You invited me for a drink to give Joe McCord time to stage his brother and his pal Lerner in my garage. And when I left the bar too soon, you had me pulled over to buy time for the setup."

A wicked smile etched across Wendt's face. "Even if I did, you can't prove anything."

"I don't have to; I'm not a court of law. Take a look in the envelope, why don't you?"

Wendt opened the envelope. It was full of 8x10 high-resolution photographs. Sergeant Randy Wendt was depicted in every one of them.

"I initially thought it was McCord who set me up," Farrell said. "So I went to his house in Pinole to begin a tail to get some dirt on him; I wanted some leverage to make him leave me alone. But the funniest thing happened; not five minutes after he left for work, you showed up. You went into his house and you stayed there for almost two hours."

Wendt's face turned red. He sifted through the pictures. Farrell went on.

"You'll notice from the first several pictures," Farrell pointed out, "you're wearing your suit when you go in. But when you come out, you're putting on your shirt, just like today." He grinned. "I believe we're standing in front of the late Officer McCord's house right now, aren't we?"

Wendt's face went from red to white.

"Those last few pictures, on the bottom of the stack," Farrell explained, "the ones where you're playing naked leapfrog with McCord's chubby wife? I took those through the window. You should tell her to close the blinds, Randy; you never can tell who's watching." His grin widened. "With a telephoto lens."

Wendt finally shuffled through the stack to the last photograph. His hand trembled slightly when he held it.

"That last one I took of your wife and kids in Antioch," Farrell said. "To prove that I know where you live."

"You son of a bitch," Wendt snarled. He dropped the pictures and threw his right fist at Farrell's head.

Farrell knew the punch was coming before Wendt did, and his hand darted out from his pocket. He was wielding the leather sap McCord's ex-cop brother had used on him. Farrell slammed the blackjack against the inside of Wendt's right forearm, and then his left, as he swung punches. Both of the detective sergeant's arms fell limply to his sides. He gasped in pain.

Farrell wasn't finished. He raised the lead-filled sap as high as he could, and with all his might brought the blackjack down on Wendt's right knee. This time Wendt didn't gasp; he screamed and fell to the sidewalk.

Wendt tried to reach the revolver on his hip, but his numb fingers fumbled the draw. Farrell smacked his hand with the sap and the gun fell to the pavement. He leaned over and recovered the revolver. Farrell ejected the cartridges and tossed it to the lawn twenty feet away. Wendt looked up at him in agony, holding his knee with both hands.

"Here's the deal," Farrell said. He pocketed the sap and withdrew an unfiltered Camel. "You're going to turn in your badge today." He put the cigarette to his lips and lit it with his trusty Zippo. "You don't deserve it."

"Like hell I will," Wendt said through clenched teeth.

"Then I'll show up at your house this afternoon and introduce myself to your wife. Is she a photography fan?"

"Fuck you."

"I'll also show up at McCord's funeral tomorrow." He exhaled smoke. "Cop funerals are typically very popular events. They're usually attended by the mayor, city council members, business and civic leaders, and cops from every corner of the state. Can't wait to see their faces when they get a peek at my photo collection."

Wendt stared bullets at Farrell but remained silent.

"What's the matter, Sergeant? No 'fuck you' for me this time?"

"Don't," Wendt said weakly.

"And finally, to really show you how much I care, I'll mail the pictures of your rendezvous with Joe McCord's wife to Dennis McCord. He's only got one testicle, I hear. Apparently, some guy you sent him to rough up shot the other one off. I'll bet he'll be thrilled to open that special-delivery package from the post office. Especially when he finds out you were porking his dead brother's wife the day before he was put in the ground."

"Please don't," Wendt pleaded.

"What am I thinking?" Farrell said, slapping his thigh. "I don't have to mail the pictures to McCord's brother; he'll be at the funeral tomorrow, won't he? I can save myself a stamp and deliver them in person."

Wendt started to cry. "Please," he repeated.

"It doesn't have to happen," Farrell told him. "Turn in your badge. Today."

"I'm ten years from my pension," Wendt begged. "I'll have nothing."

"Then file for a bogus medical retirement, like your deadbeat, malingering pal Lerner. Worker's compensation fraud among cops is epidemic these days."

"But I don't have a disabling injury," Wendt said.

Farrell suddenly withdrew the blackjack once more from his pocket and struck Wendt's knee again with all his might. Wendt howled in pain, his anguished cry ending in sobs.

"Now you do," Farrell said.

CHAPTER 52

When Farrell opened the door to his apartment, he found Kevin Kearns standing there. A week had passed since the shoot-out at Judge Callen's house in Alameda.

"Hi, Kevin," Farrell greeted him. "Come on in."

"Howdy, Bob," Kearns said, shaking his hand.

"What brings you to my humble abode?"

"Came by to get the rest of my stuff."

"Actually, I was half expecting you to move back in," Farrell said. "But it sounds like you found a place of your own."

"I'm staying at Paige's condominium." His face flushed.

"Nicely done," Farrell chuckled.

"It's only for a couple of weeks until I start the Alameda County Sheriff's Academy."

"So I heard. Congratulations. I guess I'll be calling you 'Deputy Kearns' again before too long."

"I guess so."

"Won't that create a conflict of interest between you and Paige?" Farrell teased. "You two lovebirds working for the same county?"

"That won't be an issue, at least for a while, anyway. Paige is taking a sabbatical from the district attorney's office. She's got a lot of unused vacation to catch up on."

"No kidding?"

"For a few months, at least until her condominium gets repaired, she's going back to Napa to live with her aunt."

"Good for her," Farrell said. "Lord knows she deserves some rest and recreation."

"And that's not all," Kearns added. "Her dad's going with her. Until his mansion is rebuilt, Judge Callen's going to stay at the ranch in Napa also."

"I'll be damned," Farrell said, shaking his head.

"Undoubtedly," Kearns said. "What does a guy have to do to get a drink around here?" he asked.

"Now you're speaking my language." Farrell slapped him on the back. He led Kearns to the kitchen table and grabbed a beer from the refrigerator. "Anchor Steam OK?"

"If it's cold and wet, it works for me."

Farrell poured himself a Jim Beam over ice and sat down across from Kearns.

"To a job well done," Farrell toasted, lifting his glass.

"To surviving a job well done," Kearns added. They clinked glasses.

They drank in silence a while. Kearns finally spoke.

"I want to thank you, Bob."

"What the hell for?"

"You know what for. I didn't want to take this job, and you brought me in kicking and screaming. Thanks to you, I now have a law enforcement career back on track and a lot of money in my pocket." He looked into his beer. "And I met Paige."

"You have Judge Callen to thank for the career and the money," Farrell said. "Paige was all your doing."

"Judge Callen made good just like you said," Kearns said. "He made a call, and next thing you know, I'm hired by the sheriff's department. I'm scheduled for the upcoming academy. He also paid me. A lot. Wouldn't take 'no' for an answer."

"How much did he pay you?"

"Enough to make me feel guilty."

"Hell," Farrell quipped. "If you knew how much the Judge paid me, you wouldn't feel guilty; you'd feel cheated."

"I still feel guilty."

"Because of the money," Farrell grinned, "or because you're banging his daughter?"

"Jesus, Bob!"

"Take it easy," Farrell laughed. "I'm only pulling your chain. I had to lighten things up; I thought for a second you were going to give me a hug."

"I ought to strangle you," Kearns said, shaking his head.

"I almost forgot," Farrell said, snapping his fingers and standing up. "Wait here." He left the kitchen and went into the bedroom. When he emerged a moment later, he was carrying a box the approximate size of a book. "I got you a present."

"What's the occasion?"

"Just open it," Farrell ordered, reaching for his cigarettes.

Kearns did. Inside was a brand-new, five-shot, blue-steel, concealed-hammer .38 special Bodyguard revolver, identical to the one Farrell had been using since a rookie.

"The sheriff's department will issue you a duty gun, but I figured you needed an off-duty piece. Smith & Wesson," Farrell beamed. "Workingman's gun."

"I don't know what to say," Kearns said. "Thanks, Bob."

"You know," Farrell began, lighting a cigarette, "just because you're working full-time as a deputy sheriff doesn't mean you can't moonlight doing private investigation work with me on the side."

"I should have known there'd be a catch," Kearns groaned.

"Just think it over," Farrell said. "It's all I'm asking. We do good work together. Once you graduate the academy and get settled in at the sheriff's department, you'll have loads of free time."

"You can drop the sales pitch, Bob," Kearns relented. "When that time comes, I'll give it some thought."

"That's the spirit. Don't forget, we're a team, you and me," Farrell reminded him. "Like Cisco and Pancho."

"More like Dracula and Igor," Kearns muttered.

"Shut up and drink your beer."

ACKNOWLEDGMENTS

My thanks go out to my stalwart literary agent, the inimitable Scott Miller of Trident Media Group. He always gets it done. His counsel, stewardship, and support are deeply appreciated.

I cannot convey how grateful I am to my outstanding editor, Emlyn Rees. I was reluctant to attempt this book, and Emlyn convinced me to plunge ahead. Without his encouragement, this work would not have come to be. He prodded me out of my comfort zone. This made me a better writer and I hope a better person. Thanks, Emlyn, you inspirational bastard; I'm truly in your debt.

A nod goes out to the Calaveras Crew and the Usual Suspects; one group I treasure and the other I fear. Good luck figuring out which.

Most importantly, inexpressible thanks go to Denise, Brynne, and Owen. Today, tomorrow, and forever. You know the rest.

ABOUT THE AUTHOR

Sean Lynch was born and raised in Iowa. When not outdoors shooting his BB guns, Sean could be found reading crime and science fiction, paranormal and military non-fiction, and trying to persuade his parents to let him stay up past bedtime to watch the late-show creature feature.

After high school Sean obtained a Bachelor of Sciences degree and served in the U.S. Army as an enlisted Infantryman. He migrated to Northern California's San Francisco Bay Area, where he recently retired after nearly three decades as a municipal police officer. During his Law Enforcement career Sean served as a Sector Patrol Officer, Foot Patrol Officer, Motorcycle Officer, Field Training Officer, S.W.A.T. Team Officer, Firearms Instructor, S.W.A.T. Team Sniper, Defensive Tactics Instructor, Juvenile/Sexual Assault Detective, and Homicide Detective. Sean concluded his career at the rank of Lieutenant and as Commander of the Detective Division.

A lifelong fitness enthusiast, Sean exercises daily and holds a 1st Dan in Tae Kwon Do. He still watches late-night creature features. Sean is partial to Japanese cars, German pistols, and British beer.

SeanLynchBooks.com.com
twitter.com/seanlynchbooks

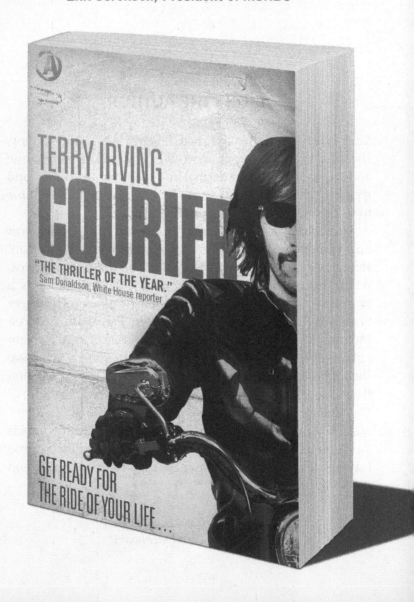

Your worst nightmare just went viral...

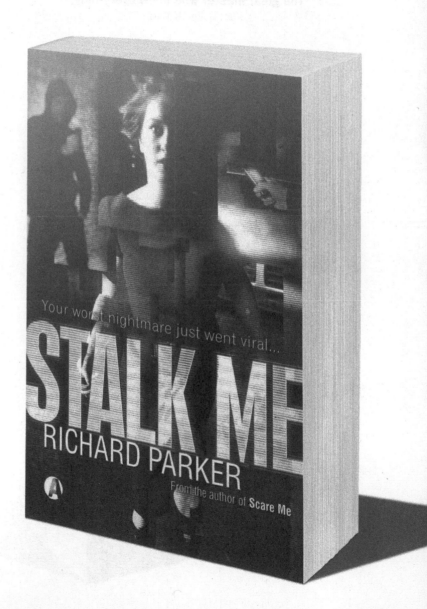

Introducing Wm. Shakespeare: Detective.

"The great master who knew everything."
Charles Dickens

BARTHOLOMEW
DANIELS

Introducing William Shakespeare: Detective

ROTTEN
AT THE
HEART